He did not move or say anything, but the witch slowly bent before him like a candle too close to heat. Her eyes widened; she staggered to the table and clutched it, one hand gripping the edge, her knuckles white.

"This is pain," he said quietly, coming up behind her. "This is how it feels. And these are nightmares—see them? This is silence. This is fear."

Also by Catherine Fisher

✠ CONTENTS ✠

BOOK ONE

The Snow-walker's Son

To Rachel

The door was the last one in the corridor.

As the flames flickered over it they showed it was barred; a hefty iron chain hung across it, and the mud floor beneath was red with rust that had flaked off in the long years of locking and unlocking.

The keeper hung his lantern on a nail, took the key from a dirty string around his neck, and fitted it into the keyhole. Then he looked behind him.

"Get on with it!" the big man growled. "Let me see what she keeps in there!"

The keeper grinned; he knew fear when he heard it. With both hands he turned the key, then tugged out the red chain in a shower of rust and pushed the door. It opened, just a fraction. Darkness and a damp smell oozed through the black slit.

He stepped well back, handed the stranger the lantern, and jerked his head. He had no tongue to speak with; she'd made sure he kept her secrets.

The stranger hesitated; a draft moved his hair and he gazed back up the stone passageway as if he longed suddenly for warmth and light. And from what I've heard, the keeper thought, you won't be seeing much of those ever again.

Then the man held up the lantern and pushed the door. The keeper watched his face intently in the red glow, and his great hand, as it clutched a luckstone that swung at his neck. The man went in slowly. The door closed.

Outside, the keeper waited, listening. No sound came out of the room and he dared not go too close. For six years now he had locked it and unlocked it, letting in the witch Gudrun and the sly old dwarf she brought with her. No one else in all that time—until today, this gruff red-beard.

For six years he had left food at the door and taken it away half eaten, had heard rustles and movements and had never looked in. But there had been that night, nearly a year ago now, when halfway up the corridor he had looked back, and in the dimness seen that hand, thin as a claw, lifting the platter.

Suddenly the door opened; he stiffened, his hand on his knife. The big man was there, carrying something heavy, wrapped in old bearskins. He cradled it with both arms; whatever it was moved in the folds against his shoulder. It made a low sound, wordless and strange.

The man had changed. His face was pale, his voice quiet. "Tell her," he muttered through his teeth, "that her secret is safe with me. I'll keep it better than she did."

Shoving the keeper aside, he strode through the flames and shadows of the stone tunnel.

The keeper waited; waited until the echoes of distant chains and gates were still. Then, furtively, he slid his lantern around the door and looked into the room.

He saw a small cell, with one window high up in the wall, icicles hanging from its sill, a low bed, straw, a fireplace full of ashes. He stepped in warily. There were a few scraps of food on the floor, but nothing to give any sign of what had been here.

It was only when he turned to go that his eyes caught the patterns: the rows and rows of strange, whirling spirals scrawled on the damp wall next to the bed.

One

Young and alone on a long road,
Once I lost my way:
Rich I felt when I found another . . .

The hall was empty.

Jessa edged inside and began to wander idly about, pulling the thick furred collar of her coat up around her face. She was early.

It had been a bitter night. The snow had blown in under the door and spread across the floor. A pool of wine that someone had spilled under the table was frozen to a red slab. She nudged it with her foot; solid as glass. Even the spiders were dead on their webs; the thin nets shook in the draft.

She walked to the great pillar of oak that grew up through the middle of the hall. It was heavily carved with old runes and magic signs, but over them all, obliterating them, was a newer cutting: a contorted snake that twisted itself down in white spirals. She brushed the frost off it with her gloved fingers. The snake was Gudrun's sign. A witch's sign.

She waited, grinding the ice to white powder under her heel.

Light gathered slowly. Corners of tables and tapestries loomed out of the shadows; a cart rumbled by outside, and the carter's shout echoed in the roof.

Jessa kicked the frozen fire. Why hadn't she come late—sauntered in sweetly when the Jarl was waiting, just to show him that she didn't care, that he couldn't order her as he wanted? It was too late now, though.

Five slow minutes slithered by.

Then a hanging was flipped back; a house thrall came in and began to take down the shutters. Frost cracked and fell from the empty windows; a raw wind whipped in and rippled the tapestries.

He hadn't seen her. Jessa was annoyed. She shuffled, and watched him whirl around, his face white. Then the terror drained out of him. That annoyed her even more.

"I'm waiting to speak to the Lord Jarl," she snapped in a clear voice. "My name is Jessa Horolfsdaughter."

It was the voice she always used with servants, cold and rather distant. Old Marrika, her nurse, used to say it was the voice of pride. What was Marrika doing now? she wondered.

The man nodded and went out. Jessa scuffed the floor impatiently. She hated this place. Everyone in it was afraid. They were littered with amulets and luckstones; they glanced around before they spoke, as if someone was always listening. Gudrun. The Jarl's strange wife. The Snow-walker. They said she knew what you thought, even as you stood before her. Jessa shivered.

The man came back and kneeled at the hearth. She saw the welcome flicker of flames and hurried over, warming her hands and rubbing them against her face until her cheeks ached. The thrall propped some logs on the blaze and went out. Jessa did not speak to him. People said all the Jarl's servants were dumb. Whatever the truth of that, they never spoke.

Crouched over the fire, she looked down the high hall. The trestles and stools were toppled here and there on the straw. At the far end was a raised platform; here the seats were piled with red cushions, the tables littered with half-empty plates. Jessa went over and picked up a pewter jug. The wine in it was frozen. She put it down with a bang.

As she turned, one of the tapestries behind the dais was drawn aside and an elderly man came in, with a boy of her own age behind him. She knew the boy at once. Thorkil Harraldsson was her first cousin; they'd brought him here about three months ago. His clothes were very fine, she thought scornfully. Just like him.

The other was Jarl Ragnar. He was still tall, but his shoulders stooped; the splendid blue quilted robe hung loose on him. He looked like a man dried out, sucked dry of all life, his eyes small and cold.

She made him the most careless bow she could.

"You have your father's manners," he said wryly.

Silent, she watched Thorkil drag up two stools and the Jarl's chair; he caught her eye and gave her a brief, wan smile. She thought he seemed uneasy, and very pleased to see her. No wonder. Prison was prison, even with fine clothes.

They sat down. The Jarl stared into the flames. Finally he spoke, without looking at them.

"Your fathers were two brothers. I had thought they were loyal to me, until they joined that last foolish march of the Wulfings. All my enemies together. It was a pity they both died in the snow."

Jessa glared at him. "Your wife's sorcery brought the snow. She won your battle for you."

He was angry, but Jessa didn't care. "The Lord Jarl has always come from the family of the Wulfings. That's why they fought you. You have no right to be Jarl."

She caught Thorkil's nervous, warning look, but it was done now. She had said it. Her face was hot; her hands shook.

Grimly the Jarl stared at the flames. "The family of the Wulfings are almost all gone," he said. "Those that are left lurk in farms and steads and byres, their women and children disguised as thralls, hurried indoors when riders come by. Gudrun knows. She sees them. One by one, I am hunting them out. The leader, Wulfgar, was taken two days ago; he's in a room under your feet, with ice and rats for company. And now there's you."

His hands rubbed together, dry as paper.

"I left you alone. I left you on your farms, fed you and let you be, until now. Now you are old enough to be dangerous."

Jessa watched his eyes on the leaping flames. She

wanted him to turn and look at her, but he would not.

"Your land will be given to men loyal to me, and you will have somewhere else to live."

"Here?" Thorkil asked.

"Not here." He smiled briefly. "Far from here."

Jessa was glad. She had been here for two days and that was enough. But she didn't trust that smile.

"Where then?"

The Jarl moved, as if he was suddenly uneasy. The silver amulets and thorshammers around his neck clicked together.

"I'm sending you to live with my son," he said.

For a moment they couldn't realize what he meant. Then Jessa felt sick; cold sweat prickled on her back. Slowly her hand sought the amulet Marrika had given her.

Thorkil was white. "You can't send us there," he breathed.

"Hold your tongue and let me finish." Ragnar was looking at them now, with a hard, amused stare.

"Your fathers were traitors; they wanted to bring me down. Many men remember them. Do you expect me to set you up on farms, to give you herds of reindeer and dowries of silver?"

"Why not?" Jessa muttered. "You took ours."

He laughed. "Call it exile, and think yourselves lucky.

At least you'll have a sort of life. You leave tomorrow for
Thrasirshall, at first light. I'll supply a ship and an escort, at
least as far as Trond. I don't suppose my men will want to
go farther."

Jessa saw Thorkil was trembling. She knew he couldn't
believe this; he was terrified. It burst out of him in a wild,
despairing cry.

"I won't go! You can't send us out there, not to that
creature!"

With one swift movement the Jarl stood and struck
him in the face with the full weight of his glove, so that he
staggered back on the stool and fell with a crash onto the
stone floor. Jessa grabbed him, but he shrugged her off.
Tears of fury glinted in his eyes as he scrambled up.

"Take a lesson from your cousin," the Jarl said. "Look
your fate in the eye. I'd thought you were stronger, but I
see you're still a boy."

Jessa took Thorkil's wrist and held it tight. Better to
keep quiet now.

The Jarl watched them. "Gudrun is right," he said.
"Traitors breed traitors."

Then, slowly, he sat down, and ran one hand wearily
down one cheek.

"There's something else."

"What?" Jessa asked coldly.

He took something from inside his coat and held it out: a thick piece of sealskin. She saw the blue veins in the Jarl's hand.

"It's a message." Ragnar looked at them almost reluctantly. "I want you to take it with you. It's for Brochael Gunnarsson . . . the man who looks after the creature. Give it to him. Tell no one." He looked wearily around the empty hall. "Whatever sort of thing Kari is, he is my son."

There was silence. Then he said, "Take it."

For a long moment Jessa did not move. Then she reached out and took the parcel. The parchment inside it crackled as she slid it into her glove.

The Jarl nodded and stood up, straightening slowly. He walked a few steps and then stopped. Without looking back he said, "Come here tonight, after the lawgiving. Gudrun wishes to speak to you. There's nothing I can do about it."

He looked over his shoulder at them. "Keep my secret. I can do nothing else for Kari. Maybe, years ago, if I had tried . . . but not now. She would know." He smiled at them, a bitter smile. "I've never seen him. I do not know what he is."

In the silence after he had shuffled out, a pigeon fluttered in the roof. One glossy feather whirled down through a shaft of light.

"Why did you take it?" Thorkil asked.

Jessa was wondering too. "Not so loud," she murmured.

He went to the fire and kneeled near the dirty hearth; Jessa followed. "We must escape," he said.

"Where?"

"Your farm—Horolfstead."

"His men have got it." She pulled at her glove. "Three days ago."

Thorkil glanced at her. "I should have known. Well, why bother to talk? There's nothing we can do—he's sending men with us."

"To Thrasirshall."

"Mmm."

Jessa was silent for a moment. Then she glanced around. "Thorkil . . ."

"What?" But he knew what.

"You've been here longer than I have. What do they say about Kari Ragnarsson?"

"Nothing. No one dares." Thorkil dropped his voice. "Besides, no one has ever seen him, except the woman who was there when he was born. She died a few days later. They say Gudrun poisoned her."

Jessa nodded. "Yes, but there are rumors. . . ."

"The same as you've heard." Thorkil edged nearer to

the fire. "She kept him locked up here somewhere, in a windowless room. He has a pelt of fur like a troll. He tears his skin with his teeth in his fits. Others say he has eyes like a wolf. There are plenty of stories. Who knows which is true? Now she keeps him in the ruin called Thrasirshall. They say it's at the edge of the world, far out in the snow-fields. No one has ever been there."

She stood up. "Neither will we. We'll get away. How can they watch us all the time?"

"Gudrun can. And where can we go in a wilderness of ice?"

But Jessa had crouched suddenly, her gloved fingers on his lips. "Quiet!"

Together they turned their heads. The hanging on the far wall was rippling slightly; the faded bears and hunters stitched on it seemed to move under the dirt.

"Someone's there," Jessa whispered. "Someone's been listening to us."

Two

Shun a woman wise in magic.

They waited for a long minute. Then Thorkil walked over and carefully pushed the musty cloth. It gave under his hand.

"There's a space here," he muttered. "No wall."

As there was no sound, he pulled the deep folds of the hanging apart and slipped inside; after a quick look around, Jessa followed. In the dimness they saw a stone archway in the wall, and beyond that a staircase twisting up. Footsteps were climbing it lightly.

"I told you," Jessa whispered. "Who is it?"

"I don't know. Probably . . ." Then he stopped.

Behind them someone had come into the hall, someone silent, without footsteps, someone who froze the air. Jessa felt sudden crystals harden on her face and mouth, felt a cold numbness that pieced her skin. Thorkil was still; frost glistened on his lips.

"It's Gudrun," he breathed.

And as if the walker on the stairs had heard him, the footsteps stopped, and began to come back down.

Suddenly Jessa had never felt so afraid. Her heart thudded; she wanted to run, had to fight to hold herself still, clenching her fingers into fists. Before them the foot-steps came closer; behind in the hall some terrible coldness loomed. Grabbing at Thorkil, she tugged him between the heavy tapestries and the wall; there was a black slit there, filthy with dust. Something brushed his coat; the tapestry whirled, and a small bent figure, much muffled in cloaks and coats, slipped past them into the hall.

"Gudrun," they heard him say, "you move like a ghost."

"But you heard me."

"I felt you."

Their voices withdrew into the room. Coldness ebbed; the freezing fear slowly loosened its grip. Jessa heard Thorkil's shudder of breath, saw his hand was shaking as he gently moved aside a fold of the cloth so they could see part of the hall.

Someone was sitting in the Jarl's chair, looking no more than a bundle of rich fabrics. Then he pushed his hood back, and Jessa saw it was a very old man, thin and spry, his hair wisps of white, his look sly and sidelong.

"They leave tomorrow," he was saying. "As you expected."

Astonished, Jessa stared at Thorkil.

The woman laughed, a low peal of sound that made a new surge of fear leap in Jessa's stomach.

The old man chuckled too. "And they know all about Thrasirshall, the poor waifs."

"What do they know?" she said.

"Oh, that the wind howls through it, that it's a wilderness of trolls and spirits on the edge of the world. Not to speak of what the hall contains." He spat, and then grinned.

They could just see the woman's white hands, and her sleeves. Gently Thorkil edged the curtain a little wider.

Gudrun stood in the light from the window. She was tall and young, her skin white as a candle, her hair pure blond and plaited in long intricate braids down her back. Her ice blue dress was edged with fur. Silver glittered at her wrist and throat; she stood straight, her sharp gaze toward them. Jessa felt Thorkil's instant stillness. Even from here, they could see her eyes had no color.

"How did they take their news?"

"The girl, quietly. Master Thorkil squealed, but Ragnar stopped that."

Gudrun laughed. "Even the Jarl needs his pleasures. I allow him a few."

"But there is one thing you may not know."

Her eyes turned on him. "Be careful," she said lightly. "Even you, Grettir."

He seemed to shift uneasily in the chair. Then he said, "Ragnar gave the girl a letter. It was for Brochael

Gunnarsson. It was a warning."

She laughed again, a murmur of amusement. "Is that all? What good will that do? Let them take it, by all means." With a rustle of silks she moved to sit by him; Thorkil edged the curtain to keep her in sight.

"None of it matters." She rested her white fingers lightly on the old man's shoulder. "Everything is ready. Ragnar is sending them there because I slid the idea of it into his mind, just as he speaks my words and eats and sleeps as I allow him."

"But the letter?"

She shrugged. "He has a corner of himself left alive. As for those two, I have my own plans for them."

She put her lips near his ear, dropped her voice low. Jessa strained to hear. "I'll have my hand on them," the woman said. Then she whispered something that made the old man grin and shake his head slyly.

"You have the great powers, Gudrun. Not many can touch you."

Instantly he was silent, as if he knew he had made a mistake. She leaned forward and ran the sharp point of one fingernail gently down his cheek. To her horror Jessa saw it leave a trail of white ice that cracked and fell away, and a blue scar in the skin as if some intense cold had seared it. The old man moaned and clutched his face.

Gudrun smiled. "Be careful, Grettir. No one can touch me. No one."

She ran her fingers lightly through his hair. "Remember that."

She got up and wandered to the table, then to the fire. "As for the creature in Thrasirshall, you and I know what he is."

She stretched one hand over the flames; thrust it close. Jessa saw a single drop of clear liquid fall from the white fingers, as if, she thought, they had begun to melt in the heat. As the drop hit the flames they hissed and crackled, leaping into a tower of fire. Smoke drifted around the hall; it hung in long snakes that moved around the woman's waist and feet, slithering over the flagged floor, blurring sight, so that to Jessa the fire faded to a halo of red, and Gudrun and Grettir were shadows without edges. Staring hard, she thought she saw something form among the flames, the dim outline of a building, a window, a room full of light, and someone sitting there, turning his head. . . .

Then the door of the hall slammed open. The thrall that Jessa had met earlier stood in the doorway, his arms full of wood. He stopped, frozen in terror.

Gudrun whirled in the smoke. She was furious; snakes of gray mist coiled and surged around her. "Out!" she hissed, her voice hoarse with rage.

The man stood there rooted, as if he dared not move. Jessa felt a pang of fear shoot through her—Get out! she thought, but he stayed, staring with horror at Gudrun as she jerked her hand toward him.

Logs cascaded to the floor with hollow smacks of sound. The man crumpled, soundless. He crouched on his knees, sobbing and shaking. Gudrun walked up to him. She stood a moment, looking down, then bent and lifted his chin. Pain convulsed him; he shuddered as she ran her long fingers across his throat. "Out," she whispered.

He staggered up and crashed through the door. They could hear the echoes of his flight for a long time, hanging in the smoky air.

Jessa breathed out with relief, but at the same time she touched the edge of the tapestry, and it rippled and swished. Instantly, Thorkil dropped it and flattened himself against the wall. There was silence in the hall. Jessa's heart thumped against her ribs.

Then Gudrun spoke. She was so close that Jessa almost jumped.

"Kari won't escape me, either. I've let him be far too long, to see what he would become. And yet, Grettir"—her voice turned away from them—"I have almost a desire to see him, to taste him, to use what he has."

Her hand came around the tapestry. Jessa almost

screamed. The white fingers were inches from her face.

"But they'll be here tonight, both of those two. That will be my time."

Grettir must have moved; they heard his chair scrape the flagstones.

"I will come."

"You must please yourself, old man, as ever." Then she turned and flashed past them, under the archway and up the stairs, her light steps rising into silence above them.

Thorkil let his breath out in a gasp and clutched Jessa's arm. They were stifled; both wanted to run out, to breathe clean air, but the old man was still there, standing silently by his chair. Slowly he crossed to the courtyard door and unlatched it. Cold air rippled the tapestries to a storm of dust. When Jessa had wiped her eyes and peered out, the hall was empty.

They ran straight to the door, squeezed through, and closed it. Smoke coiled out after them, dissipating in the wind. The watchman, half asleep, stared at their backs as they walked, too quickly, between the houses, among the children and the squalling hens. Once Jessa turned, feeling herself watched, but the windows of the Jarlshold were dark and empty.

THREE

With a good man it is good to talk,
Make him your fast friend.

"'I'll have my hand on them.' And she meant us." Jessa watched Mord Signi stack the slabs of peat carefully onto the back of the fire, and jerk his hand out as the sparks leaped. "What do you think she meant?"

"I don't think," Mord said, straightening. "Not about her."

He was a tall man; his gray hair brushed the low turf roof. He glanced over at his wife, folding Jessa's clothes into a leather bag. "But I can't let this go. Not without a murmur."

His wife put her hand on his shoulder. "It's no use talking to Ragnar," she said quietly. "Why should he listen?" Then she bent forward and whispered, so that Jessa only just caught the words. "Stay out of it. You have your own children to think of."

He turned aside, silent. Jessa felt sorry for him. He had been a kinsman of her father; he was a marked man in the

Jarlshold. And his wife was right. No pleading would move Ragnar, and anyway, she, Jessa, wouldn't have it.

Mord came back to the fire. The hearth was a large, square one in the middle of the house, and around the walls were the sleeping booths, with their wooden screens and warm, musty hangings. By now the fire was a hot blaze, licking and spitting over the new peats, throwing glows and shadows around the room, over Thorkil's face, and Mord's, worried and upset. Outside, the afternoon sky was darkening with snow. Winter lingered late, as usual, in the Jarlshold.

Thorkil said, "Mord, tell us about Gudrun."

"Best not to, lad. I'd rather keep my tongue."

"But we need to know." Thorkil glanced at Mord's wife, with her youngest daughter pulling at her skirts. "We're going there, after all."

She turned away from him. "He's right, Mord."

Mord put down the peat he had been crumbling, got up slowly, and locked the door. Coming back, he sat closer to the fire.

"It's a stranger story than any skald's saga. Much of it you'll know, I'm sure. When Ragnar was a young man, the Wulfings were the ruling kin in the north. He was just one of many small landowners; your fathers were two more. But he was ambitious. He bought land where he could, stole it where he couldn't, ruined his enemies in the Althing—that was the old law court—and gathered ruthless, cruel men about him. Still, he might have stayed as he was, if it hadn't been for her."

Mord paused. Then he said, "Beyond the Yngvir River and the mountains, there's only ice. It stretches, they say, to the edge of the world, into the endless blackness. Travelers—those that have come back—speak of great cracks that open underfoot, of mountains smooth as glass, of the sky catching fire. Beyond the icebergs even the sea freezes. No animals live there, not even the white bears, though I have heard a tale of a long glistening worm that burrows in the ice. It may not be true. But certainly there are trolls, and ettins, and some sort of spirit that howls in the empty crevasses.

"In those lands live the White People, the Snow-walkers, a race of wizards. No one knows much about them, except that sometimes they would come to the northern borders and raid. Children would disappear from farms, and it would be said that the White People had taken them. Cattle too, and sometimes dogs.

"One year the raids were so bad, the old Jarl sent Ragnar with a war band to march up there and settle it. They crossed the hills by way of the old giant's road that passes Thrasirshall, and marched down the other side, straight into a white mist. It was waiting for them there, a solid whiteness that even the wind couldn't blow away. Fifty men marched into that devil's trap, and only one came out."

"What was it?" Thorkil asked.

"Sorcery. Rune magic." Mord shrugged. "Who knows? But three months later a ship came into the harbor at Tarva, a strange ship with dark sails and twenty oarsmen—tall white-haired men who spoke a fluid, unknown language. The old man, Grettir, led them—he was younger then, of course. Then Ragnar came out of the ship, and with him a woman, white as ice, cold as steel. To this day no one knows who she is, or what godforsaken agreement he made with them to save his life. But we soon found out what sort of a creature had come among us."

Jessa glanced at Thorkil. He was listening intently, his fingers working at the laces of his boots, knotting and unknotting, over and over.

"The first thing," Mord went on, "was that the old Jarl died one night in a storm. He was hale enough when he went to bed, but in the night he gave a sudden scream, and when they got to him he was dead. There was a mark, they say, like a spread hand, in the skin of his face; it faded away, till in the morning there was nothing left."

Thorkil's head jerked up and his eyes met Jessa's. Mord did not notice. "And his fingers—there was a web of ice all over them. . . . After that, it was easy. Rumors flew; fear built up. The Jarl had left no son. The Althing should have chosen another of the Wulfings, and there were plenty of good men—but they didn't. Fear made them fools. They chose Ragnar.

"Two disagreed, I remember. One was killed by a bear, the other froze in a drift on a dark night. None of his family knew why he'd left the house, but the little boy said a 'white lady' had called him through the window. . . ." He looked up. "You must have heard much of this."

Jessa shrugged. "Some of it. No one tells you much when you're small. But what about Kari?"

Mord glanced at the door. His voice was quiet now, barely heard. "It happened I was with Ragnar when the news came; we were in the forest, watching them cut timber for the hold. 'A son,' the messenger said, but there was something about the way he said it. Ragnar noticed too. He asked what was wrong. The man muttered something about the midwife screaming; he seemed too terrified to answer. The Jarl almost knocked me over as he rode off. The gods help me, I've never seen a man look so stricken."

"Did the messenger see the baby?" Jessa asked.

"No, but he didn't need to. Rumors soon got around—you know them. The child is a monster. For myself I think the High One struck at Ragnar's pride, and her sorcery. That's the god's way. They kept the child here for a while, called it Kari, but no one ever saw it except Gudrun and the old man. Ragnar has never set eyes on him."

"So he told us," Thorkil muttered.

"And she hates it. She'll never even hear its name—Kari. When the creature was about five years old she got Ragnar to send it away, to the ruined hall in the north. I think she hoped it would die of cold. Brochael Gunnarsson was in prison—now he was one of the Wulfings' men, and he had said something against her—so Ragnar took his land and sent him to be the child's keeper. It was a hard revenge." He sighed. "I was fond of Brochael—a good man. He may be long dead. No one has been near them in all this time."

"Until now," Thorkil said grimly.

There was silence.

"If no one has seen him," Jessa said suddenly, grasping at hope, "how do they know he's so terrible?"

"Why else would she lock him up?"

It was a good answer.

"Well," Thorkil said, "we'll soon find out."

Mord frowned at him. "Be careful, lad. Be discreet. They say she can bend your mind to her will."

Thorkil laughed coldly. "Not mine."

Jessa had been thinking. "Kari and this Brochael must

be dead by now. How can they live up there?" How will we? she thought.

"Gudrun would know. She has ways of knowing. That's why, in these last years, your fathers and the Wulfings stood no chance. She was too much for them."

Thorkil stared bleakly into the fire. Jessa pulled absently at the ends of her hair. Mord caught his wife's eye. "But that's enough talk. Now we should eat."

The food at the Jarlshold was good and plentiful; they had broth and fish and honey cakes. Despite her worries Jessa was hungry. What would they eat, she wondered, at the ruined hall in the mountains? No crops would grow there; no animals would survive. She had never known real hardship; their farm had been a rich one. What would it be like?

When they had finished, Mord rose and pulled on his outdoor coat. "Come on. It's wise not to keep her waiting."

Outside, the sky was black, frosted with stars glinting in their faint colors. The moon was a low, silvery globe, balancing, it seemed, on the very tips of the mountains far off, lighting their frozen summits with an eerie bluish shimmer.

By now the Jarlshold was quiet, and very cold. A few dogs loped past them as they walked between the silent houses; once a rat ran across the frozen mud. Like all the houses Jessa had known, these were low and roofed with turf, boarded and shuttered now to keep the warmth of the fires in. Smoke hung in a faint mist over the settlement.

Only the hall was noisy; they could hear the murmur of sound grow as they walked toward it. The shutters were up again, but a circle of light flickered in the ring window high up in the wall. Laughter floated out, and voices.

A doorkeeper sat outside, polishing a sword with a whetstone; a great wolflike mastiff sprawled at his feet. Mord nodded to the man and put his hand on the latch. Then he turned. "Don't eat anything she gives you," he breathed. "Don't drink. Avoid her eyes. I don't know what else to say. If she wants you—she'll get you." Then he opened the door.

FOUR

Never lift your eyes and look up in battle
Lest the heroes enchant you, who can change warriors
Suddenly into hogs.

It was as if some runemaster had waved a hand and transformed the place. All the fires were lit, roaring in the hearths, and candles and rushlights glimmered on stands and in corners, filling the hall with a haze of smoke and light. Long hangings, woven of red and green cloths, hung over the shutters, and the trestles were scattered with scraps of food and bones that the dogs pulled down and snarled over in the straw. The hot air stank of smoke and spices.

Mord pushed them both forward through the crowd. Jessa glimpsed rich embroidery on sleeves, the glint of gold, furs, heavy pewter cups. The Jarl's court was rich, rich on other men's land. She lifted her chin, remembering suddenly her father's grin, his raised hand. She had been only six when he rode out. His face was fading from her mind.

And there was Ragnar at the high table with the witch next to him, her face pale as a ghost's with its long eyes, her gaze wandering the room. Grettir sat beside her, watching Thorkil push through the crowd.

Mord found them seats near one of the fires; a few men stood to make room and some of them nodded slightly at Jessa. So the Jarl still had enemies then, even here. Mord seemed uneasy; she caught him making discreet signals to someone across the room. Then a steward shouted for silence.

Noise hushed. Men settled back with full cups to see what would happen—a skald with some poem, Jessa thought, or a lawsuit, considered entertainment just as good. A tall, very thin man across the room caught her eye. He grinned at her and tugged a bundle of herbs tied with green ribbon from a bag at his feet and held it out. A peddler. She shook her head quickly; the man laughed and winked. Then he moved out of sight among the crowd thronging the hearth.

Thorkil nudged her.

A prisoner was coming in between two of the Jarl's men. He was a tall, dark, elegant man in a dirty leather jerkin, with a gleam of gold at his neck. He looked around with cool interest.

"That's Wulfgar," Thorkil said. "They caught him last week up at Hagafell. He's the last of the Wulfings. If anyone should be Jarl, it's him."

As the prisoner came through the crowd, the silence grew. Jessa saw how some men looked away, but others held his eye and wished him well. He must be well liked, she thought, for them to risk even that much, with Gudrun watching.

"Wulfgar Osricsson," Ragnar began, but the prisoner interrupted him at once.

"They all know my name, Ragnar." His voice was deliberately lazy. A ripple of amusement stirred in the room.

"You have plotted and warred," Ragnar went on grimly, "against the peace of this hold—"

"My own," Wulfgar said lightly.

"And against me."

"You! A thrall's son from Hvinir, where all they grow is sulphur and smoke holes."

"Be careful," Ragnar snarled.

"Let him speak!" someone yelled from the back of the hall. "He has a right. Let him speak."

Other voices joined in. The Jarl waved curtly for silence. "He can speak. If he has anything worth hearing."

The prisoner leaned forward and took an apple from the Jarl's table and bit into it. A guard moved, but Ragnar waved him back.

"I've nothing to say," Wulfgar said, chewing slowly. "Nothing that would change things. You're like a dead tree, Ragnar, smothered with a white, strangling ivy. It's poisoning you, draining you of yourself. Shake her off now, if you still can."

Jessa, like everyone else, stared at Gudrun. She was sipping her wine and smiling. Ragnar's face flushed with rage. His reply was hoarse. "That's enough. Rebellion means death. As you were a landed man it will be quick, with an ax. Tomorrow."

Men in the smoky hall looked at one another. There

was a murmuring that rose to a noise. Gudrun's eyes moved across their faces as she drank.

"He can't do that!" Thorkil muttered.

Mord's hands clamped down on his shoulders and stayed there. "Wait. Keep still." His fingers dug into the soft coat. "Don't draw attention to yourself."

Wulfgar spat an apple pip onto the floor. At once, with an enormous crash, one of the shutters on the windows suddenly collapsed, flung open in a squall of wind that whipped out half the candles at a stroke. In the darkness someone yelled; Wulfgar twisted and hurled himself through the guards into the crowd of confused shadows. Strange blue smoke was billowing from the fires. Jessa coughed, half choked; in the uproar dogs were barking and Ragnar was shouting orders. Then the doors were open; men were running among the dim houses of the hold, letting the bitter wind stream in and slice through the smoke like a knife.

"Is he away?" Thorkil shouted, on his feet.

"He ought to be. If he was ready."

"It was all planned. You knew!"

"Hush. Keep your voice down."

Jessa turned; Gudrun's chair was empty. Then her eye caught sight of something lying half in the fire, smoldering; it was a small bunch of some herb, tied with a green ribbon.

The stifling blue smoke was drifting from it. Jessa looked around, but the peddler was nowhere to be seen. She bent down quickly and pulled the singed bundle out of the ashes, stamped on it, and pushed it into the deep pockets of her coat so no one saw.

"Will he really escape?" Thorkil was asking.

"If he gets out of the hold, there's every chance. Not many who search will want to find him. He should head south, overseas."

"And will he?"

Mord gave her a half smile. "I doubt it. He wants to be Jarl." He sighed. "There are plenty of others who want it."

Suddenly it seemed the hall was almost empty. Then Mord stood up. "Ah. This is it."

One of Gudrun's men was beckoning them across. As they walked over, talk hushed. Jessa saw Thorkil's back stiffen.

They followed the man through a wooden archway crawling with twisted snakes. Beyond was a room lit by lamplight. Mord had to stoop under the lintel as he went in; Jessa came last, her fingers clenched tight to stop them shaking.

They were all there: Ragnar, Grettir, a few white-haired men with eyes like chips of ice—and Gudrun. Close to, she was almost beautiful. Her eyes were like water in a shallow pool, totally without color. Cold came out of her; Jessa felt it against her face.

Outside in the hold the search was going on; they heard running footsteps, shouts, the barking of hounds. Everywhere would be searched. Here the silence seemed intense, as if after some furious argument. Gudrun stood, watching them come; Ragnar barely turned his head. She knows, Jessa thought in a sudden panic; she knows everything. Gudrun smiled at her, a sweet, cold smile.

"The preparations for the journey are made," Ragnar snapped. "The ship leaves early, with the tide." His hands tapped impatiently on the chair arm, a smooth wolfshead, worn by many fingers.

As Gudrun moved to the table, Jessa glimpsed a peculiar glistening wisp of stuff around her wrist; she realized it was snakeskin, knotted and braided. The woman took up a jug and poured a trickle of thin red liquid into four brightly enameled cups. Jessa picked at her glove; Thorkil's strained look caught her eye. But they would have to drink it—it was the faring cup, always drunk before a journey. One after another, silent, they picked up the cups. Gudrun lifted hers with slim white fingers and sipped, looking at them over the rim all the while. Playing with us, Jessa thought, and drank immediately, feeling the hot sour taste flame in her throat. Thorkil tossed his off and banged the cup down empty. Mord's lips barely touched the rim.

"And we have these for you both." She nodded to a thrall; he brought two arm rings, thin delicate silver snakes, and gave them to Jessa and Thorkil. The silver was icy to touch; it had come from her mines where men died in the ice to find it. Jessa wanted to fling hers in the woman's face, but Mord caught her eye and she was silent, cold and stiff with anger.

Gudrun turned away. "Take them out."

"Wait!"

Every eye turned to Thorkil; men who had been talking fell silent. "Don't you mind?" he asked, his fingers clenched on the ring. "That we'll see? That we're going there . . . ?" Despite himself he could not finish.

Jessa saw a movement in the corner; it was the old man Grettir. He had turned his head and was watching.

Gudrun stared straight at Thorkil. All she said was "Thrasirshall is the pit where I fling my rubbish." She stepped close to him; he shivered in the coldness that came out from her.

"I want you to see him. I'll enjoy thinking of it. I'll enjoy watching your face, because I will see it, however far away you think me. Even in the snows and the wilderness nothing hides from me."

She glanced down, and his eyes followed hers. He had

gripped the ring so tight the serpent's mouth had cut him. One drop of blood ran down his fingers.

Five

Better gear than good sense
A traveler cannot carry.

The ship lay low in the water, rocking slightly. In the darkness it was a black shadowy mass, its dragon prow stark against the stars. Men, muffled into shapelessness by heavy cloaks, tossed the last few bundles aboard.

Jessa turned. From here the Jarlshold was a low huddle of buildings under the hill, the hall rising taller than the rest, its serpent-head gables spitting out at her.

"Did you sleep?" Thorkil asked, yawning.

"Yes." She did not tell him about the dreams, though; the dream of walking down those endless corridors full of closed doors, the dream of Gudrun. Or that she had woken and opened a corner of the shutter at midnight, gazing out into the slow, silent snowfall, while Mord's youngest daughter had sighed and snuggled beside her.

Now Mord was coming over, with the young man called Helgi, who was to be captain of the ship.

"Well . . ." Mord kissed her clumsily and thumped Thorkil on the back. "At least Wulfgar got away. They won't find him now. The weather looks good for you. . . ." For a moment he stared out over the water. Then he said, "Words are no use, so I won't waste them. I will try and get Ragnar to revoke the exile, but he may not live long, and Gudrun will certainly not change things. You must face it. We all must."

"We know that," Jessa said quietly. "Don't worry. We'll manage."

He gazed down at her. "I almost think you will."

Releasing his gloved hand, she turned to the ship. As an oarsman lifted her over she saw the frosted scum of the water splinter and remake itself on the beach, and felt the splashes on her face harden and crack. The ship swayed as Thorkil sat down beside her, clumsy in his furred coat. The helmsman raised the call, and on each side sixteen oars swiveled up, white with their fur of frost. Then they dipped. At the first slap of wood in water, the ship shuddered and grated slowly off the shingle. The wharvesmen stepped back as she rocked and settled. Mord shouted, "Good luck!"

"He's relieved to see us go," Thorkil muttered.

"That's unfair. He's very bitter about it. Good-bye!" she yelled, leaping up, and Thorkil scrambled up into the stern and clung to the dragon's neck. "Don't forget us, Mord! We'll be back!"

He seemed almost too far off to hear. But he nodded bleakly. Then he turned away.

All the cold morning the ship coasted slowly down the Tarvafjord toward the open sea, carried by the icy, ebbing tide. There was little wind and the oarsmen had to row, their backs bending and knees rising in the long, silent rhythms. Fog rose from the water and froze, leaving delicate crystals of ice on spars and planks. The ship was heavy, cluttered with sea chests and baggage, casks of beer, and cargoes for the distant settlements. All around them the fog drifted, blanking out land and sky, and the only sound it did not swallow was the soft dip and splash of the oars.

Jessa and Thorkil sat huddled up in coats and blankets, slowly getting colder and stiffer. Now there seemed to be nothing to say, and nothing to do but stare out at the drifting gray air and dream and remember. Their fingers ached with cold; Jessa thought Thorkil would have been glad even to row, but no one offered him the chance. She had already noticed how the crew watched them curiously, but rarely spoke.

Gradually the fog rose. By midmorning they could see the shore, a low rocky line, and behind it hillsides dark with trees, the snow lying among them. Once they passed a little village swathed in the smoke of its fires, but no one ran out from the houses. Only a few goats watched them glide by.

"Where are they all?" Thorkil muttered.

"Hiding."

"From us?"

"From the Jarl. It's his ship, remember."

At midday the sun was still low, barely above the hills. Helgi told the helmsman to put in at the next flat stretch of shore.

Slowly the ship turned and grazed smoothly into the shallows. As Jessa climbed out, she groaned with the stiffness of her legs; the very bones of her face ached. She and Thorkil raced each other up the beach.

The oarsmen lit a fire and handed around meat and bread, throwing scraps on the wet shingle for the gulls to scream and fight over. Jessa noticed how Helgi kept close. Sudden running would be no use at all.

"How long will the journey take?" she asked, stretching out her legs and rubbing them.

Helgi laughed. "Three days—longer, if the weather turns. Tonight we travel down to the sea, tomorrow up the coast to Ost, then up the Yngvir River to a village called Trond. After that—over the ice."

Thorkil pulled a face. "Why not go by land?"

"Because the hills are full of snow and wolves. You're anxious to arrive, are you?"

Thorkil was silenced. Looking at him, Jessa noticed the glint of silver on his arm. "Why are you wearing that?" she asked, surprised. It was the arm ring that Gudrun had given him.

He looked down at it and touched the snake's smooth head. "I don't know. I hadn't really meant to. I just put it on. . . . It's valuable, after all. Where's yours?"

"In the baggage, but I've a good mind to throw it over the side. It's bad luck. I don't know how you can wear it."

Thorkil scowled. "I will if I want. It's mine."

Jessa shook her head. "It's hers," she said, thinking how vain he was.

"Well, don't throw yours in the sea." Helgi laughed. "Throw it to me instead. The sea is rich enough."

"I might."

Thorkil looked up suddenly. "Your men. Are they coming with us all the way?"

"To the very door," Helgi said grimly. Behind him the oarsmen's talk faltered, as if they had listened for his answer.

The ship reached the coast late that evening, the

watchman of Tarva challenging them suddenly out of the darkness, his voice ringing across the black water. Jolted awake, Jessa heard the helmsman yell an answer, and saw the lights of the settlement ripple under the bows as the ship edged in among the low wharves.

They spent that night in the house of a merchant named Savik, who knew Helgi well, warm in his hall with three oarsmen sprawling and dicing near the only doorway. Where the rest went to, Jessa did not ask. She managed a brief word with Thorkil at the table.

"No chances yet."

He threw her a troubled look. "You heard what he said. We won't have any chances."

"Yes, but keep your eyes open. You never know."

"I suppose we could always jump overboard," he said savagely.

Later she slept fitfully. In her sleep she felt the rocking of the boat, as if it still carried her down the long, icy fjord, and there at the end of it, floating on the sea, was a great, dark building, the winds howling in its empty passages like wolves.

In the morning they left early, as the wind was good, and as soon as they reached open water the sail was dropped with a flapping of furled canvas and the slap of ropes—a single rectangular sheet woven of strong striped cloth. The wind plumped it out into a straining arc; the ship shuddered and plunged through the spray. Jessa climbed up into the prow and watched the white seabirds wheel overhead and scream in the cliffs and crannies. Seals bobbed their heads out and watched her with dark, intelligent eyes; in bays their sluggish shining bodies lay like great pebbles on the shingle.

She turned to the oarsmen squatting in the bottom of the boat out of the wind, some sleeping, others gaming with dice for brooches or metal rings—Thorkil with them, and losing badly it seemed.

After a while Helgi clambered over and sat beside her.

"Do you feel well? No sickness?"

"Not yet."

He grinned. "Yes, it may well come. But we have to put off some cargo at Wormshold this afternoon—that will give you a chance to go ashore. It's a big, busy settlement, under the Worm's Head."

"Worm's Head?"

"Yes. Never seen it? I'll show you." He took out a knife and scratched a few lines into the wooden prow. "It's a spit of land, look, that juts out into the sea. Like this. It looks like a dragon's head, very rough and rocky—a great hazard. There are small islets here, and skerries at the tip. The Flames, we call them. The currents are fierce around them.

That dragon's eaten many a good ship. But you'll see it soon."

And she did, as the ship flew through the morning. At first a gray smudge on the sea; then a rocky shape, growing as they sped toward it into a huge dragon's head and neck of stone, stretched out chin-deep in the gray waves, its mouth wide in a snarl, dark hollows and caves marking nostrils and eyes. The wind howled as they sailed in under it, the swell crashing and sucking and booming deep in the gashed, treacherous rocks.

Wormshold was squeezed into a small haven in the dragon's neck. As soon as Jessa saw it, she knew this would be their chance, perhaps their only chance. It was a busy trading place, full of ships, merchants, fishermen, peddlers, skalds, thieves, and traveling fraudsters of every kind. Booths and trestle tables full of merchandise crowded the waterfront; the stink of fish and meat and spices hung over the boats.

Here they could be lost, quickly and easily; she had coins sewn into the hems of her skirts; help could be bought. She tried to catch Thorkil's eyes, but he seemed silent and depressed.

"It'll never work," he said.

"What's the matter with you! We can try, can't we!" He nodded, unconvinced.

They wandered stiffly about, glad to walk and run, even though two of Helgi's men, the one called Thrand

and the big noisy one, Steinar, trailed around behind them. Jessa felt excitement pulse through her. Only two. It might have been much worse.

They stared at the goods for sale. Strange stuff, most of it, from the warmer lands to the south: wrinkled fruits, fabrics in bales and bolts, shawls, belts, buckles, fine woolen cloaks flapping in the sea wind. Rows of stiff hides creaked and swung; there were furs, colored beads, bangles, and trinkets of amber and whalebone and jet. One booth sold only rings, hundreds of them strung in rows; rings for fingers, neck, arms, of all metals, chased or plain or intricately engraved.

With a word to Steinar, Thrand stepped into the crowd, pushing his way to a man sharpening knives. Jessa saw him pull his own out and hand it over. So that left one.

She bought some sweetmeats from a farmwife and she and Thorkil ate them, watching a blacksmith hammer out a spearhead and plunge it with a hiss into a bucket of water. As Thorkil fingered the hanging weapons enviously, someone jolted gently against Jessa's shoulder.

"A thousand apologies," murmured a low voice.

A thin, lanky man stood beside her, his coat patched and ragged. He winked slyly. Astonished, she stared at him, then glanced carefully around. Steinar was a good way back, trying to buy ale.

"You travel fast down the whale's road," the peddler said quietly, examining a brooch on a stall.

"So do you." Jessa gasped. "Where is Wulfgar? Is he with you?"

"That outlaw?" He grinned at her. "That prince of the torn coat? What makes you think I would know?"

She took the fragments of herbs out of her pocket and rubbed them thoughtfully between her fingers, until their faint scent reached him.

"These."

The peddler glanced at them quickly and made a soundless whistle. "Well. You have very good eyes. As for Wulfgar, people are saying he's fled south. They may be right."

"That's not what I think." She watched Thorkil weighing a sword in his hand. Then she said, "Others might want to escape. This might be a good time."

The peddler dropped the brooch and picked up another; his eyes swept the crowd with a swift glance. "I had heard where they were sending you. But the snake woman has eyes that see too far."

She stared at him angrily. "If you won't help, I'll try anyway. I don't want to spend the rest of my life starving in Thrasirshall with . . . whatever's there. I can pay you, if that's what you want." He put the brooch down and turned to her.

"I thought you were braver," he said.

"Only about some things."

"Then listen." His voice was suddenly sharp and urgent. "Don't do anything. Trust me. You must wait until you hear from me, no matter how long it takes. *Don't* try to escape. Promise!"

"But—"

"Promise! I won't let you down."

She gave a sigh of bewilderment. "All right. But we leave here soon!"

"It won't be here. Don't worry. When you see me again, you'll understand everything."

As she stared at him she saw the man Steinar push nearer.

"I'm afraid not," she said loudly. "It's too expensive."

"Ah, lady," the peddler said at once, scratching his cheek, "please yourself. Next time I'll bring you better goods. Trust me."

With a wink he turned away into the crowd.

Thorkil touched her arm. "There you are. Steinar's coming. He's had too much to drink, by the look of him."

"Rubbish." The man was behind them; his breath stank of beer. One heavy hairy hand clamped down on Thorkil's shoulder. "Back to the ship."

Helgi was waiting for them rather anxiously. He gave

Steinar a few sharp words, but the man just shrugged and sprawled into his place among the oarsmen. Thrand came late, cursed by everyone.

The men rowed out into the current. The wind was freshening and the sea seemed much rougher; white flecks topped the waves.

Looking back, Jessa saw no sign of the peddler. She leaned her chin on her hands thoughtfully. She had promised to wait, and she would, but she couldn't help feeling they'd missed their chance. Now every day took them nearer to Thrasirshall. But there had been something in the man's look that had comforted her, some hidden spark of knowledge and, yes, laughter. He'd been laughing at her. He knew something that she didn't, that was why.

SIX

Short are the sails of a ship,
Dangerous the dark . . .

By late afternoon the storm was on them. Icy rain pelted down, hurled like glinting spears into eyes and faces. Jessa was already drenched, although she and Thorkil sat in the bottom of the boat with a sheet of sailcloth around them. When the water began to lap their ankles, they had to move and help bail. The ship rose and fell, toppling into enormous troughs, buffeted by waves that curled high over the deck. Through the spasms of rain and hail, Jessa could barely see the oarsmen clenched over their oars, or Helgi, hanging half out of the prow, dripping with spray, yelling when they swerved too near the rocks. The iron gray cliffs hung over them; the boat crashed and rose through the floundering seas, every spar and timber straining and shrieking. Sick and numb, Jessa flung water over the side. Time had gone; she had been doing this forever. Cold nailed her feet to the deck; every bone ached; the world rose and fell and floundered around her.

As darkness fell, the rain froze into masses of ice on the timbers, so that they had to hack it off with knives and fling it overboard. Once Helgi gave a great yell; the helmsman jerked the rudder and the ship skimmed a bank of shingle, grating horribly, flinging them all down. Then the wind came about and hauled the ship into a trough, and out, swinging her around. Staggering up, Jessa saw that they had cleared the headland; the rain drove now from an empty sky.

Night thickened quickly. Shields and baggage and casks of beer were flung out into the black hollows. Jessa's eyes were stinging with the salt and hail that bounced from the deck; her arms ached, frozen to her sleeves, and however hard she bailed, the water still rose, lapping the ankles of the oarsmen, who spat out curses and sardonic remarks.

At last, exhausted, she sank back on her heels, clinging to the rail. The storm roared around her; she heard strange wailings in the sea, voices on the wind, screaming, whispering spells, spinning the boat with their breath. Closing her eyes she saw Wulfgar standing in the hall; the hangings of the Jarlshold flapped; something walked and padded on strange feet through corridors and locked rooms, a creature with Gudrun's eyes that held out a thin silver arm ring, pressing it into her hands. She could feel it; she had it out of the bag where it had been hidden. It seemed to her that she turned to the sea, opened her numb fingers, and let the weight of it, the enormous weight, slide swiftly over the side. Then she lay down among the wet baggage. She was asleep when Helgi saw the harbor fire at Ost.

In the morning, she wondered what was real and what was dream. Ost was a filthy place; a squalid mess of huts and muddy pens, the people shifty-eyed and half starved. Behind the settlement the mountains with their ice white cliffs plunged straight down into the fjord; the pastures were icebound most of the year, the animals lean and hollow-eyed. The chieftain was a small greasy man who called Helgi "sir" and Thorkil and herself "lord" and "lady," his greedy eyes always on their cloaks and amulets. Helgi stayed with them all the time, and the oarsmen kept together, starting no fights and wearing their weapons conspicuously. The Jarl's hold on the land was weakening as they traveled north; they were coming to wild country full of outlaws and hunted men.

As the ship was being repaired, Jessa rummaged through her bag.

"What are you looking for?" She hadn't heard Thorkil climb aboard behind her. He looked tired, and the fine stitchery of his coat was already soiled and stained.

She closed the bag up. "The arm ring. Gudrun's. It's not here."

"Do you mean it's been stolen?"

"No." Jessa shrugged and half laughed. "I think I threw it over the side after all. Last night. I suppose I must have been half asleep."

He glared at her angrily. "Jessa, that was silver! We could have found a use for it!"

She shrugged. "I'm glad to get rid of it. I hardly thought I'd ever see you wearing her favors, either. Are you going to sell yours, then?"

His fingers ran over the smooth silver head.

"Not yet."

"You're keeping it?"

"For now. It does no harm, does it?"

"I suppose not," she said uneasily. But she didn't tell him about the peddler, as she had meant to.

They were glad to leave Ost, but as they entered the fjord and turned inland, the menace of Thrasirshall was creeping nearer. And still the peddler had not appeared. Jessa tried not to think about him. What if he had been in Gudrun's pay and had tricked her? She was furious with herself.

All morning they rowed on the still water, watching the jagged cliffs rise up on each side, scraped sheer by the retreating glacier.

Thorkil sat silent, fingering his arm ring. The men too were morose and watchful; they only spoke in mutters. Helgi stood in the prow, his hand rubbing the great dragon's neck, rarely turning his head. Silent and ominous, the narrow craft slid into the harbor of Trond at noon.

The place seemed deserted. A few boats were dragged up on the shingle. Wisps of smoke drifted from the small turf houses, their roofs green with grass. Helgi climbed out and waited. Finally he called out. No one answered. Jessa could hear the faint lap of the tidal water against the boat; skuas and gulls screamed in the crags.

Then a dog barked, and a tall man stepped up onto a rock above them, a long fishing spear glinting in his hand.

"What's your business?" he asked, after a long stare.

"Messengers," Helgi said curtly. "From the Jarl Ragnar."

"To us?"

Helgi hesitated. Then he said, "To Thrasirshall."

It must have been a great shock, but the man barely showed it. "Can you prove that?"

Helgi took the Jarl's token from his pocket—a ring, in silver, marked with one rune—and flung it up. The man caught it and looked at it carefully. Then his eyes moved over the ship. Jessa heard the whisper of a sword slowly unsheathing behind her.

"Keep that still!" Helgi hissed without turning.

Quickly the man scrambled down the rocks, soil and pebbles slithering away under his feet. He was a tall, gray man, with a weathered face. "I'm not alone. There are many of us, as you'll guess, so I advise you, friend with the sword, to hold your hand. Your token, master."

The silver ring was dropped into Helgi's hand. Steinar slammed his sword back in its sheath.

"Now," the man said, "what do you want from us?" There was a change in his voice; Helgi heard it too, and gave a wry smile. "Your hospitality, chieftain, for a few nights. Also safe haven for the ship and the men left with her. Most important, sleds, dogs, and if you have them, horses for those of us going on to the hall. This will all be paid for on our return."

"Your return!" The man raised an eyebrow. "Master, you'll pay for it before you go. No one takes that road and returns."

Suddenly he turned and shouted. Men seemed to spring up, a silent crop from the rocks. There were some young lads, but most were older like their leader; hard, coarse-looking men, but strong, and probably handy, Jessa thought, with those axs and spears. They came down and stared at the strangers, especially Jessa and Thorkil. A few women leaned in the doors of the houses.

"Come with me." The tall man led Jessa, Thorkil, and Helgi to a small hall, warm and dark inside, with a good fire blazing in the hearth.

"Now," he said, sitting down. "Dogs and sleds we have aplenty, but the way you wish to take is far too treacherous for sleds. You'll need horses. And those are precious, this far north."

"But you have them?"

"For the right price." As he spoke, a few other men came in. Warmed wine was served out by a thin woman with untidy hair. Jessa sipped hers thankfully.

"My name is Sigmund—they call me Graycloak," the man added.

"You are the chieftain?"

The man looked at him over his cup. "Indeed no. We have no chieftains here, master; no one man better than the others. I am elected to speak. We still do that here."

Helgi frowned. "The Jarl —"

"Did I mention the Jarl?" Sigmund said at once, looking around with pretended surprise. The other men laughed.

Helgi looked uneasy. "What price, then, for these horses?"

"First, my duty as a host. This young lady must be looked after."

He called one of the girls over and spoke to her quietly. Then she came up to Jessa. "Come with me," she said with a shy smile.

As she followed, Jessa saw Helgi's anxious look and grinned at him. Then the door closed between them.

Warm water was wonderful after so long without it, and clean clothes made her feel ten times better. The girl looked on curiously, fingering a brooch.

"This is nice. Did you get it at the Jarlshold?"

"No."

"Is the Jarlshold splendid? And the Snow-walker,

Gudrun, is she as evil as they say?"

"Yes, she is," Jessa said absently as she laced her boots. "She's also very powerful. I'd be careful what you say, even here."

"Oh, we are protected from her here."

Jessa looked up. "Protected?"

"Yes." The girl came and sat on a bright tapestry stool next to her. Her fingers picked absently at the stitches. "We knew you were coming."

Jessa was astonished. Then she thought of the peddler.

"How did you know?"

"Through the runes. And my father has given me a message for you. If you are really prisoners of those men, you and the boy, then you must tell me. We will release you."

Jessa's mind was working quickly. "Has the peddler arranged this?"

The girl looked puzzled. "What peddler?"

"Never mind. . . . How could you release us?"

"The crew would be killed. No one would be surprised if they never went back. Longships are often lost in storms. And no news ever comes out of Thrasirshall. The Jarl would never know if you'd got there or not."

It was all so sudden. Jessa thought for a while. The peddler could never have gotten here before them. And if these people knew "by the runes," that meant sorcery.

"How do we know it's not a trap?" she said at last. "Why help us?"

The girl shrugged. "Because of your father."

Jessa got up and wandered over to the fire. So that was it. They were Wulfings' men. She thought about the promise she had made the peddler—that stupid promise!—and then about the black, monstrous building somewhere far out there in the snow. Not to have to go there, all that long journey. But he had seemed so sure. And Gudrun—would she really be fooled?

"What do you mean, that you're protected here?" She turned quickly. "What protects you? Is it sorcery?"

The girl's black eyes looked up at her. "The shamanka does it. When Gudrun looks at us here, she sees only mist. The shamanka knew you were coming."

"Can I speak to her?"

The girl thought, then nodded. "Very well. Tonight. I'll arrange it."

"Good. And tell your father"—she paused—"that I thank him, but he must do nothing. Not yet."

Again the girl nodded.

"And you can keep the brooch, too," Jessa said, "if you like."

SEVEN

Now is answered what you ask of the runes.

Jessa woke suddenly, her eyes wide. In the darkness someone was crouching next to her; a hand was gripping her shoulder tight.

"Come with me," the girl's voice whispered in her ear.

With a sigh Jessa heaved off the warm covers, slipped on her coat and soft leather boots. Then she followed, silently, through the swinging curtain of the booth.

It was dark in the hall, and smelled of ale and meat. The fire had smoldered low, and some of the oarsmen lying in the corners snored. Carefully the girls slipped between them. One dog raised its head and watched. As they passed Thorkil's booth, Jessa paused, but the girl shook her head. "Only you. No one else."

At the door Helgi's guard was breathing heavily, slumped against the wall. All at once Jessa realized that the men had been drugged—no trained warrior would sleep as heavily as this. She stepped over him thoughtfully.

Outside, the world was black. Water lapped against the

shingle far off, and up on a hill a breeze rustled stiff branches. The girl led Jessa between the houses to one by itself at the edge of the settlement, and as they walked, their feet splintered the puddles on the open ground. Above them the sky suddenly rippled and broke into light. Looking up, Jessa saw the eerie flicker of the aurora above the trees; a green and gold and blue haze over the stars, its gauzy shape flowing and rippling like a curtain.

"Surt's blaze," the girl remarked. "The poets would say they were feasting in Gianthome."

Jessa nodded, caught in the strange light that made the snow glimmer. Then she ducked her head and followed the girl into the low doorway.

Inside, it was dim and smoky; at the far end she could see someone sitting over the fire. She fumbled forward slowly, and sat on an empty stool. The room was stiflingly warm; around her the walls were hung with thick tapestries, dim woven webs of gods and giants, trolls and strange creatures.

Opposite her sat an aged woman, her face wizened and yellow. Her thin hair was braided into intricate knots and plaits; amulets and luckstones were hung and threaded among her clothes. She wore a stiff cloak sewn with birds' feathers, glossy in the dimness. As Jessa watched, the old woman's hand, its skin dried tight over the knuckles, drifted among the stones on the table in front of her, moving one, turning another over—small, flat pebbles, each marked with its own black rune.

"Wait outside, Hana."

The curtain flickered as the girl moved through it.

Jessa waited, watching the hands turn the worn pebbles. Then, without lifting her eyes, the woman said, "It is not that I have her powers. You must know that. I do not know what sort of a creature she is, this Gudrun No-onesdaughter, or what gods she worships, but she is strong. Still"—and a pebble clicked in the dimness—"I have something, some slight skill, gathered over the years. I have spread my mind like a bird's wing over this kin. Here, we are safe. She cannot see us."

"Then if we were to stay here—Thorkil and I . . ."

"She would not know of it. But you would not be able to leave. Her mind is the surface of a lake—all the world's reflections move across it."

Jessa edged away from the fire, which was scorching her knees.

"Yes, but escape . . . it would mean the men would be killed?"

"Men!" The old woman looked up, her mouth twisted in a grim smile. "What are men? There are plenty more."

Chilled, Jessa was silent a moment. Then she said

quietly, "I won't have them killed. I won't have that."

The pebbles turned. "There is no other way. They cannot go back—she would make them speak."

"That's it, then. We must go on." She said it as firmly as she could. Only her word was keeping a dagger out of Helgi's ribs, yes, and the others too. And this wasn't the way.

The old woman turned a last pebble and gazed down at it. "So the runes tell me."

Jessa edged forward. The room seemed darker; something rustled behind her. The old woman's amulets clicked as she moved.

"Do you know," Jessa whispered, "what lives in Thrasirshall? Is there anything there still alive?"

"There is fear there. Yours. Your cousin's. Gudrun's."

"Hers?"

The woman chuckled. "Oh, hers above all. Her eyes are always this way. Nine years ago Brochael Gunnarsson landed here. There was one with him, so muffled in coats and furs against the ice that no one could see him. So it has always been. But I have felt her thought stretching out like a hand, touching, jerking back. Oh yes, there is something in the hall, something alive, and she fears it, as she fears her mirror."

Jessa touched one of the stones. It was cool and smooth. "What do you mean, her mirror?"

"Gudrun never looks in a glass." The shamanka turned and spat into the fire. "The runes have said her own reflection will destroy her. There are no mirrors in the Jarlshold."

And then with a rustle of feathers the old woman reached out and caught Jessa's wrist—a tight, cold grip. "One thing: she will have not let you go without some link, some tie to bind you to her. Find it. Break it. Whatever it costs you.

"As for Kari Ragnarsson . . . sometimes, in the darkest part of the night, I have thought that I felt . . . something. A cold, strange touch on my mind." She shrugged and sat back, gazing at Jessa. "But I do not know what he is. When you find out, you might come and tell me."

The road was an ancient one, built by giants. No one used it now—after only a few miles it dwindled into a frozen track wandering through the boulders and scree of the fjordshore. The six horses and the pack mule picked their way along it, sometimes sinking fetlock-deep in the icy bog. Jessa was stiff from jerking forward to keep her balance.

They were already four hours out from Trond, the wind howling at them down ravines in the steep rock face. They had started before dawn, but even now it was barely light enough to make out the track as it began to turn inland, toward the hills. Muffled in cloaks and coats, only their eyes visible, the riders had spread out in a straggling line, urging on their slithering, nervous horses. Helgi went first, with Thorkil and Jessa close behind him. Then came the three men who had drawn the marked stones out of Helgi's glove at Trond, when the oarsmen had argued about who was to go farther. Thorgard Blund and his cousin, the thin man called Thrand, and the big, loud-mouthed Steinar, called Hairyhand. Jessa wondered how they felt now; there had been some bitter words back there. Now the three kept together, watchful and resentful.

The track climbed up, moving slowly above the snow-line. Now the horses strode in one another's hoof holes across a great snowfield, dazzlingly white, broken only by streams that gurgled under their seamed, frozen lids. These were invisible, and treacherous; once Thorkil's horse lurched forward into one, almost throwing him. After that they kept direction only by the sun, but the sky slowly clouded over. By late afternoon they had lost the track altogether.

Finally Helgi stopped and swore. The narrow valley down which they had come was closed by a sheer rock face, glistening with icicles and glassy twists of frozen water. He turned. "We'll have to go back. This isn't it."

Jessa saw Steinar glance at his colleagues. "What about a rest?" he growled. "The horses need it."

Helgi looked at Jessa. She tugged the frosted scarf from her mouth. "I'm in no hurry."

They found an overhang of cliff and sat under it; Helgi fed the horses, then he joined Jessa and Thorkil. They ate slowly, listening to the bleak wind in the hollow rocks. The other three sat apart, talking in gruff, quiet voices. Helgi watched them. Finally they called him over, and when he came they stood up. Steinar was bigger and heavier than the younger man. He put his hand on Helgi's shoulder. Talk became hurried, noisy, almost an argument.

"I don't like the look of that," Thorkil muttered.

Jessa raised her eyes from a daydream. Helgi was shaking his head angrily. He snapped something sharp and final.

"They're scared," Thorkil said. "They don't want to go on."

"I don't blame them."

They watched the bitter, hissed argument. These were soldiers, Jessa thought, trained how to fight, to deal with things, but how could they deal with this? The horror of whatever was in Thrasirshall had caught hold of them; it was wearing at their nerves.

"Do you think he'll make them go on?"

"He'll try. But it's three to one."

"Three to three."

Thorkil flashed her a brief grin. "You're right. But remember, if we were . . . out of the way, they wouldn't have to go on at all. They've probably been thinking about that."

Helgi flung Steinar's hand from him and turned away. He marched past Jessa and caught the horse's bridle.

"Ride close to me," he muttered. "And pray we find the place soon."

Eight

A wayfarer should not walk unarmed,
But have his weapons to hand:
He knows not when he may need a spear,
Or what menace meet on the road.

It was a hard thing to pray for. Jessa swung onto her weary horse and gathered up the reins, moving out hurriedly after Thorkil. Looking back, she saw that Steinar and Thorgard Blund were still listening to the thin man, Thrand. His voice was a quiet echo under the cliff. Steinar laughed and turned, catching her eye. He put his huge hands up to his horse and hauled himself up.

Jessa and Thorkil rode close together. Neither spoke. The path ran along the edge of a vast pine wood, its branches still and heavy with snow. In there it was dim and gloomy, the trees receding into endless aisles, only a few birds piping in the hush. Once a pine marten streaked across the track.

Helgi was guessing the way now, and they all knew it. The sun became a cold globe, sliding down into mists and vapors; twilight turned the world black and gray. The snow lost its glare and shimmered blue; crystals of ice hardened on the tree trunks.

Without turning his head, Helgi muttered, "Thorkil. Can you use that knife of yours?"

"What knife?"

"The sharp one you've been keeping under your coat."

Thorkil grinned. "It's not the only thing that's sharp. Yes, I can use it."

Jessa glanced back. Three wraiths on shadow horses flickered through the trees. "Listen, Helgi—"

"Don't worry. It may not come to that. It wouldn't help us if it does." His eyes moved anxiously over the dark fells. "I'd be glad to see that hellhole now, troll or no troll."

Silence, except for the swish of snow. Jessa loosened

the blade in her belt, warm under her coat. Night fell on them, like a great bird; the stars glittered through the trees. She thought of the peddler, his urgent voice saying, "Wait for me." But where was he? He had abandoned them.

Then the voice came from behind.

"Captain!"

With a clink of harness, Helgi drew his horse to a halt. He sat still a moment, his back rigid. Then he turned around.

The three horsemen waited in a line. Their swords gleamed in the starlight. Ice glinted on their clothes and beards.

"We've come far enough," Steinar said. "We're going back."

"Go on. I should have brought braver men."

The man laughed. "What's courage against trolls and monsters? Come back with us, man."

"What will you tell the Jarl?" Helgi asked, his voice clear across the frost. "And what will you say to *her*?"

Steinar glanced at Thrand.

"My father was a poet," the thin man remarked. "I can feel a story coming to me, too. It concerns two children who fell overboard in a storm."

With a slither of sound Helgi drew his sword. "Not while I'm alive."

Suddenly the pack mule jerked. A black shape flapped down through the branches, dusting snow into Jessa's hair, and another followed it; two enormous, glossy ravens that clung and settled on the bouncing branches.

Helgi laughed grimly, his hand tight on his horse's mane. "Look at that. The High One has two birds like that. He sends them out to see everything that happens in the world. My job is to take these two to Thrasirshall and keep them safe on the way. If you're coming, come. Otherwise go back. But don't think I'll keep your cowardice quiet."

Steinar's harness creaked as he moved forward. "It's a waste, lad. Though I suppose the wolves won't think so."

The ravens karked. Snow swirled in the darkness. "Better ride, Jessa," Helgi growled, but she was ready; she dug her heels in and the horse leaped forward into a sky that tore itself apart in front of her. The aurora crackled into a great arch of green fire and scarlet flame; Jessa thundered into it over the hard snow, could feel the eerie light tingling on her face. Branches loomed at her and she ducked, lying low and breathless on the warm, sweating skin of the horse. Voices yelled; Thorkil shouted; something whistled over her head and thudded into the snow.

She kicked hard; the horse burst through the edge of the wood, leaped a black stream hanging rigid on its stones, and began to flounder up the white sides of the fell. The sky crackled and spat light; her horse was green, then gold, then scarlet. Behind her Thorkil galloped, coat flapping, his face shimmering with colors. Up and up through the deep snow, kicking the horse, urging it, swearing at it, and then, at last, the top!

She came over the lip of the white hill through the stars and an arch of flame. A great wind roared in her ears; the horse stood, snorting clouds of breath.

"Go on!" Thorkil was yelling. "Don't stop now!" His own horse fought and floundered up the slope.

But Jessa did not move. She sat, looking ahead, her hair whipping out in the gale.

"There's nowhere left to go," she called grimly.

Beside her, he gazed breathlessly down into the valley.

At Thrasirshall.

It was huge even from here: a mass of black, broken towers hung with ice. The aurora flickered silently over it, tingeing glassy walls, dark window slits. A thin moon balanced on the hills behind, its light piercing the shattered roofs, stretching the hall's long shadow over the blue unbroken snow.

No smoke rose from the roofs; no animals lowed in the byres. It was a silent ruin.

Jessa heard Helgi's horse snort behind her, and then the other three came to a slow, doubtful stop. She didn't move, or care. All the danger from behind had gone. It had been sucked down into that black, glittering ruin below them.

After a long silence Thorkil said, "It's empty. There are no lights, no tracks in the snow. They must be dead long since."

"Maybe." Helgi turned his head, the colors of Surt's blaze flickering on his face. "Well?" he said quietly.

The three men were staring at the hall, their horses fidgeting uneasily. Then Steinar sheathed his sword with a snap. He glanced at the others; Thrand shrugged.

"We should keep together." They seemed to have lost all will; Jessa saw how their eyes kept straying to the tower.

"Nothing will be said?"

"Nothing." Helgi's voice was rich with contempt. Without another word he turned his horse and moved forward. The howl of a wolf broke out in the wood behind them; then another answered, not so far away. The horses flicked their ears nervously.

The riders moved together in a tight knot, down the long white slope of the hill. No one spoke. Behind them the pack mule floundered, its rope slack.

As they came down to the ruin, they could hear the wind moaning through the broken walls. The snow down here had drifted into great banks; they pushed cautiously through it, into the shadow of the walls. At the first archway, its keystone hanging dangerously low, they halted.

"Torches," Thrand muttered. "The more light the better."

Helgi nodded. The gaunt stones behind him were coated in ice; frozen in smooth lumps and layers. Nothing moved.

They had brought torches of pitch from the boat. It took an age to make flame, but then the soaked wood flared and crackled, making the horses start in the acrid smoke. "Two will be enough," Helgi said, bending and picking one up. "I'll go first. You, Steinar, at the back. Take the other light with you."

They moved through the arch. Its gates were long gone, rotted to one black post that stuck out of the snow like a burned finger. Torchlight gleamed on frozen stone, on shapeless masses of ice that might once have been carvings. As they came to the inner gate they saw it was blocked; a row of long smooth icicles of enormous thickness hung down to the ground. Helgi and Thrand had to dismount and hack at them with sword and flame; each snapped with a great crack that rang in the ruins.

One by one the horses squeezed through. Now they found themselves in a courtyard, a great square of white.

Winds and breezes moaned in the outbuildings, sounding like voices, creaking a timber door somewhere out of sight, gusting snow from the sills of windows in the hall. The silence held them still; the silence and the emptiness. Kari is dead, Jessa thought. Whatever he was.

Helgi turned. "There's a door there, look. We might be able to get inside."

He dismounted and waded over, knee-deep in snow. As he held the torch up, the flames lit the door. It was made of ancient wood, studded with nails, and had once been repaired with planks hammered over the weak places, but even these were now green with rot. Helgi kicked it; it shuddered but held. In the darkening air they waited, stiff with fear, but there was no sound or stir from within.

Helgi drew his knife. At the same time, something black screeched from the sky. Helgi yelled with fright and dropped the torch; the horses reared and plunged. In sudden blackness dim shadows flapped overhead.

Jessa shrieked. Someone caught her arm.

"Quiet! Helgi?"

Steinar had pushed forward, torch in hand. In the red light they saw Helgi scramble from his knees, his face white. "I'm all right."

"What was it?"

He looked up. "Birds. Two of them."

They were perched on the sill above him; the two ravens from the wood. Their eyes followed every movement.

Steinar gripped the thorshammer at his neck. "This is a place of sorcery, or worse. Let's get out, man. While we can!"

But Helgi snatched the torch from his hand and turned, holding it up. Then he stopped, stock-still.

Jessa's fingers clenched on the frozen reins.

Before them, the door was opening.

It was tugged open, jerking and grating against the stones as if the wood was swollen.

Firelight streamed out, as if a slot had opened in a dark lantern. It fell on their faces, glinted in the horses' eyes. A scatter of snow falling through it turned red as blood.

A man stood there. He was a giant; his head reached the lintel of the door, and though he was wrapped in furs and patched cloaks, they saw his strength. His face was flushed with the fire's heat; his beard and hair dark red, cut close.

Helgi gripped his knife, looking suddenly small and pale on the cold steps. The big man gave him a glance, then pushed him aside and shouldered his way down among the horses. He went straight to Jessa. She could feel the warmth of the fire glowing from him as he gripped her horse's mane.

"You're late, Jessa," he said. "A good soup is almost spoiled."

Ding

Greetings to the host. The guest has arrived.
In which seat shall he sit?

The chair was too big for her, and had once been covered with some embroidery; the firelight glimmered on a patch of trees and a threadbare reindeer. She snuggled back and sipped the soup. It was so hot it scorched her tongue.

They were in a small room, very dark. There was another ragged chair, a table, and in a corner some empty shelves, their shadows jerking in the firelight. By the hearth a stack of cut logs oozed dampness. The window was boarded up, and some torn shreds of green cloth were nailed across it to keep out drafts.

Jessa's knees were hot; she edged back. Her coat was dripping into a puddle on the floor.

On the table lay two fishing spears and a knife, thrust deep into the timber. Thorkil was trying to pull it out, but couldn't.

"That's another thing," he said, tapping the empty platter. "Enough food for six. Everything prepared. How did he know?"

She shook her head.

Outside, voices approached; the door shuddered open. The big man, Brochael, came in, and Helgi trailed behind him, glancing quickly into the shadows. They had all done that. No one forgot that the creature was here, somewhere.

"We're going, Jessa," Helgi said quickly.

She stared at him. "Tonight?"

He shrugged unhappily. "You've seen. They won't stay here. To be frank, neither will I. There's too much strangeness in this place." She nodded, wordless.

"I'm just sorry to have to leave you both here."

"Don't be." Brochael planted himself in front of the blaze. "They'll be safer here than in any hold of Gudrun's."

Helgi gave her a wan smile and went to the door. Suddenly Jessa wanted to go with him; she leaped up, spilling the soup, but he caught her eye and she stopped.

"Good luck," he said. Then he went and closed the door.

In the sudden silence they heard the clink of harness,

the muffled scrape of a hoof in snow. After that there was only the wind, howling over the sills and under the doors into all the empty rooms and spaces of the hall.

Brochael sat down. He cleared the table with one sweep of his arm, tugged out the knife and thrust it in his belt, and leaned both elbows on the bare wood. "Now. I already know your names and I'm sure you can guess mine. I am Brochael Gunnarsson, of Hartfell. I knew your fathers, a long time ago. I also know that Ragnar has sent you here into exile."

"How do you know?" Jessa demanded. "How could you?"

Brochael took down a candle and lit it. "I was told," he said. There was something in his voice that puzzled her, but she was too tired to think about it now.

She took the letter out of her inner pocket and held it out.

"Were you told about this?"

He took it, looked at her a moment, then put the candle down and tugged open the knots that held the sealskin. A square of parchment fell out; he unfolded it on the table, spreading it flat with his big hands.

They all leaned over it. Spindly brown letters were marked on the rough vellum. Brochael fingered them. "It's brief enough."

He read it aloud. "'From Ragnar, Jarl, to Brochael Gunnarsson, this warning. When I die she will come for the creature. It may be to kill, or it may be for some reason of her own. Take him south, out of these lands. I would not have him suffer as I have suffered.'"

There was silence. Then Brochael folded the parchment. "Does he think I don't know?" he said roughly. He picked up the candle.

"Come with me," he said. "All this gossip can wait until morning."

He led them to a thick curtain in one corner and pulled it back. Beyond it was the usual sleeping booth—it was well paneled in wood, the blankets patched and coarse. "The other is next to it." Brochael put the candle down. "Not the silks of the Jarlshold, but just as warm. Sleep well, for as long as you like. We'll talk tomorrow."

"Where do you sleep?" Thorkil asked, looking at the damp blanket with obvious distaste.

"Elsewhere." Suddenly the big man turned, his shadow huge in the flame light. "The door will be locked—don't let that alarm you. If you hear anything—voices, movements—far off in the building, ignore it. You are safe here. No one can get in."

There was a cold silence.

"Good night," Brochael said calmly.

The curtain rustled. A moment later the key grated in the lock. "Well," Thorkil muttered after a moment. "It's almost as bad as I thought. Dust, fleas, rats." He rubbed at the soiled red cloth of his jerkin and went off to find his own sleeping place.

Wearily Jessa lay down in her clothes and wrapped herself in the rough, damp-smelling blankets. "But I didn't expect Brochael," she muttered quietly.

"What?"

There was no answer. When Thorkil came back and opened the curtain she was already asleep. He watched her for a moment, then reached out and snuffed the candle, and the flames in the eyes of the serpent on his wrist went out.

Jessa threw two crumbling squares of peat on the fire and chewed the stale bannock that seemed to be breakfast. She watched Thorkil stagger in with the empty bucket and drop it with a clang.

"That water froze as I threw it out." He sat down and looked at her. "We didn't get many answers last night. No one could have got here before us, could they?"

She was thinking of the peddler. "I don't know. Who would?"

"And have you seen this?" He tapped the slab of goat's cheese they had found.

"Cheese," Jessa said drily.

"Yes, but where did it come from? Where are the goats?"

That surprised her. She shook her head, thinking of the empty outbuildings and the untrodden snow. "Perhaps in some building at the back—"

"They'd freeze. And Kari. Where's he?"

Jessa swallowed some crumbs. "I don't want to know that." She wiped her hand in her skirt. "Locked in some room, I suppose."

A scrape interrupted them; the key turned and Brochael ducked in under the low doorway. He had snow in his hair. He grinned at them cheerfully "Awake! Sleep well?"

"Yes, thank you."

They watched him stand in front of the fire, his clothes steaming.

Thorkil glanced at Jessa. "Look," he said. "Are we prisoners here? Can we go anywhere we want to?"

Brochael gave a gruff laugh. "We're all prisoners, lad, but I'm not your keeper, if that's what you mean. But there's not much to see here. Empty rooms and snow."

He watched them for a moment, and they waited for some word of Kari, some warning of one door not to be opened, one corridor not to be explored. But all he said was

"This was a palace once, centuries ago. They say a troll king built it of unhewn stone, and the great road that led up here too. Perhaps the world was warmer in those days."

He turned and began banking up the fire. Jessa couldn't wait any longer. "What about Kari?"

"Kari's here," he said, without turning. "But you won't see him."

Afterward they put on coats and went outside. The sky was iron gray; a stiff wind cut into them down the side of the fell. On the white slope they could see the frozen tracks of Helgi's horses, climbing up into the fringe of trees. And all around, like a white jagged crown, were the mountains.

One courtyard at the back of the building had been swept clear of snow; in the center was a deep well, with faint steam rising from it. As they gazed down they felt warmth on their faces. Thorkil dropped a stone in. "A hot spring. Now that's useful."

They tugged open doors and gazed into stables and barns and byres. Everything was held in a web of ice, glistening with a faint film of soot, as if the entire hold had once had its roofs burned. There were no animals, not even a trace of them, but in one storehouse they found a few casks of dried apples and nuts, some cheese, and two hares hanging next to a row of smoked fish. Thorkil looked up at them.

"Fish! But where's the lake? Where are the fruit trees? Under the snow? I tell you what, Jessa, they should have starved here a long time ago. That's why she sent them here. And yet somehow they're getting this food." He put a finger inside the silver ring on his wrist and eased it around. "Someone must be bringing it."

Then they went into the hold itself, down a long corridor paved with stone and frost. Icicles hung from every lintel and sill. There were stairs leading up; they led to more corridors and passages, and empty rooms where the wind blew in through the bare windows.

Passing one room, Jessa stopped. This one was very small and dark, with a narrow window opposite the door, through which the gray daylight fell like a wand on the floor.

Something about the window puzzled her. Thorkil was far ahead, rummaging in an old rotting chest, so she stepped in and crossed the floor. Then she put her hand up to the window and touched it.

Glass!

She had only seen it before in tiny pieces, polished, in jewelry; never like this in a thick slab. Brushing the frost from it, she took her glove off and felt the surface, saw the trapped bubbles of air deep inside.

"Jessa?" Thorkil called.

"I'm in here."

She put her eye to the glass and looked through it. There was a courtyard below her, with trampled snow. A movement caught her eye; someone was walking through the clutter of buildings. Someone smaller than Brochael. As she tried to see, the shape warped and bent in the thick glass, slid into queer contortions. She stepped back suddenly. Had that been Kari?

"What are you looking at?" Thorkil was at her elbow.

"Quick! There's something out there!"

He looked out, blocking the light with his hands.

"Can you see him?" Jessa asked impatiently.

He shrugged. "Maybe. For a second I thought there was something. Just a flicker." He looked at her. "Was it Kari?"

"I don't know. Someone small . . . it was all bent and twisted."

They were silent. Then Thorkil said bleakly, "I think I'd rather know than wonder like this."

That evening, sewing a tear in her sleeve, Jessa said quietly, "How did you know we were coming?"

Brochael looked up from the fire, his face flushed with heat. "My business." He stirred the oatmeal calmly.

"Someone came before us?" Thorkil ventured.

Brochael grinned. "If you say so. I just knew, that's all. Ragnar sent you here because of your fathers. His idea of a pleasant exile. And to deliver his guilty little message."

"Did you know," Jessa said, biting the thread, "that Gudrun wanted us to come as well?"

That startled him. "She wanted it?"

"We overheard," Jessa explained. She looked up at him closely. "She not only knew we were coming, she said to the old man that it was her idea—that she'd made the Jarl send us."

Brochael stared back. "Did she say why?"

"Not really . . . it was hard to hear. She said she would have her hand on us. . . . I don't know what that meant."

"Don't you?" His face darkened; he looked older and grimmer. "Did she give you anything to eat or drink?"

"Yes, but she drank it too."

He shook his head. "She's a sorceress, Jessa. That means nothing at all."

She looked at Thorkil. "And when can we see Kari?" she asked, trying to sound calm.

Brochael went back to stirring the porridge. "When you're ready. When I think you're ready." He gave them a strange, sidelong look. "And if you really want to."

Ten

It's safe to tell a secret to one,
Risky to tell it to two.
To tell it to three is thoughtless folly,
Everyone else will know.

Time at Thrasirshall passed slowly. Despite the mysterious supplies, food was short and Jessa often felt hungry. After a while she got used to it. The cold was still intense; they were so far north the snow had not begun to melt. The weather made it difficult to get outside, but sometimes she and Thorkil scrambled up the fell and wandered into the silent woods. On one afternoon of pale sunshine they climbed a higher crag and gazed out at the desolate miles of land carved by slow glaciers. Brochael had told them there was nothing more to the north but ice, until the sky came down and touched the earth. Even the road ended here, at the world's end.

They ran all the way back to keep warm, floundering and giggling through the snow, Jessa in front, so that she struggled across the courtyard and burst into the room without warning. Then she stopped instantly, letting Thorkil thud into her back.

The opposite door was closing; soft footsteps shuffled on the other side, fading to an echo in empty spaces. One chair was pushed back; a knife and a piece of carven wood had been flung on the table.

Brochael leaned back and watched them, as if he was waiting for the questions. After a moment Jessa went to the fire, warming the sudden cold from her back. She watched Thorkil pick up the wood and run his fingers over the skillful carving.

"Is he afraid of us?" he said at last.

Brochael took the wood from him. "In a way. Remember, he's seen few folk besides me. But it's more than that. You're afraid of him."

And they were. They knew it. They kept together most of the time, never went alone into the dim corridors. They spent time playing chess, mending their clothes, snaring hares, or at the unending task of fetching wood and kindling. Brochael watched them, as if he was biding his time. Some days he would vanish for hours at a time and come back without any explanation, and every night he locked the door with the iron key.

Once late at night, hauling water from the well, they

thought they saw candlelight flickering in one window high in the tower, and the two black birds that had startled Helgi always seemed to be flapping and karking up there, wheeling against the greens and golds of the aurora that flickered here every night.

It was on one of those nights that Jessa had her dream.

She had fallen asleep in the warm huddle of blankets and she dreamed the peddler came out of the darkness and put his hand on her shoulder. He shook her. "Wake up. I haven't let you down. Look, I've melted the snow."

She got up and crossed to a large glass window and looked out. She saw a green land, a blue sky. Flocks of birds wheeled and screamed overhead: gulls, skuas, swifts. In the courtyard horsemen were riding; each horse had eight legs, like the horse of the High One; each was black with fiery eyes.

She looked around, but the peddler was gone, and only a white snake moved across the stone floor and under the raised bed.

Then she dreamed that the curtain opened and someone looked in. The figure crossed the room to her, looked down at her, and she saw it was Gudrun, her white hand stretched out. One finger touched Jessa's cheek with a stab of ice.

She woke at once and sat up, heart thudding.

The curtain billowed. In the next room the key was grating in the lock.

She leaped up, ran out of the booth, and flung herself on the closing door. The latch jerked in her hands.

"Thorkil!" she screamed, feeling the door shudder; the wood cut her fingers. Then he was there, pulling with her. "It's locked." He gasped. "Too late."

And she knew he was right. She released the latch and stood there, listening. There was no sound, and yet they both knew he was there, standing just beyond the door.

"Kari?" Jessa said softly.

Nothing moved. There was a small knothole in the door. She could look through; she could see him. But she dared not.

Then they heard him walk away, into silence.

After a while they went and crouched by the hot embers of the fire; Thorkil stirred them up to a brief blaze.

"Tomorrow," Jessa said firmly, "we'll find him. We'll search every room and corner. Everywhere. Brochael needn't know, either."

He sat down, easing the tight ring around his arm. "If he's insane," he said at last, "he'd be dangerous."

"Well, at least we'd _know_. We've _got_ to find out." She glared at him. "Are you coming?"

He ran a sooty hand through his hair and frowned

with annoyance. "Of course I am. Someone has to keep an eye on you."

In the morning they sat at the gaming board, waiting for Brochael to go out into the courtyard. At last, after five minutes, he had not come back. Jessa looked up. "Ready?"

He shrugged. "It's that or lose."

They had decided to start right up at the highest part of the tower and work their way down—there was still one staircase that was complete from battlement to floor, although even that had holes. They climbed slowly, their lungs aching with the cold, opening every door, prying into the forgotten crannies of the hall. Everything was the same as before: dark, frozen, echoing.

"The candlelight was from a window this high," Jessa said at last. "If we really saw it."

"Not these rooms. No one's used them for years." Thorkil sat wearily on the stairs, grinding the frost with his heel. After a while he said, "Perhaps Kari is kept underground. If you think about it, it might be. Brochael has always been so sure we won't find him."

She nodded reluctantly. Nowhere had been forbidden to them. Wherever Kari was, they were unlikely to find it by accident.

Thorkil got up. "Come on."

"Wait!" She turned quickly. "Did you hear that?"

The corridor was a dim tunnel of stone. Dust moved in drafts over the floor. One drop of water dripped from a sill.

"What?" Thorkil muttered.

"A scrape . . . a screech. I don't know. Something alive."

He glanced at her; her lips were pale, her gloved hands clenched in tight fists. "I didn't hear anything."

"But I did!" Then her eyes widened.

"Look!" she breathed.

Far down in the dimness, a door was appearing. It was forming itself out of nothing on the damp wall; a tall outline of dark wood, its latch shiny from use. A thin line of sunlight flickered underneath it, as if the room beyond was bright.

Very quietly, side by side, they approached the door. Jessa half expected it to fade away again, to be just a trick of the shadows, but it remained, waiting for them.

She reached out and put her hand on the latch. Something shifted inside; there was a rustle and a step and that peculiar low screech she had heard before. The latch was cold and hard under her fingers. She lifted it and let the door swing wide.

At first she thought she was looking into her dream. The room was flooded with sunlight streaming in through an open window, a window leaded with tiny panes of thick, bubbly glass. On the sill the ice was melting; a raven perched there looking out, until the bang of the door startled it, and it leaped into the blue air with a screech. Someone was sitting near the window, hunched up in a chair, his back to them. A mirror was propped in front of him, and as Jessa glanced in it she saw herself and Thorkil framed in the dark doorway. Then the figure moved; he bent closer to the mirror, his straight silvery hair brushing the bronze. A throb of panic shuddered through her. He had no reflection, nothing! She saw only herself and the glitter of sunlight that filled the room.

Then Kari turned and looked sidelong at them. She drew a sharp breath, heard Thorkil's stifled mutter.

His face was Gudrun's. They were identical.

Eleven

What I won from her I have well used.

He uncurled himself quickly and stood up. They saw a thin boy no taller than themselves, his skin pale and his eyes colorless as glass. With two steps he was across the room, staring at Jessa, her hair, her coat, feeling the fur on it with a murmur of delight, touching amulets and luckstones lightly; then fingering the rich red cloth of Thorkil's jerkin as if he had never seen such color. With a shock Jessa realized that he probably never had. She flicked a glance around the room and back. This was not the terrible creature of the stories. She felt foolish, confused.

Suddenly he stepped back. "Come inside," he said. "Come and see where I've been hiding from you."

Slowly Jessa stepped forward. Thorkil hung back, near the open door. They were both alert, wary of this strange thin creature, his quick eagerness. Kari seemed not to notice. He caught Jessa's arm and made her sit on a bench, pouring water for her from a wooden jug, showing her chess pieces he had carved—tiny, intricate things. His king was a perfect copy of Brochael, standing stoutly with folded arms. Despite herself, Jessa laughed.

At once Kari's mood seemed to change. He drew back. She felt as if all the excitement had suddenly drained out of him; now he was uncertain, nervous.

"I'm sorry," he murmured. "I took you by surprise. I'm not what you expected."

"No," she said, her voice a whisper.

He picked up a knife from the table and fingered it.

Jessa stood up. Behind him she saw suddenly that the long room was hung with chunks of glass threaded on thin ~~ropes~~; like crystal spiders they twirled and swung, speckling the walls with sunlight. And the walls were drawn all over with strange spirals and whorls, in dim colors. He turned and picked up the mirror. "Come and see," he said rather sadly. "This is why I had to let you in. Everything has begun." He held up the polished metal. Jessa saw only herself, her face blank with shock, and Thorkil behind her like a shadow. Kari looked at them.

"Can you see him?" he asked. "The man in the mirror?"

She felt Thorkil tremble. Her own hands shook. When she spoke she hardly recognized her voice. "Yes. We can both see him. Clearly." She watched her own mouth mumble the lie. Then Thorkil gripped her arm and drew her back.

To their surprise the boy smiled and shook his head. "You think I'm insane," he said. "I'd forgotten the rumors she puts about." He caught Jessa's eye and his face was grave again. "But the man is there. Look, Jessa, both of you. Look hard."

Sunlight glimmered in the mirror, stabbing her eyes like white pain. The polished surface blurred; she saw a sudden glint, a candle flame in a dark room, ominously dark, hung with rich, heavy cloths. In the middle of the mirror, on a great bed, lay a man richly dressed, his eyes open, his hands clasped rigid on an unsheathed sword. She recognized him at once.

Then the sun glinted; the mirror was yellow and smooth.

Before Jessa could speak, footsteps came along the corridor, and Brochael blocked the doorway. His face was a study in astonishment.

"I had to," Kari said quickly. "All our plans will have to begin, Brochael. The snow will melt, and she'll come for us."

"Gudrun?" Jessa stammered.

"There's nothing to stop her." He put the mirror down and spread his thin white fingers out over it. "He's dead, Brochael. The Jarl is dead."

Without a word or a murmur of surprise Brochael sat down on an old chest near the door. Then he thumped the door frame. "She's finished him! I knew she would!"

Jessa went cold.

"How was he when you saw him?" Brochael asked.

She thought back to the Jarl sitting in his carven chair, his hard stare into the flames of the fire. "The last time," she remembered, "he was shrunken. Dried up. But he was well, still strong. There was nothing wrong with him."

"Exactly. Nor with the Jarl before him—until she

killed him." Brochael reached up and caught her arm. "Sit down, girl. You look bewildered."

She sat herself down next to him; his great arm crept around her shoulders. "I can understand it," he said. "And it's the shock of seeing such a monster and creature of horrors as this, I suppose."

He gave Kari a wide grin.

The boy smiled back, then got up and wandered over to the window. He was very thin; his clothes, like Brochael's, were a cobweb of patches, sewn here and there with large, irregular stitches. He sat on the windowsill and leaned out.

"I watched you from up here many times."

"We didn't see you," Thorkil said.

"No." Kari turned to look at him, Gudrun's look of secret, close knowledge. "And neither did you see the door to this room, though you passed it more than once."

Thorkil frowned, fingering the arm ring.

Brochael's arm was warm and comfortable; Jessa leaned back against it. A sudden wave of relief washed over her. A shadow had lifted. Only now could she realize how she had dreaded to meet Kari—how she had not let herself imagine what he might be.

"So it was you who knew we were coming," she said, thinking aloud.

With a kark and a flap one of the ravens flew in through the window onto the sill. Kari held out a finger, and the bird tugged at it gently. "I watched you come. I saw you in the storm, and then again, at the village called Trond. There is some power there; that old woman sits in a web of it. She often thinks about me." He stroked the bird's stiff feathers. "I've watched her thoughts."

"Is it the mirror?" Thorkil asked curiously, picking it up and turning it over. "Can you see things in that, anything you want to?"

Kari seemed lost in thought; it was Brochael who answered. "Not just the mirror. Anything will do—ice, water, the side of a cup. He has her powers, Thorkil. That's what she's afraid of, the reason she brews all those filthy rumors." He glanced at Kari and lowered his voice. "The reason she locked her son away and never even let him be seen."

Jessa felt him quiver, as if anger seethed in him. Kari turned. "You shouldn't speak of it if it upsets you."

Brochael stood up suddenly and crossed to the fire. He began to fling kindling onto it, hard and fast, as if he hardly saw what he was doing. Watching him, Kari said, "She kept me in a room at the Jarlshold. I saw no one but her, and the old dwarf, Grettir. Sometimes I think I remember a woman, a different face, but only briefly. There was only darkness and silence in that place, long years of it, of shadows and sunlight moving slowly down the walls. Ice and sun and ice again, and voices and pictures moving in my head. She would come and speak bitter, fierce things, or she would just watch me stumbling away from her.

"Then Brochael came. I don't remember the journey, or the snow—isn't that strange? Just this room instead of that one, and this great shambling man who came and talked and put his arm around me." He half smiled at them. "No one had done that before. It felt strange, and yet I liked it. He taught me to speak, and to run, and to go outside without feeling terror of such open places. When she came and tormented my dreams, he woke me. Thrasirshall was no prison for me, Jessa. It was my freedom."

He paused and looked down at the mirror. "Now we have to leave it."

"Are you certain he's dead?" Thorkil put in abruptly.

"Yes."

"She may not have done it," Jessa muttered.

Brochael shook his head. "Oh, it has her mark. She has chosen her time; she's ready. And you read his message—that was from a man expecting something. Now she'll send her swordsmen out here. They may already be on the way. We have two, maybe three, days." He looked at Kari. "Was the death today?"

Kari nodded. They were silent a moment.

"Where can we go?" Jessa thought of the ice-covered fells and moors.

"Oh, I've still got a few friends." Brochael gazed artlessly out of the window. "We're not entirely alone."

"The ones who bring your food," Thorkil muttered.

The big man turned and grinned at him. "I knew you were puzzled by that. It's been goading you like a gnat, hasn't it?"

"Who are they?"

"Wait and see."

Jessa was chewing the ends of her hair. She thought how sudden everything was. "But there's nowhere we can go where she can't see us."

"Or where I can't see her." Kari sat on the chair by the window, his knees huddled up. "She'll hunt us, yes, like a wolf, sly and sudden, but I'll know. She and I are the same." He glanced up at Brochael, a bleak, swift look. "And we have no choice, do we?"

"None at all," Brochael murmured.

TWELVE

Brand kindles brand till they burn out,
Flame is quickened by flame.

They spent the rest of the day preparing for a hard journey. All the supplies of food were brought in from the outhouses; two hares that Brochael found in his snares were cooked and cut up. Water would not be a problem. The snow still lay here on the high ground, and as they traveled down, Brochael said, they would find the rivers awash with meltwater. Still, Jessa took care to bring in a few buckets from the hot spring and wash in luxury. She knew it would be a long time before that would happen again.

Kari moved about downstairs, watching Brochael for a while, then he wandered outside, the birds flapping and hopping after him. Thorkil followed; Jessa closed the door behind them. Sitting down at the table next to Brochael, feeling clean and warm, she said, "You misled us, didn't you? Deliberately."

"Not me. They're Gudrun's stories. You should blame her."

After a moment Jessa said, "It's hard to believe she could spin such lies, even her . . . Kari is so . . ."

"Ordinary?" Brochael asked slyly.

"Well, no. Of course not . . ."

Brochael laughed. "Exactly. He's her image, Jessa, her copy. They say when he was born the midwife screamed out in horror—she could see, I suppose, that this was another of the Snow-walkers, another sorcerer. And Gudrun—I often wonder what she must have thought about this rival, the only one who might ever threaten her. So she shut him away and let the rumors run."

Jessa looked up. "And why didn't she kill him? Many babies die. It wouldn't have seemed so strange."

Brochael stopped his work. For a moment he did not answer; then he said, "That's what worries me, Jessa. It's worried me for years. She wants him for something. And I don't want to think about what."

Later, as she picked out her warmest clothes and squashed them into a pack, she heard Thorkil come in behind her. He closed the door of the room softly.

"Brochael says take as little as you can," she said. "We'll have to carry everything ourselves, remember."

He muttered something and sat down. She turned her head.

"What's wrong?"

Thorkil laughed briefly. "Nothing! We're leaving this place, for a start. That makes me happy enough."

"Does it?" She threaded the laces of the bag swiftly.

"I didn't want to come here either—I think I was more frightened than you even—but since I've been here, I've been happy, in an odd sort of way. And now we know Kari's not . . ."

"Yes!" Thorkil breathed a sigh of exasperation. "Kari! Thinking he was some sort of deformed creature was bad, but I'm not sure the truth isn't worse. He's *her*, Jessa. Every time he looks at me I shiver."

"No," she said, shaking her head. "He's not her. He just looks the same. But that doesn't mean they *are* the same."

For a moment they both sat side by side, thinking.

Then she pulled his hair playfully. "Worrier. Be a warrior. And I see you're still wearing the lady's present, anyway."

He shrugged, and touched the arm ring. "That's because it won't come off."

Surprised, Jessa looked at it. "I thought it was loose enough before."

"A bit looser. Perhaps the cold here has made it shrink. Anyway, it won't come off, and it doesn't matter. No one can steal it this way."

She put her hand on the smooth snake and tugged at it, but he was right. It gripped his wrist without a gap.

"Perhaps it's swallowed a bit more of its tail." He laughed.

There was something in his voice for a moment that was new to her; a strange tone. But when she looked at him he laughed and stood up, his longish brown hair brushing the collar of the red jerkin. "Don't worry, Jessa, I won't bring much. I may like fine things, but I'm too lazy to carry them far!"

And they both laughed in the cold room.

That evening, around the fire in the darkness downstairs, they made their plans.

"We'll go south," Brochael said. "After all, it's the only way you can go from this godforsaken place. To the north is nothing but ice, mountains and seas of it, and mists. Beyond that, Gunningagap, the rift into blackness. Only sorcerers could live up there."

Jessa flicked a glance at Kari; he sat curled up against Brochael's knees, his face a shifting mask of firelight and shadows.

"And then where?" Thorkil asked. "A ship?"

"No ship would take us," Brochael said curtly. "And I don't intend to try. The weather's beginning to turn milder. Spring is coming. We'll go overland—it will be hard, but safer. And there's a place—an old hall, one of the Wulfings' hunting halls in the mountains. That's the place we're going."

"Will we be safe there?" Jessa asked, surprised.

Brochael shrugged. "As anywhere. But that's the meeting place. It's all been arranged, long ago. The Jarl's death will bring them."

Kari shifted, as if the fire scorched him. One of the ravens gave a low croak; the flames crackled and hissed over damp wood.

"And after?" Thorkil insisted. "What then? Will these mysterious allies of yours have swordsmen, horses, axmen? Will they fight against Gudrun?"

"We'll see." Brochael gave his rich laugh. "You're very curious, aren't you, lad."

Thorkil shrugged. "Wary, that's all."

And then Kari said, very quietly, "We should start tomorrow."

Brochael looked at him.

After a moment he said, "What is it?"

"A ship." Kari watched the flames; his voice was quiet. "A ship with a dragon prow. She's beached, on a rocky shore."

"Can you show us?" Brochael kept his voice low.

Kari did not answer. His gaze seemed to be on something deep in the fire; Jessa stared too, trying to see.

And then, in the shifting of a burned log, the ship was there. She saw it through the flames, as if it was behind them, a little beyond. Horses were being led off, down a steep ramp into the water that swirled and sank through the shingle. Men stood about, some holding torches that guttered and spat. She could smell pitch and resin, the salt tang of the fjord, hear a gull crying, far off.

"That's Trond." Thorkil's voice came out of the darkness. Jessa nodded. She had already recognized the steep cliffs, and among a group of men, Sigmund Graycloak, his hair swept across his face by the night wind.

But the men coming from the boat were some she had seen about the Jarlshold; silent, rough men, each with a serpent mark tattooed down his cheek—Gudrun's own choice. She counted ten or more. An ashen shield was flung down, then spears, heavy packs. Then the flames flickered in the draft, and there was only darkness behind the fire.

She looked at Brochael. "How can they have gotten so far already? It's impossible. It took us three days to reach Trond. . . ."

His bleak expression answered her; she caught her breath as the thought leaped into her mind. "She sent them out *before*? Before Ragnar was dead?"

Brochael nodded silently, rubbing his beard. For a while no one spoke, each of them thinking. Jessa felt again that sudden urge of panic that she had known so long ago in the Jarlshall; could almost think she smelled Gudrun's sweet scent, hear the drift and rustle of her movements.

Raising her head, she stared at the flames.

Gudrun looked back at her.

The sorceress was surrounded by candles; a halo of light that lit the sharpness of her smile, the eager glint of her eyes.

Transfixed with fear, Jessa hardly breathed, but Kari stretched out his foot and nudged a log. It shifted with a shower of sparks. Wood fell, settled. The fire leaped up; it showed Jessa the dark room, Kari's face with a bleak pain in it, Brochael's grim and angry.

"Did she see us?" Thorkil whispered.

"No." Kari's fingers shook; he clenched them. "She tries—often. But I won't let her. Not anymore."

Behind him something shuffled in the darkness. The raven, with a hop and a flutter, perched on the chair behind Brochael's shoulder. Its eyes were tiny red sparks in the flame light.

Thirteen

Odin, they said, swore an oath on his ring;
Who from now on will trust him?

They left at midmorning. Brochael had food ready. They ate it quickly, in a tense silence. Jessa watched Kari until he glanced at her with his sharp look, then she smiled. Doubtfully he smiled back.

When everything was ready Brochael flung water on the fire and hauled a heavy pack onto his back. He picked up an ax and shoved it into his belt. "Well, I brought little; I'm taking away less." He grinned at Jessa. "It will be interesting to see how the world has changed."

Outside they wrapped themselves in cloaks and hoods and thick gloves. The wind was cold; it was coming from the north and brought flecks of snow. Overhead the two ravens flapped against the clouds.

"They'll miss you," Jessa said.

Kari looked up. "They're coming. They go where I go."

He turned and looked back at the hall, at the black walls trapped in their gleaming coats of ice. "It's strange," he whispered. "I feel as if I'm stepping out of myself, like a snake out of its skin."

"Come on." Brochael caught his arm. "If her men

catch us here, that's just what we'll all be doing."

Kari pulled a dark, ragged scarf up around his face. Then Brochael led them across the courtyard and under the broken archway, out into the snow.

All that long afternoon they walked, one in the footsteps of the other, up the long slopes of the mountain. The wind whistled against them, as if it would push them back; the snow underfoot was soft under the top layer of thin, crunchy ice. They crossed the glacier carefully, slithering on the flat snow swirls, watching for cracks and crevasses, moving swiftly on the scree and tumbled stones. Once over, they climbed again, along the sheer side of the fell, heading south, floundering through the soft, wetter snow. By the time they reached the top, the sky was dark purple, with a few stars scattered across it, faint as dust. Far off in the north, a pale aurora flickered over the mountain peaks.

Jessa was wet through and breathless. She paused, looking back at the long blue scar they had torn through the snow.

Brochael looked too. "It's a dry night," he muttered. "That will still be there tomorrow—maybe even the day after. They'll see it."

She looked at him. "They'll be here tomorrow?"

"Bound to be. They'll ride hard." He turned and

trudged on after Kari and Thorkil. "When Gudrun wants a thing done, Jessa, it's done."

By about midnight they had come back down to the treeline. Brochael let them sleep for a while in a thick pine wood, where the trees clustered so closely there was no snow; they lay on a centuries-thick quilt of needles and leaf mold, richly scented and full of tiny, scurrying beetles. Too tired to notice, Jessa slept.

The ravens woke her, croaking in the trees above her, sending down showers of dry powdery snow. She sat up. Brochael and Kari were out at the trees' edge, talking. She saw Brochael mark something on the ground with a stick. Thorkil lay nearby, still asleep, his fur hood up over his face, one arm thrown out carelessly. She shivered; it was barely light and bitterly cold.

Brochael turned. "About time. Come and have something to eat."

It was the same cooked meat, and some black, hard bread. She chewed it slowly, looking out over the still, white country wrapped in its fogs and mists, the forests marching over slope and hillside like a motionless and silent army. Kari stared out too, as if his eyes feasted on this different place. She caught the same vivid excitement in him as when he had first seen Thorkil and herself; his fingers clenched in their gloves, his eyes paler than ever in the early light. Finally Brochael stirred and flung a handful of rotten cones at Thorkil.

"Get up, lad. This is no place to sleep late." He turned to Jessa. "Get your things. Time's wasting."

It took them a while to wake Thorkil; he seemed deep in dreams and hardly knew where he was for a moment or two. Brochael grinned down at him.

"Perhaps the young lord could get off his bed now? And take his scented bath?"

Thorkil smiled back, but Jessa thought he was still quiet and tired.

Once they had begun to walk, none of them spoke very much; it was easier to trudge in silence through the empty land and the wide, bitter sky.

Suddenly, at about midday, Kari stopped. Then, slowly, he looked back. Jessa looked too.

Smoke was rising over the skyline far off—a great black column of it, the underside lit with a faint red glow. Silent, the four of them watched it. It could only be Thrasirshall. They'd been quick, Jessa thought, quicker than she'd dreamed. Gudrun must have chosen them well, men who wouldn't fear the place and its hidden creature— perhaps she'd even told them something of the truth. They'd have searched, then burned, and even now they would be galloping down the fellside. She turned, straight into Brochael.

His face was grim. "Yes, you're right. Kari! Come on!"

He pushed them into the trees and along the hilltop. The snow was thinner here, and in the tangle of undergrowth their tracks would be harder to see. Jessa knew he was worried; he urged them on tirelessly all afternoon. Kari walked swiftly, and she wasn't tired herself. Oddly enough it was Thorkil who held them back. More than once she had to call the others to wait for him.

When he caught up, his breath came in gasps and he clutched his side.

"Can't we rest?" he said at last.

"What's the matter with you?" Brochael snarled. "Are you ill?"

"I don't know!" He seemed puzzled, and in pain. "I can't seem to get my breath . . . perhaps it's the cold. Just a few minutes, Brochael."

But Brochael shoved him on. "We haven't got that long. A spear in the back will be a harder pain to put up with."

But after a while Thorkil stopped again. He collapsed onto his knees, dragging in air. Jessa crouched beside him.

"He's really in trouble. We'll have to wait."

Brochael stormed and cursed. Then he turned and marched off through the trees.

"Where's he gone?" Jessa asked.

"To look back." Kari kneeled beside her. He took his thin hand from its glove and gripped Thorkil's shoulder.

"Look at me," he said.

Shuddering, Thorkil looked up. Their eyes met. They were still for a moment, a long silence, and then Thorkil began to breathe easily and freely. At the same time Kari shivered, as if something had chilled him. He put his glove back on and pushed the lank hair from his eyes.

"What was it?" Jessa said to him.

"Nothing." His pale eyes searched through the trees. "Nothing. He'll be all right."

With a floundering of branches Brochael was coming back. "No sign of them yet," he snapped. "The forest ends ahead, then the land is open moor. We'll have to cross it before tonight." He looked at Thorkil. "Can you manage?"

"Yes." Jessa helped him up; he straightened slowly. "It's easier now. . . . I don't know what caused it."

"Never mind! Just move."

They pushed their way out through the trees, the wet, heavy snow sliding from the branches onto their shoulders. Beyond, the land was a dim slope, frozen into stiff hillocks and littered with boulders under the snow. It was treacherous, but they scrambled down. Far overhead the two birds circled; they swooped down, cawing and karking over

Kari's head as he slipped and stumbled at Jessa's side. Below, Brochael was close to Thorkil, both of them sliding on the loose scree that lay invisible under the snow. Horses would find this hard to manage. That would help surely.

By the time they had crossed the great moor, the short day was darkening. They were tired; their ankles ached with the bruising of the stones. Before them lay a small lake, frozen white, but at its edge the land made an overhang where rock outcropped. The bitter wind brought tears to their eyes. Jessa's ears ached and her toes were an agony.

Brochael pushed his way through the scrub and under the overhang and they followed, squatting in a breathless row against the rock.

In the shelter and the quiet they coughed and spat and caught breath. Jessa felt Brochael's warmth at her side. She tugged her boots off and rubbed her wet feet. After a while a faint glow touched her face and fingers.

"Well," Brochael said at last. "Here is as good as anywhere."

"You mean we'll stay?" Thorkil said doubtfully.

"We can't outrun them. We must hide." He looked at Kari. "Will the birds warn us?"

The boy nodded, tugging pine needles from his silvery hair.

"Then we sleep," Brochael said. "All of us. While we can."

"It's too cold," Thorkil objected. "We'll freeze—or we will later."

Brochael gave him an irritated glance. "I don't think you'll find that, if you're as tired as you should be. You were the one who wanted to stop."

"Yes." Thorkil looked uneasy. "Yes, I know."

They ate some dried meat from Brochael's pack, but it was hard to swallow and there was nothing to drink but snow. Then they lay down, huddled together for warmth. Jessa felt Brochael pull his coat around Kari. Then she slept, suddenly and completely.

When she woke it was still dark, the sky in the east glimmering with wan light. She was unbearably stiff and cold. Carefully she moved away from the others and sat up. Brochael lay on his back against the rocks, one hand on his ax even in sleep. She could just see Kari in the depths of his coat. But Thorkil was gone.

She scrambled up, easing the pain from her back and arms. Then, quietly, so as not to wake the others, she pushed through the bushes and crouched down.

The landscape was bleak and silent. Far off some bird was calling, a lonely cry over the miles of tundra. The wind was cold, but she knew it was milder than last night;

already the frost on the branches under her fingers was beginning to drip.

But where was Thorkil? She was worried about him. The pain yesterday, which seemed to fade so quickly—that wasn't like him.

She slipped out from the bushes and stood up. Below, over a shallow slope of scree, was the shore of the lake, its black reeds poking up from the frozen lid. Perhaps he was down there.

She went down, the tiny stones trickling underfoot, and saw at the very edge that the ice was receding, thinning to a frill where bubbles of trapped air slid and wheezed. She crouched down and drank; the water was bitterly cold and stagnant.

Then a sound froze her. It was the slow clip-clop of hooves. It came from her left, somewhere nearby. As she looked around, she saw him, a horseman coming down the track, an armed man, with ring mail that glittered in the pale light. She kept perfectly still. If she moved now, he would see her.

The man drew rein. He looked across the dimness of the moor, at the flat glimmer of the ice. Where were the rest of them? she wondered. Probably not far.

His head turned; she held her breath, flattening against the wet stones, but he kept looking beyond her.

Then he urged the horse on.

At the same moment, she saw Thorkil.

He was crouched behind a rock halfway up the slope. He hadn't seen her, but he was watching the rider intently, and then he did something that astonished her. He stood up and called!

The rider's head turned swiftly; the horse whinnied with fright. As the horseman struggled with it, Jessa leaped to her feet, and Thorkil looked down at her. He stared, as if she was a stranger. At the same time, the horseman dragged the horse's head to stillness. He looked up, and she saw him stiffen.

He had seen her!

FOURTEEN

If aware that another is wicked, say so:
Make no truce or treaty with foes.

The horseman stared at Jessa. After a moment he urged the horse with his knees, and it picked its way toward her over the stones. The man's eyes slid from her; he paused as if puzzled, and then came on again.

"Keep very still," Kari's voice said from somewhere behind her. "He can't see you now, but if you move, it will be more difficult."

She waited as the horseman rode nearer. Now she could see his face, the blue snake mark in his skin; he looked wary, almost afraid. His eyes took in the moor and the lake; they moved across her without a flicker. It was uncanny, unbearably tense. She moved her foot; a stone clicked.

Again the man stopped, his gaze exploring the lakeshore. She was so close she could have reached out and touched the horse. It turned and looked at her, nuzzling at her shoulder.

Suddenly, as if his nerve had snapped, the rider whirled his mount around and urged it hurriedly back up the track, slithering and scrambling over the loose ground. He rode up to the top of the slope and over it, without looking back. The noise of hooves on stones died away to silence.

A warm hand gripped her. "It's all right. He's gone."

Brochael was there, holding his ax, looking at her angrily. "Why did you stand up? If he'd seen any one of us, one shout would have brought them all over here. Are you mad?"

"I thought he would see Thorkil!"

"Thorkil was well hidden," Brochael snorted, watching him come down the slope. "Think next time!"

Furious, she pulled away from him. She glared at Thorkil angrily. "Why did *you* stand up?" she snapped.

He glared back. "I was calling you. I hadn't seen the rider."

"But—"

"Anyway, it doesn't matter," he said. "I climbed up there to get a look around. You can see the line of the old road across the hills. It looks as if it heads south."

While he and Brochael discussed the route, she turned away, puzzled. She saw Kari watching her. He sat on a rock, with one of the great birds at his feet, the other behind him, picking at something red on the snow. For a moment he looked so like Gudrun that she shivered.

"How did you do it?" she asked.

"I don't know." His eyes met hers calmly. "It wasn't easy—for a moment he saw you. I had to make him believe that he was wrong. That there was nothing there."

"Like the door in the hall?"

"Yes."

She turned and looked out at the coming sun lighting the clouds and the white mountains. "Is it the runes, the magic the old woman has? Is that the same?"

He shrugged. "I don't know any runes. This is in me, I haven't learned it." He looked over at the lake. "I've never seen so much frozen water like that. It has a strange beauty. . . ."

"Has it?" Jessa asked. "It tastes foul."

They ate some meat and smoked fish and drank the brackish water. Then Brochael outlined his plans.

"We'll head directly south, keeping near the line of the road, but staying in the forests as far as possible. We'll be harder to follow there; we might even risk a fire at night."

"What if they have dogs?" Jessa asked.

"They don't. We would have seen them by now. It will be rough country, but if we move quickly we could be at Morthrafell in two days, where the river called Skolka cuts through the mountains down to Skolkafjord and the sea." He glanced at Kari. "We can wait at the hall of the Wulfings, as arranged."

"Wait for who?" Thorkil asked.

Ignoring him, Brochael pulled the pack onto his back and stood up. "Now, take care. They may still be about."

It took them all morning to cross the open moor, going cautiously over the boggy, treacherous ground. Finally the land rose a little, and they came into the forest, scattering a herd of elk.

Here the snow was thin; ice glistened and hung from the dark branches. They moved easily through the scattered trees, and as the sun climbed, it became warmer. A few birds sang, far down in the aisles of the wood.

Jessa tried to speak to Thorkil but he was never near her. He kept near Kari, always talking and asking questions that Kari rarely answered. But when they stopped to eat at midday, Jessa saw her chance. Pulling Thorkil away, she shoved him hard against a tree trunk.

"What were you thinking of?" she snapped.

"What do you mean?"

"You know! You called out!"

"To you."

"But you didn't see me until after!"

He looked at her. His eyes were blue and clear; there was a hard look in them that was new. "You're wrong, Jessa. I called you. Who else would I have called?"

She was silenced. She wanted to say "the horseman" but it would be wrong; it would be foolish. But that was what was in her mind.

He pushed past her and went back to the others. She stared after him. It was unthinkable that he should betray them. Why should he? He hated Gudrun.

All afternoon the forest went on endlessly, full of the piping of invisible birds. They traveled along tracks and

winding paths, always keeping the sun on their right as it
sank among clouds and vapor. Once Kari cried out;
Brochael raced back. "What is it?"

The boy stood stock-still, his face white. "She spoke to
me. She knows where we are. She has a hand on us, gripping us tight." He looked up at Brochael; Jesssa saw a
strange glance pass between them.

After that they moved more carefully. Twice the ravens
karked a warning, and they plunged off the path, hiding in
scrub and spiny bushes, but no one passed. Once, far off in
the forest, Jessa thought she heard voices and the jingle of
harness, but it was so distant she could not be sure.

At sunset they were still traveling over the high, bare
passes of the hills. Jessa was desperately tired; she stumbled
and her ears ached with the cold. She longed for shelter
and hot food.

But now Brochael would not stop. He hurried them
on over one ridge and another, perilously outlined against
the black horizon. They spent part of the night in a cave
high up on a cliffside—a chilly crack in the rocks so cold
that they had to risk a fire of wet wood. It smoked so much
they could hardly breathe. Brochael was anxious, Thorkil
silent and morose. Each of them had a weapon to hand
except Kari, who slept silently and completely on the hard
floor, with the two birds sitting hunched by his side.

They left the cave long before it was light and climbed up over the highest crags and passes, until at last they stood looking down on a distant green country cracked open by a great fjord of blue water.

"Skolkafjord," Brochael said, easing the weight on his back. "We've done well."

The wind roared in their ears, whipping Jessa's hair out of her hood. She watched Kari as he stared with delight at the snowless country, at the expanse of water and the distant glimmering sea. Brochael watched him too, grinning, but Thorkil stood slightly apart, looking back.

Coming down was easier. Soon they came to country Brochael recognized: thin woodlands where the snow was softer, and where small, swift streams bubbled and leaped downhill. By midafternoon they reached the place he had called the hall of the Wulfings.

It rose among the trees ahead of them as they came down the valley of a swift stream—a ruin without a roof and with the walls broken and blackened. Charred timbers rose from tangles of briar and bramble, and openings that had once been doors and windows were choked with black, tangled stems. Thorkil touched a window shutter that hung from one hinge; it slithered and fell with a crash that sent echoes through the wood.

Forcing his way through, Brochael led them in.

Even now they could see where the great hall had been; the large square hearth in the center was still black with ashes, its stones fire-marked under the pine sapling that grew out of it. Jessa threw down her pack and sat on a stone; from the charred ash she pulled a half-burned wooden spoon, its handle carved with a zigzag line.

"What happened here?"

"This was Wulfings' land," Brochael said. "The Jarl's men would have cleared it, and then burned it."

With a squawk and a flap a raven landed on the high crumbling wall. Thorkil looked up at it. "Is it safe?"

Brochael handed out broken bannocks. "Safe as any-where it's probably been long forgotten." Jessa noticed his glance at Kari; the boy nodded slightly.

"That witch can probably see us anyway," he went on cheerfully, stretching out his legs.

They found a sheltered place under the wall and made it as comfortable as they could, tugging out the brambles and flattening the ground. But there could be no fire until after dark, and even then it might not be wise. Jessa and Kari scrambled down to the stream for water. As he bent over it, she saw him pause, and then squat slowly. He watched the moving water with a strange fixity, always one spot, though Jessa could see nothing but the brown stream over its stones.

After a moment she asked, "What do you see?"

Slowly he put his hand out and spread it flat on the surface, letting the icy stream well around his fingers. Then he pulled them out and let them drip. "Nothing."

Absently he filled the bowl, and she knew he was going to ask her something. She was right.

"You met her, didn't you, in the Jarlshold?"

"Yes." She had already noticed that he never called Gudrun his mother.

"You told Brochael she knew you were coming."

"Yes."

He looked at her intently, a sudden swift glance. Then he said, "We're carrying something with us, Jessa, something extra. Some burden. You know that, don't you?"

She wanted to tell him about Thorkil, but she couldn't.

In silence he stood up, holding the bowl steady, so as not to spill a drop. They walked back without speaking.

That night they risked a fire and sat around it. The heat was a glorious comfort; Jessa felt it warming her chapped hands and sore face. But she was tired of smoked meat and dry, hard oatcake, and longed for something fresh and sweet. Apples from Horolfstead, or one of Marrika's sweet honey cakes.

As she rolled in her blanket she noticed Thorkil

moving up next to Kari. There was something anxious pushing at the back of her mind, something important that she could not quite grasp, and as she reached for it, it slid away, into a deep dark hole under the earth. Her mind slid after it, into sleep.

A bird screech woke her.

She sat up in the darkness. Something moved beside her; she saw the flash of a knife and she yelled. Quick as an eel, Kari rolled over, but the knife slashed him across shoulder and chest. Then Thorkil was on him, struggling, holding him down. Jessa was already on her feet, but before she or Brochael could move, Thorkil was flung backward with a force that astonished them. He screamed, dropping the knife and shuddering in apparent agony on the charred ground. "Stop it!" he screamed. "Stop him! Stop him!"

Kari scrambled up and looked down at him, his eyes cold and amused, like Gudrun's.

FIfTEEN

A coiled adder, the ice of a night . . .
A witch's welcome, the wit of a slave,
Are never safe: let no man trust them . . .

"Let him be," Brochael said.

Kari glanced at him and seemed to do nothing else, but with a gasp Thorkil was released. He lay sprawling in the brambles, sobbing. Jessa moved toward him, but Brochael caught her by the arm.

"Not yet," he said gruffly.

Carefully Kari went forward, blood seeping through his shirt. He crouched down and touched Thorkil's hair very softly. Thorkil did not move. Gently Kari's fingers moved over the heaving shoulder, down the arm to Thorkil's wrist; then he tugged the sleeve back and touched the ring. "This is it."

Brochael edged forward. "An arm ring?"

"It looks like one."

He fingered it curiously; in the darkness Jessa saw the silver glitter. Then she clutched Brochael's sleeve.

Under Kari's touch the metal had begun to move. It softened into a long, lithe form, writhing around Thorkil's wrist, unwinding and gliding with a tiny hissing sound that chilled them. Thorkil squirmed, but Kari held him down. "Keep still!"

Slowly the long white worm slithered out, leaving a bloodless ring on the skin. It lay on the charred soil, twisting and kinking itself, hissing and spitting, its tiny eyes like pale beads. As they watched it, it faded to dull smoke, then to a stinking smear on the soil, then to nothing.

Silently Jessa touched all her amulets in turn. Brochael scuffed at the ground with his boot, but nothing was there. Whatever it had been, it was gone. After a moment he let her go, and she went over to Thorkil and helped him to sit up. He seemed half-dazed, scratching at the white scar on his wrist as if it itched or ached unbearably. When she spoke to him, he did not answer.

After a while Brochael had to come over and carry him back to the blankets, where he sank instantly into sleep.

"It wasn't him . . . ," Jessa said.

"I know." Brochael looked down at him. "It was her."

He crossed to Kari and began to examine the knife slash—it was long and shallow, in places barely breaking the skin.

"We knew she had her hand on him," Kari said.

Jessa was silent. She sat down, and handed Brochael the bowl of clean water. "You didn't trust us. That's why we didn't see you at Thrasirshall."

"Not until you had to." Kari watched as Brochael wiped the thin line of blood away.

"It's not deep," Jessa said.

"No," Brochael snapped, "but it could have been. It could have been deep enough to end all her worries."

She was silent. She knew he was right.

"And you!" the big man growled fiercely. "You knew about this ring, but you said nothing!"

She felt the heat rise in her neck and face. "I thought it was just his greed. I didn't think it was harmful. . . ."

But it wasn't true. She was furious with herself because she had doubted Thorkil and she had been right.

Kari was watching her closely. "There were two. You threw yours into the sea," he said suddenly.

She shrugged, not bothering to ask how he knew. She felt ashamed and bitter.

"The ring explains a lot," Kari said after a while. "That pain he had—it was real enough, but she made him feel it. She's done that to me . . . long ago. It was to slow us down. And then it explains the red cloth."

"What cloth?"

Kari put his hand into the pack at his side and pulled out a few frayed strips of cloth; a rich, red fabric with skeins of gold woven through it.

"Recognize it?"

"It's Thorkil's tunic."

"He's been dropping bits of it," Brochael muttered, flinging the bloody water from the bowl into the bushes. "Stabbing pieces onto thorns, snapping branches. He was leaving a clear trail for them."

She was aghast. "But he hates her!"

"Even so. She moved his will; she can do that. He'll hate her even more after this."

"Brochael found these at first by accident. Then I told the birds to pick them up." Kari eased his arm back into his shirt. "They like bright things. They brought them to me."

Jessa looked out into the black forest. So this was why he had stood up that morning by the lake—so that the horseman would see him and know. She frowned, thinking of it. All this time the witch had held him by the wrist, moved him like a piece in a game.

"Do you think he knows," she said. "Does he understand what he's been doing?"

But Kari was staring across the ruined hall. "Brochael . . ."

"I know. I heard it." The big man already had the ax in his hands; it glinted in the dark.

Jessa strained her ears to catch any sound, but the forest outside the wall seemed utterly still, the breeze barely moving the branches.

Then a twig cracked.

Brochael's fingers closed slowly on the wooden shaft.

Someone was coming, rustling through the leaves. She could hear it now even after the thudding of her heart, the pliant branches of alder and blackthorn whipping back into place.

Brochael crouched lower. "Keep still," he breathed, "and do nothing." She saw movement in the broken doorway of the hall; a deeper shadow in the shadows. It paused in the tangle of branch and stone. Then, to her astonishment, it spoke.

"You can put that ax away, Brochael."

The voice was familiar, a sly, amused tone. Brochael gave a great guffaw of laughter, and even Kari smiled.

"You rogue," the big man roared, standing up. "Come in here and let us see you."

A thin shape detached itself from the shadows and pushed through the bushes. Brochael tossed down the ax and gripped him by both shoulders.

"Not so hard," the man laughed.

"You won't snap. You're early—we hadn't expected you yet."

Jessa looked at Kari in astonishment. "It's the peddler!"

"What peddler?"

The peddler grinned at her. "That's how she saw me

last, spellmaster. I was flinging a few herbs in the Jarl's fire. A certain outlaw escaped at the time."

"And then at Wormshold," Jessa muttered.

"Indeed. Where you were so unwilling to take the sea path, the whales' way, the house of the skerries. Frightened of what was waiting in the grim hall." He winked at Kari. "She was so urgent I almost told her."

"You're a poet," Jessa said with sudden understanding. She knew now why they had not wanted her to escape.

Brochael laughed. "Of course he is. You've heard of Skapti Arnsson? He was the Wulfings' skald. Talks in riddles and cryptic lines." He pounded the man on the shoulder. "A peddler of words!"

The skald glanced down at Thorkil, who was lying still against the wall. "What happened to that one?"

"She had hold of him," Brochael said tersely. "A sorcery, in the shape of a silver ring."

The skald whistled. Then he said, "We heard Ragnar was dead two days ago. We've traveled west since then, mostly by night. The forests are full of the troll wife's men."

"Is Wulfgar with you?" Kari asked.

"Not far off."

"Then why doesn't he come?"

The skald grinned. "He's waiting for the signal. And

he's wary of you, ravenmaster. I told him you were no monster, but the story sticks. Shall I call him?"

Kari nodded, pulling his coat about him. He looked paler in the darkness; the thin moon rising over the branches glinted on his hair. The skald went out into the wood. They heard a swish of branches, the low murmur of voices. Then he came back, followed by the man Jessa had seen in the Jarlshold, the lithe, dark-haired man in the leather coat. He came forward quickly, his eyes glancing over Brochael and herself until he came to Kari, and he stopped. They stood staring at each other, one pale and one dark.

Wulfgar spoke first. "She's an accomplished liar," he said almost admiringly. "You have all her looks."

Kari looked down absently and then gazed at Wulfgar. "Not her heart," he said.

Wulfgar nodded slowly. "And your powers—these things the skald told me about—are they as great as hers? Will you use them against her?"

One of the ravens fell from the trees with a shriek that startled them all, even Brochael. It perched on the branch above Kari, its eyes glinting. He held his hand up to it and let it peck at his finger. "I'll try. That's all I can say."

Wulfgar stared at the bird. "Then I suppose that will have to do."

Sixteen

Too many eyes are open by day.

Brochael woke Jessa before dawn. As she struggled up she saw Thorkil sitting and talking with Wulfgar. He laughed and waved to her.

"He doesn't seem to remember anything about last night," Brochael said quietly. "Best not to speak of it at all."

"How can he not remember?"

"Who knows. But don't mention it."

She nodded. "Is Kari well?"

"Well enough. He'll carry the scar, that's all."

Later, as she rolled her blanket, Thorkil came over. He grinned at her, and she saw that the restraint and silence that had grown on him lately was gone. He was easy, pleased with himself. The old Thorkil.

"Feeling better?" she said, suddenly glad to see him.

He shrugged, surprised. "A bit tired." He did not mention the missing arm ring, but she saw his fingers restlessly rubbing at the white wrinkled scar that twisted about his wrist. It had not faded in the night; she wondered now if it ever would. They'll both carry scars, she thought.

All morning they moved swiftly on through the trees, downhill, with Wulfgar scouting ahead and Brochael, like a great shadow at Kari's shoulder, keeping guard at the back. The forest was quiet, in an end-of-winter hush, brushed at its edges by a dusting of green, the tight furled buds barely splitting, the new growth of pines and firs soft and fresh among the dark needles.

When the forest ended they saw a low green valley before them, with a swift river running through it.

"This is the Skolka," Brochael said. "Beyond it, up in those rocks, is the Jarl's Gate, the pass down into the Mjornir district, where the Jarlshold is."

Jessa looked up at the narrow peaks. "I can't see any pass."

"It's narrow," Wulfgar said. "Barely a thread between the rocks. A few weeks ago it would still have been blocked with snow."

"And how do we cross the river?" Thorkil wondered.

Brochael looked at Wulfgar. "There's a ford—"

"Guarded. She's not such a fool as that."

"She's not a fool at all," the skald muttered to Jessa, with a lopsided grin.

"You and I will have to find a place to cross," Brochael decided. "The rest of you can wait, and rest."

"I'll come," Thorkil said.

Brochael's eyes flickered doubtfully to Kari, but the boy nodded. There was nothing to worry about now, Jessa thought. They could trust him again.

"All right," Brochael said. "But stay close."

When they were gone, Jessa and Kari lay in the edges of the forest, listening to Skapti's tale of his journey. The sun became almost warm; one or two early flies buzzed in the leaves. Kari fed the ravens scraps of dried meat, one perched on each side as he lay against the tree.

When the skald had finished, Jessa said, "You might have told me—at Wormshold."

"Not my secret. Besides"—he winked at Kari—"we had to find out if you were safe to trust."

"How did you know all about it?"

Skapti shrugged. "I knew Brochael years ago. When she sent him to Thrasirshall we all heard of it. No one thought we would see him again. There was much fighting at the time. . . . But later, one time when I was traveling near Trond, I decided to see him."

"You went to Thrasirshall on your own?" Jessa was astonished.

The skald grinned. "Oh, I was scared enough. When I saw the place, I thought my heart would stop. But I knew Brochael would starve unless he had food brought in. I might add, he was glad to see me. Tired of eating rat, I suppose."

Jessa giggled.

"I didn't see this creature"—he tapped Kari with his foot—"until later, but a skald knows that many things that seem true are not, and all about lying. I don't think I really believed her stories, even then. We arranged a supply line for food; some of the Wulfings' men brought it, when they could get through the snow. All secret. I was there quite often after that." He grinned. "I remember the time this one first heard music."

Kari nodded slowly. "So do I. . . ."

When the others came back they were wet and hungry.

"There's a place," Brochael said, swallowing a great chunk of oatcake, "a little way upstream. Plenty of rocks, though the current is swift and deep in places." He spat out a piece of cheese. "Rancid! Food is something else we need."

"There's a house over there," Jessa said. They looked in the direction she pointed at the thin trail of smoke rising into the sky.

"Too dangerous," the skald muttered.

"Unless we steal, as Odin stole the mead of Wisdom."

"I don't steal from my own people," Wulfgar said sharply.

Skapti laughed, rubbing his long nose. "Then just ask, my lord. When they know it's the next Jarl at the door, they'll give."

Wulfgar laughed at Jessa. "Do you see the impudence I have to put up with?"

The crossing place Brochael had found was sheltered, with a few trees. The bank shelved down, but the bed of the stream was choked with rocks, the swift brown water roaring over and through them. That would be easy. But between the last rock and the farther shore was at least six feet of empty, swirling water.

Brochael took off his pack, coat, and shirt and tied a heavy, hempen rope around his waist. Thorkil wound the end around a rock and braced it. The big man laughed. "It'll take more than you. If I go in I'll want you all on there." With a glance at Kari he began to cross the rocks swiftly, with easy steps. Despite his size he was light-footed. On the last one he paused. Wulfgar and Thorkil gripped the rope. Slowly Brochael lowered himself into the icy water. It rose high against his chest. He waded forward, and the current caught him; he staggered, fought for balance, arms wide.

Slowly he steadied, the brown water racing past him, his skin tinged with blue, as if bruised with cold. He forced his bulk through the stream, gripped the other bank, and heaved himself up, the water running from him.

"Well stepped!" the skald yelled, flinging over Brochael's clothes.

Shaking with cold, Brochael dressed, then he whipped the rope up from the water and tightened it, a dripping, taut line over the river. They threw the baggage over, then Kari crossed, gripping the rope tight with both hands, the birds cawing anxiously over his head. He had to drag himself, hand over hand, the current tearing at him, Brochael leaning out so far to help that he almost overbalanced. Jessa saw the raw blue scar on Kari's chest as he was pulled out. He flung his cloak on and crouched, coughing, on the bank.

Skapti crossed next, then Thorkil. As he was halfway over, the ravens croaked and rose up, circling. Kari looked up. "They're here!"

At the end of the forest something was moving; as Jessa turned she saw a man step out, the weapon in his hand gleaming in the sun. He turned at once and shouted.

"Hurry up!" Brochael roared, leaning over and hauling Thorkil out. "Jessa! Quick!"

With a slither of steel Wulfgar had his sword out. He turned to face the wood; already a line of men was running toward him. Jessa pulled off her coat and flung it over, scrambling from rock to rock. She tugged her boots off, threw them to Thorkil, and jumped straight into the stream.

The icy water drove the breath right out of her; she grabbed the taut rope and hung there, gasping, feeling the flow of the river against her body, filling her nose and mouth. Hand over hand, she pulled herself through the stream; her feet dragged again and again off the stones, her clothes heavy with the icy water. She heard a splash behind her; a shout. Wulfgar was on the rocks. Her hands were sore on the rope; she slipped, and grabbed tight. Then Brochael's arm gripped her. She reached up to the bank and hauled herself out, coughing and shivering. Someone flung a coat around her. She pushed the wet hair from her eyes.

Two men had outrun the others. Swords out, they were hacking at Wulfgar. Dodging, he kicked one in the ribs; the man gasped, and slipped backward. Wulfgar leaped across the rocks; with an enormous splash he was in the water.

Brochael whirled around. "Run. Get up to the pass!"

Already Wulfgar was halfway across, the water roaring over his clenched hands and the tight, thrumming rope. Gudrun's man slipped and slithered on the rocks, ducking stones that Skapti hurled at him. His knife flashed. With a sharp slash he brought it down on the rope, slicing through it. In an instant Wulfgar was downstream, whirled away in the roaring brown flood, battered against the rocks, clutching at the roots of trees and the brown soil.

Brochael raced after him, flung himself at full length, and grabbed. Wulfgar sank and surged up, gasping. Their hands met, gripped tight; Brochael was jerked forward.

"Hold me!" he yelled, and Thorkil and Skapti threw themselves over him, clawing at his feet, and at the stems of bushes and thorns. Stones were falling on them like hail; on the far bank Gudrun's men clambered swiftly over the rocks.

"Pull!" Brochael roared. "Pull!" Tugging on his belt and feet and shoulders, they dragged at him; hauling his own weight and Wulfgar's painfully in, inch by inch. A stone hit Thorkil on the chest; he gasped, but hung on.

Then a man screamed. Looking up, Jessa saw the ravens hurtle down, stabbing at the men's faces, fluttering and beating them with their heavy black wings, shrieking high karks of anger. The men ducked, covered their eyes. One had blood running from his forehead.

Jessa grabbed at Thorkil and heaved. Slowly Brochael was squirming and wriggling back, and then Wulfgar grabbed the skald's hand, and with a great rush of water they dragged him out, blue with cold and shivering uncontrollably. He collapsed onto his knees, coughing and retching, but Brochael hauled him up. "You can drown later. Come on!"

Then he turned his head.

Jessa realized with a sudden chill that the clamor of the birds had stopped.

Kari was standing at the bank of the stream, one raven on a rock above him, the other at his feet, silently wiping its beak in the grass. On the other side of the river, Gudrun's men were gazing at him. They stared, silent and fascinated.

"Ah," said the skald softly. "Look at that. Gudrun's wordhoard works against her."

The men stood silent; one touched an amulet that swung from his coat. Then their leader whirled on them. "Move! Get down to the ford!"

The men turned. "You'd better hurry," the man said grimly. "No outlaw reaches the Jarlshold, not while I hold the passes." He was a tall man; his eyes blue. He wore the silver snake ring around his arm. He ran after his men. Wulfgar coughed and spat, watching him go.

"No outlaw will," he remarked.

Seventeen

Fire is needed by the newcomer
Whose knees are frozen numb;
Meat and clean linen a man needs
Who has fared across the fells.

As they ran toward the hills they were all numb with the cold. Kari kept coughing. Brochael watched him anxiously. Their clothes clung to them; the icy winds coming down from the pass froze the sodden materials and frosted coat and shirt with tiny crystals. In the shelter of some rocks they stopped and crouched.

"We should keep on," Thorkil said. "They'll be coming. . . ."

"It's a good long way to the ford. And we need food, and a fire," Brochael told him.

"Then we try the homestead we saw." Skapti stood up. "It was this way."

As cautiously as they could, they came through the undergrowth and saw before them, as if it squatted among the rocks at the base of the mountain, a small, crooked house built of turves, its roof green and overgrown. Thorns and brambles grew up around the door; the byres looked empty and unused. Smoke drifted from the hearth hole.

"Hardly a palace," the skald remarked.

Wulfgar shrugged. "I'll try and put up with it."

The skald turned to Brochael. "Let me go. Poets wander in strange places."

"Not alone," Brochael said. "We don't know how many live there, or whether they're Gudrun's men or not. Jessa, go with him. His daughter, shall we say?"

She gave him a wry smile. "I suppose I look poor enough."

"I'm honored." Skapti laughed.

Brochael clapped him on his shoulder. "Now look, if there's danger, get out. Don't mention us until you're sure."

The skald nodded. He stood up, tall and thin, and Jessa followed him, the almost empty pack slung over her shoulder. They trudged up through the rocks and the soft, wet tussocks of grass.

A bleat in the bushes startled her. She turned and saw two goats, sitting away to her left. Their slitted eyes watched her as she walked, their jaws chewing without pause.

When he reached the door, Skapti winked at her. Then he thumped twice on the soft, rotting wood. He stood as tall as the eaves.

A shuffle inside kept them silent. Then, without

warning, the door opened. The man who stood there was so small he scarcely reached to Jessa's shoulder. He had a narrow face and tiny sly eyes that hardly seemed to open, hooded with heavy lids. A white stubble of beard sprouted from his chin. He looked up at them both warily.

"I'm a skald, stranger," Skapti said briskly. "This is my daughter, Jessa. We're seeking a fire and some food."

The dwarfish man eyed them narrowly. Then, without speaking, he shuffled aside. The skald shrugged and went in, and Jessa followed him. They were both alert for an ambush, but there was none. The room was dark, cluttered, with greasy rags and rushes on the hard mud floor. They sat down by the fire, a smoky blaze that made the room stiflingly hot, but Jessa was glad of it.

The old man handed them each a slice of hard black bread and some cheese. The cheese was very strong, but Jessa ate it quickly. Faint steam rose from her wet clothes.

"Your girl's damp," the old man remarked, squatting on a stool.

"The ford," Skapti said, chewing his bread.

"Ah." The old man stirred the fire. "That's odd. I thought you came the other way."

There was silence for a moment. Jessa, thinking of the others out in the cold, and Gudrun's swordsmen hurrying to the ford, wished the skald would hurry. The old man glanced at her. "Now your girl's restless," he said. She smiled warily.

At last Skapti said, "I hear the Jarl Ragnar is dead."

The old man looked up. "News travels fast."

"To those who are interested. You didn't tell us your name."

Scratching his shoulder with a long hand, the old man grinned. "You're the strangers. You speak."

"My name is Skapti Arnsson. I was the Wulfings' poet."

For a moment Jessa thought he had made a mistake, but she knew time was short.

The old man gave him a hard look. "The Wulfings. I thought they were all dead."

"All but one. Wulfgar. He should be Jarl, by right."

Suddenly the old man stood. He fetched a small stone bottle, uncorked it, and poured out a hot red liquid into three cups. They drank, and it burned Jessa's throat and glowed inside her. The old man slammed his cup down and wiped his beard. "That's what I keep for enemies of the witch. Now, let's grip like wrestlers and stop the circling. My name is Asgrim; they call me the Dwarf. How many of you are there, and who pursues you?"

Astonished, Skapti stared at him. Then he laughed. "Well, I'm not as sly as is thought, it seems. There are four others. One is Wulfgar."

"Outside?"

"Not far. Gudrun's men are behind us. We need to cross the pass, but first we need food and warmth."

"Then get them in! Girl, go and get them."

She glanced at Skapti, who shrugged. "Do as he says." He grinned at the old man. "Six to one is good enough odds."

Jessa tugged open the door and ran across the grass. Instantly she saw them coming, rising like ghosts from the bushes. "Come on!" she called.

"How many?" Brochael asked as he came up.

"One old man."

He nodded and tugged her hair.

The old man glanced at Thorkil and Brochael as they ducked under the low door. Then he stabbed a finger at Wulfgar. "You're the Wulfing, lord?"

"I am."

"Then remember Asgrim when you're Jarl. But if they catch you, forget you ever knew me."

Wulfgar laughed and nodded and pushed past him to the fire. As he moved, the old man saw Kari. Jessa had never seen anyone stand so still. After a while Kari said, "You'll know me again."

"Who on the gods' earth are you?" the old man whispered.

Brochael hauled Kari toward the fire. "Get the wet clothes off—all of you! Hurry." As he unlaced his own great shirt he grinned at the dwarf. "He's Kari Ragnarsson. As you've guessed."

Asgrim sat down. His eyes followed Kari with fascination. "He's her image," he muttered. "Every hair of his head. Every look of his eyes."

Kari gave him a quick glance. "That's enough," Brochael snapped. "Now, we'd be grateful for something to eat."

Shaking his head, the old man got up and put more bread and cheese and cups on the table. "Poor fare for lords," he said, "but it's all that's here."

When they were dressed and warm, they ate hungrily. Wulfgar swallowed a crust and said, "If I can ever repay you, master, I will, and generously. Rings and horses will be yours for this."

The old man grinned. "I can't eat promises. Nor do they keep me warm." He pointed down at the heap of wet clothes on the floor. "I'll take these, to be going on with."

He fingered the fine cloth of Thorkil's shirt, then picked up Brochael's tattered one. The big man roared. "It'll go around you twice!"

"All the warmer." The Dwarf winked at them, and they laughed until Kari said, "Quiet."

He lifted his eyes from the wine in his cup. "They're outside."

"I heard nothing," the old man began, but Brochael waved him silent.

At the window Skapti eased back a corner of the shutter. It was getting dark outside. The trees were black shadows.

"Can't see anything."

"They're out there," Kari muttered. "A lot of them."

In the silence, they heard a strange, quiet rattle and caw from the roof. "Send the birds off," Brochael snapped. "They may follow." He turned to Asgrim. "Is there a back door?"

"They'll see you."

"We've no choice."

"He could hide us," Thorkil put in.

"And have that witch torment me for it?"

Skapti laughed. "No hero this, is he? There'll be no songs about Asgrim, I can see that."

With a sliver of steel Brochael drew a long knife. "Decide now. And be quick."

"No." Wulfgar caught his arm and forced it down. "No. Let him choose freely. I'll not raise my hand against my host."

For a moment Brochael glared at him. Then he nodded, and put the knife away. "As you say. But you may have doomed us all."

"I don't think so." Wulfgar turned to the Dwarf. His

voice was slow, almost lazy. "Now. Where's this loyalty to the Wulfings that you boast of?"

The old man scratched his beard and laughed ruefully. "It's over here, lord, behind this wall." He led them through the dark room into the cow byre next door, its floor covered with filthy straw and smelling of rats. One wall was boarded with wood; he pulled a plank away to show a large space behind. "My bolt hole. I've used it myself before now. You may not all fit."

Brochael pushed Kari in without a word, and then Jessa. Skapti followed, folding himself up, and then Thorkil and Wulfgar. When Brochael squeezed in too, there was barely room. Hurriedly Asgrim put the plank back; they heard him fling straw against it.

There was a loud thump on the outer door. Then it burst open. Voices came through, loud and threatening.

"Be ready," Brochael whispered. "We may have to take them by surprise."

Jessa heard knives drawn in the darkness. Useless, she thought. If he betrays us here, we're finished. Some light filtered through a knothole in the wood. Brochael leaned forward and blocked it, putting his eye to the hole. "Six . . . seven," he mouthed. "More outside."

"Outlaws," they heard a voice saying. "Traitors to the Jarl."

"I've not seen them." Asgrim's voice sounded near; in the doorway to the byre. "And why should they come here?"

"They'd need food."

"I don't have enough for myself, master, without giving to passersby."

"I see. And so what are these?"

Brochael jerked back from the hole.

"What is it?" Jessa asked. She saw him turn his head in the dimness.

"We left the clothes by the fire," he breathed. "They've found them."

Eighteen

After nightfall I hurried back,
But the warriors were all awake.
Lights were burning, blazing torches,
So false proved the path.

Asgrim didn't hesitate. "All right. I stole them."

"Where from?"

"Out near the river. Behind some rocks."

"But you didn't tell me."

They heard the Dwarf laugh. "I'm a poor man, master. That's good cloth—well, some of it is. Your quarry must have whipped off their wet clothes and dressed in dry, then sped off and left these. They'll be halfway up the pass by now."

There was a pause. He doesn't believe it, Jessa thought.

Then they heard Asgrim yelp in pain. "You're a poor liar," the warrior growled. "They've been here, haven't they? Any idea what she'll do to you for this? I believe the silver mines beyond Ironwood always need men."

"Believe me," the Dwarf gasped, "I can imagine. But no outlaws have been here, I can say that for a truth."

"Back!" Brochael muttered. "They're coming in."

"Search this!" The leader's voice was so near it made Jessa jump. "All of it. Burn the place if you have to." The noise of smashing wood and flung furniture made Wulfgar grit his teeth.

"We can't let them do this."

"I think," the skald remarked drily, "I can let them, if I force myself."

The noise came nearer. Something began to thump the panels of their hiding place. Jessa bit her lip. No one breathed. The hand slithered along the wood, feeling.

Brochael raised his ax; it glinted in the dimness.

But before he could move, there was a sudden commotion and yells from outside. A breathless voice rang in the byre.

"The birds! They're up over the pass!"

Scuffles, the slam of a door, running footsteps. Then silence.

Brochael moved first. "Now," he growled. He kicked down the panel with one blow and was out, pulling the others after him. A shuffle in the next room made Wulfgar turn, but it was only the old man, his head around the door.

"Hurry," he said. "They may be back."

Wulfgar gripped his hand. "I don't forget my promises."

The small man grinned. "You'll probably be dead. And I'll get no horses from her, either."

Wulfgar thumped his arm and was gone. As the others passed, Asgrim spoke to Kari. "She must fear you. You must be the one who can defeat her."

Kari turned bleakly. "What about my fear of her?" he said.

Then Brochael pushed him out. "Will you be safe, old man?"

"Safer than you."

Brochael nodded ruefully. "There may be songs about you, after all," he said. Then he raced after the others.

They ran through the trees until the ground began to slope upward. Behind a pile of boulders Brochael stopped them. He crouched, one great arm around Thorkil's shoulder. "Listen. We go silent and we go swift. They're ahead of us, and will have men watching every path. They'll also be waiting at the pass, but there's no other way over, and we must take it. Be wary; keep your eyes open."

They nodded.

"No one is to carry anything. Throw those empty packs in here." He pulled some bushes apart and they tossed in the bags, the springy growth swishing back as he let it go. "Now. Take care."

They climbed slowly, following the course of a narrow rocky stream that tumbled down the slope into the river. It cut deep into the peaty soil; thick tangles of gorse and bramble sprawled across it. They went carefully in the gathering darkness, often on hands and knees, keeping their heads low, below the level of the bank, splashing through the brown tumbling water chock-full of rocks. When the stream became smaller and dwindled to a trickle things were more difficult. This high up, the ground was open; only boulders and the shadows of stunted trees offered cover. They crawled in the dark over the boggy ground, flattening at any sound, until Jessa's clothes were wet and her nostrils full of the smells of the mosses and the tiny creeping plants, the tussocky grass and the sundew that clung to her hair.

As the mountainside rose and became rockier, they began to clamber among the loose boulders that dislodged and tumbled underfoot, and scree that slid treacherously. Once, the skald nearly fell, and only Thorkil's quick grip kept him up. The wind became colder, the air damp with thin rain. There were few signs of Gudrun's men. Wulfgar thought they had crossed the mountains already, but Brochael just grunted. Jessa knew he was worried about the pass, that the danger would be up there, in the narrowest place.

He was right.

As midnight crept on and the sky turned black, they saw up ahead of them in the rainy air the red sparks of fires, the flickering shadows of watchers.

Finally, crouching behind a tower of rock, they saw the pass. It was a very narrow place, where the path dwindled to a thread between two pinnacles of the mountain, sheer and jagged. In the very middle of the path a fire had been lit; men sat around it, talking, the edges of their faces red in the flame light. Beyond, in the darkness, the path must run on, over the lip of the hill, down and down, into the flat marshy country of the Jarlshold.

Brochael took a long look, then turned his back and leaned against the rock, stretching out his legs in front of him. "We'll need the High One himself to get us through this."

Thorkil turned to Kari. "Why don't you do what you did before—make us invisible?"

Kari shook his head. "That's not what I did. I made one man think he had not seen you. There are far too many of them for that. I can't touch all their minds."

Thorkil shrugged. "So what can you do?" There was a touch of scorn in his voice. Jessa remembered the unwinding arm ring and frowned at him. But then, he didn't remember.

"I don't know," Kari said. "Not yet."

After a silence Wulfgar rubbed his wet hair. "We can't get by with stealth, so we must attack."

"No." Brochael shook his head. "We'd be cut to pieces."

"Well, do you have any other ideas?"

"None."

There was another silence. Finally Jesssa said, "I've got an idea." They all looked at her. She was fiddling with the laces on her boots. "It's the fire."

"What about it?" Wulfgar asked patiently.

"It's the only light they've got. And it's what blocks the way. If the fire went out suddenly, it would be dark, very dark, in that crack in the rocks. Their eyes wouldn't be used to it. We could take them by surprise, if we were near enough."

Brochael was nodding. "Yes, she's right."

"But listen, little shamanka," the skald said, pulling gently on her hair, "how do we put it out? Throw rocks at it?"

She shrugged. "Kari must put it out."

Kari looked at her. "I've told you, I can't—"

"I don't mean make them believe. I mean put it *out*. You, yourself." She shuffled around to look at him, her voice urgent. "She could do it, and if she could, you can. You must. You must know your own powers."

Kari stared into the darkness. He let Brochael put a hand on his shoulder. "What do you think?" the big man asked gently.

"I don't know. I'll try, but—"

"You can," Jessa said quietly. "And you know it."

He smiled. "If you say so."

"If it was possible," Brochael said slowly, "we could be through in seconds. Wulfgar and I will hold the pass until you're down." He grinned at the dark man sprawled elegantly in the mud. "What do you say, my lord? We'd have some good fighting."

Wulfgar nodded, but the skald said softly, "I thought the point of this was a new Jarl. Not much use to us if he's dead."

Wulfgar ignored him. "So it depends on you, runemaster," he said to Kari.

Kari turned and gazed over the rocks at the blaze of fire. "Let's move up closer, then."

Shadows in the darkness, they drifted from rock to rock, silent as ghosts. Now they were so near they could hear the soft speech of the watchers and the crackle and spit of flames. A sentinel moved past them; they waited, flat against rock. Kari, a darker shape in the darkness, edged out so that he could see the flames. Jessa saw the light of them glimmer on his face.

They waited, unmoving. For a while nothing changed; they had time to know they were crouched in a dark, damp place high up on a mountain, pinned down by the wind.

And then Jessa began to feel it, a slow accumulation of darkness, a gathering up of night from all its cracks and holes and crannies. Kari was conjuring with black air; as he lay flat against the rock, unmoving, she could sense his mind searching, gathering, piling night on night.

The fire glimmered. A man muttered something and threw on kindling; sparks flew and went out. Above the flames the air seemed a web of blackness, descending, drifting down. The red light grew less. The flames sank. Kari clenched his fist, his face intent. "Go on," Jessa breathed, half to herself. "Go on." Slowly the fire was dwindling, shrinking to small cold blue flames. Someone shouted angrily; the charred sticks were stirred into a cloud of ash. Kari gripped Brochael's sleeve.

"Now," he said. And the fire went out.

It was gone so suddenly that Jessa was barely ready. In the blackness someone pushed her. She sprang up and ran up the steep path, slipping between shadows in a confusion of shouts and the clash of swords. Someone grabbed her; she thumped at his chest and shoved him away, and then she was over the pass and racing downhill over loose stones that clattered and spilled under her feet, down and down into the darkness of the land below. Breathless with speed, she slid and rolled and grabbed at the scree to steady herself, hearing the stones rattle down and fall a long way. She crouched on hands and knees. Someone was kneeling at her side. "All right?"

She recognized Thorkil's voice. "Yes." She scrambled up. "Where are they?"

The top of the mountain was black against the dim sky. Figures moved up there; there were shouts, the ominous clang of metal.

"Brochael's holding them." Thorkil sounded breathless, choked with excitement. "He and Wulfgar, like they said!"

"They'll be killed! Where's Kari?"

"I don't know."

She looked up. "We must do something!"

But as they watched it, the sky split open. An arch of blue light flamed suddenly over the hilltop, and under it they saw Brochael clearly, wielding his ax, scattering men, and Wulfgar, his sword flashing blue and purple. Then out of the arch shot strange shafts of eerie fire, glimmering down like a net of light. Gudrun's men leaped back, one yelling, as the blue flames scorched him, until the rippling curtain of light had closed the pass. Wulfgar and Brochael were already hurtling down the path to where Jessa and Thorkil waited.

"Where's Kari?" Brochael gasped.

"Here." He was standing farther down the slope, the skald at his side.

In the eerie blue light Brochael stared at him. "Did you do that?" he said, his voice gruff. "How could you have done that?"

Kari was silent. Then he said, "I didn't want you to be hurt."

Brochael shoved his ax into his belt. For a moment Jessa thought she saw something new in his face; some fear. But when he looked up at Kari it was gone. "Let's get on," he said.

NINETEEN

Learned I grew then, lore-wise,
Waxed and throve well.
Word from word gave words to me,
Deed from deed gave deeds to me.

They moved down the hillside, a line of shadows in the darkness. No one pursued them. For hours, looking back, they could see the strange gate of blue light on the hilltop, dwindling behind them, until they came down to the trees and it was lost among the branches. Jessa was at the back, near Brochael. "What happened up there?" she asked quietly.

He shrugged. "It came down between us—between

her men and us. Fire, sparkling, spitting, crackling. It was like lightning that stayed. I tell you, Jessa, it scared me. I never thought he could do that."

Silent, she nodded. But it didn't scare her. It filled her with secret, fierce delight. Oh, Gudrun, she thought, wait until you see what we're bringing you!

That night they stopped and slept near the banks of a stream, lulled by the wind in the trees and the trickle of meltwater. In the morning they moved on, always down, into the endless forests. As the day went on the sky darkened. A coldness in the air seemed to thicken and drift together; it made a low mist that wrapped itself around the boles of trees. As the travelers walked it swirled cold and wet about their legs, soaking coats and cloaks and Jessa's skirts.

"Witch mist," the skald remarked over his shoulder. "This is her welcome."

Brochael called them to stop and looked, as he always did, at Kari. "Is he right?" he asked.

Kari was leaning against a tree. He seemed to grow more silent the farther they went. As he nodded, drops of dew ran from his hair. "She's watching us. Her face is white among the candles. She'll deal with us herself now."

As he spoke the mist drifted between them, muffling

sound, ice-cold on the skin. "Keep together," Brochael said quickly. "Within touch, or we're lost."

Jessa felt his strong fingers fasten on her belt. She gripped Thorkil's wrist. "Where's Wulfgar?"

"Right here." A shadow moved at the skald's side; his voice strangely echoless in the murk.

"What now?" Thorkil said.

"We go on. Hand in hand, if necessary."

"We can't move in this, Brochael," Wulfgar said quietly. "We've no way of telling our direction; we could go miles out of our way."

"We can't afford to wait either," Jessa put in. "Not if you want to be the next Jarl."

She heard Skapti chuckle. "Sharply put," he whispered in her ear.

She turned to Kari. "What about the birds? They'll fly above this—can't we follow them?"

She saw him nod. He gave a call and the two black shapes dropped heavily through the trees, one with its huge talons digging into the leather of his gloves. The other hopped to a fallen log and screeched.

"What are these creatures?" Wulfgar asked. "Birds or spirits?"

Kari glanced at him. "They say Odin has two ravens. One is Thought, and one is Memory. They see all that passes in the world." He threw one up into the mist and the other followed.

When they moved on they kept together, following the high, distant kark of the two ravens. Fog clung to their faces and drifted into their mouths when they spoke; it slithered about them, cold and white. None of them could see where they were going or noticed that the forest was beginning to thin out, until the ground underfoot became marshy, with tussocks of grass that tripped them up. Their feet sank into soft mud.

The croaks of the ravens were growing fainter, far to the left. Then they faded away. Kari called, twice, but nothing answered.

Finally they stopped. Silence and cold closed in around them, like a silver ring. Jessa remembered Mord's tale of the white mist that had swallowed the Jarl's men long ago, of how they marched into it and not one had come out. Was that how it would be now, for them? A crystal of snow floated down onto her glove, a strange star with seven points. It melted slowly into the soft leather.

"We're out of the woods." Brochael pulled his hand from his glove and rubbed his beard and hair. "No more than a few miles from the Jarlshold. There will be men waiting."

"How do you know?" Thorkil asked curiously.

"Salt, lad. I can smell the water of the fjord. I've been a long time away from it."

He grinned at Jessa, but she only said, "It's snow."

They stared at her.

"She's sending snow." Jessa looked up. "And the birds are lost in it."

Silent, they watched it come spinning down around them; soft wet flakes falling on hair and in the folds of clothes. It glittered, like silver.

"Don't taste it," Kari said slowly. "Don't let it touch your lips."

Wulfgar untied the scarf from his neck and wrapped it around his face. They all did the same, muffling nose and mouth.

"Now keep on," Brochael snapped. "This witchbrew won't keep us back." He pushed Thorkil forward and they hurried behind him, splashing into freezing pools and marsh mire. Already the snow was horizontal; it was a white storm in their eyes and faces.

Jessa saw Kari slip, and waited. "All right?"

He nodded, his eyes shards of gray. "This is for me."

"This?"

"The snow. All of it." For a moment he stood still. "And the worst will be seeing her. All those silent days . . ."

"That's all over."

He shook his head. "That silence lives with you. You can never fill it."

She nodded, not knowing what to say. They moved on slowly, behind the others.

"What do you want," he said, "if we get through all this?"

"Wulfgar to be Jarl. And my farm back. Horolfstead. It's near the sea. What do you want?"

Snow stuck to his hair and eyelids. "I want not to be like her."

"But you're not!"

"I am. I'm afraid she will make me part of herself." He turned to her. "Does that sound strange? But she can do that. Suck you in, burrow into your heart—"

A yell interrupted him. As Jessa whirled around she saw men leap out of the snow. Two of them clung to Brochael, who roared and flung them off, but before he could tug out his ax they had grabbed him and pulled him down.

"Keep still," Kari muttered.

Wulfgar and the skald were already surrounded; Thorkil had his sword knocked scornfully into the marsh—he swore and struggled, but a blow in the chest silenced him.

"Only six," Kari muttered.

"Can they see us?"

"Not us."

They were Gudrun's men; they wore the snake rings on their wrists. One of them dragged Thorkil up. "The Jarl's son. Where is he?" Breathless, Thorkil shook his head. The man flung him onto Brochael. "Spread out. She said we might not see him."

They moved quickly, making a ring of swords. Kari and Jessa were inside it.

"Cut the air. Use your swords. He's here."

"You're wasting your time," Brochael snarled, but they took no notice and began to close in, moving together through the blizzard. Blades sliced the swirling snow.

Jessa took a step back. "The one on the left," she breathed.

But the man heard; his eyes widened with terror. "Here!" he yelled, flinging one arm out. He touched Jessa's hair and grabbed at it. She screamed and kicked him, and as he staggered back Skapti stuck out his long leg and tripped him so that he crashed to the ground. At once Jessa and Kari had leaped through the gap and raced into the flying web of snow.

"Run!" Brochael yelled.

They ran blindly, stumbling through the wet fen, the cries and shouts behind them dying into wind and silence;

ran until their lungs ached, and they collapsed behind a heap of stones, coughing and dragging in breath.

"We can't go back for them." Kari gasped. "There's no time." She saw him turn, his hands clenched.

"Can you hear it?" he asked savagely.

"The wind?"

"It's not the wind, it's her, taunting me. She's waiting for me to come. She wants it!"

Jessa shoved the knife back in her belt. "I know. And we've all helped her."

"You?"

"Even me," Jessa said bitterly. "I was so proud—I thought I'd outwitted her. I wouldn't let her use me—I threw the arm ring away. But it didn't matter. She made us bring you—she's let us come, through the snow and the mist, through the fingers of her men. She wants you for something."

Kari gave her a strange look. "You think so?"

"So does Brochael."

He lifted his head. "Then let's not disappoint her."

It was her snow. They walked through a white moving tunnel of it, and it stung on the skin like venom. Dimly, on each side, shapes flickered, shifted, and came to nothing—wolves, worms, troll shadows that danced in the corners of their eyes—but they walked on swiftly to the place where the snow ended and stepped through the edge of it, into darkness.

Before them the sky was purple, dotted with faint stars. They looked over a wide stretch of marshy ground, misty with gases and smokes that rose from the earth, the smell of them drifting on the wind. Not far off the plop of some creature into a pool sounded loud and strange.

Across the marsh stood the Jarlshold: a cluster of black roofs, with the carven ends of the hall gables clear against the sky. There were no lights down there, no sounds. Not even the barking of a dog.

Without speaking, they began to move forward, helping each other over the treacherous mire. The water was brackish and icy, with a sharp smell of weed and decay. Strange tiny lights, purple and green and blue, moved among the reeds and mists, always at a distance.

Jessa's skirt slopped against her boots; her hair was muddy and clung to her back. The fumes of the marsh made them cough, and the sound echoed through the stillness.

Gradually the ground rose, became drier. They climbed a long slope of thorn and black, spiny bushes, and pushed through them onto a track paved with flat stones.

As they followed it between the first houses, their footsteps sounded loud in the stillness. There was no watchman, no challenge. Jessa wondered how late it was, whether everyone was asleep, but the silence was not normal. And no smoke. That meant no fires in the houses.

They passed Mord's house, but the door was closed and she dared not try it. The shadows between the buildings were black; as they came silently under the walls of the great hall, Jessa saw that the windows were shuttered, and no light leaked from them. The two ravens, like gargoyles, were perched on the roof. One gave a short kark.

"Where is everyone?" she asked. "What's she done with them?"

"Nothing. They're here."

"How do you know?"

Kari did not seem to hear. He took her hand, and they moved silently along the black wall.

At the door the watchman's stool was empty, and there was no dog. Jessa put her hand to the door and lifted the latch. It moved easily, with a tiny creak that made her wince. Both together, they pushed it ajar, and slipped inside.

Twenty

Offered, myself to myself.

Gudrun was waiting for them.

She was standing with her back to the fire; the smoke of it hung about her in the dark spaces of the hall.

No one spoke. Kari leaned with his back against the door, hands behind him; then, slowly, he walked out into the firelight. Jessa stayed where she was.

He stopped a few yards from Gudrun and they stared at each other in silence. To Jessa the likeness they shared was astonishing: the same thin paleness, the same sense of hidden power—even the same straight, shining hair, though Kari's was ragged and muddy, and Gudrun's arranged in long elaborate braids.

Then the woman moved with a rustle of silks.

"Where are your friends?"

"Your men have them." Kari's voice was low, but his hands were clenched and trembling. "You should have known that."

She shrugged lightly. "Perhaps I did."

"No," he said slowly. "You didn't."

A flicker of expression crossed her face, as if she was surprised, but it was gone before Jessa could be sure.

Gudrun moved nearer to Kari. She was taller. She ran a narrow finger down his patched coat. Jessa saw, tied around her wrist, a wisp of dried snakeskin.

"Not the clothes for the Jarl's son."

"You took that away from me."

"I could give it back." She smiled with real amusement and touched his hair. Jessa saw how he stiffened.

"It's too late." He pulled away and went to the fire and tossed on a handful of kindling. Then he stood close up to the flames. The new wood crackled and spit; the sound echoed in the roof.

"You're afraid of me." He said it steadily, but with an effort, looking into the leaping web of flame. "Because I'm the same as you—just the same. You invented all those lies so that no one would know it, but they only have to look. Any powers you have, I have too."

She smiled, smoothing her dress. "But I know how to use them. You don't."

"I've been learning."

"Tricks played on fools. Not the real spells, not the twisting of minds, the webs of fear and delight."

She had come after him and reached out again, fingering the ends of his hair as if she could not leave him alone. "As for fear, I'm afraid of nothing."

"Except your reflection," Jessa said.

Gudrun turned quickly, as if she had forgotten her. "Silence!"

"It's true." Kari looked up. "And you know it's not the one in the mirror. I'm your reflection."

Gudrun was still a moment. Then she said, "Indeed you are. You and I are the same."

"No." He shook his head, but she went up to him, clutched his hands.

"Look at us. Together we could make the north such a kingdom of sorcery as has never been dreamed. I have let you live for this, watched you, to see what you would become." Her cold eyes glittered. "And you've become me."

"No!" Kari stepped back. "You're wrong. I would never join with you."

Gudrun straightened; her fingers stabbed the air; she snapped out a rune. Kari caught his breath. To Jessa's horror, he staggered with a gasp of pain.

"Stop it! Leave him alone," she cried.

But already he was lifting his head, straightening, white and unsteady. When he spoke, his voice was bitter. "You won't do that again. Now feel its reflection."

He did not move or say anything, but the witch slowly bent before him like a candle too close to heat. Her eyes widened; she staggered to the table and clutched it, one hand gripping the edge, her knuckles white.

"This is pain," he said quietly, coming up behind her. "This is how it feels. And these are nightmares—see them? This is silence. This is fear."

Gudrun shuddered, shaking her head. She beat off something invisible with her hand; quick, nervous snatches. Kari stood and watched. Then he touched her hair. Jessa felt her heart thump with fear.

"Are these the webs you mean?" he said softly. "You see I can weave them too."

Gudrun buckled into a chair. Her long hands lay on the table—Jessa could see them trembling. The hall was dark and silent.

Then Kari turned away, and Gudrun's hands were still. He went back to the fire. After a while he said in a sharp voice, "It's over, your time of power. There are two of us now—a balance. I think you should go back to the place you came from; leave the Jarlshold to choose its own leader."

"You?" she said scornfully, raising her head.

"Not me. They won't want me." He rubbed his hair wearily. "I'm too much like you."

"Kari!" Jessa cried.

He turned and saw that the witch was standing, tall and pale. Her white gown fell in straight folds; it glinted like frost.

"It's not finished," she said. "Has he told you about the serpent, this Brochael you're so fond of? The serpent hugs the world; it devours itself. It will never be destroyed until the end of the world, when the great wolf of darkness snaps its binding, and the ship of monsters sails into the harbor. Far from here, far to the north, is a hall, all woven of white snakes; its doors face out to the eternal ice."

She held out her hands; drew them slowly apart. Jessa saw light gleam between them. The hall seemed to shudder; the shutters creaked as if something was pressing against them.

"That is the place I come from," Gudrun said. "The serpent is what I serve. And now it strikes."

She was close to him; her hands moved in a flash of light. Jessa screamed and grabbed Kari, hauling him aside as the knife slashed down. Gudrun turned and struck again; the blade whistled past Jessa's face, slicing through strands of her hair. Kari grabbed it. With an effort he wrenched it out of her hand and flung it onto the fire.

At once the flames roared up, higher than his head. Long coils of smoke poured out, twisting around his neck and arms. Smoke swept around Jessa's waist, squeezing her tight, even though her hands went through it as she beat at it. She yelled and squirmed, but the serpent of smoke held her, hugging the breath out of her. Its tongue flickered at

Kari, pinning him against the wall, blackening the stones and scorching the tapestry behind him into smoking holes. As he dodged, the cloth caught alight; a line of flame ran up the edge, crackling through the dusty threads.

Kari scrambled through the smoke to Jessa. As he caught hold of her the weight on her chest seemed to burst; she breathed in, sick and dizzy.

"Where is she?" he yelled, but Jessa shook her head and jerked back as the tapestry fell, a roaring sheet of flame, from the wall.

"This way!" she screamed.

They ran to the door and tugged. It didn't move. Jessa slammed her palms against it and whirled around. "The windows, then!"

But the windows were shuttered, the hall a closed cage of burning cloth. Smoke stung their eyes; they were coughing and retching. High overhead the roof tree crackled, spilling sparks like blossoms.

Outside, a voice was yelling. Something thumped on the door.

Jessa slammed and kicked at it. "How can we get out?"

"We can't."

He dragged her down and they gasped the cold air near the floor. Then she looked at him. To her astonishment she saw he was half smiling. She forced herself to be calm.

"What are you going to do?"

"This."

He kneeled in the smoke, his hands gripped into fists.

And the smoke turned white. It gathered itself together into hard grains and fell silently. It fell from the darkness up there in the rafters; fell as a gentle, relentless snow, onto the flames, onto Jessa's hair and upturned face. The air grew cold; the water on her cheeks froze. Soot hardened to a black glaze, and the flames sank. Tapestries stiffened into rigid folds and hard, crumpled masses on the flagstones.

Slowly, easily, the snow fell, whitening floor and tables, hanging like frail lace on their clothes, and on Gudrun's, as she sat in the center of the hall, watching them.

She sat calmly in a great chair, her face expressionless. On a stool at her feet huddled the wizened old man Grettir, looking more ancient than ever. His long eyes watched them both carefully. Jessa stared back. Had they been there all the time, in all that flame and smoke?

Suddenly someone outside yelled. The door shuddered, as if something heavy had struck it.

The witch stood up and came forward. The old man followed her like a dog. She seemed slightly smaller, almost as if something had gone from her. Close up, Jessa saw the faint lines on her face as she kneeled thoughtfully by Kari.

"It seems you're right," she said. "There are two of us

now." She smiled at him. "So I will do you the greatest harm I can. I'll give you what you want."

"What do you mean?" he muttered.

"I leave it all to you," she said. "With this curse. They will never love you, never trust you. Power like ours is a terror to them. You'll see that. Your new Jarl will want to be rid of you as soon as he can." She touched his shoulder lightly. "And you'll use them, as I did. It's what we always do."

Then she was on her feet, walking to the black folds of tapestry. She tugged them back, and there was the small arch Jessa remembered. The door shuddered again. Gudrun ignored it, and turned and tossed something down that rolled and lay on the stone flags. "Keep this," she said. "One day I may come back for it."

As she turned he said, "You're wrong about me. I'm not like you."

"We'll see," she said. Jessa thought she was smiling. Then she was gone, the old man close behind, into the stone passages behind the curtain.

After a moment Jessa turned and ran to the door. She pulled the latch and it lifted easily; she tugged the heavy door wide. The men outside stared at her, but someone gave a great shout and grabbed her arms. She saw it was Brochael, with a crowd of others at his back.

"Where's Kari?"

"Inside."

They surged past her. She saw Gudrun's men standing uncertain outside, but she left them and followed Thorkil.

"Where's Gudrun?" he asked.

She shook her head, suddenly tired.

Wulfgar had picked the object off the floor. He gave it to Kari, who fingered the knotted snakeskin.

"Search the hold," Brochael said, but Kari shook his head.

"You won't find her. She's gone."

"But where?"

"Back. Wherever she came from."

"For good?" Brochael asked gruffly.

Kari shrugged. "That's more than I can say." Suddenly he turned to Wulfgar. "Well. Here we are in your hall. It seems the Wulfings have come home at last."

The skald went over and kicked the frozen mass of the fire.

"And not a moment too soon," he remarked.

———————————— ✠ ————————————

Twenty-One

Silence becomes the son of a prince.

By morning the whole of the Jarlshold had been searched, but there was no sign of Gudrun or Grettir. How she had vanished from among them no one knew, but it was said later that a man who farmed up on the fells to the east had seen a woman, dressed all in white, walking swiftly and tirelessly over the snow, with a dark figure like a shadow behind her. Terrified, he had hurried indoors to the firelight.

First thing in the morning the men of the Jarlshold and all the surrounding settlements had gathered in the great hall, staring at the travelers curiously. Many of them could not tear their eyes from Kari as he sat quietly talking to Brochael and Wulfgar. Jessa knew that the presence of so many people was making him uneasy; she caught his eye and smiled and he did the same. Wulfgar was voted Jarl with a great roar of approval, no one disagreeing, but afterward, in the crush and excitement, Kari was missing. She searched for him, pushing her way to Thorkil.

"Have you seen Kari?"

He shook his head. "Elsewhere, I suppose. Not used to all these people."

But when she asked Brochael, he paused for a moment and shrugged a little unhappily. "I have an idea where he might be. Come on."

As she followed him out of the hall, she heard silence fall behind her, and into it came the skald's voice, clear and sharp, chanting an old song in praise of the Wulfings, a chain of words, lilting and proud. Looking back, she saw Wulfgar sitting in the Jarl's chair, relaxing in it lazily, his fingers moving over the worn arms as Ragnar's had done. Behind him, Thorkil leaned.

She followed Brochael. They went down into a part of the Jarlshold she had never seen: a long dark corridor at the foot of a flight of damp steps. On each side were small rooms, their windows barred, and the stench from them stale and fetid.

"Her prisons," Brochael growled. "Full, till this morning."

His voice echoed in the stone tunnel.

She followed him to the very end, deep in the rock under the hold. The door of the last room was ajar, and he pushed it open. They saw a very small cell, long neglected. The walls were dark with grime and soot. Old straw rustled under their feet; one tiny window let in the light.

Kari stood at the far end of the room, looking at something on the wall. Jessa saw it was some faint scrawl of circles and spirals, almost worn away with age. His hair shone pale and clean, and he wore the new clothes that Wulfgar had given them all from the Jarl's store. He turned around when he heard them.

"Why come here?" Brochael asked gruffly.

"Just to look. To see if I remembered it right." After a moment he took the snakeskin bracelet from his pocket and fingered it, dropping it silently into the cold ashes in the fireplace. Then he came out and closed the door.

Brochael put an arm around him. "Come on. The lord Jarl will be having his first feast tonight. Everyone will want to stare at you as he loads you with gold and gives us all rings and horses. Asgrim will be here within days, when he hears."

"I don't want his gold," Kari said. "But I would like Thrasirshall—whatever is left of it."

Brochael nodded. "You'll get it! Who else would want it?" He grinned at Jessa. "And the new lady of Horolfstead will be wearing her best, I expect?"

"All borrowed." Jessa laughed.

Kari laughed too. Then he turned and raised his hands, and made a small movement.

As they watched it, the door faded out of sight.

BOOK TWO

The Empty Hand

To Joseph

Oης

*Darkness drowns everything
and under its shadow-cover shapes . . . glide
dark beneath the clouds.*

The creature moved down from the north, traveling quickly. All the long night it had blurred and flickered through blizzards, leaving its prints briefly on the open tundra, until the snow clogged them. It was a gray wraith on the glaciers, a shadow that trudged under black, frosted skies.

Hunger drove it—aching hunger. And a voice, a clear, cold voice that had called it out of some unremembered darkness, had knotted and woven its atoms together with spells and words and runes, and had sent it south tormented by this emptiness nothing could fill. Who the voice was, it did not know. It hardly knew anything, even where it was going.

The creature made a low moan that rang through the ice chasm around it. Sharp edges of snow fell soundlessly through its body. It climbed up and paused, turning its head north wearily, but the voice was still there, silent, insistent. It turned and trudged down the fellside.

There had been a feathered thing on a frozen lake

days ago, but that had been stinking and tasteless, a picked skeleton. Silver shapes under the ice had flicked away, unreachable. Head down, the rune beast stumbled on without thought. Stars glinted through it.

Then it stopped and lifted its head.

Dark shapes crowded the hillside below. The creature had seen nothing like them before. They stood, huge and rigid, sighing in the raw wind. The voice put a word, like a cold drop, into the creature's ear.

Trees.

Dimly it realized that the air had been changing for a long time. Days ago there had been bitter roaring winds at the uttermost ends of the earth, high snows and glacial emptiness. Now it was less cold. Down here things grew.

The rune creature glimmered between the trees and paused, deep in shadow. The wood was silent. There were strange new smells, teasing pleasures that tore at its hunger; pine and rotting wood and leaves and fungi; rich, decaying sensations. And beyond that, small, musky scents.

Animals.

The voice told it about animals, the sweetness of meat, the warmth of blood.

It hurried on, eager, drifting and glinting through

the tangled undergrowth. Snow fell through its body silently.

Two

. . . Caught sleeping by the cunning of the thief.

Oh, the fish was fresh all right. She wondered if it was even dead, it glared up at her so balefully from the wooden plate.

And the ale was worse. Grimly she swallowed one mouthful and turned on the man mending nets on the step.

"You'd better get me something else. Water, even."

"Water! Lady, you'll poison yourself!"

"I think I already have." Jessa poured the thin pale liquid deliberately onto the straw. "I wouldn't give this muck to my worst enemy."

Unruffled, the man stood up, gathering the torn net in his arms. "There's another cask. It'll cost you, though."

"I thought it might." She pushed the platter across the table. "And while you're there, you can do something to this. Cook it, preferably. If I'd wanted it raw, I could have speared my own."

The innkeeper nodded sourly. "With your tongue. It's sharp enough."

He gathered up the plate in disgust and disappeared behind a woven blue curtain.

Grinning, Jessa leaned her elbows on the table and folded her fingers together. It had been a good day. The market had been the best for a long time—they'd sold all the livestock, and the men had gone back to the farm with spices and yarn and leather and new swords. Under her coat hung a full pouch of silver. And Skapti was coming to meet her, the Jarl's tall, thin, sarcastic poet. In fact he should have been here by now. They were sailing to the Jarlshold on the next tide, and she was looking forward to it.

Someone came in, and she glanced up, but it wasn't the skald. A small, scrawny man. He sat in a corner and called for ale.

The room was warm; it smelled of food and dogs and smoke. All day it had been thronged with traders and peddlers and market women, but now she was the last of them. She gazed idly out over the wharf. The sun still hung above the horizon; a cold red globe, steaming over the sea. The nights were already getting shorter. Through the uncurtained doorway she could see the keels of upturned boats in the lurid light; gulls screamed and fought over the drying nets. As she listened, the clang of metal on metal from the smithy stopped, leaving a sudden stillness of sea wash and birds.

The innkeeper came back and dropped the platter on the table without ceremony. "It's well cooked now."

Jessa flicked the fish over with her knife. "Charred, I'd say."

"You would."

He put the cup of ale next to it and turned, straight into the blunt end of a knife that cracked viciously down. He crumpled and crashed among the tables.

Halfway to her feet in astonishment, Jessa froze.

Then, slowly, she sat down.

"Wise. Very wise."

The scrawny man watched her for a moment. He had very small eyes, dark and beady, and his face was thin and stubbly around the chin. A rat's face.

He reversed the weapon easily and let the point flicker toward her in the red light. "Over there. Against the wall. Don't scream."

She got up and moved in front of the table, her hands sliding smoothly behind her for the knife.

"Leave that!" He reached out and grabbed her arm. "Over there."

Furious, Jessa shook him off. She walked to the wall

and stood there, arms folded, icy with rage. But she had to be calm. She had to watch for her chance. There would probably only be one.

The man backed quickly, slammed the door, and dropped the bar of wood across it. The room went dim, with only the window now to give light, but he left that unshuttered and kneeled by the innkeeper, his free hand rummaging deftly among the man's clothes.

"Have you killed him?" she snapped.

"Not yet." He dragged out a handful of coins, thrust them into a leather sack that hung around his neck, and heaved the heavy body over.

"Well flattened, like all his kind." He gave her a swift, evil look. "Why didn't you go when everyone else did?"

"I'm waiting for someone." She said it firmly, taking quick glances around the dark room, but always meeting his eyes when he looked up. "They'll be here soon."

"They will, will they?"

"Why else would I stay?"

He wasn't listening. He got up and stepped over the still shape. "Where's his money? He did good trade today. Where does he keep it?"

"I've no idea," she said coldly.

Suddenly he turned, ran to the hearth, and rummaged there, clearing it of cooking pots with one sweep. Grabbing the lid of a nearby chest, he wrenched it open and threw out clothing and belts and fishhooks into a great heap by the smoldering fire.

Jessa took one step toward the window.

"Keep still!"

He was upright, with a small metal box in his hands. Jamming the point of the knife into the lid he forced it back with a crash. Then he grinned, showing broken teeth.

Jessa edged another step. Skapti must be here soon! And yet maybe that wasn't such a good thing. He wouldn't be expecting anything, and this scum looked murderous. She glanced at him thoughtfully as he poured a rain of small silver coins through his dirty fingers.

"You'd better go now you've got what you want. My friends will be here."

He slammed the box shut and scuttled toward her through the dimness. Close up his skin was gray with dirt; his breath stank. "And you must have some coins too, with a coat and boots of such nice soft leather." He narrowed his eyes. "A wealthy lass, by the look of you."

Icily Jessa glared at him. "The men I'm meeting are the Jarl's men, I warn you. The Jarl's poet himself. He and I are friends."

She had thought that would make him pause, but to her surprise he grinned, thin-lipped. "Jarl Wulfgar himself!

So we both have important friends. Just give me the money you've got, now."

"Kari Ragnarsson is also my friend." She said it at random, but just for a second caught a sudden wariness, even fear, in the thief's eyes.

"That one? The sorcerer? The Snow-walker?" He touched a greasy amulet quickly. "Well, it's a pity he's not here, then."

"He can see things that happen far off. He may be watching us. Remembering you."

Nervously the man's eyes shifted. His tongue flickered over his lips. "I'll have to take my chance." He held out his hand. "The purse."

The knife glittered in the firelight. Jessa clenched her fists hopelessly.

But before she could move, there was a rattle at the door. The latch jerked. "Anyone there?" a voice called.

She whirled around but the rat-faced thief had the knife to her throat in an instant. "Not a sound!" he hissed.

The door shuddered as Skapti thumped it again. "Jessa! Thorgard! Open the door!"

She could smell the man's warm breath behind her ear, and see the filthy nails that clutched the knife. He was small, not much taller than she was, but scrawny and tough. She cursed him silently.

Outside, Skapti's footsteps shuffled. Then they heard him walk away. Jessa almost despaired. She knew that her last chance was ebbing and that she had to do something now, at once. Recklessly she pulled away.

"All right. You can have the money."

He watched as she pulled the pouch from under her coat, weighing it reluctantly. He grinned and stepped forward, and then she drew back her arm and flung the purse at him hard; as he grabbed for it she shoved the table against him and heaved it up and over so it fell on him with a crash, spilling salt and fish and plate and ale. She was halfway out of the window before the knife thudded into the frame beside her. With a scream of anger she jumped, picked herself up, and raced into the dark shouting, "Skapti! Skapti, wait!"

A lanky figure ahead of her turned. "Jessa? Is that you?"

"He's armed! Quick!"

The skald caught her and put her behind him, then drew his sword, staring uneasily into the twilight. "Who is?"

Jessa gasped out her story.

"He's alone then?"

"Yes."

"And you're all right?"

"Yes, yes, but the rat's got my money!"

The skald grinned down at her. "Then we'd better try and get it back. Come on. Though he's probably gone." He rubbed his long nose. "Some dark unwarriorly corner of me hopes so, anyway."

"Well I don't. And I'm right behind you."

He stalked back down the wharf; she followed, hearing the planks creak beneath them, and the tide slapping the wood.

The door was wide open. Skapti peered around it carefully, his lean face sharp in the dying firelight. Then he straightened. "Sorry, Jessa. Your rat has run."

She stormed past him. The room was a mess. The table lay on its side, food scattered over the straw. She kicked a chair in frustration. "If only I hadn't thrown the wretched purse! What a stupid, stupid thing to do! Some of it was Wulfgar's money too!"

"You had no choice. He was armed and you weren't."

"That's another thing. Carry two knives, my father always said."

"He was wise."

"If I ever see that rat again . . ."

"You won't. We sail tonight, on the tide." Skapti kneeled by the innkeeper, who was groaning softly, and turned him over. "Get some water for this fellow, will you . . . and some of his ale."

"His own ale!" she muttered sourly. "That'll finish him off for sure."

Three

There was a handsome hall there.
And high within it sat a king of great courage.

Jessa pulled her coat around her and gazed out over the waves. The boat dipped, splashing spray high into the spring sky; eggshell blue, paler than snow shadows. She was cold, but the fresh smell of the morning fjord filled her like a second breakfast.

Skapti staggered down the boat, falling against oarsmen who handed him off good-humoredly. He sat by Jessa, hugging his long knees. "Soon be there. A good morning for voyaging, this."

She nodded, watching the green banks slide by, bright with tender grass. Snow hung in the clefts of the hills, but here the day might be warm enough later to do without gloves.

The poet flexed his long fingers. "Talk to me, Jessa.

Unlock your word-hoard. Spill your thoughts like pebbles into my silence."

She took her gaze from the green land and gave him a wry smile. "Still spinning word chains."

"It's my job."

"And Wulfgar's is to rule the land. What's he doing, to allow thieves and footpads in his markets?"

"There are always thieves and footpads."

But he seemed uneasy, she thought.

Then he said, "Wulfgar has done a great deal of good since he became the Jarl—you'll see that when we get to the hold. People aren't afraid to speak out now—there are courts again—on wergild, on property. Justice is done. All the witch's prisoners—and there were many—have been released. The farms and herds she took have been given back—those that have owners still alive, that is. The Jarlshold is no longer a place of terror, Jessa."

"That's as it should be. And Wulfgar. Has he changed?"

Skapti shrugged and looked out over the water. "All men change. Power's a heavy robe. You need to be very strong to wear it. Wulfgar is as honest, and noble, and fierce of heart as ever he was."

"But?"

"But what?"

"That's what I want to know." She stopped playing

with the laces of her boots and glanced at him sideways. "Come on, Skapti. I know you. What's wrong?"

"Nothing." The skald pulled a strange face. "At least, only in my own overbright imaginings. Maybe power isn't a robe but a honeypot, attracting wasps. Or maybe poets just like riddles. After all, after a witch like Gudrun anything is better. Now, what about you?"

She saw he wanted to change the subject and laughed. "Oh me! I'm fine. The farm is mine now, and Thorkil has his father's land too, so we're a wealthy family— or we were until yesterday." Irritated by the memory she glared at the oarsmen's straining backs.

Skapti nodded. "And have you heard nothing of Kari?"

She looked at him. "I . . . I think so,"

"*Think* so? Jessa, you say *I* talk in riddles!"

She grinned and leaned back against the wooden chests stacked in the bow. "Well, I know Kari and Brochael went back out to Thrasirshall to live, far off in the north. But a month ago, when I was in the fields at home, looking at some lambs, all of a sudden I . . . felt him. He was there. I was so sure that I turned around, but there was only the empty grass on the cliff top, and the sea. But he'd been watching me, Skapti. I knew it."

Skapti shrugged. "No doubt he was. Kari's powers are beyond guessing."

"Has Wulfgar heard from them?"

"Twice. Brochael sent a messenger asking for men from his own hold to go and work at Thrasirshall with him. Why Kari wants to go back and live in that troll-haunted ruin I can't think! A few men went north to them. Food was arranged—nothing grows up there, as you know."

"And the second time?"

"Wulfgar sent a man last autumn. He wanted Kari to have his father's land—not that it's worth much. Kari told him to keep it."

Jessa laughed. "Well, he's no farmer."

"No. The messenger said they were living their old strange life up there, Brochael rebuilding parts of the hall, and Kari in that peculiar tower room of his most of the time. There were odd sounds at night, the man said; flickers of light from the windows. He was scared, glad to get away."

They were silent. Jessa thought of the witch, Gudrun, Kari's mother, who had locked her son away in Thrasirshall for years because she feared that his powers were the same as hers; the strange sorcery of the White People, the Snow-walkers who lived beyond the edge of the world. Gudrun had used her own power for evil, to kill and enslave and torment. She had hoped her son would do the same. But Kari had refused, and now Gudrun had gone, no one knew where.

"What do you think he's doing?"

"I don't know," Skapti said. "I'm no runemaster."

"I miss them both." She thought of Brochael's great hug as he had left, and the way the boat had dipped under his weight as he climbed in. "Will you travel up to see them?"

"Not yet," he said. "I want to keep an eye on the Jarlshold."

There it was again, that glimmer of worry. But it lifted from his face as he looked up. "And here we are, anyway."

The low wharves and the turf-covered houses of the Jarlshold were rising from the fjord shore, smoke from their hearths wreathing high into the clear sky. Among them, high and gray, was the Jarlshall, the only stone building, its roof carved with writhing gargoyles and wide-snarling dragons. Beyond the marshland the mountains gleamed white.

As the oarsmen slid the ship smoothly across the gray waters, Jessa hugged her knees and smiled to herself, remembering how she had come here first, as a prisoner, cold and angry. Things were different now. The witch was gone.

She had meant to stay with Mord Signi, her kinsman, but Skapti wouldn't hear of it. Helping her out of the boat, he told her she was the Jarl's honored guest and would stay in the hall itself.

He took her baggage from one of the oarsmen. "Is this all?"

She nodded, and he slung it over his shoulder.

"Traveling light, Jessa."

"Lighter than I'd expected," she said sourly. "And what do you think Wulfgar will say? We can't pay him back now—some of that money was a loan of his."

Skapti jumped from the wooden landing stage. "He'll put a price on your thief, for a start."

She followed his tall, spindly figure through the cluster of houses. Someone called and he waved to them. Jessa felt the sun warm her; she slipped off her gloves and let her fingers feel the cool spring air. Looking around, she could see the Jarlshold was thriving. There seemed to be more people than before; new houses had been built and there were at least five longships on the fjord, not to mention a whole fleet of fishing craft bobbing and bumping against the shingle. Children screeched and giggled, their high voices hanging in the air. Hens ran clucking from Skapti's feet.

The Jarlshall looked just the same, tall, grim, and strong. But the door was wide open, and when she followed the skald inside, the spring sunshine streamed down on her through the high windows, softening the edges of the great space, filling it with light.

"Jessa!"

Wulfgar was before her in an instant, both hands on her shoulders. "You've grown!"

"A bit." So have you, she thought. He looked as if power suited him. Still dark, elegant, with a lazy authority, but better dressed, richly even, his coat trimmed with thick dark fur, a gold collar glinting at his neck.

"Come to the fire. You must be cold." He led her over the stone floor to the central hearth. Skapti dropped the pack lightly onto a bench.

"She's had some trouble."

"Trouble?"

A thrall brought enameled cups, the steam rising from them. Jessa sipped at hers and let the warmed wine slide down her throat. Then she said, "I was robbed, Wulfgar, by a noisome little wretch in an inn at Hollfara. A purse of silver—I'm afraid most of it was yours."

A hardness came into his eyes. "You weren't hurt?"

"She didn't give him the chance." Skapti sprawled on the bench and drank thirstily while Jessa told her tale, kicking mud from her boots.

When she had finished, Wulfgar turned angrily. "Do you hear this, Vidar?"

The man who came forward from the group listening by the fire was a stranger to Jessa. He was older than Wulfgar; a small, graying man, his beard clipped to a point.

He had a thin, clever face, and as he looked at Jessa she saw that an old scar drew down one side of his mouth slightly. His heavy coat was sealskin, dyed blue, and hung with amulets and luckstones and the boars of Freyr. He took her hand. "I've heard of you, Jessa Horolfsdaughter. I'm sorry such a thing should have happened."

"Jessa, this is Vidar Paulsson—Vidar Freyrspriest, they call him. He'll be leading the Freyrscoming in a few days."

She smiled at him briefly, then turned back. "I want this man caught, Wulfgar."

"He will be. I promise you."

The gray man glanced past her. "Did you see him?"

"No." Skapti gave Jessa a lopsided grin.

"Pity. Still, we should send word to the holders at Karvir and all the ports along the coast. Someone will know him."

Wulfgar nodded. "And don't worry about the silver, Jessa. I owe you a lot more than that. Now, Vidar will show you where you're sleeping."

She took her bag from the bench. "It's good to be back, Lord Jarl."

He smiled at her lazily. "It's good to have you, Lady Jessa."

Vidar led her between the tapestries and up some stone

steps that led to the private rooms, rooms that had once been Gudrun's. His heavy blue coat dragged on the stair in front of her.

"Wulfgar often talks of you," he said. "The strange way you met, when he was an outlaw, without friends."

"Does he?"

"Indeed. And of your other friend, the witch's son."

She looked up. "Kari?"

"The same. This is your room." He opened the door to a tiny chamber warmed by a brazier of coals. The walls were hung with thick tapestries. One small unshuttered window spilt sunlight on the floor.

She went in. "Thank you."

"If there's anything you want, the house thralls have orders to bring it. Wulfgar will hold a feast tonight to honor your coming." He smiled at her, turning the scar away. "I confess I'm curious. I would have liked to have seen this Kari Ragnarsson. They say he's a sorcerer of enormous power, that he can reach into minds and twist them, change shape—"

"He's not a sorcerer." She snapped it out before she thought.

Vidar stared.

"I'm sorry. But just because Gudrun was, don't think Kari is. He's not like her."

"I had heard," the priest said slowly, "that they were very alike."

"Only to look at."

He opened the door. "I'm glad you think so." Then he smiled pleasantly. "Welcome back to the Jarlshold, Jessa."

When he was gone, she sat on the wooden chest by the window and looked around the room. It was very fine. Her room at home was nothing like it. And suddenly she felt quite lonely, and that surprised her.

FOUR

The fen and fell his fastness was,
the marsh his haunt.

The forests were endless.

Ranks of motionless trees stood weighted with snow, deep in unprinted drifts. Far above, the pale sky was streaked with cloud, unmoving, as if claws had scored it.

Crouched in a snow hole, the rune creature watched with its pale eyes. It watched a small, white thing with a scampering run. The creature had no name for it. Stiff with hunger, it let the nervous, furred thing run nearer and pause.

The stoat lifted its head and blinked. It turned, eyes alert, but before it could even tense, the claws struck, killing it without a sound. Blood splashed onto the snow, sinking in, melting.

The creature ate greedily. Warmth moved in its throat; a welcome fullness flushed momentarily inside it. When it moved away, it left nothing but small bones and the stained, trampled snow.

Now it slid and slithered downhill, into a small valley where a stream ran deep under the ice. Smashing through the thick, bubbled lid, the creature bent and drank, crystals of ice forming instantly on its lips, thin icicles that snapped as it raised itself and roared. It tore berries from bushes, twigs and needles from pinon, chewing them and spitting them out. Thought stirred in it; it crouched and scrabbled at the roots of a tree, flinging snow aside, but the topsoil was frozen deep and nothing lived in it.

The rune beast hugged itself, rocking silently. Snow from the branches above drifted down on it, dusting its limbs and shoulders. It was growing stronger. Slowly, meal by tiny meal, it was hardening, becoming less a web of runes and shadows, more a thing of hunger and teeth and frost. The voice in its head spoke endlessly to it, sometimes comforting, sometimes mocking.

Reluctantly the creature gathered itself and stood, swaying. It staggered on, always south. For long hours it trudged through the aisles of trees, torn at by brambles, soaked with falling snow. Somewhere far ahead was something it must have, a distant tugging at its nerves.

Only when the noise came did it stop.

The noise was strange, and the smell that drifted with it made the creature whimper with excitement and pain. It crouched in the snow, clenching and unclenching its long, clawed fingers. The sound was high, an echo, a clang. Not a tree murmur, not one of the feathered whistlers. In all the leagues of its journey the shadow maker had heard nothing like this. Silent, it dragged itself to a tree and stared around, clutching the mossed trunk.

It saw an animal, large, four-legged, gray-white. Branches sprouted from its head. The sound came from a tiny round thing that clanked and jangled on its neck. There were others too, behind, tearing lichen from the trees with their long, quick tongues.

This is good, the voice told it, laughing. *You must strike now. You must feed. This is your strength that has come to you.*

FIVE

There was laughter of heroes; harp-music ran,
words were warm-hearted.

She was kneeling by a small pool. Around her the courtyard was deep in snow, but the pool was liquid, silver-gray. Reflections of cloud drifted across it.

"Where?" she asked.

"I don't know where," the voice behind her said quietly. "But look, Jessa, look harder. Please."

She bent closer. Her own face stared back, the long ends of her hair brushing the surface. And then, far under, far through, she saw the movement of something through trees, something large, pale, undefined.

"I can't see it clearly."

"Because I can't, not yet. But it's coming. It's coming closer every day."

A coal shifted. She opened her eyes quickly.

"Kari?" she murmured.

But the small room was empty and dim. The draft from the window had blown the rushlight out.

Stiffly she got up from the chair and crossed the room and looked out. The Jarlshold was dark. Stars glimmered over the smoke; the pale mountains on the other side of the fjord were jagged and immense against the black sky. She let the cold air freshen her. It was strange to have fallen asleep like that, though she hadn't slept much the night before, what with talking to Skapti and then lying bundled in fur in the stern, feeling the ship rise and plummet beneath her.

And the dream. Already it was fading, and she groped after it. Kari had been there, and had said . . . but she couldn't remember what. She wondered if he could be watching her now and made a face at the empty air. "That's for Brochael," she said aloud. But the room was silent, and wherever Kari was, he wasn't here.

She slammed the shutter suddenly and latched it and went downstairs. The Jarlshall was busy, and the feast was for her. It was Wulfgar's welcome, and rightly so, she thought wryly, after all the things they'd been through in the past, both outlaws, both hunted. She smoothed the embroidery on the scarlet dress old Marrika had sewn for her; it was tasseled and laced with sealskin and hung with ivory. On each shoulder she had pinned the two great discs of interwoven gold that had been her mother's, and her grandmother's before that, the last treasures of the family hoard. They felt heavy, and reassuring.

The hall was warm as she pushed her way through the crowd. Many of them knew her, some were old friends of her family, and it took her a long while to get to the high table, already tired with polite talk. Skapti had a chair ready for her, next to Wulfgar's empty one.

"Place of honor."

"Quite right," she said, sitting. "So where's the host?"

He grinned and sat beside her. "Down there talking. He'll be along."

"I hope so. I'm hungry."

And the word broke the dream and she remembered it, the pool, and the white shape Kari had tried to show her, and the hunger. That most of all. But what she had seen was vague; she put it to the back of her mind. Later she'd remember.

She leaned her chin on her hands and looked down at the crowd, talking, arguing, carving meat, laughing. All those hands and faces. All those words. The three fires were well ablaze, roaring out heat; smoke rose straight to the roof where it hung about the smoke holes and the ring window. Doves flapped up there, restless. On the walls hung heavy tapestries, and Jessa remembered how some of them had burned with Gudrun's rune fire on the night the witch had left. In the center of the hall stood the roof tree, a mighty pillar rising into the dark, its trunk carved with ancient signs for power and luck. In Gudrun's time a white snake had been cut deep into the timber; Jessa could still see parts of its sinuous outline, scored over with new runes cut by Wulfgar's priests and shamans.

She looked past and saw Wulfgar coming, but then Vidar caught his arm and came with him, talking all the time.

"Now what's so urgent?" Skapti muttered.

"You don't like him, do you?"

"Who? Wulfgar?"

She smiled impatiently. "You know who I mean, clever. This Vidar."

The skald ran one long finger around the lip of his cup. "Sharp, Jessa."

She thought of the innkeeper and frowned, but Wulfgar was sitting beside her now. "I'm sorry, Jessa." He waved to the house thralls to serve, and great dishes began to appear, bobbing through the crowd. The food was good, and Jessa began to enjoy it. As they ate, Wulfgar told her he had begun a search for the thief.

"I'll have no footpads—not if I can get rid of them."

"Which you won't," Skapti muttered.

"We'll see." He looked down the long hall thoughtfully. "Things have begun to change, Jessa, and there's so much more I want to do. Gudrun nearly destroyed us; she tainted us with evil, with the stink of witchery. No one dared speak out—you remember how it was. Sorcery doesn't need weapons, or a knife in the ribs; it poisons courage, robs men of will, makes them fear shadows, things that move in the dark. We've finished with all that."

She nodded, but was silent, thinking of Kari. Sorcery was in him too. Sorcery that had won Wulfgar his land. Had he forgotten that? Was that why Kari kept away?

Vidar was watching her. He'd been listening; that annoyed her. Now he said, "Wulfgar is right. We can do without such things."

She couldn't help it. "What about Kari?"

Vidar shrugged; Wulfgar looked uneasy. "Kari is different, of course."

"And far away," the priest added.

And you want him to stay away, she thought, watching him speak quietly in the Jarl's ear. His eyes watched the men in the hall, darting from group to group.

"Well," Skapti whispered, "I don't think you like him either."

She pushed him away. "Rubbish."

"Not so, Jessa."

"Is he one of the wasps you mentioned?"

Slightly, he nodded.

When the conversation came around to Gudrun, everyone was listening.

"Nothing has been seen of her since that day she

went," Wulfgar said. "It's as if she walked off the world's edge."

"We wouldn't be that lucky," Skapti remarked.

"And the White People?"

"Nothing. Except that a man from Thykkawood was here last week—that's well up in the glacier country. He says a strange mist has been seen up in the mountain passes, full of sparks and colors, curling into shapes, as if something walked there. The local wise woman says the White People are brewing some sorcery. No one has seen them—but then no one ever does."

"Do you think," Jessa said slowly, "that they—that she—might take some sort of revenge on us?"

"Sometimes I think it." He drank from the cup. "Sometimes."

Vidar said, "She was very beautiful, they say."

Jessa stared at him. "You never saw her? Yes, she was, and deadly too."

"A frost candle," Skapti muttered, standing up and reaching for the kantele. He turned a peg on it and a string hummed quietly. "A woman with an ice heart. That was Gudrun."

Silence fell in the hall as they saw him stand.

While he sang, Jessa let the lilting words warm her like the wine; a song of praise for Wulfgar, for the new order that had come to the land, for peace. The words, woven in long complex lines of rhythm and kenning and music, filled the silent hall, and when the last complicated chain of sound ended, there was a pause before the storm of noise, as if he had somehow reached their hearts and hushed them.

Jessa realized she was sleepy. She leaned over to Wulfgar.

"I'm going outside for some air."

He nodded. "Take my coat."

She brushed the scraps from her, dragged the heavy robe from his chair and pushed her way to the outer door. Near the biggest fire a juggler was tossing three axs recklessly around his head, his friends cheering him from a safe distance. He dropped one, and it thudded into the straw as he leaped aside to a roar of derision.

Jessa slipped outside, tugging the heavy door shut behind her. The sky was black, frosted with stars. She took a deep breath of the air, felt its cold shock clear her head of wine fumes and smoke, and she pulled Wulfgar's big coat tighter, her hands well up inside the sleeves.

The night was silent. Smoke drifted from the turf houses; a few hens clucked. Even the dogs seemed asleep. She wandered a little way between the buildings, her boots quietly crunching the frozen mud. Above her, abruptly, the sky rippled into an aurora, a curtain of colors drifting silently over the stars as if a wind moved it. Scarlet, green, faintest blue. She had seen this a hundred times but it always surprised her. Some said a giant named Surt made this light; others that it was the walls of Asgard glimpsed in the sky. Skapti believed it was caused by frost in the air, but that was surely poet's nonsense.

The hall door behind her opened; a burst of talk and laughter drifted out, and with it a figure that moved quickly into the shadows of the wall. Then the man stepped out, and a flicker of blue-green light stroked his face. She realized it was Vidar. He made his way cautiously between the houses and, as a woman came out of one, Jessa saw him jerk back into shadow, as if not to be seen.

That surprised her. What was he doing?

She watched as he moved behind the smithy and then slipped after him carefully. The priest walked on, his coat swaying, the amulets at his neck and sewn to his collar making tiny clinking noises against each other. He walked hurriedly to the farthest end of the settlement to a small crooked-looking hut built against another. Goats bleated from behind it. Not far off the waters of the fjord rasped the shore.

Jessa watched from the corner of a wall.

Even in the frosty silence the knock seemed quiet and secret. The door opened slightly; a face peered out, lit briefly by the green ripples of light. Then Vidar slipped inside and the door closed.

Jessa turned and leaned back against the wall and whistled a silent cloud into the air. She was too astonished to be cold. She had known that face, recognized it at once. She would have known it anywhere. It had been the little rat-faced thief who'd robbed her at the inn.

Six

It was with pain that the powerful spirit
dwelling in darkness endured that time.

Sleep was a new thing. Obeying the heaviness in its stomach and head, the rune creature had hidden all day in a cleft on a fellside, and the strange darkness had come down inside its eyes and taken its mind away.

When it woke, the daylight had gone. All the stars looked down at it. For a moment the thing lay there, still curled. Then the voice came out of the whiteness and spoke sharply, and coldly; it uncramped its limbs and staggered up, stiff with frost.

Outside the cleft was open land, far below. This was a different country. There were trees, yes, but among them open smooth slopes, white and untrodden. The land folded into valleys, running south.

The creature began to trudge. It had come through long weeks of weariness and ice, and there was a long way to go yet, but the desire inside it was sharpening. Somewhere ahead, there was something it must have. *Yes,* said the voice quietly. The voice ruled it. She would never let it go, let it escape—dully, the creature knew this. She . . . when had it first known the voice was she? Recently. Memories and thoughts were confused, stirring into being like a pain.

Half sliding, half tumbling down the smooth slopes of snow, the spell-sending watched the moon with pale eyes. The silver ball bobbed high, out of reach. Angry, the creature tried to climb a tree, a tall pine, but the lowest branches snapped under its weight and it tore at the trunk with its claws in wrath, slashing the bark into deep parallel gashes. Again and again it struck, tingling with peculiar pleasure; not stopping until the tree bole was flayed bare, its fibrous clots of bark littering the snow.

After that it went on, lumbering through the dark, crashing through branches, dim thickets, the long blue shadows of the arctic night. It had eaten well in the last days. Hare, stoat, marten; the rich juices of the reindeer herd. It murmured at that memory, floundering through the steep empty slopes, through drifts as high as its chest, tearing a long scar through the dim ghostly snowfield. Above it the moon hung, a perfect silver hole in the sky.

When dawn came, the creature paused under a bush heavy with red berries. Shaking the snow off, it crammed them into its mouth, sharp bubbles of taste that burned and hurt and burst. Then it stopped, sniffing the air.

Something was coming.

Something so strange, so deliciously and muskily scented that the rune beast dribbled red berry juice and swallowed without thought.

Cautiously it drifted to the edge of the trees.

On the snowfield a thin, gangly thing was moving. It had long flat feet, and it slid them over the top of the snow. In its muffled paws long sticks splayed to each side. A scrawny, biped thing, heavily furred, laboring up the slope.

The creature watched with ice-pale eyes. Then it moved out of the trees and stood up.

The skier turned his head. His lips moved soundlessly.

SEVEN

Too few supporters flocked to our prince
when affliction came.

"It's not that I don't believe you, Jessa," Skapti said carefully. "Of course I believe you. But you may have been mistaken. Much as I dislike Vidar I can't imagine him as a thief's benchmate."

"So you do dislike him." Jessa put her boots up on the rock in front of her. "I knew."

"You would." He leaned back against the mossy boulders and frowned down at the Jarlshold, the huddle of roofs and ships, the dragon heads of the hall. "It's just that he wasn't here, you see."

"When Gudrun ruled?"

Skapti nodded, rubbing the side of his nose and the edge of his long hand. "In all the troubles, when Wulfgar and I were outlaws, when we were running from Gudrun's men like kicked dogs, when we were scavenging on snow and fish bones, where was Vidar then?"

"Out of it?"

"Well out. And safe. Living in Stavangerfjord with his wife's family. Keeping his head down. Obeying. He didn't lose any land. None of his family disappeared, or ended on her soldiers' swordpoints."

Jessa looked at him. "And he came back when Wulfgar was made the Jarl."

"Oh yes. When it was safe, when all the danger was over." He glanced at her and laughed sourly. "Oh no, Jessa, I don't like the man, Freyrspriest or not. But there's no doubt his counsel is good. And Wulfgar trusts him. But theft! Unlikely."

"Well," she said slowly, "I don't know about that. But I saw that rat's face, Skapti, and it was the same man. Vidar can't know he's a thief. In any case, I think we should tell Wulfgar."

The skald nodded, his lank hair ruffled in the spring breeze. He stood up and hauled her after him. "Come on, then. Let's find our friend with the knife."

As they walked back down the rock-strewn pasture, goats scattered before them, bleating. Voices rose from the fishing fleet drifting into shore; the foremost ship ground its keel into the shingle with a hoarse scrape.

Coming into the hold, they saw that preparations had begun for the Freyrscoming. Kindling was being unloaded from two wagons at the back of the hall; great logs, freshly cut, oozing with sap and the rich smell of forest damp. House thralls were carrying them in and stacking them in crisscrossed heaps, their shaven circles of timber ridged with age rings. Sawdust and splintered wood were trampled into the mud.

The hall was empty, its shutters thrown wide and the great roof tree standing stark in the dimness. They ran upstairs. Skapti thumped on the door of Wulfgar's chamber and they went in.

The Jarl was sitting in a chair with a selection of swords spread over his knees and at his feet. A plump, sleek merchant with black, oily hair perched nervously on the bench.

"Skapti!" Wulfgar sprang up, sending weapons everywhere. "Now which of these do you think is the best?"

He gathered up a long heavy blade with a leather-bound grip and held it against another, shorter weapon with fine engraving along the blade. Jessa wandered to the fire.

"This one handles better, but the other is more . . ."

"Showy," Jessa put in.

He tugged her hair gently. "That's the word."

Skapti took the swords and swung them one by one. "The plain one has better balance."

"Ah, but the other," the merchant said quickly, "is more fit for the Jarl. A fine sword, crafted in the south, beyond the Cold Sea. Hammered from finest twisted steel."

"And a higher price." Skapti grinned at Jessa.

"A little . . ."

"A lot, I'd say."

The merchant frowned. "But the runes on the blade have the properties of protection. No enemy could touch the Jarl."

Skapti tossed the swords onto the bed. "Well, buy that one then, Wulfgar. With your skill you might need it."

Wulfgar glared at him. "Sometimes I think you forget who I am."

"Not me," the skald snapped. "I've watched your back in too many battles."

For a long, amused moment Wulfgar gazed at him. Then he gave his lazy smile and leaned back in his chair, turning graciously to the merchant. "As my friend points out in his poetic way, a Jarl should be dependent on his war band, not on sorcery. I will buy the plainer sword, at the price you mentioned. Now if you go down to the hall, Guthlac will give you something to eat."

Recognizing his dismissal, the merchant gathered up his swords, wrapping each in fine oiled cloth. Skapti opened the door and watched him stagger carefully down the steps.

"Smooth as his blades," he muttered.

Wulfgar laughed and poured out a cup of wine.

Jessa sat opposite him. "Wulfgar, I want to tell you something. That thief who stole the silver. I've seen him. He's here at the hold."

He stared at her in surprise, eyes dark. "Here? Jessa, you should have said."

"I only found out last night." She flicked a look at Skapti, who shrugged. "I saw Vidar go into one of the houses here. The thief opened the door to him."

"Vidar!"

"I'm sure it was the same man."

He gazed at her thoughtfully, fingering the fine gold neck ring at his throat. "There must be some mistake. Vidar can't know this."

"Probably not. But we should ask him."

Wulfgar turned to the window, then leaned out, his hands on the sill. He called below for someone to send Vidar Freyrspriest up and then wandered back to the fire.

"Well, if your thief is here we'll get our silver back at least." He smiled at her. But she knew he was puzzled.

After a few moments there was a tap on the door and Vidar came in, frost melting on his coat. In daylight the scar on his face was grayer, drawn tight. "You wanted me?"

"Sit down," Wulfgar said.

He sat, glancing quickly at their faces. "What is it? Is something wrong?"

Wulfgar put one foot on the bench and leaned over him. For a moment Jessa sensed his authority, hidden behind that easy, lazy manner. Vidar looked tense, as if he felt it too. But Wulfgar spoke quietly.

"You went to a house last night."

"A house?"

"Here in the hold."

"I watched you," Jessa put in. Impatiently she stood up. "Look, the man who opened the door to you was the one who stole money from me in Holltara two days ago."

Vidar stared at her. "Snorri? Impossible!"

Furious, she glared back. "I know what I saw!"

Vidar stroked his narrow gray beard. "I'm sure you think so, Jessa, but I can't believe this. Snorri used to be a bondsman of mine. He bought his freedom years ago. He lives here now, and part owns one of the fishing boats. He'd never thieve. For one thing, he hasn't the wits."

"The only way to settle it," Skapti remarked, "is to send for him."

"Of course." Vidar nodded and went to stand, but Wulfgar pushed him back and stalked to the door. They heard him shouting orders down the stairs.

"If this is true," the priest murmured to Jessa, "I will personally see to it that every coin is paid back."

She nodded, gave him a tight smile, but she knew

quite well he thought she was mistaken. She glanced at Skapti but he seemed lost in his own thoughts, so she turned to the fire and watched Vidar from the corner of her eye. What if he did know? What if he and the thief were accomplices? She had to admit, it seemed unlikely. And yet she remembered the way he had crept between the houses, stepping back into shadow when that woman passed.

Wulfgar came back. "I've sent for him. Take some wine, Vidar. Is everything ready for tomorrow night?"

Vidar nodded. "The kindling is here, for the fires. The ritual meats for the feast are ready; a boar is being slaughtered tomorrow. The image of the god has reached the village of Krasc, just over the hill. He'll be brought here by boat. Everything for the ceremony is ready." As he spoke he poured wine carefully into a cup. One red drop fell on his fingers and he sucked it away. "I intend to spend this afternoon alone in the hills, preparing myself, speaking to Freyr in my heart. The omens are good. He'll bring us a good crop and a good harvest this year."

Wulfgar nodded, then turned as his steward, Guthlac, came in.

"The man Snorri is in the hall. He was found on the wharves."

Wulfgar swept out and the others followed. They clattered down the stairs, through the tapestries and into the hall.

A man waited, a warrior discreetly behind him.

"That's not him," Jessa said at once.

Behind her, Vidar said, "But it is, Jessa. This is Snorri, the man I went to see. His child suffers a small ailment, which I have medicines to ease."

"It's not the man who opened the door," she said icily.

The fisherman glanced nervously from face to face. He was small, yes, with straggly brown hair, but it wasn't the same man. She knew it! And that meant Vidar was lying.

Calming herself, she turned to him. He stood at Wulfgar's shoulder, his face slightly puzzled, watching her carefully, the scar dragging at the corner of his mouth. "I'm sorry, Jessa, but it is," he murmured.

There was a tense silence. Then Wulfgar took her arm. "Anyone can make a mistake, Jessa," he said gently. He jerked his head at the fisherman. "You can go."

Relief lit the man's eyes. He scurried to the door.

"Wait!" Jessa took a few steps after him. "Vidar Paulsson came to see you last night?" she said quietly.

The man nodded hurriedly. "My son is ill. Vidar knows runes, has things that help. . . ."

"No one else lives with you?"

"No one," he muttered uneasily.

"Are you sure?"

He looked away, faint sweat on his lip. "No one."

She was silent a moment. Then she said, "Thank you."

As the man hurried out, Wulfgar said, "Don't worry about it, Jessa. After all, it was dark, and this whole thing was on your mind. We'll find the man, I promise you."

She gripped her hands into fists and turned with a smile. "You're right. It was just a mistake." She crossed to Vidar and gave him a bright glance. "I'm sorry. I shouldn't have doubted your word."

"Not at all," he said, rubbing his stubbly beard. "Not at all."

As she left them talking she wondered if she had convinced him. It was important she did. Because if he was lying—and he was—she would have to find out why without him knowing, or even suspecting her. As she turned, before the tapestry fell behind her, she saw Vidar and Wulfgar talking about the feast—they seemed to have put it out of their minds already. But Skapti was gazing after her thoughtfully.

Eight

The company came to its feet.

It was late that night, very late, when the uproar began.

Jessa was awake in an instant, hearing the doors crash open below, the shout and murmur of raised voices in the hall. She snatched the knife from her belt, tugged on coat and boots, and ran outside, straight into Skapti.

"What is it?"

"I don't know. Where's Wulfgar?"

"Here." He was behind them, looking sleepy, some of his men clustered about him. "What's going on?" he snapped. "Are we being attacked?"

A thrall raced up the stairs. "There are men below, in the hall. Strangers. They've come a long way—they want to speak to you."

"At this hour!" Wulfgar gave Skapti his sword and ran a hand through his tangle of hair. "Won't it keep?"

"They insist. They seem . . . terrified."

For a moment Wulfgar stood still. Then he put the man aside gently and walked down the stairs, his bodyguard about him. Jessa followed, curious.

The hall was almost in darkness. A few torches still guttered at one end, and the only fire that had not gone out was being banked up with dry wood so that it spit and crackled and gave little light. Argument hummed in the great stone spaces; the war band who normally slept there were on their feet, surrounding a group of about five strangers.

Wulfgar pushed through to them. "All right," he said wearily. "I'm the Jarl. Who are you?"

The men fell silent; they glanced at one another. Finally one of them spoke. "Farmers, lord, some of us; others are freedmen. We come from the Harvenir district, about two days' journey from here to the north."

"And?"

The man threw an imploring look at his companions. The thrall had been right, Jessa thought; these men were more than frightened.

"Lord." The man grabbed Wulfgar's arm. The bodyguard jerked forward but he waved them back. "Lord, speak to your watchmen! Double the guard on the ships and the approaches to the hold!"

"Why?"

"Do it, please!" The man was sweating. "Please! The thing may be close behind us."

His words rang in the flame-lit, shadowy spaces; the men of the hold felt amulets and thorshammers discreetly.

"Thing?" the Jarl said quietly.

"A creature, a great troll, who knows what it is!

Something that kills without mercy."

The silence was deep. Then Wulfgar turned easily and murmured names, commands. Some men left quickly, still consumed with curiosity.

Jessa beckoned two of the house thralls. "These men need food," she said, "and some hot, spiced ale. Hurry with it."

The strangers stared at her, restless, unfocused.

"Sit down," Wulfgar said to them. "Bring those benches here, to the fire."

The five men sat silent, flames licking their spread fingers. They seemed spent, worn out with weariness and some heavier dread that dried up their words. When the food came, they ate quickly, among the whispers of the war band.

Wulfgar was patient. When the ale was poured, he came and sat on the bench opposite them, leaning forward.

The spokesman had recovered a little. He shook his head, his face haggard. "Forgive me . . . Jarl . . . the way I spoke . . ."

"Forgotten," Wulfgar said. "Now tell me what has happened."

Jessa picked up a blanket from the straw and threw it around her shoulders. The hall was a great darkness behind her.

"My name is Thorolf of Harvenir," the man said wearily. "These are my neighbors. Karl Ulfsson, Thorbjorn the Strong and his sons. We came to warn you."

"Of what?"

The man gripped his hands together tightly. "We don't know," he whispered. "None of us have seen it clearly. Glimpses. Movements in the snow. Above all, prints and tracks. It must be huge, ferocious, an evil sending."

"A bear?" somebody said.

Thorolf shook his head doubtfully. "It thinks," he said quietly.

Jessa glanced at Skapti. His face was alert against the flame light. Beyond him Vidar was listening too.

"Two days ago," the farmer said, "one of my bondsmen, a strong reliable man called Brand, went out to look for some stragglers from the reindeer herd. By nightfall he hadn't returned. We feared some accident; the snow is still deep up there in the high pastures, and there are crevasses. . . . In the morning, as soon as it was light, I took men and dogs to look for him."

He rubbed his face wearily. "It took us all morning to find him. What there was left of him."

There was utter silence in the hall. His voice sounded very small when he spoke again.

"In a wide snowfield we found marks, blood, a

smashed ski. Something had been dragged to a scatter of trees. The dogs wouldn't go near, but we did. You can imagine how it was. . . . We buried him and hurried home. At first we thought, like you, that some bear had had him, some wolves, but when we saw the prints—"

"What were they like?" Skapti interrupted.

"Too big. A long foot with five splayed toes. Almost human, but . . . clawed." After a moment he went on, "At the farm we brought the cattle indoors, shuttered the windows, barred the doors. The weather closed in at dusk; snow fell thickly, and the wind roared and howled. All night strange noises moved and shuffled around the house, snuffling, banging, scratching, as if some great beast was out there. We sat awake, all of us, my wife, my children, the men armed with axs. Once it tore and shoved at the door; the whole thing shuddered. No one dared sleep; we kept the fire banked up; the room was heavy with smoke. Even the cattle were still, as if they smelled it out there, the thing that prowled. . . ." He glanced around at their attentive faces. "I never want to see another night like that. Finally morning came. Things seemed quiet; we dug ourselves out. Prints were everywhere. The byre had been smashed open, clawed apart. Snow had frozen everything, white and hard."

He paused, and Wulfgar said, "But you didn't see it?"

"No. Just the footprints. But since then, there have been other times." He drank, as if parched, and the man beside him leaned forward, the one called Thorbjorn, a great black-bearded man.

"It was at my farm too. Two goats vanished; there's no trace of them. The dogs howling in their chains. Karl here lost reindeer, sheep, a dog. None of us dare go out, master! Our children can hide indoors but men have to tend the flocks; spring is coming. . . ."

"I understand that," Wulfgar said quietly, "but you say it thinks?"

Thorolf raised his head. "Yes."

Jessa stepped closer to the fire. The cold at her back made her shiver; Skapti eased aside for her.

"We set a trap," the farmer explained, "at Karlsstead. We dug a pit in the floor of a byre and covered it with loose sticks and straw. A goat was tethered at the back. For a bear, that would have been unlikely to fail, don't you think?"

Several men nodded.

"If you were careful," Vidar murmured.

"We were careful."

"So what happened?" Jessa urged.

Thorolf looked at her as if he had only just noticed her. "For two nights, nothing. Then on the third, a night of silent snowfall, Karl's youngest daughter opened the corner of the shutter and looked out. She says she saw a shape moving in the drift, glimmering. A big, pale shadow."

"It still could have been a bear."

"It could. But in the morning the goat was gone. Neither hair nor bone of it remained. The covering over the trap was still in place. Instead the planks from the back had been torn wide. And, masters, the child said the shape carried something squirming under its arm."

They were all silent. Wind creaked through the rafters high up in the hall; the fires crackled loudly. What sort of bear carried its prey away like that? Jessa wondered. Wulfgar glanced at Vidar, his face edged with firelight.

"What do you think?"

"A bear can be cunning," the gray man said slowly, fingering the scar at his lip.

"But like that?"

"If not a bear, then what?"

No one answered. No one wanted to put words on it.

"Has it been about in daylight?" Wulfgar asked. He glanced at Skapti. "They say there are things—trolls, snow beasts, mere dwellers. . . ."

The skald shrugged thin shoulders. "In sagas, yes. Things that throw a shadow on the heart."

"Jarl," Thorolf interrupted, "whatever it is, we need

help. One man is dead already."

Wulfgar nodded. He brooded for a moment, then said, "Men will ride back with you. Tomorrow is the Freyrscoming. After that, I'll come myself."

"You don't understand." The farmer put the cup down and gripped his big fingers desperately together. "I haven't explained myself well. I knew I wouldn't. . . . I said the creature thinks. It plots. It's journeying with a purpose, not just scavenging here and there. We plotted its progress through our lands; it moves on, always south. Hard terrain doesn't stop it." He looked up. "We rode here swiftly, on horseback, without stopping. The thing walks, hunts, sleeps maybe, but it won't be too far behind us."

Wulfgar stared at him. "What do you mean, behind you?"

"I mean the creature is coming here, lord. It's coming directly toward the Jarlshold."

DING

I was little equipped to act as bodyguard.

Hakon Empty-hand paused in the doorway of the shieling. Outside, the moon shone through a vivid purple aurora, silvering the trees that crowded close about the field. He stared anxiously into the dark, crowded aisles of the forest

"Inga! Don't run off!"

She came around the corner of the building and glared at him. "I wasn't."

"Where's your brother?"

"Here." Kilmund had another lamb on his shoulders; he was staggering under its weight. The ewe followed, bleating in alarm. "This one was at the other end of the field."

Hakon eased it awkwardly off the little boy's back; it ran into the dark byre and gazed around at the straw. Carefully they pushed the ewe in after it.

Hakon shut the door and nudged the latch home with his good hand, the left one.

"That's all we can do. Now let's get home."

He was worried—the darkness had fallen before they'd finished and the news had made him uneasy. Gripping Inga's arm, he said, "Stay close to me now."

Crossing the pasture, the little boy kicked and danced. "Don't tell me you're afraid of the troll, Hakon."

"He is!" Inga cried.

"I'm not." Kilmund kicked a small rock in the grass. "Father says those things are skalds' lies and only thralls believe them."

"Well, I'm only a thrall," Hakon growled, "so keep quiet and come on."

By now they were in the forest, and the light was dimmer. Ever since the group of men had ridden by that morning, Hakon had been uneasy. Perhaps he should have taken the children home straight away. But it had been too easy to imagine the master, ranting because the work hadn't been done. "Can't even round up a few lambs, boy, without scurrying back for orders!"

Skuli Skulisson was a good farmer but a hard man; not a man with imagination. Not really a man who knew about fear. Hakon did. He peered into the green gloom of the wood. Those men had believed their tale of the troll. They'd been riding to the Jarlshold, sweating, afraid. And they'd had good swords, and two hands to use them.

"Do we have to go so fast?" Inga asked him. "My side hurts."

He stopped and looked down at her. "Much?"

"It hurts," she said tearfully. "Carry me, Hakon."

Hurriedly he kneeled and gathered her up. She was light, a bundle of frail bones. With his good hand he gripped Kilmund's shoulder. "Come on now. Hurry."

It was well into the wood, in the clearing by the stream, that he heard the noise. Not stopping, he turned his head quickly, ignoring the children's high voices. Something rustled; in the dark tangle of undergrowth to his left he sensed the slightest stir of its presence. It might be anything, but he walked faster, pushing the boy on. Two miles to the farm. A knife on his belt and a rusty sword, but he'd never been good with his left hand and he was thin and hadn't the weight behind the thrust. Already Inga felt heavier, making his arm ache.

In the windy unease of the wood there were many noises—leaves pattering, the rising roar of high branches, the crisp rustle of nettle and thorn whipping against his legs. He stumbled over a stone and gasped, and Inga squealed, "Don't drop me!"

"I won't. Be quiet now."

He longed to shift her weight but he needed his good hand free. Quickly he put her down and drew the sword. It was old, notched, not much use. A thrall's sword.

"What's that for?" Kilmund's eyes were wide.

"Nothing. A game."

"What sort of game?"

Leaves gusted into his face as he crouched beside the children. "Hunting. We're going to run, fast and silent. As fast as we can."

"I don't want to," the boy said stubbornly.

Hakon gripped the sword tight. "We're late. And if you're late, your father will have me beaten. And you too, probably, if I tell him you were idling. You don't want that, do you?"

"No."

"Good. Then run. Now!"

They hurried through the straining wood, branches cracking under their feet, but it wasn't fast enough, and Hakon, behind his snatched breathing, knew that the peculiar movement was still out there, somewhere in the dark. It kept level with them; once or twice among the trees he thought he saw a pale glimmer, a shadow in the tangle-wood.

At the edge of a clearing bright with moonlight they stopped, breathless. He glanced around, his heart thumping. The trees here were closely grouped—old gnarled oaks, their branches and boles green with mosses and lichens that grew even on the rocks, soft cushions, sprawling yellow splashes.

In the wood, something breathed. Like an echo of himself he heard it, rasping, strange and heavy.

A branch swished. Stones clattered.

"What's that?" Inga whispered.

In the silence the whole wood murmured and creaked and stirred in the rising gale. Pale cloud dragged across the moon.

Hakon grabbed her. "Up the tree. Hurry!"

"I don't want to!" She began to cry with terror and he shoved her fiercely up into the branches, wishing he could lift her. "Hold tight! Now, Kilmund! Move!"

But the boy was staring into the breathing darkness. "Is it the troll?"

"Get up there!" Hakon jerked him off the ground. "Hold your sister. Hold her tight!"

Above him the branches swayed, dropped leaves on him. Legs and arms moved in a flurry of snow that had begun to fall slowly, like ash drift from a fire. Inga's cry came down from the dark.

"Come on, Hakon!"

"Quiet!"

He turned, his back against the tree, clutching the sword that felt hot and heavy in his hand. And then, among the undergrowth, among storm-stirred leaves and snow, something shifted, and he knew he was looking at a face, a narrow, inhuman face among splintered branches and shadow. It watched him, its small eyes pale as ice, a big, indistinct shape, and he swore for a moment that the snow drifted through its body.

Like a man, but bigger. Like a bear, but . . . not. As it watched him he knew that it thought, that it hungered, and he felt a sudden pulse of terror that he squashed at once, deep down.

Barely opening his lips he said, "It's here. Don't move, Kilmund. Don't speak. Whatever happens don't let her make a sound."

But it could probably smell them. Best not to think about that. Facing into the dark he knew his own life was lost. Nothing could get him up that tree in time, not with one useless hand. If he turned, it would come, crashing out . . .

Odin, he thought, if you love me, do something.

The branches moved. It was coming; snow blurred it but it was coming out, toward him. And at that instant the moon leaked from its cloud and lit the wood with sudden bars of silver.

Breathless, Hakon pressed himself back. He saw a gray pelt, a thick, heavy body, eyes lit with savage hunger. His sword glimmered like frost; the air before him was a whirlwind of white, dissolving flakes.

The creature made a sound, wordless, tense.

Sweat running, Hakon raised his sword.

And then, from above, came a screech that made him jerk his glance up; the night fell on him in two black pieces, flapping and screaming. As he ducked, they stabbed at the rune beast's face, scratching, fluttering, and it clawed them off, roaring, swinging away.

In an instant Hakon was scrambling up the tree, hauling himself up clumsily, dragged by small invisible fingers, torn, scratched, shaking all over with unstoppable fear. "All right!" he whispered. "It's all right!"

Below they heard the roars of furious anger. In a whirlwind of shadows the thing crashed back into the undergrowth, slashing and splintering. They heard it howl and stagger through the wood, farther and farther off into the rising gale.

His arm around Inga, Hakon tried to stop shaking. He stared into the dark, listening, intent for the distant sounds. Soon only wind shook the wood. Snow gusted about them.

After a long time the little boy whispered in his ear, "What was it? What scared it away?"

For a moment Hakon could not speak. Then he managed a word.

"Birds."

"Birds?"

"Ravens. Two great ravens."

"Where did they come from?"

Dazed, Hakon watched the moonlight glitter on his rusty, useless blade. Then he said, "Odin sent them."

Ten

At the speaking of the wise
. . . the hall was silent.

Jessa shuffled her feet. It was cold, standing out here in the growing dusk. Far off to the west the sky was a deep velvet blue, slowly being marred by a great pile of purple swelling cloud. The first stars glimmered, almost too faint to see unless she stared hard at them.

Out there on the hill above the fjord the beacon was burning, blazing over the black water, its reflection rippling like a dragon's tongue, the explosions of wood at its heart loud even from here. Miles away another fire burned, a mere point in the sky.

The fires burned for the god's journey. The image of Freyr, keeper of the harvest, lord of boars and horses, was coming to the Jarlshold last of all, as he did every year, on his gilded wagon. All through the last of the winter, the god had traveled, bringing spring with him, dragged from hold to hold, village to village, over the snowdrifts and through the dense forests, rowed on boats to the ends of the narrowest fjords. Every year Freyr visited his farmers and brought them luck, and heart—the promise of plenty. And last of all he came to Wulfgar's hall.

She scuffed her feet impatiently against a tussock of grass. Around her the crowd waited—women and thralls, bondsmen, freemen, children, warriors, some laughing and talking, some silent. Skapti came pushing through them.

"Well?" she said at once.

"Nothing. The patrols went a day's journey to the north and east—the last came back a few minutes ago. Nothing. Though they said the woods were strangely silent." He scratched his ear with a long hand.

"Do you believe it?" Jessa asked.

"They believed it, didn't they? Those men were terrified. As for trolls and mere dwellers, who knows? Something killed the stock, that's sure."

"And the man."

He pulled a face. "Wulfgar will have that looked into. Men are mostly killed by other men."

She stared at him. "You think that?"

"I'm a hardheaded poet, little valkyrie, and I think

appalling things. But don't worry, Wulfgar believes in this creature. A bear, he thinks, a big one, driven south by hunger. He's put men on all the approaches. And he says he'll ask the god about it."

Uneasy, she turned away. But those men had been gripped by terror. And there was still that little rat-thief somewhere about. She clenched her gloves into fists. She couldn't let that rest. Vidar would have to be followed again, and more closely.

She could see him now, waiting down there on the shore, a dim figure on the beach. And as the crowd around her murmured and pointed, she saw the boat.

A longship, blazing with torches. It slid out of the dark mist without a ripple, and shadows moved on its deck among the flare light, as if it truly came from a realm beyond the world—Asgard or Niflheim—a ship of spirits. As it ground into the shingle, the figures on deck and beach became a mass of black and scarlet, confused flickers, lifting something among the smoke and flame crackle. Then in the growing dark they moved up the hill toward her and the muddle became a long line of torchbearers, escorting the wagon of Freyr to the Jarl's welcome.

Six men pulled it; as they drew near she saw their masks: boar, horse, the black holes of their eyes. These were men who had given a year to Freyr's service, to guard his image. When their time was up, others would take their place; there were always eager men. Farmers would send their sons—it would bring them a good harvest.

And hauled behind them, dragged with thick ropes that had frayed and worn against the wood, came the great gilded wagon, swaying and rattling, with the crowd pushing it and holding children up to touch it and laughing.

In it sat the god himself. The image was unknowably ancient, centuries old; a crude, wooden shape, seamed and split with time and the rain.

A young head, its eyes narrow slits roughly hewn and a massive collar of gold around its neck, it rattled past her, and she turned to follow the crowd jostling into the Jarlshall, coughing in the streaming smoke from the pits where the feast meats baked.

The hall too was smoky with torches, the windows shuttered. The image was dragged between the filthy, billowing tapestries, over the flagstones, right up to the hearth where Wulfgar waited, alone in his carven chair, his picked men ranged behind him.

Slowly he stood up.

Still swaying in its gilded seat, the eyes of Freyr stared into the darkness of the hall.

Wulfgar put his hand out; a woman put a horn into it, a heavy ox horn banded with amber and gold. He lifted it and looked up at the towering head.

"I greet your image, Freyr. Bring plenty on the hold."
And he drank a little and gave the horn to Vidar. Slowly it
was passed from hand to hand, mouth to mouth, everyone
sipping at the rich red wine, even the smallest children.
Jessa let its bitterness slide over her tongue, heat her throat.
Then she pushed to the front and found a bench by the
wall and sat there, leaning back in the shadows.

Vidar Freyrspriest stood by himself now. He wore a
light coat threaded with amulets of boars, open at the neck.
From a small bowl held by a thrall he took the last pieces of
toadstool and swallowed them, his hand shaking. Already
he looked strange, his face pale and sweating, his eyes unfocused, the pupils swollen and dark.

The thrall took his arm and led him to the image, and
he stood before it, head bowed.

Talk died away. All the torches were put out. The hall
was black, one pale circle of sky high in its east wall. Only
the fires burned, and in their leaping light the god seemed
to take life; shadows blurred on his face, the dark gashes of
his eyes flickered and moved.

"Sit down," Wulfgar muttered.

There was a rustle in the straw. Outside, a dog yelped.

"Freyr has come," Wulfgar's voice said simply, "and we
have questions to ask him. Most of you will have heard the

rumor the men of Harvenir brought here yesterday. We need to know about this. Vidar Freyrspriest is ready. Freyr will speak through him. He may be able to tell us what this thing that prowls is."

There was a hush in the hall. Jessa looked for Skapti and couldn't see him. It was too dark. Only the nearest faces were lit by the sharp, uneasy red light.

Wulfgar sat on his chair, leaning forward. He said softly, "Does Freyr hear me?"

Vidar stepped from the fire. His face was a mask of shadows. He lifted his head, staring blindly into the dark.

"I hear you."

Jessa went cold. His voice was hoarse, a rasp, totally transformed. It was slurred as though he had forgotten the use of words. Not Vidar's voice.

No one moved. Wulfgar said, "We welcome you, Freyr. We ask your advice."

There was silence. Then words came, breathed harshly, with difficulty.

"I give no freedom from danger." The figure by the fire barely stirred. "The gods are bound by weird as you are. By the fate of Asgard."

Wulfgar nodded. "We know this. But you have knowledge. There is something prowling in my land. Something out there in the darkness. It kills men and beasts, brings terror and shadows of fear. Do you know of it?"

The figure that was Vidar, and yet not Vidar, stood below the wagon. Firelight danced on him, black and red, and on the great image above him, and both their eyes were dark gashes; they were fragments of faces, masked with smoke.

The voice came suddenly, abruptly.

"Sorcery moves here. It approaches slowly, through the forests, over the snow-bound ridges and the passes. It is a terrible, driven hunger."

"Hunger for what?" Wulfgar whispered.

"For something here. Something left here. Something that is death."

And the figure shuddered and fell on his knees, gripped with sudden convulsions. Wulfgar leaped up and ran to him, propping him up, and as she came close behind, Jessa heard him mutter, "Whose death, Freyr? Whose?"

Face gray, eyes set, Vidar opened his mouth, struggled for breath. "Yours," he hissed.

No one else could have heard. Wulfgar flashed a look at Jessa, but before he could speak, the priest's back arched in a spasm of pain; he lifted his head and cried out, "Listen! It comes from the north—a pale thing, evil, a creature of runes! Beware of it!"

Wulfgar shook him. "Vidar!"

But the priest crumpled and was silent.

After a shocked moment the Jarl nodded. "I hear your warning, Freyr," he murmured, "and I thank you for it, believe me." Raising his voice, he said, "Light the torches. Mord, help me with him. The trance is over."

But before anyone could move, the door at the back of the hall slammed open. Every head turned.

In the dim starlight two figures stood. For a moment they waited there, then pushed forward, the crowd moving apart for them silently, as if in fear.

One was a big man; his hair and beard were russet. A great bearskin coat hung to his knee, an ax glinting at his side. But it was his companion that everyone stared at, as he dragged off his hood and gazed around at the throng of faces.

A thin, pale boy, his hair silver-white, his eyes colorless as frost.

Jessa stared at him in amazement.

"Kari?" she breathed.

ELEVEN

The black raven
. . . shall have much to speak of.

He was taller, she thought, as they sat in the cleared hall with the torches being lit around them. But still as frail-looking, as brittle as ice.

Brochael, the big tawny man, was talking and eating at once, Skapti pouring him wine that he gulped down almost without noticing. "So it was a bad time to arrive then? I wondered what you were all doing there in the dark!" He grinned at Jessa, flung an arm around her, and squashed her against him till she punched him. "It's good to see you again, little lass. Not so little now either. Married yet?"

"Idiot!"

Letting her go, he drank again.

Skapti glanced at Kari. "And you, runemaster. How are you?"

"Oh, well enough." But Kari was watching the thralls who tended the fire, their terrified sidelong glances.

"You can go," Jessa said to them sharply. They hurried out.

"Don't mind them," she said. "They're new here. Wulfgar's own men. Most of the people here won't have seen you before. They're bound to stare."

"I know." He gave her a quiet smile. She saw again that stunned silence in the mead hall, the crowd staring at Gudrun's son, her image, the other Snow-walker, the sorcerer from the world's end. For years only rumors about him had spread from hold to hold, about a creature kept prisoner in the uttermost north, and even when he'd come here before with herself and Wulfgar and Skapti, hardly anyone had seen him. Sitting here now, Jessa remembered his struggle with the witch that only she had watched, in this very hall—the blazing flames, the rune snow, the exhausting matching of two powers. And after it Gudrun had gone, walking into the night, leaving Kari her curse, and scars on all their hearts.

"They will never love you," she said, "never trust you. Power like ours is a terror to them."

Looking at him now, Jessa knew he was remembering that too.

Just then Wulfgar came back, and Vidar with him, walking with exaggerated care. The priest still looked pale, but his eyes were focused. He too stared at Kari.

"Vidar," Wulfgar said coolly, "these are two of my greatest friends. This is Brochael Gunnarsson, and Kari Ragnarsson."

Vidar's eyes flickered briefly to Brochael. He nodded.

"I'm honored. I've heard much about you . . . both."

The big man slapped him amiably on the arm. "Feeling better?"

"A little." Vidar moved away stiffly. "The aftereffects of the trance echo in my mind for a time."

"I'm sure they do." Brochael leaned back and stretched his legs out to the fire. "One soul is enough for any man, without inviting the gods in."

Everyone hid smiles, except Vidar, who stared at Brochael coldly.

"Have you eaten everything, Brochael?" Jessa asked him. "Because it's about time you told us why you're here. Not just to see me, I suppose?"

He laughed gruffly, but she saw him look quickly at Kari. "You tell them."

Kari turned the cup in his thin fingers. He seemed to be searching for the right words. At last he said, "We came to warn you."

"You too?" Wulfgar leaned forward. "What about?"

Kari looked at him strangely. He looked so much like Gudrun that Jessa felt cold, and suddenly uneasy.

"Something's coming," Kari said slowly. "Something evil. She sent it."

"Your mother?"

Vidar asked that, and they all frowned at him.

But Kari only nodded after a moment.

"How do you know?" the priest persisted.

"He's seen it." Brochael flung a bone to a hound under the table.

"Seen it?"

"That's what I said."

Nobody spoke. Jessa knew well how Kari could see things—in water, in shiny surfaces—things that were happening far off, or in the past. She also guessed he had some strange remote knowledge of Gudrun, wherever she lived out in the wilderness of the north.

"Kari," she murmured, "we've already heard of this thing. Men came from an outlying district yesterday. They said it had killed a man up there, and livestock. They seemed to think it was coming here."

"It is." He rubbed dust and a smudge of mud from his face. "She's formed it out of spells, deep spells, and runes and cold, out of snow and the dark between the stars. Out of her anger with us. I know it's coming here—something here draws it. I've come to find out what. I've seen it twice, not clearly, blurred, but each time closer to the hold. It's changing; I think it's growing stronger."

Vidar stirred. "I cannot always remember what the god says through me, but did not Freyr himself speak of a pale approaching evil?"

"He did," Wulfgar muttered.

Vidar looked dubiously at Kari. "It might be this creature."

Jessa looked up quickly, caught up by something in his tone. She saw he was staring at Kari in fascination. It made her angry, and the memory of the thief's face in the doorway leaped back into her mind. She wanted to be rid of him, to talk to Kari.

"You two must be tired out," she said quickly. "We can leave all the talk till the morning. Then we can decide what to do."

Brochael heaved himself up at once. "That's the girl I know. Bossy."

"And she shows me what a poor host I've become," Wulfgar said. He stood too, tall and dark. "You're both welcome, you know that. And I think we'll need you, Kari. There are still ghosts and echoes here, it seems."

Kari nodded.

"And where are the birds, those strange followers of yours?"

"In the roof."

Everyone looked up. Two hunched shadows shuffled on a high rafter. Their small eyes glinted in the red light. One of them gave a low croak.

Vidar stared at them. "What are these? Spirits?"

"Ravens," Skapti said slyly. "That's all."

"Indeed." The priest turned slowly to Wulfgar. "Jarl, can I speak with you now?"

As Skapti led the others out, Jessa glanced back. Wulfgar was sitting in his chair and Vidar was leaning over him, talking rapidly and quietly, his hands spread. What was he up to now?

Upstairs, after some searching, they found an empty room with two sleeping booths built against the walls. Most rooms in the Jarlshold were empty, untouched since Gudrun's time. This one was both cold and damp.

"Never mind! It's a palace after Thrasirshall," Brochael muttered.

"You weren't expected," Skapti said. "We've no farseers in this hold." He grinned at Kari.

"Freyr forgot to mention it, then," Brochael said drily.

"Yes."

They exchanged an amused look.

"Well, you'll need a fire lit."

Jessa turned to the door but Kari said, "No. There's no need."

He squatted by the pile of sticks and peats in the square central hearth and did not touch them, did not even seem to move at all, but suddenly she caught the glint of flame deep among the kindling, and in a second it had caught and was a red line crackling down the edge of the dry wood.

He looked up at her.

"Now, if Vidar had seen that," Skapti muttered, sitting down, "it really would have made him nervous."

Jessa couldn't laugh. She was amazed and a little frightened. Kari sat back watching her. He looked tired. "I've been doing what you said. Remember? You told me once that I should know what my powers are. Find out what I can do. So I've found out."

Pulling her down beside him, Brochael gripped her cold hands. "You should see, Jessa! All these months, dreaming and sleeping and experimenting until I thought I'd never get a word out of him again! And then—fires lighting, yes, and voices and movements drifting outside the windows all night, as if visions hung there, or the Aesir themselves. Branches breaking into blossom." He laughed gruffly, with a look at Kari. "And all sorts of things he won't even tell me about."

There was a hint of worry in that look, she saw. "But this creature. What about that?"

Kari stared at the new, noisy flames. "She may have sent it to destroy us. And it's close, Jessa, somewhere very near. Yesterday the birds attacked it."

"And how do you know that?" she said.

He gave her his brief, sidelong smile. "Because they told me."

twelve

*Nor did he let them rest
but the next night brought new horrors.*

The night had many small, red eyes.

They shone, glinting and winking, far off in the dark miles of land. Squatting in the loose rocks and rubble of the pass, the creature gazed down at them. *They are fires*, the voice instructed it. *They are dangerous, a fierce pain, a spirit that leaves dark prints deep in the flesh. Keep away from them. They are all that can harm you.*

The rune beast nodded, scratching its face and eyes. It was weary; it had come a long, bitter way. And hungry. Always hungry.

Below, a great stretch of water glinted under the moon; the creature could see the tide flooding in, the gleaming currents surging upstream. Sharp smells of salt and fish and seaweed drifted up to it; the bleat of goats on the shore made it stir with pangs of memory.

Nearer, on this side of the fjord, a smoky huddle of dark shapes clustered on the fellside, with one bigger shadow in the center. These were the houses men built; the creature had prowled about several in the last weeks. But never so many together, nor huddled so close.

The still air stank of men, of smoke; the rank smell of crowded cattle rose up to it. And something else: the thing it had searched for, all the long miles. Attentively it considered the minute sounds of the night: the water's lap, the cluck of sleepy hens, a rattle of pebbles. Then, silent, moving from rock to rock, it began to edge down the fellside. Marshland lay to its right, silver pools among black, broken reeds, soft bubbles of unknown underwater stirrings. Skirting the soft tussocks and the mud, it prowled over a black slope scattered with boulders, down to the track that led in among the houses. There it waited, breathing harshly.

A man moved among the houses, a shadow in shadows. The moon lit the sharpness of metal in his hand. Without moving, the creature watched him pass.

This is the place, her voice said. The voice was cold and remote. It seemed to come from a great distance, and yet it was close, somewhere inside, heart-deep. The words held hidden, fierce delight. *This is the place. Go on! Go in!*

Stirred, the creature shook its head, rocked itself, shivered. It felt eager, and afraid. Something was there that burned with power.

But later, when the moon had slid under a great swelling of cloud, the thing moved down into the settlement. It prowled silently among the shadows, from house to house, drifting like a ghost by shuttered windows, the rattling doors of byres, to the very walls of the stone-built hall, where the grim dragon heads roared silently down upon it. All the windows were barred, the doors secure, a building of blank eyes, holding secrets. Here was the end of its long journey. But the hunted thing was safe, locked in here, untouchable.

Wrathful, the rune beast swayed upright. Its eyes glinted; moonlight touched its snow-pale hands. Then it turned, swift as thought, and crouched in the lee of the wall.

When the watchman came around the corner, he had no time even to scream.

Thirteen

Along the wide highroads the chiefs of the
clans came from far and near to see the foe's footprints.

Jessa opened her eyes and lay stiff. Not again, she thought. But the hold was silent. Across the dark room the brazier threw a dim light into the rafters. She lay there a moment, trying to find the small noise that had woken her; then she turned over and curled up, comfortably warm.

Outside, something shuffled and slid in the wind.

She thought about Vidar. Tomorrow she would tell Kari all about it—about the thief in the inn and the man who had opened the door. As she remembered, the cold point of an invisible knife touched her throat. She rolled over angrily. Yes, Kari would be able to help. They could certainly try that house again.

Below the window something scraped along the wall. She thought of Wulfgar's men, watching the fences and gateways, their swords sharp in the frost. Then she thought about Kari. He had grown, somehow. He was more silent, though he'd never said much, and there was a new aura about him, a hidden tingle of power, an invisible coat. It reminded her of something, and sleepily she searched caves and hollows for the memory until the shock of it made her open her eyes in the dark. Gudrun. Of course.

Then she sat up. For a moment she thought she had heard a low sound outside, almost a moan, an eerie murmur.

Pushing the bedclothes aside she went to the window and tugged open the shutter. Moonlight flooded her face; a cold wind blew her hair back, and putting out her head she looked down. The stone wall of the hold glittered with frost; at its foot a pool in the dark mud glinted.

No one was about.

The houses were dark masses of shadow, the sky overcast, dragging cloud over the moon. For a moment she waited there, listening, but the wind was too cold, and soon she latched the window, slammed the shutters, and leaped back into bed, shivering, her feet like ice. It took her a long time to get back to sleep.

In the morning she was halfway into her coat when the door thumped wide. Skapti called, "Jessa!" and was gone, racing along the wooden floorboards. Grabbing her boots she ran after him, into Kari's room.

Brochael, bare chested and tousled with sleep, had the ax in his hands already. "What's wrong?"

Hurtling in behind him, Jessa heard the skald say, "Your creature. It's been here."

Kari jumped down from the windowsill, the ravens rising outside.

"Not ours!" Brochael snapped.

"Listen!" Skapti's hiss silenced him. "There are tracks, all over the hold. Big, spread prints. And one man is missing."

Brochael flashed a glance at Kari. They all did.

He shook his pale hair quickly. "I don't know anything."

"We still need you." Skapti turned. "Wulfgar's going after it now, while the trail is fresh. He's furious."

Lacing up her boot, Jessa said, "I'm coming too."

Brochael gave a quick snort and grabbed his shirt and coat. "There's nothing to eat, I suppose?"

"No time." Skapti was already halfway down the stairs.

Brochael scowled after him. "If I was as thin as a worn-out bowstring, I don't suppose I'd care either!"

The courtyard was chaotic. Ponies were waiting, men were running, shouting. Wulfgar, on his black Skarnir horse, swung around and looked down at Kari. They could see how upset he was.

"Your warning was barely in time," he snapped. "Look."

But Jessa was already crouching over the prints in the mud. They were close under the wall, large and splayed, five toed. As Kari kneeled beside her and touched the spoor lightly, she whispered, "I think I heard it."

He looked at her.

"In the night. I was half asleep. I heard a sort of . . . whimper."

His colorless eyes looked through her for a second.

"Hunger," he said.

"What?"

"Hunger, Jessa."

Puzzled, she wondered if he was talking about himself, or Brochael, or . . . but there was no time to ask. Wulfgar was bitterly impatient, and when they were all on horseback, he led them out at a gallop, their hooves ringing on the cobbled track.

The morning was cold; the grass and mud stiff with frost. The prints were set hard, leading into the marshy land behind the hold, but once in there the horses sank fetlock-deep into the soft mud, stumbling over tussocks of wiry grass. Finding the trail here was impossible, the riders spread out in a wide fan and moved quickly up to firmer ground, the dogs running and snuffling in all directions.

Jessa stayed close to Kari, but neither of them spoke. He was unused to riding, but the pony seemed to understand him; Jessa noticed how it moved and paused when he wanted it to, without rein or spur.

A shout from the left brought them all galloping over; one of the men pointed to the prints. Half full of water, the marks were still soft, recent. Something heavy had been dragged here; the grass was flattened, its stems broken, the mud scored smooth.

Brochael leaped down and tugged something from the mud. He wiped it on his sleeve and saw it was a sword hilt, snapped clean in half. There were dark stains on the leather grip.

Grimly Wulfgar stared down at it. Then he looked ahead. Before them the ground ran uphill to the edges of the forest; boulder-littered turf with a small stream leaping down over the stones.

"Up there."

The dogs slithered and slunk around the rocks. Jessa knew they were behaving strangely. Most of them would have been racing into the wood by now, barking and yelping.

"They're scared," she said to Brochael.

He leaned over and looked at them. "You're right. They've got the scent and they don't like it."

The trail led high into the hills, winding along the bank of the stream. At the end of the valley they climbed higher, and all the way up, the horses were nervous.

At the fringe of a dark rank of trees they stopped.

"Spread out," Wulfgar ordered. "But stay within sight of those on either side."

"We'll just drive it out ahead of us," Vidar muttered,

peering into the green dimness.

"Maybe. But I don't want to corner it. There aren't enough of us here for that. It's Halldor we need to find."

He knew, they all knew, that the man was dead. No one said it. Anger and a cold fear hung over them all, subduing the dogs, unnerving the horses. Riding close to Brochael, Jessa moved her horse among the narrow, silvery trunks of birch, hearing the unnatural silence of the wood, no breeze, no birdsong.

They rode slowly, the horses crushing the new shoots of bracken, tall bare stems curled at the top like shepherds' crooks, cracking the winter's fallen twigs. The smell of fungi and cold damp soil rose among the fresh growth; above, the leafless trees let gray light filter down.

On each side of her, riders moved: Skapti far off to the left, and nearer, on the right, Brochael, and beyond him Kari. The big man was keeping them both close to him, and that was wise, Jessa thought, because if the creature came roaring out of the wood, they'd need him and his ax. Her fingers tightened as she glanced nervously around. The ground was uneven. Now the trees were mixed; spruce and fir massed in heavy banks. The light became gloomier, greener. She lost sight of Skapti and called out to him in alarm.

"All right. Here." He drifted back into sight around a tree, his voice hanging in the silence. Hooves made no sound here, muffled on deep springy cushions of needles, centuries deep.

"We're going to lose one another," she muttered to Brochael, but before he answered, a call came from the depths of the wood, from man to man.

Brochael waved to Skapti, then turned his horse. "They've found something."

The men were gathered by a small hollow. Jessa looked down at Wulfgar, who was standing, and saw a fragment of cloth in his hands: a green strip of cloak, slashed and wet. Another was trampled in the mud at his feet.

No one said anything for a moment.

Then Vidar murmured, "I suggest, Jarl, that we go back. There aren't enough of us here, as you said yourself."

"No."

Wulfgar put the cloth in his belt and swung himself up. "Not without the body," he said with cold fury.

Vidar hesitated. Then he nodded.

They pushed on, following broken branches, a ragged scar torn into the wood. The trees were much thicker, hard to force through. Branches, tangled and low, swept close to the ground, swishing back into the riders' faces.

Finally Wulfgar stopped. He dismounted and crouched, peering into the utter blackness among the trees. After a while he said, "There's some sort of cleft in there; a rock wall. We'll have to go in on foot. Gunnar, tether the dogs and keep them back; they're no use. Keep two men with you and guard the horses. Jessa, stay here."

"Wulfgar, you're not thinking!" Brochael jumped down. "Maybe it's waiting in there!"

The Jarl gave him a cool look. "That's never bothered you before."

"We should be careful."

"He was one of my men," Wulfgar said levelly. "My war band. You know what that means."

Brochael glared. "Of course I do! All I'm saying is take care! We don't even know what it is!"

Behind him, Kari stirred. "It doesn't matter. It's not here."

They all turned and looked at him on his shadowy horse. Some of the men touched amulets unobtrusively. Suddenly Jessa felt their unease. They didn't know whether to believe him. Perhaps he felt it too, for the birds dropped from the trees as if to aid him, one clutching his shoulder with its great claws.

It flapped away as Wulfgar asked, "Are you sure?"

"Yes. It was there, not long ago. But now it's not." He gave a slight shrug and slid down from his horse. "I'll go in, if you want."

"No, we will." Wulfgar half turned, then glanced back. "You are sure?"

Jessa watched in surprise. It was unlike him to ask twice.

Kari spread his fingers. "I can't feel it."

"Wulfgar." Vidar pushed forward urgently. "You must be careful." He glanced past the Jarl's shoulder at Kari, a rapid glance, but Jessa saw it. "Remember Freyr's warning! And what I said to you last night."

It seemed to her then that Wulfgar was really unsure, as he gazed for a moment into the wood. Then he shook his head. "We're going in. Will you come with me, old friend?"

The priest sighed and nodded. He drew a long sword, took off his heavy pale coat and tossed it over the horse.

"Stay at the back, Jessa," Wulfgar warned.

Then he bent low, and they followed him in under the branches.

It didn't take long.

Stumbling under a swinging branch, Jessa thumped into Brochael's broad back; he turned, deliberately blocking her view.

"Don't look, Jessa," he said gently, holding her shoulder. "They've found him."

"Alive?"

He shook his head.

She had known that, anyway. Behind him the men talked in low, shocked whispers.

"Go back to Kari," the big man muttered. "We'll deal with this."

She turned and pushed through the spiny branches quickly. She felt cold and sick.

Kari hadn't come. He sat on his own with the two ravens. The men guarding the horses had moved away; they watched him, whispering.

She sat beside him. Neither of them spoke; he pulled a dead leaf from his hair and rolled it in long, frail fingers.

"Did you hear Freyr's warning?" he asked quietly.

Jessa dragged her mind back to the dark, smoky hall. "Yes. Just before you came, last night."

"That some pale, evil creature was coming to the hold?"

She looked at him, suddenly wary. "Yes."

"The thing that killed this man."

She shrugged. "What else?"

He dropped the leaf. It fluttered down against a mossy rock and lay there, still.

FOURTEEN

He was more huge than any human being.

They rode back toward the hold in a silent cavalcade. No one felt inclined to talk; the only sounds in the empty land were the jingle of harness and the wind, humming in the high fells.

Wulfgar rode far out in front, as if he wanted to think, and everyone else followed in a straggling line. Brochael's ax glinted on his saddle bow; they had had to use it to hack a deep, hasty grave in the frozen soil. It had taken them a long time, Jessa thought. She wondered if the creature had been watching them.

She wondered about it, this thing Gudrun had sent. Unseen, ferocious, spell-forged. The thought made her uneasy; she turned in her saddle and looked back up the fellside.

The wood was a black fringe, hiding its death and its secret. Deep in the tangle of branches it must be lurking, breathing, bloodied. Surely this was what Freyr had warned them about. What else could he have meant? She wondered why Kari had asked.

Then she narrowed her eyes into the snow glare. Two small shapes were moving down the hill toward them, obviously horsemen.

"Wulfgar!" she called, and everyone turned, staring where she pointed.

Brochael brought his horse back to her. "Now, who are these?" he muttered.

They waited, watching the two horses pick their way down the steep, boulder-strewn slope. Farm ponies, scrawny and unkempt. The first was ridden by a coarse looking black-haired man, his leather jerkin hacked into rough holes at neck and arms, soiled and sweaty. Behind him was a boy about Jessa's age, riding awkwardly, she thought, until as they came close she noticed he only used one hand, the other resting uselessly in his lap.

"Who are you?" Brochael asked bluntly.

The black-haired man scowled at him. "I should ask that. You've been on my land." Then he saw Wulfgar riding back and his look changed at once; he slid from the horse hurriedly. "Lord Jarl. I didn't see you."

Wulfgar nodded tight lipped; he hated servility. "I'm sorry we've been on your land. Your name?"

"Skuli Skulisson of Kordamark." The man saw the boy was still on the horse and glared. "Get down, fool."

The boy dismounted and stood, watching them all quietly. He wore a thrall ring around his neck; he looked uneasy, glancing from face to face—a quick look at Jessa, and then his eyes widened; a flash of terror filled them, and she knew he had seen Kari.

"I was coming to the hold, lord," Skuli said, rubbing the black stubble of his beard with the back of one hand. He too had seen Kari; his eyes kept darting to him nervously. He swallowed. "I have some news that will interest you. This creature—"

"You've seen it?" Wulfgar asked quickly.

"Not myself, lord, no, not me. But this boy has. Last night he says he saw it. Come and tell your story. Answer the Jarl."

The thrall came forward. He seemed wary, but not afraid.

"What's your name?" Wulfgar asked easily.

"Hakon, lord."

"You don't have to call me 'lord.' Where did you see the thing?"

Hakon stared, surprised. "In the pastures above Skulisstead, about four leagues east of here. It was last night, just at dusk. I was bringing the children home—the master's boy and girl. I'd heard the rumors and I was worried—"

"So you should have been!" his master snarled.

"Be quiet," Wulfgar said sharply. "Let him finish." He sat on a boulder and let his horse crop the sparse turf. "What did you see?"

Hakon glanced at the listening horsemen, at Jessa, Brochael, Skapti. Not at Kari. He looked tired, she thought, and there were bruises on his neck and face. Skuli must have made his anger felt.

"At first nothing. Then in the wood I knew it was there—sounds, rustles, following us. I got the children up a tree. Then it came out at me." He shrugged, searching for words. "It was . . . whitish, the color of an ice bear, but bigger, upright. Bigger than a man. Heavier."

"An animal?" Wulfgar said.

The boy hesitated. Then he said, "An animal, yes, I think . . . it's hard to say. Snow drifted across it; it seemed blurred."

"For how long?"

"Just seconds, lord. Not clearly. It had small, bright eyes."

They were silent.

"And do you think it could reason, this creature?"

Kari's question was quiet and unexpected. Hakon jerked his head up with a glint of fear. Then he glanced away, back at Wulfgar. "Yes. It was . . . it had something. Some sorcery." Defiantly he looked up at the pale boy on the horse. "An evil sorcery."

"It attacked you?" Wulfgar asked. "How did you escape?"

"Odin saved me." He stammered into silence.

One or two of the men glanced at each other.

Skuli sneered. "I'm sorry, my lord. The fool thinks that the god cares for him. Warrior Odin, of all the gods!"

"He does." Hakon looked straight at Wulfgar. "My lord, two great black birds fell from the sky. They fought off the beast, screaming at it, driving it back into the trees. Who else could have sent them?"

"Who else indeed?" By an iron effort of will Wulfgar did not look at Kari. Skapti grinned, and Brochael snorted with laughter.

"There may be some other explanation for the birds," the Jarl said quietly. "But why didn't you climb the tree with the children? It was dangerous to stay below."

Hakon was silent.

"He couldn't," Skuli said bluntly. "We call him Hakon Empty-hand. He can only use the one. The other's useless."

Jessa saw the thrall straighten. Both hands hung by his sides. He looked at no one.

After a moment Wulfgar stood up, giving the farmer a cold glare. Then he said, "Thank you—both. This creature has been in my hold and killed one of my men. If it can be killed, I intend to kill it. I'll need all the men I can get. Come back to the hold with us and have something to eat." He glanced up, but the ravens were nowhere to be seen. "You may even see something that will surprise you."

On the way back Jessa maneuvered her horse next to Kari's. "Slow down. I've got something to tell you."

He gave her a sidelong look. "Jessa, you've had

something to tell me since I got here. It doesn't take sorcery or runemasters to know that."

She laughed and took off a glove, flexing her fingers. "The weather's getting warmer. Have you noticed?"

"It's warmer than Thrasirshall."

"Anywhere is." She looked at him. "It's about Vidar Freyrspriest."

The ice-pale eyes glanced at her quickly. "What about him?"

Briefly she told him about the thief at Hollfara, and the man who had opened the door of the house in the Jarlshold.

"It was him, I know it was, but when they sent for him another wretch came, a man called Snorri. Vidar backed him up. It was all lies, and all planned. That's what worries me. It means Vidar knows the rat-thief and probably what he does. More than that, he knows where he is."

"In the hold?"

"Or just outside. He's hiding him. Maybe even takes a share of the money. And what sort of adviser does that make him for Wulfgar? What sort of man of honor? Not only that, Skapti doesn't like him."

"Doesn't he?" He smiled wanly. "Then it must be serious. Did Wulfgar believe you, about the thief?"

She shrugged, looking out over the landscape. "I pretended I was mistaken. I didn't want to put the priest on his guard.

He's a clever man—he watches people. Have you noticed?"

His smile went. "I'd noticed." He pushed the hair from his eyes and glanced at her. "And I'll tell you something else about him. This man Skuli—"

"A real charmer!"

"Yes, well, Vidar knows him. They gave each other one look, just one, but I felt the knowledge of it tingle in my fingers. They know each other. Your Vidar keeps bad company." He shrugged. "Maybe you should watch him."

"I'd hoped you'd say that. We could follow him. . . ."

Kari laughed then, something he rarely did, so that Brochael looked back, curious.

"Jessa," he marveled, "do you think that I could slip about the hold unnoticed? The witch's son, the sorcerer, the master of ravens? None of them trust me, you saw that. They can't take their eyes off me. The Snow-walker's son." He shrugged bitterly, a little proudly. "Besides, I don't need to follow him."

She dragged hair from her face. "I know you don't."

"Then tonight, we'll see what we can see. If your thief is in the hold, we'll know. I'll show him to you."

"Thanks." She nodded quickly. But the echo of Gudrun was in his voice, and though she hated herself for it, just for a moment, she feared him.

Fifteen

He could not away from me;
nor would I from him.

Crouched between two pines on the ridge of the forest the creature watched them go.

Even from here it could see the different shapes of them, her voice whispering each description in its ear. *The dark one; the tall one; the big, bearded one; the one with long hair; the one with the scarred face. And the small, silvery one. My son,* her voice murmured.

The creature lurched down to a pool in a hollow, smashing the thin linkings of ice with its claws. Peat brown water lapped at the soil.

Her face looked up at it as it drank, narrow and pale; silvery hair braided about it, her eyes colorless and bright as glass. *My enemies,* she said. *Especially the last one, Kari. He and I are the same, and yet opposites. Once I cursed him that no one would trust him, not even his dearest friends, and he hasn't forgotten that.* She smiled, a sad, bitter smile. *That's the sorrow of power, and its delight.*

The rune beast lapped at the brackish water, barely understanding. Water dripped from its raised face, soaking its pelt and the clots of old blood. It felt as if it had been drinking her, taking her coldness into itself. She reached out as if to touch it, and the pool rippled, wave-blown. *There are plans working here,* she whispered, *and not only mine.*

Confused, the rune beast tried to summon questions; the patterns of sound slid through its mind and were lost, and she laughed. The creature swung its slow head at the sound.

And each one thinks he plans for himself and is unseen. But I see.

Her reflection dissolved and shimmered; only her voice, like a cold echo of its own hunger, tickled the creature's ear so that it scrabbled and scratched. *Leave thinking to me. I am your thoughts. You've done well already. Now take as many as you can. Feast yourself. Take the dark one if you want, the Jarl, the arrogant one. But leave my son alone.*

The beast swayed dizzily.

I'd see him betrayed by his friends first. I want him to feel that. Then he'll act. He won't be able to help it.

When she had gone from its mind, it crouched, its small pale eyes gazing deep into the trees, breathing the wet, earthy scents of the forest, the far-off taint of blood and men and horses. Weariness surged in its brain, a dark unthinking pain that masked even the hunger.

The rune thing stumbled far down into the forest,

over roots and rocks, fumbling through the tangle of branches; down black aisles of stark trees to the fresh mound of turned earth. Trampling over that, it climbed into a deep split between two rocks and curled there, heaving its huge bulk around in search of comfort. It was growing daily; its body would hardly fit here now; its skin was scratched and smeared and sodden with the forest's damp. Deep among mosses and lichen and unfurling bracken, eyes closed, it waited for sleep.

When a small bird landed on a stone and picked at its fur, the creature did not move. Deep in dreams, the voice whispered to it all the long afternoon.

Sixteen

Fatal bonds were fettered for him.

"I've called you here to discuss what to do," Wulfgar said.

They sat in his room, Jessa and Kari by the fire, Brochael on the bench, Skapti and Vidar opposite. Wulfgar turned from the window and leaned his back against it.

"Then come and sit down," Skapti muttered. "We can't talk with you prowling."

Wulfgar came over, but without his usual amusement. He sat on a chair and leaned back grimly.

"First, what do we know about it? Gudrun sent it." He glanced at Kari. "That's certain."

The boy nodded.

"Second. It kills. Apparently to eat." For a moment he was silent as they all thought of Halldor; then he pulled his thoughts back and snapped, "It's big, has no weapons but its hands, may or may not be intelligent. And it's coming here. Why?"

Some eyes and most thoughts slid to Kari.

"Because there is something here that draws it," he said simply. "I don't know yet what it is."

"A person?" Vidar asked smoothly.

"Maybe."

"And what will it do when it comes back to the hold? Perhaps tonight? Or tomorrow?"

They were silent. Flames crackled in the room; someone yelled at a dog outside.

Kari said, "Didn't Freyr tell you?" He looked strangely at the priest through his silver fringe of hair, and Vidar shrugged uneasily.

"The god spoke of death."

"Whose?"

Vidar glanced at Wulfgar and didn't answer.

"Mine," the Jarl said softly.

Brochael swore softly under his breath, and Skapti drew himself up sharply. "You? It's come for you?"

Wulfgar shrugged.

"Then you can't risk yourself hunting it!"

Angrily the Jarl stood up. "It's killed one of my men. I have a responsibility to his family and to the rest of them. I have no choice but to hunt it. Tomorrow. This afternoon I'll send messengers to all the holdings. We need every man they can spare."

"But—"

"Don't argue with me, Skapti! I have to go. You know that."

They all knew it.

Into the silence Vidar said, "I agree. It kills like a beast—we must hunt it like one. Despite the danger." He glanced at Wulfgar then; a dark flicker of a look that made Jessa uneasy.

Kari stirred beside her. "I don't think hunting it is the answer."

Wulfgar glared at him. "Why not?"

"Because it's not a thing of flesh and blood."

"Then what? Fight sorcery with sorcery?"

Slowly Kari nodded. "Perhaps. If I knew what it searches for. But there's one thing about it that I do know, that I can feel right now. It's hungry."

Wrathfully Wulfgar sat down. "Do you expect me to feel sorry for it? Do you?"

Kari shook his head. His eyes were bright and sharp. "Not just hunger. I mean this."

And for one piercing second he made them all empty, without heart or thoughts or memories, so that inside each of them was a black, raging nothing that swelled out and engulfed them, and they had no names anymore, no friends, nothing but a searing hunger that tormented like flame.

And then it was gone.

White-faced, Jessa let her fingers slowly stop trembling. She glanced at the others' shocked faces.

"I'm sorry," Kari said quietly. "But I wanted you to know. That's what you will be hunting. And whatever it hungers for is here."

Wulfgar stirred, brushing hair from his forehead. He looked sick and shaken but his voice was steady. "Then destroying it would almost be a mercy. I won't change my mind, Kari. Tomorrow, early, we leave."

He stood up, and everyone else did the same. "Stay

here, Vidar," the Jarl said, "I want to talk to you. Skapti, ask the thrall Hakon to come up, will you?"

Hakon ate the bread slowly. It was the best and softest he had ever tasted, but he didn't want anyone to see that. And the Jarlshall was so huge, all built of stone like the halls of Asgard, the meat spitted and crackling over its fires. And the tapestries! His eyes followed them as they gusted and stirred; great dusty faded hunts, the intricately sewn adventures of the gods, Odin with both his ravens, Hammer-Thor, Loki, Freyr. There was nothing like this at Skulisstead—a dark, greasy house, full of cooking smells and fleas and drying fleeces. This was how lords lived.

Skuli was drinking at the nearest fire. Drinking too much. He'd be here for the afternoon at least, downing the Jarl's hospitality, and then, Hakon thought with a brief smile, he'd probably sleep it off. For him it was a day free of work, and that was so strange he hardly knew what to do with it.

Then the tall man, the poet, came over and beckoned him with a long finger. "Come with me, Odin-favored. The Jarl wants you."

Following him, Hakon muttered, "Don't mock me, master."

Skapti grinned. "They say Odin isn't to be trusted.

Those birds that saved you belonged to Kari Ragnarsson."

"The Snow-walker?"

"The same. So you owe him for your rescue."

Hakon set his mouth in a tight line and said nothing.

Jarl Wulfgar was waiting for him in a small room with a fire. He waved Skapti away and told Hakon to sit down. The skald went out and closed the door reluctantly.

"Now, I want to hear it again. What you saw."

Hakon nodded. He already liked this dark, lazy, almost dangerous man. After he'd finished, Wulfgar asked a few sharp, relentless questions. Then he sat still.

There was one other listener there—the one they called the priest of Freyr, with the pale coat and the scar down his face. Hakon hadn't noticed him at first; now he saw how the man held that cheek away, in shadow, and he understood that. His own useless hand lay on his knee; he had learned how to make it look normal. Until he tried to pick anything up.

The man listened and said nothing until the Jarl turned to him. "Well?"

"I don't know. Freyr spoke obliquely, as the gods do."

"But if you don't think it was this creature he was warning me against, then what, Vidar? And even if it threatens my death, I can't let it win."

"Jarl." The priest came forward. "You know what I

think. May I speak again, of things you won't like?"

Almost angrily, Wulfgar glared at him. "I'm not Gudrun. You can say what you want."

Vidar nodded and sat down. "Then let me say this. I don't think Freyr meant this creature at all. Perhaps it is just an ice bear, driven south by hunger. I think Freyr was warning us of a nearer danger, an evil, sorcerous threat."

The Jarl turned his head quickly. "You mean Kari."

"Yes."

Wulfgar clenched a fist but Vidar said, "Listen, Wulfgar, hear me out. I know you trust Kari. But you're the Jarl, and my friend, and I can't let any harm come to you. I have to say this."

Hakon sat silent. They both seemed to have forgotten he was even there. He was just a thrall, after all.

Wulfgar gazed into the fire bitterly. "Kari's my friend, too."

"Is he?" Vidar pressed him closer. "How much do you really know about him? Really?"

"He drove Gudrun away. Jessa saw it. There was some sorcerous battle of wills. You can't deny he did that for us."

"No!" Vidar said eagerly. "He did that for himself! Now that she's gone he is the most powerful. He's her son, her image. You saw how he twisted our minds just now—he has her blood, her secret, evil guile. You can't ignore that. And his father was the Jarl before you—perhaps he feels he should have been chosen. He wants to be Jarl himself!"

Wulfgar shook his head, but slowly. "He had his chance."

"No, he didn't. He was too young then, not ready. What has he been doing up there in Thrasirshall for two years but gathering his powers, weaving runes, knotting the forces of air and darkness together? Now he's ready! And the words of the god mean him. A pale creature, come from the north. Remember that he arrived then, at that moment."

Barely breathing, Hakon watched the Jarl. He was staring grimly at nothing. "I won't believe this."

"You must! You must, Wulfgar, and not let what you see as a debt of honor blind you! Kari is strange, ambiguous, dangerous! And the creature may even be his!"

The priest gripped Wulfgar's wrist with his hand; the Jarl stared at him. "His?"

"He does not want us to hunt it. Why not? What other reasons can there be but that he brought it here? To kill you. Then he will take over."

Wulfgar shrugged him off. "And Brochael? What about him?"

The priest spread his hands. "It would be better not to trust either of them."

"Not Brochael too . . ." Raising his head wearily, Wulfgar saw Hakon and glared at him. Then he said, "Get out."

Hakon went to the door quickly.

"Wait!"

Wulfgar stood up slowly, as if a great burden was on him. "You've been helpful to me, Hakon, and I thank you for that, but you've heard words here you shouldn't have heard. That should not even have been spoken. I want you to forget them."

It could have been a threat. With Skuli there would have been a blow, to reinforce it. Not just this uneasy sadness.

You won't forget them, Hakon thought. But he nodded and went out of the room.

Halfway down the stairs he realized that he was free. Let the Jarl worry about traitors. He had some time without work!

Slipping through the hall, he saw Skuli loudly voicing some slurred opinion, so he edged through the door into the sunlight and wandered into the hold. Freedom washed over him—no one giving him orders, no backbreaking fetching and carrying! In a dream of delight he explored the Jarlshold, watched the boats unload fish and casks and bales of cloth, climbed aboard merchants' longships and fingered their silks and engraved silver rings. There were swords there he would have given almost anything to own, to be able to use them, to wield them well. As he watched Wulfgar's picked men whetting their blades and laughing on benches in the sunshine, something moved in him like an ache of hunger. He forced himself not to feel it, and with long practice, almost succeeded. None of that was for him. He was a thrall, a possession, something owned. And seared by a cold sorcery.

As he turned bitterly away he saw the skald again, sitting with his long legs stretched out, touching the strings of the kantele into soft, tuneless notes. Next to him sat the girl Hakon had noticed that morning, her long hair loose, her sharp, clever eyes watching him.

Jessa Horolfsdaughter. The sorcerer's friend.

She beckoned him over.

For a moment he hesitated; then habit took over and he went.

"How can I serve you?" he asked sullenly.

"I don't want you to serve me." She laughed. "We thought you might like some wine."

Astonished, he watched her pour it. The cup was gilt, with tiny red enameled birds around it, wingtip to wingtip. He picked it up, left-handed, awkward.

"We saw you watching the war band," the skald muttered, twanging a string near his ear. "A short life, the warrior's."

"But a proud one."

They both looked at him.

Jessa said, "We think you did well, saving the children. Skuli should have been grateful, though by the look of him I doubt that."

He shrugged.

"Have you always been with him?" Her tone was friendly, and though he resented the question, he answered it. "Not always. I was born a free man. But my parents died and I was no use on my uncle's farm, not after . . . Well, I was sold to Skuli to pay off a debt."

They were both silent. Distaste, he supposed. Good, let them feel it.

"But your hand." The poet turned his thin sharp face. "You can't use it?"

"No." Hakon was used to this curiosity. He lifted it with the other, feeling the cold of the skin. "There's no feeling, nothing, from the wrist down."

They didn't ask, but he told them anyway. "It was done to punish me. For theft."

Jessa looked startled. "You stole?"

"I was five years old. I took some food from a plate when my uncle had guests. Important guests. I was beaten, but then she said that wasn't enough. She gave me her own, lasting punishment."

Skapti sat up. "She? You don't mean . . ."

"Yes. The Jarl's wife. The witch. She touched my hand with one long finger, and it turned to ice. There was no pain, nothing, but I couldn't open my hand and I never have been able to since. She seared me with her sorcery and she laughed. I remember her, every look of her, and when I saw him today I saw her again." He stood up. "Your friend's mother did this, lady."

Jessa frowned at him. "She did worse to her son. You can't blame him."

Hakon nodded calmly. "But he's still her son. He has her blood, her powers." Remembering Vidar's words, he echoed them, deliberately mocking. "You can't ignore that."

Seventeen

The fleetness of the serpent
wound itself together.

Jessa knocked on the wooden door and Brochael opened it.

"Come inside," he said abruptly.

The small room was dark, with only the fire to light it.

The shutters hung half open; a few stars glittered in the deepening blue sky.

Kari sat on the floor, his knees drawn up and his thin arms wrapped around them. His eyes were closed.

"Is he asleep?" she whispered.

He looked up at her then and said, "No. Just a bit tired. Sit down, Jessa."

Brochael had eased his weight down on the bench, so she sat on the floor, leaning back against his knees. In the warm comfort of the room they were all silent for a moment, but there was an underlying unease, as if the two of them had been quarrelling before she came in, though she could hardly believe that.

Kari watched the flames. Their light flickered on the pale edges of his hair.

"Can you see anything?" she asked eagerly.

"Not yet. Give me a while."

She flicked a satisfied look at Brochael, but it faded instantly as she saw how he was watching Kari, with an unhappiness in his face that shocked her. Then she saw the reason.

Tied around Kari's wrist, half-hidden by his dark sleeve, was a small, knotted bracelet made of snakeskin.

She recognized it at once, with a kind of horror.

It was the bracelet Gudrun had worn. Two years ago

the witch had taken it off as she left and thrown it down on the floor—a reminder of her power, her long tyranny over them all.

"Keep it," she'd said.

But Kari had thrown it away; he'd locked it in the dungeon far below the hall, the damp cell where he had been a prisoner as a small child; a child without speech, unable to run, not knowing what people were, what the outside air was like. It had been there ever since, she supposed.

And now?

Jessa's mind raced. He'd obviously been down there. He'd opened the room, picked the snakeskin from the ashes . . . but why? Why would he? She tried to catch Brochael's eye, but he wouldn't look at her. His usual cheerful smile was gone; she had never seen him look so confused, so miserable. She glanced back at the bracelet. Kari must have a reason for this. They shouldn't start thinking stupid, unforgivable things. He wasn't Gudrun. He wasn't.

"Look!" he said to her suddenly, and she jerked her bewildered gaze back to the flames and saw there was something there. It drifted and blurred; became shapes that moved behind the peats and black, smoldering chars of wood, but she couldn't see it clearly. And then suddenly, it was Gudrun.

The sorceress was looking out at them, as if reflected in a pool or a lake, the water rippling over her face, her silvery hair, the ice blue dress she wore glinting with crystals and snow shards. She was speaking, and Jessa heard the words close, almost inside her ear, so that she put up her hand and scratched at it.

There are plans working here. And not only mine. And each one thinks he plans for himself and is unseen. But I see.

Jessa looked at Brochael and saw that he heard it too; his lips were tight with distaste. Kari sat silent, knees bent, looking away. Then the image dissolved into flame light and the ripple of heat over wood, but her voice still hung and echoed as if from somewhere far distant.

Feast yourself Take the dark one If you want, the Jarl, the arrogant one. But leave my son alone.

Kari looked up at that. He looked so much like Gudrun that Jessa almost thought it was he who had spoken.

"Who's she talking to?" Brochael asked gruffly.

Kari shrugged. "Perhaps this beast of hers."

"So it's Wulfgar she wants dead. I'd have thought it would have been you."

Kari watched him sidelong. "So would I. We may have missed something. She may be keeping something worse for me." He twisted the laces of his shirt around his fingers. There was silence a moment, then he said, "And is this your thief, Jessa?"

Vidar sat among the flames. It was some dark, shadowy place, and he was leaning forward, and her heart leaped as she saw the thin rat-faced man drinking opposite.

"That's him!"

"Looks a skulking little cutthroat," Brochael observed.

"He tried to cut mine. Where is he?"

"I don't know." Kari watched the men. "I think he's near, in the hold or not far outside, but I can't tell. I do know this is happening now, right now."

"Vidar's got his sword," Brochael growled. "He doesn't wear that in the hold."

"But he can't be far because he was here an hour ago."

"One of the farms then. It's fair to think he'd get this scum away, if he thought you'd seen him. What are they planning?"

But the images spluttered, became burned wood. Kari shook his head wearily. "I've lost it."

Brochael looked at Jessa. "Will you tell the Jarl?"

"No!" It was Kari who answered quickly.

"Why not?"

"Because he trusts Vidar. He doesn't trust me. And we have no proof."

Surprised and uneasy, Jessa said, "Of course Wulfgar trusts you."

"No, Jessa." He gripped his fingers tight together.

"Vidar is turning him against me. I know that, I can see it, the fine threads of mistrust that he's spinning, like a web over this hold. It began long ago, before you came, before we came."

"That's nonsense," Brochael said gruffly.

"No, it isn't. Think about it, Brochael! To Vidar, I'm the pale approaching danger. I'm Gudrun's son. I was the last Jarl's son. He wants Wulfgar to see me as a threat."

Jessa clenched her fists without noticing. "But Wulfgar knows you!"

"Does he?" He turned his strange, colorless eyes fiercely on her. "None of you know me, really! Sometimes I don't think I know myself, what I might do. This is her curse, remember, that you'll never quite trust me, that I might turn on you as she did." He looked away bleakly. "And I might! I can feel it in myself."

"We can all do evil—"

"Not like I could!" He gripped her fingers suddenly; she felt him trembling, as if he suppressed fear.

"Power, Jessa. Feel it? It's burning in me. Sometimes I want to cry out with the strength of it, let it rage in a crackle of light and flame. Things call to me out of the snow, out of the endless wastes—wandering things, spirits, elements. And people—I can't be near them because I want to change them, to move them, to slide into their minds and make them do what I want them to do. And I could, and they'd never know! But I daren't, because that's how she started. . . ."

Numb, she stared at him. "We trust you."

Brochael gripped his shoulder. "I know you better than you know yourself. I taught you to speak, boy. Carried you out of her prisons myself. You'll never be like her."

Kari watched them a moment, calming himself. "So why didn't you ask me about this?"

He slipped the snakeskin band off, held it up on one long finger. "Why not, Jessa? Because you weren't sure?"

In all honesty, she couldn't answer him. No words would come.

Eighteen

The warriors slept whose task it was to hold
the horned building—all except one.

"Don't go skulking off again, thief-thrall." Skuli's breath stank; he swayed as he stood. All evening, Hakon knew, he'd been flat on his back among the dogs and the straw.

He dragged a blanket into a corner by the fire and lay

there, listening to the group gambling in one corner, the sleepy talk of the house carls about the fire. This was the man who owned him; this drunken, potbellied fool. He thought of wild, impossible things—running away, hiding out here, appealing to the Jarl—but all the while he knew he was dreaming. A runaway thrall was hunted down—everyone saw to that. None of them wanted their own thralls trying it. And what would Wulfgar want with a one-handed man? Best to go back to the sheep and learn how to forget.

He thought about them all at the high table that night, their fine clothes, their easy ways, their freedom. Going where they wanted, saying what they thought. They would all be on the hunt tomorrow, even Jessa, and he'd be left here.

Then he remembered the thing in the wood and felt a shiver of pride. He'd been the only one even to glimpse it, that pale shadow in the snow, the flicker of strange, colorless eyes that had stared into his. It had been hungry, raging with hunger. It was only now, quite suddenly, that he realized that.

And surely it would be difficult to find. The hold was full of men, they'd been riding in all day, but out there the fells were endless and the forests black. Somewhere in those snowfields the creature was waiting. Maybe waiting until now, until it was dark. He shivered, pulling the rough blanket closer. His right hand lay outside the folds, but he left it there. He could never feel anything with that, even the cold.

Deep in the night, something woke him. Opening his eyes, he saw the hall was black; the last fire had burned low, it was a red smolder in the shadows. Sleeping shapes breathed and snored about it.

Lying still, he listened, and fear prickled on his skin. Outside the hall, something was moving. It shuffled and scraped; tiny unnerving sounds in the night's silence. He lay rigid and unbreathing from noise to noise. A scrape against the wall; the bang of something heavy. Then footsteps, slow footsteps near the door.

He sat up quickly.

The windows were safely shuttered, the door barred. Men slept around them, their swords close at hand. The fire stirred peacefully. But Hakon knew it was out there. It was prowling the hold.

He wished someone else would hear it and wake up, but no one did. Guthlac, Wulfgar's steward, slept near the fire, wrapped in a warm fleece. Hakon decided to wake him.

But then a noise at the door made him jerk his head; with a whisper of terror he stared across the hall. It seemed to him suddenly that the great wooden structure was not as solid as it had been, that the bar across it was somehow less distinct. He gripped the blanket tight, stared harder through the dark. Was he imagining it? No. There was a faintness there, a fading, and suddenly he knew that the door was going, dissolving in some sorcerous mist. He turned to shout, to jump up.

And found he couldn't move.

Just couldn't. Hand or body. And couldn't speak. For a moment of terrible, sickening fear he thought the paralysis had shot from his hand through his whole body and would be there forever.

And then he saw Kari.

The boy was watching him, standing in the shadows just at the foot of the stairs. He was a pale ghost against the drift and blackness of the tapestries; Hakon could see the silveriness of his hair; his thin, turned face.

"I'm sorry," Kari murmured, "but I don't want the others woken."

Helpless and furious, Hakon watched him walk across the dark spaces of the hall, across a long circle of moonlight that stretched from the ring window, high up. Two black shadows swooped after him; with a crawling of his skin Hakon saw that they were ravens, two huge birds that flapped and rustled their great glossy wings.

What was he doing? Hakon struggled to move even one finger, but it was impossible. His body was held rigid.

Kari came up close to the door. Now there was almost nothing left of it, a mist, a blur of darkness, and beyond that something else that moved, white and indistinct.

The Snow-walker stopped. Before him a shape pushed itself through the nebulous web of sorcery, resolved itself into a great clawed limb, its pale fur clotted with water and stains of blood and earth. It was so close to Kari that it almost touched him as it stretched, groping blindly into the warmth of the hall.

Unbreathing, Hakon watched.

Gently Kari lifted a hand and reached out. He touched the very tip of the creature's claw and it was still, as if it felt him. A thin knotted bracelet hung on his wrist; Hakon saw it glisten, as if it was made of some iridescent skin.

Beyond the mist of the door the creature shifted. He could almost see it now, pale against the shadowy night, wreathed with mist and crystals of ice.

Kari took his hand away. Still he stood there, not speaking, not moving.

Hakon squirmed, fought for control over his lips, the muscles of his throat. He had to shout! He had to warn them all! But nothing would come and Kari did not even spare him a glance.

"Not yet," Kari murmured, almost under his breath, "not yet. I don't know what to do with you yet."

The thing outside made a strange, uneasy moan. Kari waited, the birds motionless at his feet, the great claw reaching for him. Then, silently, the door began to re-form, to shimmer back into existence, and the thing outside squirmed and dragged its arm back heavily, as if the air had become thicker, and it snarled and stepped away into the dark.

The door was there, solid, reassuring.

Kari turned after a moment. He looked pale, unsteady. He came over to Hakon and crouched down to him, and he was white with weariness, as if some great struggle had failed.

"You'll tell no one what you saw."

Instantly Hakon knew he was free. He grabbed the amulet at his neck. "What were you doing?" he snarled. "Trying to let it in! It could have killed us all!"

In the dimness Kari gave him a bleak smile. "As I said, tell no one. You'll find you won't be able to anyway, even if you try. For a few days. That should be enough."

He reached out then, but Hakon flung him off. "Don't touch me! That's what she did!"

Sprawled, surprised, Kari shook his head. "I don't need to touch you," he said.

And sleep came down on Hakon like a blanket: heavy, smothering, without dreams.

In the morning he sat on the empty bench outside and watched the men arm themselves, harness their horses, gather dogs and spears and skis. Jessa came over and looked down at him. "Going home?"

Home! he thought bitterly, but only shook his head.

"Skuli's going on the hunt. I have to stay here."

She nodded, as if she understood how he felt. Her hair was braided tight; she wore two knives in her belt, long sharp weapons, newly bought.

"Where's your friend?" he said warily.

"Skapti?"

"Kari."

She gave him a sudden, considering look. "I don't know. Why?"

He breathed deeply. "Jessa . . ." But it was no use. As soon as he began to speak, the same choking, cold web stifled the words in his throat. He'd already tried to tell some of the men, twice, what had happened.

"What's the matter?" She was watching him curiously.

He shook his head. "I can't . . . say. I can't."

"Are you all right?"

He shrugged hopelessly. Beware of Kari, he thought.

Be careful of him. He's a traitor. "Yes, I'm all right."

He glanced down at the pale withered skin of his right hand. "Sorcery," he said thickly. "It maims you."

For a moment she wondered, then Skuli called him wrathfully, and he got up and walked away. There was nothing he could do to warn her, he knew that. Rune power had him in its grip.

"Good luck on the hunt!" he called back. "Be careful."

She smiled, puzzled still. "I intend to."

As he strode after Skuli, she watched, thoughtful. What had that been about? What had he wanted to say? He wanted to join the hunt, to be one of them, but it wasn't that. She knew that without him saying it.

She turned to see Wulfgar standing by his horse. "Are we all here?"

"Almost." Skapti glanced around.

She put her foot into his clasped hands and leaped lightly onto the pony, gathering its reins, slapping its smooth neck. "Kari and Brochael aren't here."

"One of us is." Brochael was standing in the hall door, his tawny beard aflame with the red sun.

"Come on then!" Skapti called.

Brochael did not move. His face was grim. Then he went over to Wulfgar and looked up at him.

"We're not coming."

A stir went through the listening men. Brochael ignored it. Dropping his voice, he said, "Kari won't come. I don't really know why, but I have to stay with him. I don't understand what this is all about, Wulfgar. But it's not cowardice, you know that."

"Not on your part," Vidar put in.

Brochael swung angrily. "Nor on his! It's . . . he says it's not the thing to do."

The Jarl shrugged coldly. "Kari must do as he wants."

Vidar gave him a quick, warning look. "Remember what I said."

Wulfgar gave him a blazing glare. "I do! I can't forget it."

But everyone else was looking at the doorway. Kari stood there in the wan light; his dark coat wrapped him. He didn't smile, or even look at Jessa. His pale eyes were fixed on Vidar. Then he said, "I'll stay, Wulfgar. I have some hunting of my own to do."

Then he turned and went back inside. With a pained, puzzled glance at Jessa, Brochael stalked after him.

The darkness of the hall swallowed them both.

Dineteen

It is not far from here
in terms of miles, that the mere lies
overcast with dark, crag-rooted trees . . .

All the morning they rode, about forty riders and a pack of
dogs, high into the frosted fells. Again it had been only too
easy to find marks and prints in the soft mud all about the
Jarlshold—between the houses, down at the wharves, even
right up to the door of the hall, as if the rune thing had
prowled silently about all night. But Wulfgar had ordered
everyone to stay indoors with their livestock, and no one
seemed to have heard anything at all.

This time the prints led away clearly along the fjord-
side, among shingle patches and wet grasses. The hunters
followed, their reflections traveling with them along the
brown, rippling waters.

Jessa, near the back, turned to Skapti. "What did he
mean by that—his own hunting?"

"Who knows?" The skald's fingers tugged a dry leaf
from the horse's mane. "Who can follow the thoughts of
runemasters, Jessa, or travel down the tracks of their
minds?"

"He's up to something."

"Doubtless."

"And he's right about Vidar. About all of us. Listen, Skapti—stop thinking up word chains and listen to me! Sometimes I think about Gudrun, and I wonder." She twisted her head. "Don't you?"

He nodded unhappily. "But that's what she wants us to do. She rules us, even now."

Jessa's horse splashed through the crumbling turf of the waterside, one hoof slipping into the mud. Jerked sideways, she saw herself suddenly, a small white face far below.

"Her reflection," she muttered.

Gradually they climbed higher, through wide pastures, beside the tiny lakes and tarns of the mountains, skirting the forest that crowded below the snowline. Above, the sun glinted on the high passes, the white peaks never free from snow.

The trail was easy to follow, the dogs running free, casting about, barking. But as the forest came closer they began to slow down, reluctant.

Wulfgar waved his arm, and the group of horsemen spread out into the long line of the hunt, pacing along a grassy lakeside and into the ferns and bracken of the wood. But the ground here was too steep and broken, riven by streams that crashed and fell foaming among boulders, swept by heavy overhanging branches. Riding was impossible; after only a few yards they turned around.

"It'll have to be on foot." Wulfgar swung himself down, and hauled out the great ash spear strapped to his saddle.

"Spread out; keep the dogs leashed. Two men stay with the horses. Jessa, keep with me. The rest of you stay in twos. No one is to be alone. If you see it, or anything, shout. Remember this thing kills quickly, and it's big."

They disappeared discreetly, man by man, fading into the gloom between the trees. A crackle of leaves, a swish of branches, and they were gone, as if the forest was empty.

Close behind Wulfgar, Jessa stepped over roots that tangled the broken, rock-strewn ground. In the green light figures flickered to the left of her, but already it was hard to see who. Once someone called from that direction; everyone stopped, listening, but the word came back along the line quickly. "Nothing."

Foot by foot, the men moved on, trying to keep one another in sight. Long growths of ivy hung from the still trees, and the farther in the hunters went, the darker and more silent the wood became; sounds grew fainter, dissolved into whistles and rustles, as if the great carpet of needles underfoot crushed and muffled every sound. Breathing was all Jessa could hear now, her own, and Wulfgar's slither and push through the tanglewood. On each side of them a deepening darkness loomed, full of leaf rustle and movement.

Wulfgar slid into a hollow and stopped, dragging his foot out with a whispered curse. He crouched, peering ahead.

"It chooses the darkest places, the most difficult ground for us."

"Any animal would."

"Not like this." He glanced behind warily. "Those farmers were right. The creature can think. Or someone tells it what to do."

But Jessa was listening suddenly. "Where are they all? I can't hear anyone."

He listened too, then called, "Skapti! Vidar!"

There was no answer. His voice rang oddly around them.

"They should never be out of earshot!" Angrily he called them again.

The green silence muffled his shout.

"They've gone after it," Jessa said.

"Without us?"

"We may have been too far over. We were on the end of the line."

He glared at her. "It still shouldn't have happened."

"Or they might be ahead somewhere."

Wulfgar hesitated. Then, after a moment, he walked on.

Uneasy now, Jessa scrambled after him, her knife drawn. They pressed through the swishing, tangled briars, creeping under low branches, sometimes on hands and knees, until she realized that the ground was dropping away steeply before them. Once Wulfgar called again; his voice rang eerily back among the black, clustered trees, as if there was some barrier it could not pierce. All about them the wood was completely silent.

"There's rune lore in this," he muttered.

Jessa thought so too. She crouched in the mud to catch her breath. "Gudrun. It's her creature, after all."

"Gudrun's too far away."

"Who else then?"

"I don't know, Jessa. I'm trying not to think." He looked around at her rather strangely, she thought. "Come on. We have to find the others."

They slid down the slope, steadying themselves from trunk to trunk, their hands powdered with green lichen. At the bottom they came to a place Jessa disliked on sight.

It was a still hollow. Everything in it was thick with moss, smothered with it, as if nothing here had been disturbed for long years, but had oozed out moisture and liverworts and slow globules of living growth. Wood was rotten, splintering softly underfoot, overgrown with brown steps of fungi. At the bottom of the hollow they saw a small mere, brown and still, the branches of a drowned tree rising stark from the surface.

"A real troll haunt," Jessa muttered, rubbing green smudges off her cheek.

Wulfgar looked quickly around. "It may have been here. Something made that track to the water."

He squelched forward through the spongy moss, water oozing out and rolling in bright drops over his boots, but Jessa stayed where she was.

A rustle in the forest froze them both. Wulfgar turned like lightning, braced the spear into the ground, held the point ready, crouching. Jessa crouched too, silent.

Something was coming.

The stiff black branches stirred and swished.

She drew the other knife stealthily and held them both in hot fists.

Then the undergrowth parted.

Vidar looked out.

Wulfgar stood up slowly with a murmur of relief. "You!" he said. "And where are the others?"

"Not far." Vidar came out into the hollow, tugging his feet irritably from the boggy ground. "Gunther thinks he had a sight of the thing. It moves quickly, for all its size."

"Which way?"

"North."

All the time he was walking closer. Still crouched, Jessa watched, and as she was about to stand and ease her knees, a movement in the bushes behind Vidar caught her eye. Something glimmered there, a paleness, a crackle of leaves.

Her heart thudded.

And then she saw it wasn't the rune beast at all.

It was a thin, rat-faced man, smirking as Vidar walked closer and closer to the Jarl. Closer and closer.

Something snapped in her. Knowledge burst in her brain like light; she leaped up and screamed, "Wulfgar! *Look out!*"

He turned to face her quickly.

"No!" she yelled, but Vidar's knife was out.

It slashed down into the Jarl's back, swiftly, silently

Twenty

To elude death is not easy.

Wulfgar crumpled into the wet moss; Vidar whirled around in fury.

"Get her!" he roared.

But he found Jessa was already racing toward him, her face twisted with wrath; she hurled herself into him, catching him off balance so that he crashed into the mud.

She turned, crouched. "Wulfgar! Quick!"

Blood seeped through his coat and over her hands.

Then Vidar had grabbed her heel and thin wiry arms snatched her from behind, pinning her elbows back as she kicked and screamed and squirmed. It was useless. The thief held her tight, his wheezing laughter warm against her ear.

Slowly Vidar picked himself up.

She stood still now, breathing hard. She watched him wipe lichen from his scarred face and thin beard, all the time keeping his cold gray eyes on her.

"Traitor!" she said.

He shook his head. "Not so. Wulfgar was that. He was a friend of the sorcerers. Like you are."

She glanced down quickly. Her heart thudded as she saw Wulfgar was still breathing.

"Not for long," Vidar said sadly. "The creature will finish him."

"Creature?"

"That's what I'll tell them. That's what they'll all believe. And I'm afraid that you too will have been its victim. A few knife slashes will look very convincing. I'm sorry this had to be, Jessa, but you can see I can't have any witnesses."

He nodded. Behind her, just for a moment, a hand slackened. In a whirl of panic she tore her arms free and ran, splashing through the bog, dragging the knife from her belt. She raced around the mere, hurtling over tussocks of grass, leaping branches, dodging around rocks, and behind her the thief crashed in pursuit, in the pounding of her breath, the thud of her heart.

She reached the trees and fled in among them, with one glance back. He was close; he ran lithe and low, the long blade gleaming in his hand. She ducked branches, leaves that slapped her face and arms; her coat snagged and she tore it desperately away, hot with fear. Down a slope, around a pile of rocks, and she crumpled there, swallowing breath, the wood swinging crazily around her.

Gasping in air, she flipped over onto her stomach and peered back through the tangle of bracken.

He was coming, slowly now.

"Come on, lady," he said. "This just makes things harder."

Silent, her face set, she let him come. Anger was cold in her, a terrible icy fury that she gripped tight, like the corded hilts in her hands. Let him come. She owed him this.

He edged against the rock, tensed, his small eyes darting. She clenched her teeth; she felt wild and reckless and tingling with a bitter power. She hated him, and Vidar, especially Vidar!

He came to the rock and paused. For a moment he looked the other way.

She was out in an instant, the knife slashing down at him, so that he gave a yell of pain and fury and struck back at her, the blade slicing the air with a swift whistle of sound. As she turned he caught her sleeve; with a scream of pure anger she tore the coat right off and raced into the trees.

A stream ran down the fell, a small, noisy torrent. She leaped up from rock to rock, reckless, over the fierce falls of peat brown water, the smooth white creamy foam gathering in pools. Up and up, the roar and crash of the falls filling her ears, and the thief climbed after her, swearing and cursing.

Near the top, under low trees, she climbed deftly up into the branches.

Now keep still. Keep still.

She held herself light, among the larch leaves. He was moving somewhere below; she could hear him. How long would he search? Or would he give up, go back and tell Vidar she was dead? Maybe that, she thought scornfully. A thief was usually a liar as well.

He was slower, clumsier. She'd hurt him.

She glanced at the blade; it was clean. But he'd yelled.

Slowly the rustles of his movements grew distant. Jessa took deeper breaths. For long minutes she waited; minutes that lengthened to an infinite, unguessable time of quiet breathing, listening, watching. Rustles and breezes moved in the clustered trees; the water below roared and churned over the rocks. Noises of the forest closed slowly about her, the breeze through the topmost branches, the birdsong.

It was the birds that convinced her he was gone.

After a while she knew she had to take the chance. He might be near, he might be lurking, but she had to get back to Wulfgar. She had to tell the others about Vidar. The thought of him made her drive her nails into the soft trunk.

Cautiously she slid down the branches, her hands rasping the crumbling bark. Then she waited. No sign of him.

She pushed through to the stream and began to clamber down it again. One foot slid into the water with a splash; she stopped and glanced around quickly.

Still nothing. And yet, if he had any sense, this was where he'd wait. Anxious now, she climbed down the stream, lowering herself carefully, forced to put away weapons and use both hands. Water foamed and roared about her; she slipped again, soaked with spray.

At the bottom of the slope she looked around. Trees stood in all directions—which way had she come? Silence hung behind the race of the water. She could shout, but only the wretch with the knife would hear her. Or had he really gone? With a sudden shiver of alarm she remembered her coat. He had it! Vidar's words echoed in her head. A few knife slashes. Very convincing.

Now she was really afraid—a chill of terror she hadn't had time to feel before. She plunged into the wood, heading along the overgrown bank of the stream. It had to run into the mere.

It took her a long, anxious time to find the hollow; as she scrambled eagerly down to it her feet sank into the deep wet mosses.

It was empty.

Cold, uneasy, she ran over to where Wulfgar had fallen. The flattened mosses were still springing back into place. Two dark clots stained their fronds.

She turned, crouched, looked at the trampled ground. Men had been here, lots of them.

She forced herself to think.

Skapti and the others had come. They must have heard her scream. But had Wulfgar still been alive? And what did they think had happened to her, that they didn't even search?

She stared out at the rippling brown water.

That wretched coat!

Then suddenly she smiled, a hard smile. Wulfgar must be alive. The urgency had been to get him back to the hold. But with Vidar to look after him, how long before . . . there were lots of ways he could finish it. Poison. The pillow over the face. And the others didn't even know!

She leaped up and ran through the forest, pushing her way back the route she and Wulfgar had come, scrambling up the sliding scree, leaping through the trees without thought.

At the edge the fell was empty, the horses gone. And far, far away, tiny blurs among the trees of the valley, she saw them galloping. "Skapti!" she screamed. "Skapti!"

But they were too far to hear her.

Sinking down, she let the weariness and the fear and shock of it all flood over her; a cold trembling and sobbing that burst out despite herself. Clenching her fists, she fought for control. She was alone here. Wulfgar would die and no one would know Vidar had killed him.

But after a few minutes she raised her head, dragging a breath of sudden despair into her lungs.

She had remembered. She wasn't alone.

The creature was out here too.

Twenty-One

With such biting words of rebuke and
reminder he taunts him at every turn.

The hunters arrived back just before dusk.

Hakon, sitting on the fjordshore listlessly tossing in stones, heard the ring of hooves and scrambled up quickly. By the time he reached the hall, men and dogs and horses were everywhere, the air full of voices and angry words.

Grabbing someone's elbow, he asked, "Did you get it? The creature?"

The man shrugged him off. "It got us. Wulfgar's hurt badly. The girl's dead."

"Jessa?"

Astonished, he let the man push away, staring at him without seeing. He couldn't believe it. He thought of how he'd spoken to her right here, only this morning, in her soft leather coat, her hair braided. Jessa? And he hadn't been able to warn her. The fear of it struck him to silence.

Everyone was hurrying into the hall. He went with

them, passive, hustled by holders, women, fishermen.

Inside they gathered in a hushed, anxious throng. Hakon was crushed at the back against the tapestried wall. He leaned back against it, feeling lost. Vidar came in, a crowd of men about him. Skuli was one of them. Everyone fell silent.

"Friends." The priest's voice was low and bitter; his face gray. "There's bad news—bad for this hold and for the whole of the north. You may have heard that Wulfgar is badly hurt. The beast struck him from behind, we think. He's lost much blood. He's unconscious and may not recover."

A ripple of talk ran down the hall. Vidar watched, the scar on his cheek dragging the pale skin.

"What happened?" someone yelled.

"Sorcery." He said it deliberately into the silence.

After a moment he went on. "Wulfgar and Jessa Horolfsdaughter were at the end of the line. Only a few paces into the forest we realized that they were gone. Some rune craft, some filthy sorcery enticed them into the dark. We searched, all of us." He paused, rubbing the back of one hand down his stubbly beard. "I and one of my men found them in a hollow by a mere, a place of stinking lichens and soft, boggy ground. The Jarl lay still—slashed by its claws. Then we saw it." He stared in silent horror at the floor, as if he didn't want to go on.

The crowd kept silent, waiting.

"It was crouched over the remains of the girl—a great, pale thing, a beast of ice, its eyes burning like demons', a rune terror brought down on us by witchcraft and spells. Not a bear, no. I struck at it in my fury, but the sword passed through, as if through mist. It carried the girl off. Only this was left."

And he held up the coat. It was slashed apart, bloodied, almost unrecognizable. But Hakon knew it, and he shook his head bleakly. All over the hall, fingers felt for amulets and thorshammers.

Vidar shook the rag fiercely. "Look at it! All that's left of her! Already it's killed three of our people, and maybe the Jarl too. And friends, tell me, where can this curse have come from if not from the Snow-walkers?"

A roar of approval erupted. Fists were thumped on tables; near Hakon a woman screamed words of hate, lost in the uproar; men shouted, dogs barked frantically. Alarmed, he glanced around. There was no sign of Brochael or Kari, but he didn't care about them. Skapti was missing, probably with them. Skapti had been kind to him, he realized dismally; Skapti and Jessa. He began to shove his way to the back of the hall, filled with a sudden, cold foreboding.

"And why look to Gudrun for this?" Vidar shouted, his voice clear and harsh. "She's gone, long gone. But she was no fool—we all know that! She left us her son. And what weird coincidence brought him here the night of Freyr's warning, if it wasn't that the god was warning us of him. Of Kari!" He had to shout now, above the noise. "Kari brought this creature! Why else wouldn't he go to hunt it when Wulfgar needed him? Will we let him enslave us and torment us, like his mother did?"

The walls rang with shouting, a storm of anger, but not everyone was convinced. One, a tall man named Mord, leaped onto a bench and yelled, "Wait! Listen to me! Listen! Kari Ragnarsson helped save this hold, this whole realm, from her sorcery! We can't forget that! There's no proof he's responsible for these deaths. And above all Wulfgar trusts him."

"He does not."

Vidar said it quietly, and the shock of it brought stillness.

He spoke ominously now. "Only yesterday he told me this. He feared that Kari had only come back here to claim his father's rights, and his mother's place. To rule us all. To weave a web of sorcery around us, as she did, moving our hearts, our souls, making our minds do what he wants, think what he wants."

Hakon had reached the stairs. No one was guarding them. He raced up, hearing the noise gather again below.

There were doors, many of them, all closed. Wulfgar's men clustered outside one anxiously.

"Where's Skapti?" he snapped.

"In there."

He pushed through the ring and flung the door open.

Wulfgar lay on a bed heavy with woven coverings. He was pale, and seemed hardly to be breathing. Kari was bent over him, his long fingers touching the Jarl's forehead.

"Leave him alone," Hakon snarled.

"What do you want?" Skapti came forward and grabbed his elbow roughly. The skald looked bone weary; his eyes were hard, unremembering.

Hakon said, "Are you in it with them?"

"In what?"

"I wanted to warn you—you were . . . you and Jessa . . ." He turned nervously. "Get out, Skapti. Now. Vidar will be here."

But already the noise was loud on the stairs.

The big, tawny man, Brochael, had an ax in his hands. He caught Kari by the shoulder, pulling him back.

Skapti turned angrily. "What's going on?"

Then Vidar was in the room, backed by a crowd, among them a small rat-faced man at the back.

"We want you, Kari," Vidar said quietly. "No one else."

Brochael raised the blade. "I'll kill any man who touches him," he said evenly.

Vidar nodded. "What about you?" He turned to Skapti. "You're Wulfgar's benchmate. Where do you stand in all this?"

Skapti stared at him grimly, as if he had begun to understand. "With Wulfgar. All of us do."

"Not all." Vidar came forward. "Keep away from the Jarl," he said fiercely to Kari. "Haven't you done enough? And why kill Jessa? Why?"

Kari looked up, his eyes bright. "Jessa is alive."

"Liar! I saw it happen!"

Unmoving, Kari watched them. His eyes had no color, he looked at them each in turn and they quailed, remembering always Gudrun and her power, the cold draining of your mind as you stood before her. Then he shook his straight silvery hair. "Jessa's alive. I know that. And this creature is not my sending. It has nothing to do with me."

Vidar came up to him slowly, ignoring Brochael's threat until the ax lifted.

"We can't take the chance. We have to protect the Jarl from you."

"No," Skapti said unhappily.

"Yes."

Vidar reached out quickly, grabbed Kari's wrist. Brochael moved, but almost at once Vidar fell with a sudden cry to the wooden floor, curling, rolling in agony.

"Stop!" he screamed. "He's killing me! Stop him!"

Kari stared at him, almost in astonishment; then the men surged forward, overpowering Brochael with difficulty, two of them staggering back, the rest leaping onto him and Kari, striking with fists and hilts until Skapti pulled them off, yelling in his loudest hall voice.

On the floor Kari slowly uncurled. The skald crouched. "Leave him! This is Wulfgar's hold and under his law! He's not dead yet!"

Some of the men helped Vidar up. Ashen and shaking, he straightened out of their arms. For a moment he seemed unable to speak. Then he said, "Take them both below. Chain them."

Skapti stood up. "Not that."

"We must! Don't you see, the boy has power. He attacked me with it. He must be held secure or he could do anything."

Brochael struggled furiously in the grip of two men. "Lying fool," he muttered. "Skapti, for Thorssake . . ."

The skald bent and picked Kari up gently. "I'll carry him myself, Brochael. No one else will touch him. And I swear no one will harm either of you. Not until Wulfgar speaks on this."

"And if he dies?" Brochael snapped.

"There'll be a new Jarl," Vidar said. He turned to the door, and only Hakon glimpsed his small, hard smile.

Twenty-Two

The dark death-shadow
drove always against them.

The smell of blood was in the forest.

Raising its dripping mouth from the pool the spell-spun creature sensed it, the edges of its nostrils widening.

Blood. And more.

Men, horses, dogs. And more.

Anger.

The creature let the complex wash of fear and wrath into its mind. Excited, it roared and thrashed, tearing the branches from a young spruce, crushing the pungent leaves in one clenched fist.

Then it tossed them down and followed the scent. In

these last days it had moved always upright, rarely crouching as at first. It walked, an eerie glimmer in the murk, and the birds fled before it. Pushing between branches it came to its high vantage point and looked down. About it the forest breathed and murmured in the breezy afternoon, the cold wind strengthening ominously. Gray heavy cloud gathered in the west. The thing sniffed, recognizing the signs of rain.

And there it was, something else, something faint on the wind, a new scent. Human. Not too far away.

Find it, the voice instructed firmly.

Stalking forward, the sending moved downhill. Its head was high now, tall among the trees. Clouds of whining gnats tormented it, so that it snarled and beat them off. Among the clefts and broken hillsides of the steep wood, it slid back to all fours awkwardly, snapping boughs with its weight, dragging out a shallow-rooted sapling in a shower of soil as it steadied itself. Far into the trees the noise rang, a cracking, splintering progress.

And then the rain came, silent at first, then a steady hard beat of drops pattering among branches, rolling from leaves and stalks. The wood dropped into a blurred, trickling place; the pelt of the rune beast clotted, became sodden, water dripping into its small eyes. Oblivious, it strode out of the trees onto the lakeside. Then it stopped.

Scents drifted, faint in the wet air. Rain fell on the water, dimpling the surface with millions of dancing ripples, appearing and disappearing so that the creature gazed, half-entranced, until the voice snapped at it and the sudden, sharp hunger made it turn away.

It moved around the lakeside to a place of rocks, clefts, deep rubble. This was where the scent was. Among these slippery, wet stones. In this cliff face.

A blur in the rain, the creature slipped between the boulders. Then it crouched.

Somewhere near, its prey breathed.

The creature turned its head, and saw a small, dark cleft, a cave with a narrow entrance.

In there.

Twenty-Three

Solitary and wretched . . .

Jessa crouched absolutely still.

The cave was a tiny, dark space, the entrance just a slit among rocks. Too narrow for the creature to get in, she was sure. But she knew it was out there. She had heard the slow crack and snap of branches, heard its footsteps, and once a strange snuffle, like a dog makes after meat.

All at once something blurred past, out there in the rain; then, with a suddenness that snatched her breath, the entrance went dark.

She slammed back against the rock wall, knife in hand.

Slowly the creature put its arm into the cave.

She saw a great, heavy limb, pale with wet fur. Its hand was huge, not human, but with five thick stubby fingers, each with a curved claw that slashed across the dark, gripping at nothing.

Flat as she could be, she watched it, fascinated. The beast must be far stronger than she'd imagined. As the hand swung past her cheek she turned her head with a gasp, smelling it close, the wet, forest smell, the fur clotted with moss and rain and blood, the claws split and raw.

It roared, restlessly groping for her. She hardly breathed; her stomach and shoulders ached with taut fear, and still the hand stretched closer, the muscles straining under the thick pelt.

Then it pulled back.

And was gone.

She dared not move. For what seemed like hours she stayed there, waiting, letting her breath out slowly, shivering with aftershock. At last she peeled herself off the wall, and found the back of her jerkin soaked with sweat and running damp. Before her legs gave way she sat down, huddled in the far corner, her arms tight about her knees.

Gods, she thought. What a mess.

Was it still out there? There were no sounds now. Yes, there were, scraps of movement, rustles. Nervously she counted them off, a bird screech, rain splatter, the slither of soil.

Any of them might be the beast.

The cleft entrance showed dimness. It was getting dark. Skapti and the men would be home by now. There'd be panic about Wulfgar, lies about what had happened to her. And here she was, stuck in this hole!

She stabbed both knives savagely into the mud before her and flung her arms back around her knees. She had to be calm. She had to think! There were two choices: Go out, and try to get through to the nearest farm—probably Skulisstead. Or stay the night here, without a coat or water or any way of making a fire.

But that was only one choice really, and she knew it. The forest at night was far too dangerous to risk—wolves, boar, morasses, cliffs—far too easy to get lost in, and the spell beast might be sitting out there with its back against a tree just waiting for her. No, she'd have to stay, at least until daylight. She shook her head bitterly. Nothing to eat, nothing to drink except trickles of rain, and worst of all, the cold. The cold would be bad, but not enough to kill her. There was just room to stand, move her arms, walk a few steps. She'd be in a bad way, but it might have been worse, she told herself. A few weeks earlier, and she'd have frozen.

Laying her head sideways on her knees, she began to think carefully. Vidar had struck Wulfgar down coldly and viciously. It had been planned, the whole thing, probably for a while now. Skapti had never trusted the priest, had he—and he'd been right. And it was easy to see Vidar's next step. He had to finish Wulfgar, and then get rid of Kari.

Only Kari and Brochael could stop him now.

But even Kari might not know what the priest had done. If only she could have warned Wulfgar! But you did, she told herself sharply. And all it did was make things worse, make the priest notice you. "Stupid," she said aloud, and instantly a leaf rustle close outside set her heart thudding.

Nothing came near the cleft.

After a while she forced herself back to her thoughts. Kari was in danger, and so was Wulfgar, and everyone would believe she was dead, even Vidar. Yes! Maybe even him. And that might be the one chance, the only chance, that would save her. If he thought she was dead he wouldn't be searching for her. He wouldn't be worried. If she could get back to the hold unseen; if she could only get back in time, then everyone would believe her. She grinned, there in the dark. Her safety depended on the thief's lies. And his cowardice. Now there was an irony.

Sometime later she jerked awake, gripping the knives hard.

Something had moved and splashed down at the lake. As she sat there she felt the stiffness of cold in her back and arms, the dragging ache. After a while she scrambled up wearily and paced up and down, shivering, in the tiny space. Thorsteeth, she was cold! Bitterly cold. And hungry. Strangely, hugely hungry.

Carefully she crept to the opening. Sleet pattered against her face; she licked it from her lips gratefully. Then she reached out and tore a limp piece of moss from the rock, tugging it free and stepping back quickly into the dark.

Head back, she squeezed the water out of it; it slid down her throat and tasted foul, but did something for her thirst. She squeezed the handful dry, then looked thoughtfully at the green fronds. Reindeer ate it. It couldn't be poisonous, could it? And she was sore with hunger; it churned like a blackness inside her and around her, as if it was an enormous creature itself.

Reluctantly she nibbled the moss. It tasted wet, coarse, and bitter. She flung it down, thinking bitterly of hot, spicy

meats, steaming fish. There were plenty of fish out there in
that lake; fungi she knew how to find. But she was stuck in
this hell pit, this earth swallow . . . Skapti would have found
a string of good names for it.

She settled back on the earth floor, curled against the
cold. For a long time she lay awake; then sleep came, or a
kind of half sleep, and she drifted between her aching body
and bitter, disjointed dreams about Kari, and Skapti, and
endless forests, and Wulfgar, always falling, falling slowly
into the moss. And once she thought she dreamed of a
white snake, which crawled into the cave and twisted itself
around her wrist, so that she woke in horror, flicking it off.

After waking for the fourth or fifth time, she saw daylight outside, gray and blear. She was unbearably cold now;
her breath made clouds about her, and the edges of the
knives and her hands and face and clothes were frosted
with a fur of tiny crystals.

Painfully she staggered up. Now she had to take the risk.

For a moment she massaged the blood back into her
legs and fingers. Then, knives in hands, she glided through
the narrow crack into the dawn.

The rocks, glinting with frost, were bare. Nothing
watched her, even from above, where thin pine saplings
sprouted from the crevices. Below, the lake was still, its
waters dull as the sky. Nothing moved among the trees;

the wood was ominously silent.

After a moment of waiting she noticed the creature's prints beside her; they led into a tangle of bracken, then out, away into the wood. Had it gone, then?

Finally Jessa crept quietly down to the lake. She was too thirsty to care now. She drank hurriedly, snatching the icy water up in her palms, always watching the forest.

It had gone. Probably its hunger had been too urgent. And for the moment, she didn't care where it was.

She glanced about, working out her direction, tugging the wet, stray hairs from her face. She had to find a farm, and it might take all day. Picking out something that wriggled in her hair, she sucked cuts and briar tears on her filthy hands.

All day. And by then, she might be too late.

Twenty-Four

Daring is the thing for a fighting man to be remembered by.

Hakon staggered into the storehouse and dumped the logs onto the floor. They toppled and rolled; he kicked them to stillness and wiped the sweat from his face with the back of his good hand. Wearily he crouched, dragged the wood out, and began to arrange it crisscross.

His back ached and his shoulders felt like knots of pain and he'd only been back since last night. They'd been saving all the filthy jobs up; Gretta, Skuli's wife, was good at that. Even though it took him twice as long as anybody else . . . but then she had something to moan about. All day he'd been lugging wood, cutting peats, dragging food out for the pigs and even now, when the children were in bed and the wine jug going around, he still hadn't finished.

He threw the last log down and sat listening to the ragged singing in the house. Celebrating Skuli's luck. Skuli, Vidar's man.

Then he turned quickly. Something had stirred in the dark corner where the horse harness hung, some slight movement, a chink of metal. He backed to the door.

"Stay where you are, Hakon. And don't shout."

Something rose from the straw, a shadowy wraith. As it came forward through a slant of moonlight, he saw her, a girl, splashed and bedraggled. Shadows flowed over her. His fingers clenched with fear.

"Jessa? Gods, Jessa, how can it be you!"

She grinned at him. "Thought I was a ghost, did you?"

"You ought to be! Vidar said you were dead. He said he saw it happen!"

"The creature tore me to pieces, I suppose."

"He's even got your coat. It's all slashed."

She shook her head and sat down wearily, leaning forward over her knees.

He crouched beside her. "You mean it was all a lie?"

"Of course it was, weak brain!" She looked up fiercely. "For Thorssake, Hakon, haven't you got something I can eat? I'm dying of hunger!"

He grinned at her happily. "I'll bet you are. And look at you! Where have you been?"

She was filthy, her hair tangled, torn from its braids; her face and clothes stained and soaked with rain.

"Come into the house with me. They'll be glad—"

"No."

She watched him; he saw the sudden wariness.

"No one is to know I'm here. No one. It's vital. Is Skuli back?"

"He's still at the Jarlshold. He sent me back by myself."

"All the better."

"Jessa," he said urgently, "what's going *on*?"

"Get me some food and I'll explain."

He pulled a doubtful face. "I'm a thrall, remember. I only get what they give me."

"You'll manage," Jessa said, scratching her hair. "If you don't, I may end up eating you."

She managed a wan smile, and he laughed and nodded and went out.

Jessa waited, bone weary. She was so tired she could hardly keep awake, but the hunger was the worst. Where was he?

For a moment of panic she thought he might be telling them all she was there, and her hand drifted to the knife hilt. If he did that she was finished. Both of them, probably. It was an unpleasant idea, and it wouldn't go away. She dragged herself up, slid behind the door and stood there, aching all over.

After a few moments the door swung open. Arms full, he looked around. "Where are you?"

She stepped out. "What have you got?"

Hakon looked surprised. Then he turned and put the things down.

"So you didn't trust me?" he said bitterly.

"Trusting people isn't easy anymore, Hakon, not after what I've seen. Cheese!" She snatched a chunk before he had given her the platter. On it were three slices of barley bread, some goat's cheese, and a few strips of smoked fish. She ate quickly, glancing at the jug of water he put down. "Thanks. It's better than a feast!"

"And I've brought you some clothes. Until yours are dry."

He put down a threadbare shirt and some trousers.

"Yours?"

"Yes. You're lucky. They're clean."

She swallowed and gave him a brief smile. "Good. Turn your back."

While she dressed, she said, "Tell me what happened. First of all, is Wulfgar alive?"

Hakon nodded. "As far as I know. He was last night. Skapti is with him all the time."

She laughed suddenly, a crow of delight, then sat down and went on eating. "Is he? The rogue. Well, go on."

He broke off a corner of the cheese and nibbled it. "I should have brought a lamp."

"Never mind that! Go on!"

Hakon shrugged, turning to look at her. "Vidar told the people about how the creature attacked you and Wulfgar. He showed them your coat."

"And they believed him?"

"Of course. So did I. Jessa, if it wasn't the creature . . ."

She shook her head sharply. "There was no creature. Vidar stabbed Wulfgar in the back. Deliberately. And now I've put you in as much danger as I am, because in all the world, Hakon, we're the only ones who know it."

He stared at her, utterly astounded. "The priest is a traitor?"

"More than a traitor. A murderer. And I think he plans to be the next Jarl."

Quickly she described to him what had happened, the struggle in the muffled, mossy gloom of the clearing, her escape up the rocks, the nightmare of the cave. As she told him how the creature's arm had groped for her he looked at her strangely, but said nothing until she had finished. Then he nodded slowly.

"Skapti and the men must have got there before the priest had time to do any more. But Jessa, Vidar stirred up the people at the hold. He told them it was all Kari Ragnarsson's fault, that his sorcery had brought the creature. Then he had Kari and the big man—"

"Brochael."

"Yes . . . he had them chained up."

In the dimness, she drew a quick breath. "And Kari let this happen?"

"Could he have stopped them?"

She laughed briefly. "Of course he could, if he wanted. I see how it was—he didn't want to touch their minds."

"He touched Vidar's!" Tossing down the straw he'd been bending, he told her about the sudden power that had pushed the priest back, his sprawled, screaming agony.

"He can do that, yes. But he told me he wouldn't."

"Then he lied. As for touching minds, he almost broke into mine."

She stared at him. "You?"

"I tried to tell you at the hunt. He wouldn't let me. Jessa, the night before, Kari came into the hall with those two spirit birds of his. Everyone but me was asleep. The creature came to the door. Kari . . . did something to the door. Its arm came through, Jessa; he touched it. He spoke to it."

She was listening intently. "That doesn't mean—"

"He touched it! He was wearing a witch's band, a knot of snakeskin—"

Suddenly she jumped up. "No. We've all been wrong. We need to trust Kari."

"I don't."

"But I do! I think, last night, that I worked it out. He's my friend, Hakon, and I'd almost forgotten that. We're all under some spell, an invisible, choking net of distrust; we're all tangled in it and we have to break out, to snap it to pieces! And the first step is to get Kari free. Come with me, Hakon."

He looked startled. "I can't!"

"Because you're a thrall."

"Of course! Why else?"

She threw herself down next to him. "Gods, Hakon, we can change that. Wulfgar can change it."

"Why should he?"

"We'd be saving his life."

"And if we don't? If he dies?"

"Then it doesn't matter, really. Our lives won't be worth two brass coins anyway." She gave him a sharp, side-long look. "Although I can keep you out of it. No one knows that you know. But it's your chance, Hakon, to get out of all this! If you really want it."

She knew that she had stung him; he took so long to answer.

"Of course I do."

For a moment she watched him. Then she said, "Can you get me a horse?"

"Now?"

"Now. I've got to get back. I'll wait here, but hurry."

He looked around at the frail timber walls. "What about the beast?"

"That's a good wall Skuli's men have put up."

"You got over it!"

She grinned. "Yes. But the creature won't come here. The Jarlshold, not here. Besides"—she took out the two knives and laid them down—"I've got these. I'm getting quite fond of them."

He gathered the plate and jug and stood up. At the door he turned awkwardly. "We'll need two horses," he said.

Twenty-Five

*The hand is stilled that would openly have
granted your every desire.*

When she woke from a brief, drowsy sleep, he was latching the door; he crouched quickly in the straw.

"Get ready. Two horses are waiting, saddled, out in the field. I led them out; no one heard. They've all gone to bed."

Wearily she sat up and dragged her own shirt over his, and her stiff, muddy jerkin.

"I haven't got a coat for you."

"I'll live. Have you got a comb?"

He pulled one, with broken wooden teeth, from the small pack under his arm. She dragged it through her hair, wincing, then plaiting the long brown braids quickly. "That's better. Lead the way."

Outside, the sky was deep blue-gray, with masses of

cloud in the east. The farm buildings were dark blocks of shadow, silent but for a dog on a long chain that whimpered at Hakon.

"Quiet!" he snapped.

The dog subsided gloomily.

He drew Jessa out of the shadows. "This way."

They ran, two flickers of speed, across the yard and out of the wooden gate, down a track to where two horses grazed under a tree. Sheep bleated and looked up, watching as they chewed. The soft tearing of their tongues in the grass was the only sound.

Jessa and Hakon scrambled up onto the horses—the same scraggy ponies as before, she thought—and turned their heads southwest, into the dark. They rode without speaking, through the pastures scattering dim huddles of sheep, down the fellside, picking a careful way past boulders, leaping the tumbling streams.

Behind them the sky darkened. Storm clouds spread over the stars and a wind sprang up, gusting the manes of the ponies.

"Rain again," Jessa said, glancing back.

"Maybe snow." Hakon let his empty hand swing beside him without noticing. She looked at it, curious.

As they galloped on he said, "They'll come after us."

"Tomorrow."

"Mm. I turned the other ponies loose. It'll take them a while to round them up."

"Good. But I think we've got more to worry about ahead than behind."

"*You* might have."

She was silent, knowing he was right. A runaway thrall would be lucky to escape with his life. Guiltily she said, "Thanks for the clothes."

He shrugged. "I hope the fleas don't bite you too much."

Jessa stopped scratching and glared at him. "I think they're enjoying the change."

Coming to the wider fells, they could gallop, the horses thundering over the black grass. In a few hours they had ridden close enough to the Jarlshold to see the smoke from its fires drifting against the dark sky.

Jessa pulled the weary pony to a halt. "Let them drink. I need to think now."

A stream gushed down among dim banks of bracken; the water was icy, meltwater from the mountains, clear of any plant or fish, cascading in roars of white foam. As she lay full-length and drank, Jessa felt the cold of it burn her throat and chest; she splashed some on her face and scrubbed away dirt and stains with the end of her sleeve. She felt sharper now, more alert. Carefully Hakon lifted water in his good hand. Halfway to his lips he dropped it.

"Listen! Horses!"

Instantly they were both flat.

The sound of galloping came from the Jarlshold; a group of horsemen. Even from this distance Jessa saw them pass, shadows in the night. They crossed the stream farther down and galloped away toward the east. She thought they seemed heavily armed, with long ash spears slung from the saddles.

Jessa picked herself up. "I'll bet I know where they're going."

"Where?" he asked, worried.

"To find my remains." She gave a snort of laughter; he stared at her in disbelief.

"Jessa, it isn't funny! Have you any idea of how we felt when we heard . . . all those people? The stunned silence, the women crying. They all like you."

She was quiet a moment. Then she said, "I know. But not Kari?"

"Kari said you were alive."

"So he knows that much. Let's hope Vidar doesn't believe him." She glanced at the ponies. "Look, it'll be harder now not to be seen. I think we should leave the horses here, among the trees. They'll be all right. There's water, plenty of grass—"

"There's also a troll with claws like plowshares."

"Then we won't tether them. They can run. Don't

worry, Hakon, if it comes to the worst, I can pay for them. Though it won't."

He stood up abruptly. "It must be a fine thing to have money."

"It is." She looked at him coolly.

He gathered the ponies' harnesses and led them among the dark trees. Watching him go, Jessa thought that she'd never known a thrall so touchy about himself. But then, she told herself, turning back to the water, you've never really known a thrall at all.

Skapti opened the door and had to stoop to enter; behind him Vidar's man lingered uneasily. The dim cell was bitterly cold.

"Why haven't they got a fire?" he snapped.

"Vidar's orders."

"Let Vidar rot in Hel. Light one now."

The man shook his head, stubborn. "Not my job, skald. Get some house thrall."

Skapti crouched down by Brochael. "I'll try and get it seen to. How are you?"

Brochael lifted the chains on his wrist and let them drop. "I've been better," he said, the anger still clotting his voice.

"And you, runemaster?"

"Dizzy." Kari looked wan, even in this dimness. He sat

knees up in the straw, his thin wrists manacled with long chains to the wall. "But Wulfgar. How is he?"

"Still unconscious. He knew me briefly this morning." The skald shook his head. "I wish there was more I could do for you. But Vidar's the one giving the orders."

"Stay with Wulfgar. Look after him." Kari's voice was urgent. "Don't leave him if you can help it. I have such a strange feeling about all this. Besides"—he smiled—"I have this great bear here to look after me."

Brochael growled out a laugh. "You can look after yourself. As Vidar found."

"I didn't touch him."

They stared at him, and he looked absently across at the tiny window where stars glimmered. "He pretended. He did that himself."

"What's he planning?" Skapti mused. "This injury to Wulfgar is just what he needed. If Wulfgar dies . . ."

"He'll be Jarl. And we'll be dead. But Jessa . . ."

"Jessa?" The skald glanced at Brochael. "Do you believe all this, about Jessa being alive?"

"If Kari says so." Brochael grinned. "And about that girl, Skapti, I'd believe anything."

Halfway across the marsh, balanced on two tussocks of grass, Hakon heard them. He glanced around wildly.

There they were, waiting on the trunk of a dead, drowned tree, its smooth gray boughs like hands, grasping for the rising moon.

"Jessa!"

"What?" She turned irritably, dragging her foot from the black ooze.

"There!"

In the green gloom of the marsh, amid flickers of fume and mist, he saw her turn. Then she went on. "I see them. He's sent them out to look for us."

For a moment Hakon waited, hearing the plop and ripple of something in the black mire. Then he scrambled after her quickly.

Two hunched shadows, the ravens watched him go.

Twenty-Six

It was declared then to men and received by every ear,
that for all this time a survivor had been living . . .

He slipped between the boats to the last in the row. She sat behind it, her feet dangling over the black water. She threw the last crust in soundlessly. "Well?"

"The hall door is barred. No guard. But there'll be one outside the prison, if we go there."

She nodded. "That will be up to Kari."

Hakon stared at her through the darkness. "What can he do? He doesn't even know we're here."

She gave him a sly, amused glance. "Doesn't he? What about those?"

The ravens were perched on a nearby roof, outlined against the moon. They looked like great wooden gargoyles, until one karked, and scratched under its wing.

"Odin's birds," Hakon muttered, remembering them falling on the beast in the wood.

"Thought and Memory. The ravens that told him everything that had happened in the world. I think these two do something like that for Kari."

She stood up briskly. "Ready?"

"I just hope you're right about Kari."

"I'm right," she said simply. "Anyway, you've forgotten the spell creature. Only Kari can deal with that." She dragged the damp hair from her face, pulled on her gloves, and jammed the knives firmly in her belt. "Right. Now, I know another way into the hall. There are too many doors and passageways in that place—Gudrun's maze, they called it."

Then she paused and turned. "For the last time, Hakon, you don't have to come."

He laughed. "Jessa, I've run away from Skuli, I've stolen his food and his horses, and I can't do anything else to make life worse!"

"So?"

"So I'm coming. If a one-handed fighter is any use."

She nodded, looking up. "I'm glad."

The moon was a cold ball now, wobbling among mists. As it rose, the forests of spruce and fir on the far side of the fjord scarred it with their black tops. Slowly it drifted free of them, into mist and torn cloud.

"A wolf chases it," Hakon said, standing. "One day it will be caught and swallowed."

She nodded. "Meanwhile it makes shadows like Gudrun's monster."

For a moment they watched the darkness gather; it rose from the water and out of the trees. The water lapping the wharf was cold and restless, glinting black and silver. An almost invisible snow began to fall, clinging to their cheeks and foreheads, melting instantly. Stars glimmered in the east, until a cloud ate them slowly.

Jessa tugged the dirty hood over her face. "Recognize me?"

"Your own mother wouldn't."

She turned to the birds. "Tell him we're coming."

Head to one side, one of them watched her. Then it flapped away and the other followed. Hakon touched the amulet under his shirt furtively, hoping she wouldn't notice. All this witchery unnerved him, he knew that. Jessa probably knew it too.

They came out from among the moored boats, ran along the wharf and slipped between the houses. The night was empty. From shadow to shadow they slid, behind the smithy where the day's last red sparks glowered under ashes, past henhouses, yards, deserted stalls. Only once did a little girl open her door and glimpse them, caught in the slot of light; then the door was slammed quickly, the bar jammed into place.

They felt alone, locked out, outsiders. With the coming of darkness the Jarlshold had become a place of bolts and shutters, all living things drawn safe inside. Fear of the shadow maker drifted like the snow, invisible until it touched your skin. Whatever it was that stalked the hold at night, no one even wanted to catch sight of it.

They ran quickly, peering around corners. Snow blinded them; Hakon saw pale shapes among its slither; he spun at imaginary footsteps and the bang of a shed door in the wind.

Suddenly the hall loomed up out of the darkness. Grabbing his arm, Jessa said, "Quiet now," and led him around to the back of the building, their footsteps crunching the thin blown layer of snow. Gaping dragon mouths dripped icicles above them. Briefly the moon lit a dust of snow on dark ledges.

"Where now?"

"Down here," she whispered.

At the bottom of some steps, almost overgrown with bare, tangled stems of ivy, was a small door, green with age.

"I pointed this out to Wulfgar last time I was here. A weak point." He saw her grin in the dark. "I'm glad he didn't listen."

A sound behind made them crouch, alert. The moon drifted in white veils over the cold roofs.

"Nothing." She turned back, fumbling for the latch. It lifted easily, with a tiny creak, but the wood was so swollen that the door had to be forced open. They both dragged at it, wincing at the noise. Finally a narrow crack showed in the wall.

"Go on," Jessa whispered.

He slid in first, the sword tight in his left hand. She took one look back into the night and squeezed in after him.

The passageway was icy cold and dim. Voices came

from the hall, somewhere above. Someone must be still awake. Far down by the stairway a torch guttered on the stone wall.

"Down here," she murmured.

The steps down to the underground rooms were dank and earthy. In the bitter cold the damp on the walls had the faintest skin of ice; it cracked under a finger touch. At the bottom, around a corner, was a long passage with a row of doors, all half open.

Silently they slipped from opening to opening, room to empty room. Each smelled of decay, mold, used air. Hakon grasped his sword, rubbing dust from his eyes with the back of his empty hand. Wulfgar didn't seem to keep many prisoners.

At the bend in the passage Jessa held him back. He peered over her shoulder soundlessly.

Far down there was a man sitting on a stool, his legs stretched out, and a lamp on the floor by his feet. He was leaning back against the wall, whistling tunelessly between his teeth. His hands moved; in the dimness they could see he was whittling wood with a small knife.

"They're in there," Jessa breathed. There was an anger in her look and Hakon thought for a moment he had made some sound, but Jessa was thinking about Kari, his empty years of imprisonment down here, and how Gudrun seemed to have drawn him back here again.

"Now what?" he murmured.

"We wait."

"And what if someone comes?"

She glared at him. "Silence them. But he's armed and the passage is too long to take him by surprise unless . . ."

Even as she said it, the whistling stopped.

Turning back, they saw the man on his feet; he faced the prison door doubtfully. "What's going on in there?"

"Get ready," Jessa breathed.

He rattled the lock and chain. There was no window to see through and no answer from inside.

The keeper glanced down the long passage nervously. Then he drew out the key and unlocked the door, pulling the chain clear, but even as he pushed the door wide, someone came and shoved him hard from behind, pitching him into the dirty straw of the cell on his face. A rusty sword jabbed the back of his neck.

"Stay there! Don't move!"

Jessa pulled off her hood and grinned at the prisoners.

"Girl," Brochael said, already up on his knees, "you're a beautiful sight for someone dead three days. Around his neck, look, there in the pouch."

She had the keys out quickly and unlocked the big man's chains first, and he stood up and stamped and flung his arms about. "Thorsteeth. Another night in here would have finished me."

Unlocking Kari's wrists, she muttered, "How is Wulfgar?"

"We don't know," he said. "Everything about Wulfgar is dark to me. Jessa, what happened out there?"

She helped him up; the chain had left red welts on his white skin. As she gripped his wrists, her fingers touched the snakeskin knot; for a moment a jolt, a crackle like lightning jerked her fingers wide. She stared at him, astonished. Then she said, "Vidar tried to murder him. Vidar! There was no creature."

"*What!*"

Appalled, Brochael caught her arm.

"It's true. I saw it."

"Gods!" For a moment he was silent, taking it in; then he grabbed Kari's shoulder. "Can you walk?"

"Yes . . ."

"Right, now listen to me. If we stay here we're finished. There's no safety if Vidar thinks we know. Have you got horses, Jessa?"

"Two."

"We'll steal more." He glanced over at the thrall chaining the keeper firmly to the wall. "Is he yours?"

"No, he's a friend. Hakon."

Hakon came over; Brochael nodded at him. "All the better. Come on, now. Be silent."

"No. Wait."

They all looked at Kari; he looked at Jessa. Then he said, "If we leave Wulfgar here, Vidar will kill him secretly. Then Vidar will be Jarl and no one will be able to stop him. You have to tell them, Jessa, all the men of the hold. You have to tell them what you saw."

"What if they don't believe me?"

His pale eyes widened. "Jessa, you're alive! That shows he's been lying. We have to do it; we've no choice."

Reluctantly she nodded.

Brochael swore, but Kari silenced him with a look.

"Trust me. They'll be in the hall."

Twenty-Seven

He was my closest counselor,
he was keeper of my thoughts.

Not many of them had been sleeping; there was too much anxiety for that, too much fear of what might be prowling outside. But when they saw Kari, all the men in the hall sat still and stared with astonishment. Some of them, already wrapped in blankets for the night, rolled over to see why the silence had fallen.

Behind him, the others waited, Brochael with the prison keeper's sword, Jessa under her dark hood.

For a moment Vidar seemed lost for words. Then he yelled, "Take him back!"

No one seemed ready to obey. Kari looked tense, dangerous. He said, "This time no one touches me, Vidar, or the pain will be real, I promise you."

He walked forward into the firelight, a slight figure in dark clothes, his hair glinting. At his back Brochael seemed huge.

One of the ravens churred quietly in the roof; men glanced up, uneasy.

"What do you want?" Vidar fumed. "How did you get out?"

Kari ignored him. Turning to the men, he said, "Some of you know me—those that are Wulfgar's men. Here's someone else you know."

Jessa tugged off her hood. "So I'm dead, am I, Vidar?" she murmured.

She enjoyed that moment immensely. The flicker of astonishment that opened his face to her told her all she wanted to know. The thief had lied, even to him.

The men were standing now, silent. Some of them picked up weapons.

She raised her voice. "Listen to me, holders. There was no creature on that hunt—we never even saw it. This man," and she pointed to him with a sudden fury that made her finger shake, "this man stabbed Wulfgar Osricsson in the back. I saw him."

The hall rang with noise. Among it Vidar stood still, his face set.

"Liar!" he said.

"It's true. He would have killed me too if he could—or rather that sniveling little wretch over there would have."

Heads turned toward the thief. Jessa had spotted him at once, hunched up over a bowl of soup by the fire. Now he was gawping at her, then at Vidar. The priest flashed him a look of pure hatred, then whirled back. Facing the men, he raised his hands, palms out.

"You know I would never move against Wulfgar!"

"Not even to be Jarl!" Brochael sneered. "You men!" he roared. "You, Mord Signi, and Guthlac, and the rest of you. You know Jessa. Who would you rather believe? She even saw the knife go in!"

"They're trying to snare you in rune magic, in some sort of spell!" Vidar hadn't given up, but the scar stood out against his flushed skin. "Don't you see, the Snow-walker is moving your minds! He can do that. How do you know that's Jessa! I saw her dead in the moss—I brought you her coat, slashed to pieces! This is some fetch, some tangle of evil he's conjured. . . ."

It was then he realized they were not even looking at him. They were staring, all of them, over his shoulder. Slowly he too turned his head.

Wulfgar was standing on the steps behind him.

The Jarl was white-faced, his dark hair tousled. Skapti hung anxiously at his side, as if to steady him should he stagger, but Wulfgar just stood there, letting the blustering echoes drift away into silence.

Jessa felt a great wave of delight and relief surge inside her. The men shouted, whooped, murmured into stillness, but Wulfgar only waited, his eyes on Vidar, unsmiling.

Then, painfully, he came down the steps and faced the priest. Their faces were masks of flame and shadow.

"It seems I made a mistake," the Jarl said quietly. "I thought there was only one evil thing among us. But all the time there were two. As well as the witch's sending there was yours, and yours is worse. Lies. Treachery. Making me doubt my own friends. A net of slander spun over my own hold. Ambition. And murder, almost."

Vidar stumbled back one step. The men closed on him quickly, but Wulfgar stood still.

"And the worst thing is that I thought you were my friend, my adviser. We laughed together, hunted, ate together. I liked you, Vidar. And all the time that was a mask, was it? All that time you were plotting my death, plotting against all of us. Was any of it real? Any of it?"

For a moment the priest went to speak; then his lips closed. Wulfgar gave him a hard, bitter look.

"Not a good answer."

He turned away deliberately.

Vidar took one step forward quickly; then he screamed in pain, flung down the knife, and crumpled over his blackened hand, moaning and cursing.

On the floor the hilt smoked. The stench of burning rose from it.

Three men grabbed the priest and hauled him up.

Wulfgar, startled, glanced at Kari. "Thank you. From what Skapti tells me, you owed him that."

Kari nodded. He went over to the priest. "But you're wrong about one thing, Wulfgar. This man has no power of his own. I think this was Gudrun's doing too, in a way. Remember what she said to me. No one will trust you, she said. She sent this, just as she sent the other thing."

He came forward. Vidar clutched his burned hand

warily and tried to back away, but the men gripped him.

"Have you ever looked at reflections?" Kari asked him quietly. "I don't have one—mine is in a far-off place, far to the north, beyond the bears and the icebergs, where the world plunges into nothing. That's where she is, my reflection. Identical, yes, but opposite. Reflections are opposites. One lifts the right hand, the other the left. Haven't you noticed that?"

The priest stared at him, his narrow face blank, as if he had exhausted all feeling.

"Why did you do it?" Skapti asked.

Vidar still looked at Kari. Then he said, "Because sorcery is wrong. It corrupts. Because Wulfgar allowed you to come here and I knew that you were dangerous. I believed what I said about you. One day you will destroy us. That's why Gudrun left you here."

Kari was silent. Jessa knew he had been wounded; Vidar's words hung in the air like a dark chill.

Suddenly she spoke out. "You did it for your own ambition," she said. "No other reason."

Kari looked at her, a grateful flicker. Tension broke. The men moved, agreeing.

"Well said," Skapti muttered.

As if in answer, one of the ravens squawked oddly, and Kari glanced up at it.

"Wulfgar, we still have Gudrun to deal with. Her creature is coming. Clear the hall quickly. Get your men out. This is my fight now."

Lowering himself with a wince of pain into the chair, Wulfgar said, "You heard him. All of you, out."

"I'm staying," Jessa said firmly. She went over and kissed Wulfgar gently on the forehead.

"What's that for?" he asked, smiling.

"For being alive!"

He shrugged. "Thank a hard life. And Skapti—who'd bully anyone back to existence."

The skald folded his lanky arms. "I'm staying too. If I have to make songs about this creature I need to see it."

"That's never stopped you before," Brochael murmured.

Hakon watched the last of the men hurry out. He wondered if he should go with them, and then remembered he was free—for the moment at least. Skuli had scuttled off already. He'd make up his own mind. And though he was afraid, he wanted to stay.

"As for Vidar," Wulfgar snapped, "he can stay too. Let him see what this sorcery is."

By now the hall was almost empty, and dark.

"If this fails," Kari said, turning to Wulfgar suddenly, "you must all get out and burn the hall with the thing inside. No sword will hurt it, Wulfgar. Promise me you'll do that."

"No promises," the Jarl said lightly.

Kari shook his head ruefully. "You're a stubborn man." Then he turned to Brochael. "Go and open the door."

"What!"

"Open it. Wide. And keep yourself behind it."

For a moment the big man looked down at him, bitterly anxious. "I hope you know what you're doing, little prince."

"So do I," Kari said wryly.

"It could kill you."

Kari shook his head. "Haven't you realized why she sent it here yet, Brochael? Not to kill. To be killed."

Brochael stared at him. Then he jammed the sword into his belt and turned away without a word. As he walked down the hall his boots rang on the flagstones; he grasped the wooden bar and heaved it aside with a mighty effort, the rumble echoing in the high rafters.

Then, slowly, he dragged the great door wide.

The night was black. Stars glinted.

Snow swirled in, sliding over the door with a faint, uneasy hiss.

Twenty-Eight

Gliding through the shadows came
the walker in the night.

It strode now, through the marsh.

Water splashed its face; the green slime of algae clotted it; mud splattered the spread claws.

Snow, like a white dissolving mist, opened and closed mysterious pathways about it, gave it glimpses of stars and water and a huddle of dark buildings against the dim sky.

Ahead, low in the distance, was the hall, lit with red light. From its wide-open door a mist of flame light breathed into the dark, as if the building was a great crouching dragon, lying asleep, its fires low.

Eagerly the rune beast stalked through the mists and the cold fog wraiths that drifted from the marsh; it breathed cold clouds against the stars. Snow stuck to its sharp face.

It came to the edge of the mud, to firmer ground. Already its hunger was immense. Here it became unbearable. Hunger was the empty world about it, the vast, frosty silences of the sky. Hunger was her voice in its ears, in its belly, in its sharpening, tangled mind.

Everything is ready now, she whispered. *Everything.*

Her voice was a cold breeze among the houses. She crossed its path like a shadow, slinking into the grass. *You'll see. My snake bond grips him, and he'll use it. I left it for him. I left it for you.*

Among the houses now, the dark timbers. Inside them the rune creature sensed terror, the humans crouched and listening, the smell of fear, the snorting, restless animals. It strode down the pathways the snow made, down the long dark openings of its pain, and ahead the hall rose like a fortress unlocked, a grim black wall of snow-dusted stone.

The door was open, a red mouth.

The creature stopped, one great hand on the wall.

In that opening lay the end of all its hunger; dimly it knew that. And yet even from here it could sense him, the one who waited, the one who had reached out and touched it, a strange, cold touch. And it gathered all its strength and made the question in its mind, knotted it together from sounds and memories and fears.

"What do you want me to do?"

Whatever he says, she answered. *He will unleash you, not I. The power is his, and I've made sure he will hurt enough to use it. Feast, my friend.*

The creature stood, silent.

Then after a moment it crouched under the lintel, and went in.

Twenty-nine

The monster strained away;
the man stepped closer.
The monster's desire was
for darkness between them.

The thing loomed in the doorway.

In the dim spaces of the hall it rose against the rafters, a pale glimmer wreathed with mist and smoke, snow scattering from it.

Before it, Kari seemed very small, in a wilderness of stone.

Brochael hung back in the shadows of the doorway, watching.

It was not an animal. Not a man either exactly, but like one, Jessa thought, very like one. Its eyes moved, fixing on Kari; it roared and slashed at him viciously.

Kari flinched, but held his ground.

The creature seemed wary of coming closer. It swung quickly and looked behind it, but Brochael jerked back out of sight.

Then Kari spoke to it. "Listen to me."

The rune beast stared. For a moment Jessa thought a flicker of recognition showed in its face.

"This is what you want."

Kari held out his hand. The snakeskin band dangled from his white fingers.

The creature looked at it, making a peculiar wordless murmur in its throat.

"She left this here. She left it for me, and it drew you here. Over all the miles, through forests, over mountains, this was what you hungered for. It has enormous power. I think it has enough to enslave you or to set you free. Enough to fill all the emptiness in you."

He turned it, thoughtfully, in his fingers. The skin gleamed, fire red.

Wulfgar stirred uneasily. "Wasn't that Gudrun's?" he breathed.

Jessa nodded, unable to speak. She remembered Gudrun flinging it down like a challenge, her cold voice saying, "You'll use them, as I did. We always do."

Now Kari held the shadow bringer still, by what power she dared not think.

The creature's claw reached out; Kari stepped back. There was a tense pause; then with a roar of pain the beast struck out. With one blow it sent him reeling; Wulfgar leaped up, and Brochael raced out of the shadows with a yell.

The rune beast hung over Kari for a moment; then with a whisper of dismay it turned, bewildered, from side to side. And Jessa saw there was a cage about it; a cage of light that glittered in the dull flame light, thin filaments that ran from roof to floor, like water.

The creature crumpled, hugging itself; for a wild moment it slashed and struggled against light and sorcery, but as if it realized how useless this was, it huddled still again, eyes bright.

Painfully Kari picked himself up. He looked down at the snakeskin.

"This is the key to your cage," he said, slipping it on. "This. And she left it for me to use against my friends." He glanced back quickly at Jessa and the others, a quizzical, unreadable look. "They don't trust me. They lock me away. They're afraid of what I have, and she wants me to hate them for that and move against them. Doesn't she?"

The creature stared at him, only its eyes following his movements. He fingered the soft skin gently. "This would unleash you. You could destroy all of them, and you couldn't touch me."

"Listen to him," Vidar snarled. "He'll kill us all."

"No," Jessa said grimly. "He's just making his point."

The rune beast murmured, a strange sound.

"Exactly," Kari said, as if he understood it. "I don't hate them. They know that . . . most of them. I won't use her gift against them. But if I don't, what do we do with you? Because you're hungry."

He reached out his hand. The creature watched, its great head alert.

"I know that hunger," Kari whispered. "I knew it for years, here—the emptiness, the darkness, without faces, without language, without warmth. Dreaming of nothing, my mind walking in white snowfields."

The creature snarled; Kari jerked back, waving Brochael away.

"Be careful!" Jessa murmured.

"He knows what he's doing." But Skapti stood stiff, fists clenched.

"So you see," Kari said, "I daren't use this thing and I must. That's what power is." He seemed almost to be talking to himself now, Jessa thought, and her heart thudded as she saw him lean forward again.

"She sent you here for me to kill. For me to taste how that felt, and to want to taste it again. Oh she's clever, my mother." He looked closely at the creature, curious. "She left us both empty, didn't she?"

The beast strained away, as if it feared him.

Kari held out the bracelet.

Jessa forgot to breathe; she saw Brochael jerk forward.

"Take it," Kari whispered.

For a moment the creature's eyes met his. He stepped closer, among the bars of light.

"Kari!" Brochael's cry burst from him, but the Snow-walker took no notice. He crouched by the creature's head, and dropped the snakeskin band over one sharp claw.

"Take it. Let it feed you. Then both of us can break free."

Hands empty, he scrambled back.

Jessa gripped the back of the chair. Now, she thought, anything could happen.

The creature was staring at the tiny thing. Then it stood up and gazed intently down the smoky hall, as if it had seen all the silent, anxious watchers for the first time, had woken from a long sleep, or shaken off some nagging, insistent voice. It murmured, and there were almost words in the sounds it made to Kari, and he answered too, something Jessa could not hear.

And quite suddenly, though he did nothing, she knew that Kari was the focal point of the hall, that all the darkness and tension spread from him, and the danger too, and for a moment of sharp fear she knew he had them all in the power of his mind. Her vision shifted; for that time he was not the Kari she knew. He was someone else. A stranger. An alien.

The beast stumbled back. It shimmered; already through it she could see the doorway with its glint of stars. Thinner, frailer, the creature opened itself; snow fell through it now, it was delicate as melting ice, dissolving back into the runes and atoms the witch had forged it from. Kari wasn't doing it; the creature itself was fleeing with its prize. And as it drifted away among mists, it subtly distorted, and at the last she was almost sure it was a man's shape that was there, as if the long emergence was ended. For a second it wavered, between being and nonbeing. Then it was gone, and the hall was dark.

And they were all standing on a wide snowfield.

The sky was gray; the wind howling toward them over empty crevasses, so that Jessa's hair whipped back and she gasped with the sudden biting cold. Behind her Skapti swore; Vidar cried out in fear.

The landscape was immense, a cracked glacier pitted with ravines, the snow gusting over it.

And far off a woman was walking toward them, a woman with long silvery hair, and she walked quickly, but all the time she came no nearer, until at last she raised her head and looked at them, and stopped.

Jessa stared at Gudrun. The Snow-walker was older;

her smooth skin finely lined, her lips thin.

She glanced at them all, then at Kari.

"So you wouldn't use it?"

"I couldn't."

"Even after they betrayed you?"

"That was your doing."

"Not all of it." She shook her head, wondering. "But to give it away. That I didn't expect. Sometimes you surprise me, Kari."

He stepped toward her, through the blue shadows. "Leave us alone now. Leave them alone. We have nothing that you need."

Almost sadly, she shook her head, and Jessa's stomach tightened with fear.

"I can't," the witch said. "I need you. I find I want to draw you back to me."

Kari gripped his fists. "I'll never come."

For a moment she looked at him strangely. "No?" Then she looked beyond him, at Wulfgar and the others. "As for you, I lay this fate on you, my lord. The thing you love best, that thing I will have some day."

Wulfgar kept his voice steady. "Not if I can prevent it."

"Guard your hall well, then." She turned away to Kari with a hard smile. "Don't consume yourself with power, my son. Keep some for me."

Wind gusted snow into their faces.

Then they stood alone on the great stone floor of the hall.

Thirty

Our sole remedy is to turn again to you.

Wulfgar drank deeply, and put the cup down. "Her words are poison. I'll remember them, but not worry too much. This time we've defeated her. As for Vidar, he seems to think a little differently about you now."

Kari nodded, and Brochael gave Jessa a broad smile, stretching out his legs to the banked-up fire.

The hall was securely barred; for a moment they sat in silence again, among the crack and crackle of the flames.

Then Jessa said, "What will happen to him?"

"I'll let him try the dungeons for a day or so. Then"—Wulfgar shrugged and winced—"then the men of the hold will judge him in open court. You'll have to speak, Jessa."

"Oh, I'll speak!" She turned her cup in her hands. "I'll have plenty to say about this thief friend too. A purse of silver, Wulfgar. Vidar promised that if his man was involved, remember?"

"I think," the Jarl said evenly, "we might get that much from him."

Brochael put his arms heavily around Skapti and Hakon. "And what about this one? Can we do nothing for him?"

Hakon let the strong grip hearten him. He looked sidelong at Jessa; she was watching Wulfgar.

The Jarl nodded. "Jessa and I have spoken about it. Hakon, how much was your family's debt to Skuli?"

"Sixty silver pieces."

"Gods, that's not much for a life of thralldom," Brochael growled.

"It's enough, if you haven't got it."

"I've got it," Wulfgar said, "and I'll pay it."

"My lord—"

"Hakon Empty-hand," Wulfgar said lazily, "Don't call me 'my lord.' You and Jessa saved us all. Sixty pieces is a very small reward. . . ."

"Not to me."

"So I'll want something from you in return. Your service. Not as a thrall," he added hastily, seeing Hakon's face, "but as one of my men."

Hakon stared. Then he rubbed his nose. He knew he

was grinning like a fool; Brochael was openly laughing at him. He just couldn't believe this.

"With one empty hand?"

Wulfgar gave his lazy shrug. "The hands of other men are empty, though they may not seem so." His eyes darkened for a moment at the memory.

"But it was Kari who saved us," Hakon said uneasily. "He destroyed the beast."

"Not destroyed," Kari said, looking up. "And there were two beasts. The second one we destroyed between us. That one was invisible, and the more dangerous."

Wulfgar nodded. "I was to blame. I let Vidar persuade me. I'm sorry. I won't doubt you again."

Kari almost smiled. "Don't be so sure. Perhaps you should. A little." Suddenly he held out his hand to Hakon. "And will you forgive me for what Gudrun did to you?"

For a moment Hakon couldn't move. The memory of the long years of anguish, the strange terror of that vision of the ice field almost engulfed him. Then he lifted his hand and clasped Kari's.

The Snow-walker's grip was narrow and cool; it tingled his flesh. Hakon saw the others grinning at him, Jessa was laughing with her fingers over her lips, and he couldn't see why until he looked down at his hand and saw that it was the right one that he had offered Kari. His right hand!

He pulled it away, flexed the weak fingers, stared at the runemaster in fear and dismay and a growing, unbearable delight.

"What have you done?" he whispered.

Kari shook his head. "The opposite," he said.

And as they laughed, the wind called outside, like a cold voice, and Jessa noticed how Kari listened to it quietly.

BOOK THREE

The Soul Thieves

For Tess

One

Outside I sat by myself
when you came.

The sword was of heavy beaten iron, with a narrow groove down the center of the blade. On the pommel tiny gilt birds with red eyes watched one another, and two dragons wound their bodies around the hilt, notched and scratched.

"It's not new," Brochael observed.

"It's perfect." Hakon's voice was so stunned that almost no one heard him. He looked up at the house thrall who had brought it. "Tell Wulfgar . . . tell the Jarl that I'm grateful. Very grateful."

The man went and whispered his message in the Jarl's ear, and they saw Wulfgar grin and wave lazily down the long crowded table.

Hakon held the sword tight, turned it over, scratched with his thumbnail at a tiny mark in the metal. His right hand, still slightly smaller and weaker than the left, clasped the hilt; he slashed with it sideways at imaginary enemies.

Jessa jerked back. "Be careful!"

"Sorry." Reluctantly he laid the sword on the table, among the greasy dishes. Jessa smiled to herself. She knew he barely believed it was his.

"Better than that rust heap you had before," Brochael said, emptying the last drop of wine thoughtfully onto the floor. "Now it needs a name." He reached over for the jug and refilled his cup. "And here's the very man. What are some good names for a sword, Skapti?"

The tall poet lounged on the end of the bench.

"Whose is it?"

"Hakon's."

Skapti touched the blade with his long fingers. "Well," he said, considering, "you could call it Growler, Angry One, Screamer, Rune-scored, Scythe of Honor, Worm Borer, Dragonsdeath—"

"I like that one."

"Don't interrupt." Skapti glared at him. "Leg Biter, Host Striker, Life Quencher, Corpse Pain, Wound Bright, Skull Crusher, Deceiver, Night Bringer . . . Oh, I could go on and on. There are hundreds of sword names. The skald lists are full of them."

"You can't name it until it's done something," Jessa said firmly. She poured Skapti some wine.

"You mean killed someone?" Hakon sounded uneasy.

"Drawn blood." Brochael winked over the boy's head. "The blade must drink, that's what they say. Then you name it."

Skapti tapped the hilt. "Where did you get it?"

A burst of laughter along the table rang in the noisy hall. Then Hakon said, "Wulfgar gave it to me. To mark his wedding." He reached out and touched it lightly, and the firelight glittered in the metal, like a splash of blood.

Jessa shivered then, though the mead hall was warm and smoky, and her scarlet dress was heavy and spun of good wool. For a moment even the clatter of dishes and conversation seemed to fade; then the foreboding passed, and the talk rose about her again.

She looked along the table.

Wulfgar sat in the middle, leaning forward in his carved chair, his dark coat edged with fur at the collar. He was listening as Signi whispered something close to his ear; then he smiled and closed his hand over hers.

"Look at him." Jessa laughed. "Oblivious."

"Ah well, I don't blame him," Brochael said drily. "She's a fine girl."

Fine was the word, Jessa thought. Signi's hair was long and fine, delicate as spun silk, pale and golden. Her dress moved as she turned on the seat, gold glinting at her wrist and shoulders. A fine girl, refined, the daughter of a wealthy house. They had been betrothed to each other for years, since they were both children, Jessa knew. And now that Wulfgar had come into his land and power, now that he was Jarl, they were to be married. Tomorrow at noon. Midsummer's Day.

The table was thronged with Signi's family and kin; they had been traveling in all week from outlying farms. Wulfgar's friends had made room for them; the Jarl's guests always had pride of place.

Jessa looked around at Brochael. "Is Kari still asleep? Perhaps we should wake him."

He frowned down at her, then looked across the room toward the door. "If you like. There won't be anything left to eat if he doesn't come soon. But you know how he is, Jessa; he may not want to come."

She nodded, standing. "I'll go up and see."

Crossing the hall between the tables, she dodged the serving men and thought that Kari could hardly be asleep. The noise of the Jarl's feast was loud, and all the doors were open to the light midsummer night, the sun barely setting even now, the pale sky lit with eerie streaks of cloud. At this time of year it never really got dark at all. She slipped through the archway, up the stone stairs, and along to a room at the end where she tapped on the door.

"Kari?"

After a moment he answered her. "Come in, Jessa."

He was sitting in front of the dying fire, his back against the bench and his knees drawn up. Firelight lit his pale face with red, leaping glimmers; his hands were red, and his hair, and for a moment she thought again that it looked like blood, and went cold.

He glanced up quickly. "What is it? What's the matter?"

"Nothing." She came inside. "It was just the light on you. It's dark in here."

He looked back at the fire. "You were scared for a minute. I felt it."

The two black ravens that followed him everywhere stood on the windowsill, looking out. One of them stared strangely at her.

She perched on the bench, rubbing her foot. "I'm never scared. Now, are you coming down? Brochael's eating and drinking for ten, but there's still plenty left."

"Has Wulfgar asked for me?"

"No. He knows you." If it had been anyone else, she knew, Wulfgar would have taken their absence as a deliberate insult, but not Kari. Kari was different. Kari avoided crowds, and Jessa understood why.

Now he made no attempt to move, his best blue shirt picking up soot smuts from the dirty floor.

"There's nothing wrong, is there?" she asked anxiously.

He pushed the long silvery hair back from his eyes. "No." But he sounded puzzled, not quite sure.

"Tell me," she said after a moment.

Turning to her, his face was drawn, uneasy. "Oh, I don't know, Jessa. It's just that tonight, since the twilight began, I've felt something. A tingling in my fingers. A shiver. Coldness. It worries me that I can't think what it is."

"Do you think it's this wedding?"

"No. I think it's just me." Suddenly he stood, pulling her up. "I'm hungry. Let's go down. I'd like to see Hakon's new sword."

Jessa stopped dead. "He's only just been given it. How did you . . . ?"

His pleading look silenced her.

As they walked up the crowded hall a ripple of hush followed them, as if conversations had faltered and then gone rapidly on. People were only just beginning to get used to Kari; it took them such a long time, Jessa thought irritably. His pale skin and frost gray, colorless eyes disturbed them; when they saw him they remembered Gudrun and were afraid.

But Wulfgar was pleased. "So you came!" he said lazily. "I wondered if we'd have the honor."

Kari smiled back, glancing at Signi. "I'm sorry. Brochael says I have no manners; he's right."

The blond girl looked at him curiously. Then she poured him a cup of wine and held it out. "I'm glad you've come, Kari," she said, in her soft, southland accent. "You and I need to be friends. I want to know all Wulfgar's friends. I want them to like me."

He took the cup, his eyes watching her face. "They will, lady."

She flushed, glancing at Wulfgar. "Is that a prophecy?"

Wulfgar laughed, and Kari said, "It's already come true."

He raised the cup to drink and stopped, so still that Jessa looked at him. He was staring into the wine as if something had poisoned it, and when he looked up his face was white with terror.

"She's here," he breathed.

Alarmed, Wulfgar leaned forward. "Who is?"

But Kari had spun around, quick as a sword slash. "Close the doors!" he yelled, his voice raw and desperate over the hubbub. "Close them! *Now!*"

Skapti was on his feet, Wulfgar too.

"Do it!" he thundered, and men around the hall moved, scrambling from tables, grabbing their weapons. Jessa caught Kari's arms, and the red wine splashed her dress.

"What is it?" She gasped. "What's happening?"

"She's here." He stared over her shoulder. "Gods, Jessa. Look!"

Mist was streaming through the high windows—strange glinting stuff, full of shadows and forms, hands that came groping over the sills, figures that swarmed in the doorways. In seconds the hall was full of it, an icy silver breath that swirled and blinded.

Women screamed; angry yells and barking and swordplay rang in the crowded, panic-stricken spaces. The fires shriveled instantly, hard and cold; candles on the table froze. The mist swirled between faces, and people were lost; Jessa saw Wulfgar tugging at his sword, then he was gone, blanked out by a wraith of fog that caught her and seemed to drag her by the arms. She tore herself away and somewhere nearby Kari called out; then he was shoved against her so hard they both fell, crashing against the table. She grabbed him and screamed, "Kari!" but he didn't answer, and putting her hand to his face her fingers felt wetness. She held them near to her eyes and saw blood.

"Kari!"

In the uproar no one heard her. Pale, unearthly forms of men and dogs moved around her; a sword slapped down hard nearby as men fought among themselves, against their shadows. She scrambled up and was knocked back by a blow from something cold and hard; crumpling on hands and knees she felt the side of her face go numb and tingle; then the pain grew to a throbbing ache.

Someone grabbed her; she flung him off, but he gasped. "It's me!"

She recognized the sword. "Hakon! What's happening?"

"I don't know."

"Kari's hurt. We need to get him somewhere safe!"

They felt for him in the mist and grabbed him under the arms; then Hakon dragged him back under the table, kicking benches out of the way. They crouched over him, shocked.

"It's Gudrun!" Jessa stormed.

"What?"

"Gudrun! She's doing this!"

Around them the mist closed in. Shapes moved in it; they thought they saw huge men, tall as trolls, creatures from nightmares. A fog wolf with glinting eyes snarled under the table; the legs of distorted, monstrous beings waded past them through the hall. Frost was spreading quickly across the floor; it crunched under their feet and nails; they breathed it in and the pain of it seared their throats, clogged their voices.

"Getting cold," Hakon's voice whispered, close to her.

"Me too." She struggled to say "Keep awake," but her lips felt swollen, her tongue would not make the sounds.

Cold stiffened her clenched fingers.

"Hakon . . . ," she murmured, but he did not answer. She felt for him; his arm lay cold beside her.

Around them the hall was silent.

Now the white grip of the ice was creeping gently over her cheek, spreading on her skin. With a great effort she shifted a little, and the fine film cracked, but it formed again almost instantly, sealing her lips with a mask of glass. She couldn't breathe.

Crystals of ice closed over her eyelids, crusting her lashes. Darkness froze in her mind.

Two

A farseeing witch, wise in talismans,
Caster of spells.

Lost in the frost spell, each of them walked in a dream. Brochael dreamed he was in some sort of room. He was sure of that, but couldn't remember how he had come there. He was holding open a heavy door; a chain swung from it, rusted with age. In his other hand was a lantern; he raised it now, to see what was there.

In the darkness something made a sound. He swung the light toward it.

It was squatting on the floor, pressed into a corner. A small, crouched shape, twisting away from the light. Heavily, Brochael crossed the dirty straw toward it. The door closed behind him.

The red flame of the lantern quivered; he saw eyes, a scuttle of movement.

It was a boy, about six years old. He was filthy, his hair matted and soiled, his clothes rags. Crusts of dirt smeared his thin face; his eyes were large, staring, without emotion.

Brochael crouched, his huge shadow enveloping the corner of the stinking cell. The boy did not move.

"Can you speak?" He found his voice gruff; anger mounting in him like a flame. When the boy made no answer, he reached out for him. With that trembling touch he knew this was Kari; he remembered, and looked up, and saw Gudrun there. She put out her hand and pulled the boy up; he changed, grew older, cleaner, taller, so that they faced each other among the shadows.

The lantern shook in Brochael's hand.

He could not tell them apart.

Hakon dreamed himself in a white emptiness. As he reached for his sword it slid away from him; alarmed, he grabbed it and the whole floor rose up beneath him, became a surface of glass, slippery, impossible to grip. Desperately, palms flat, he slipped down, down into Gudrun's spell, and below him was an endless roaring chasm, deep as his nightmares.

An idea came to him, and he stabbed the sword into the ice to hold himself steady, but out of it wriggled a snake that wound around his hand, the cool scales rippling between his fingers. He lost power and feeling; the fingers were forced wide and the snake gripped his wrist so tight the sword fell from his numb fingers; it toppled over the brink, and fell, and he fell after it, into nowhere.

Skapti's nightmare was very different. For him it meant standing in a green wood, watching the mist from a distance. He knew it was a spell. Shapes moved in it; his friends, he thought, each of them lost.

Under his long hand the bark of the tree was rough; leaves were pattering down around him in the wind—at least he thought at first they were leaves, but as he looked at them again he saw they were words. All the words of all his songs were coming undone and falling about him like rain. He caught one and crunched it in his fingers; a small, crisp word.

Lost.

He let it fall angrily, chilled to the heart.

Then he saw her standing in the wood: a tall white-skinned woman laughing at him. "Poets know a great deal, Skapti," she said, "and make fine things. But even these can be destroyed."

As he stared at her the words fell between them, a silent, bitter snow.

Signi had no idea she was dreaming. A tall woman bent over and helped her stand.

"Thank you," she murmured, brushing her dress. "What happened? Where's Wulfgar?"

The woman smiled coldly, and before Signi could move, she fixed a narrow chain of fine gold links to each of her wrists. Signi stared at her, then snatched her hands away. "What are you doing?"

She gazed around in horror at the frozen hall. "Wulfgar!"

"He won't hear you." The woman turned calmly, leading her out; Signi was forced to follow. She tugged and pulled, but it was no use. "Where are we going?" she asked tearfully.

Gudrun laughed.

As they left the hall it rippled into nothing, into mist.

★ ★ ★

Wulfgar knew he had lost her. In his dream he ran through the empty hold looking for her, calling her name. Where was everyone? What had happened? Furious, he stopped and yelled for his men.

But the night was silent; the aurora flickering over the stone hall and its dragon gables. He raced down to the fjord shore, and ran out onto the longest wharf, his boots loud on the wooden boards.

"Signi!" he yelled.

The water was pale, lit by the midnight sun. Only as he turned away did he see her, fast asleep under the surface. Eels slithered through her hair, the fine strands spreading in the rise and fall of the current. When he lay down and reached out to her, thin layers of ice closed tight about his wrist.

The water held him, a cold grip.

Only Kari did not dream. Instead he slipped out of his body and stood up, looking down at the blood on his hair. Then he edged between the fallen tables and the dream-wrapped bodies of his friends to the door of the hall, flung wide. Outside the watchman lay sprawled, his sword iced over, the black wolfhound still at his side.

Stepping over them, Kari hurried out under the dawn glimmer and looked north. Down the tracks of the sky he watched shapes move, heard voices call to him from invisible realms. He answered quickly, and the ghosts of jarls and warriors and women came and crowded about him.

"What happened?" he asked bitterly.

"She came. She took one of them back with her."

"Who came?"

They stared at him, their faces pale as his. "We know no names. Names are for the living."

"You must tell me!"

"She. The Snow walker."

His mother. He wondered why he'd been so urgent; he'd known it would be her. He nodded and turned back slowly, and they made room for him, drifting apart like mist.

Coming back into the hall, he gazed across it, at the frosted trunk of the roof tree, where it stood rising high into the rafters. Two black forms sat among its branches.

"Go out and look," he said. "There may be some trace of her. Look to the north."

"It's unlikely," one of them croaked.

"Try anyway. I'll wake these."

As they rose up and flapped out of the window, he moved reluctantly back into his body, feeling the heavy pain begin to throb in his head, the bitter cold in fingers and stomach.

He rolled over, dragging himself up unsteadily onto his knees, fighting down sickness. Then he grabbed Jessa's arm and shook it feebly. "Jessa! Wake up. Wake up!"

It was all a dream, Jessa knew that. She stood on the hilltop next to the grazing horse and looked down at the snow-covered land. Fires burned, far to the south. A great bridge, like a pale rainbow, rose into the sky, its end lost among clouds.

On the black waters of the fjord a ship was drifting on the ebb tide—a funeral ship. Even from here Jessa could see the bright shields hung on each side of it, and they were burning, their metal cracking and melting, dropping with a hiss into the black water. Flames devoured the mast, racing up the edges of the sails.

And on the ship were all the friends she knew and had ever known, and they were alive. Some were calling out to her, others silent, looking back; Skapti and Signi, Wulfgar and Brochael, Marrika and Thorkil, her father, Kari. Hakon with his bright new sword and looking so desolate that her heart nearly broke.

Gudrun was standing beside her. The witch was tall; her long silver hair hung straight down her back.

"My ship," she said softly. "And if you want them as they were, Jessa, you must come and get them."

"Come where?" Jessa asked, furious.

"Beyond the end of the world."

"There's nothing beyond the end!"

"Ah, but there is." Gudrun smiled her close, secret smile. "The land of the soul. The place beyond legends. The country of the wise."

Then she reached out and gripped Jessa's arm painfully.

"But now you must wake up."

And it wasn't Gudrun, it was Kari, his face white, blood clotted in his hair. He leaned against her and she struggled up from the floor, holding his arm. Ice cracked and splintered and fell from her hair and clothes; she felt cold, cold to the heart.

"What happened? You look terrible!"

"I hit my head," he said quietly. "I can't see properly."

Making him sit down, she stared around. The hall was dim, lit only with the weak night sun and a strange frosty glimmer. A film of ice lay over everything—over the floor, the tables, the sprawled bodies of the sleepers, over plates of food and upturned benches. Wine was frozen as it spilled; the fires were out, hard and black, and on the walls the tapestries were stiff, rigid folds.

In the open doorway she could see where the mist had poured in and turned to ice; it had frozen in rivulets and glassy, bubbled streams, hard over tables and sleeping dogs.

The high windows were sheeted with icicles.

No wonder no one had been ready. Swords were frozen into scabbards; shields to their brackets on the walls. A woman lay nearby holding a child, both of them white with frost and barely breathing.

Jessa shivered. "We've got to wake them! They'll die otherwise."

He nodded, stood up and walked unsteadily to the fires. As she shook Hakon fiercely she heard the crackle and stir of the rune flames igniting behind her.

It took a long time to wake everyone. Some were deep in the death sleep, almost lost in their dreams, their souls wandering far among spells. Brochael awoke with a jerk, gripping her shoulder; Skapti more slowly, raising his head from the table and looking upward, as if the roof was falling in.

Gradually the hall thawed and filled with noise; murmurs grew to voices, angry, questioning; small children sobbed and the warmth from the fires set everything dripping and softening.

"Get those doors shut!" Brochael ordered. One arm around Kari, he parted the boy's hair. "That's deep. Get me something, Hakon, to stop the blood."

"Where's Wulfgar?" Jessa ran to the high table. It was overturned on its side. A knife had been flung in the confusion and was frozen, embedded in the wood. She scrambled over, tugging benches and chairs away, crunching the frozen straw underneath. She saw his arm first, flung around Signi, and with a yell to Skapti she tried to drag the heavy table off them, until men came and pushed her aside, heaving the boards away, crowding around the Jarl.

They helped him sit up, breathless and sore.

"What was it?" he managed.

Jessa crouched. "It looks like Gudrun's work. Some sort of spell. A few people are hurt, but none are dead. Are you all right?"

He rubbed soot and ice from his face and nodded, turning to Signi. She lay cold on the straw, Skapti bending over her. The skald looked up anxiously. "I can't wake her."

Wulfgar grabbed the girl's shoulders, his hands crushing the fine silk. "Signi!" He shook her again.

She lay still, still as death, but they saw she was breathing. Her face was clear, and her eyes opened, but there was no movement in her, no flicker of recognition.

"Signi?" Wulfgar said again. "Are you all right?"

When she still did not speak he lifted her, and Jessa righted a chair and they sat her in it, but her head lolled slowly to one side, the long hair swinging over her face.

A woman began to cry in the crowd.

Wulfgar chafed her hands. "Get her waiting women. Get Einar—"

"It's no use."

Kari's voice was harsh, and they turned, surprised. He stood by the table, Brochael's great arm around him.

"What do you mean?" Wulfgar yelled.

"She's gone. Gudrun has taken her."

"Taken her!" The Jarl leaped up. "She's not dead!"

"Not even that. Taken her soul, taken it far away." He put his hand to his head as if it ached, and for a moment Jessa thought he would fall, but he looked up again and nodded at the center of the hall. "Look. She left her mark."

The roof tree was split, from top to bottom.

Carved deep in the wood, a white snake twisted, poison bubbling and hissing from its jaws.

THREE

The gods hastened to their hall of judgment,
Sat in council to discover who
Had tainted all the air with corruption . . .

They carried Signi upstairs and laid her on the brocaded bed in her room, with a warm fur cover over her and the fire crackling over the new logs. But nothing they did could wake her, no voice, no entreaty. She breathed shallowly, so slowly that it frightened them, and both the herb woman, Gerda, and the physician, Einar Grimsson, tried every remedy they knew, filling the chamber with exotic scents of oils and unguents and charred wood. They even tried pricking her skin with sharp needles, but she never moved, though the red blood ran freely. Finally Wulfgar stopped it all and ordered them out.

When Jessa tapped on the door a little later, he was still sitting on the edge of the bed, his wine-stained coat held tight around him.

"Well?" he said, without turning.

She came into the room, Skapti behind her.

"Kari says it was some kind of supernatural attack." The skald leaned against the shuttered window. "I think he's right—there are no footprints outside, no horse tracks, no evidence of any armed force."

"But we saw them! Some of the men are wounded."

"I know, but what we saw were visions, Wulfgar, mind shapes, nothing that was real. Everyone seems to have seen different things. Some of the men may have fought one another, or against wraiths and shadows—none of us knew what was real. We were all spell blinded."

"Can you remember," Jessa said slowly, "what you dreamed?"

Skapti looked at her absently. "No. Not really. Except that it was full of pain."

Wulfgar got up suddenly and stormed around the room. "How could she do this! And why Signi? She's never even met Gudrun! If the witch wanted revenge on us why didn't she kill us all there in the hall?"

Jessa stirred, on the bench by the fire. "This is what she said she would do."

They both stared at her blankly, so she dragged the loose brown hair from her cheek and said, "Don't you remember the night we all saw her, in that strange vision? The night the creature came? She was standing in a snow-field. She said she wanted Kari to come to her, and he wouldn't. Then she turned to you."

"I remember." Wulfgar stared darkly across the room. "She said, 'What you love best, that thing I will have.' But I never thought it would be this."

He looked down at the girl on the bed. Her eyes were closed now, as if she slept.

"Sit down," Skapti said gently. "We need to think."

Wulfgar came over and slumped beside Jessa on the bench. All his usual lazy elegance had left him. He put his head in his hands and stared hopelessly into the fire. "What can we do?"

Neither of them could answer.

In the awkward silence they heard footsteps outside. Then Brochael opened the door and ushered Kari in.

The boy looked frail; he went and gazed down at Signi, and they saw the deep raw cut across his forehead.

"You should be in bed," Wulfgar muttered.

"That's what I said," Brochael growled.

Ignoring them both, Kari came and sat by the blazing logs.

"What do we do?" Wulfgar said again.

Kari watched him bleakly. Then he said, "It's only too clear what we have to do. Gudrun has made sure we have no choice. We have to go to her."

"Why?"

"Because that's where Signi is." He glanced again at the still shape on the bed. "That isn't her, it's just her body, her shell. It's empty. She's not there."

"How do you know?"

"Because I've been into her mind, Wulfgar, and it's blank!" He ran long fingers through his hair and then said, "Gudrun has done this to make me come to her."

"Come where?" Jessa asked, remembering her dream.

"I don't know. Far away."

"The land of the White People."

He shrugged. "Wherever that is."

Skapti came forward, intrigued. "They say it's beyond

the end of the world. A place of trolls, a giant haunt. They say the ice goes up to touch the sky. No one could live up there."

"The Snow-walkers live there. My people," said Kari grimly.

Wulfgar looked up suddenly. "All right. If you say that's what we have to do to get her back, we'll do it. I'll take as many shiploads of men as I can get; a war band—"

"A war band is no use," Brochael said unexpectedly. His huge shadow loomed on the wall, the firelight warm on his tawny hair and beard. "The last Jarl sent a war band up there and no one ever came back."

"He's right," Kari said. "Besides, only I need to go."

There was an uproar of protest, everyone speaking at once until Brochael's strong voice silenced them. "You can't go! Even if you got there, she'd kill you!"

"She could have killed me here." Calmly Kari rubbed his forehead. "She doesn't want that. She wants me alive."

"You're not going!" Brochael was angry now and obstinate; his face was set.

"There's no alternative." Kari looked at him hard. "Think of it, Brochael. Signi will just lie like that for months, for years, never speaking, never knowing any of us. We could all grow old and die, and she'd just be the same. Gudrun has plenty of time. Gudrun can wait for us."

Silent with pain, Wulfgar clenched his fingers.

But stubbornly the big man shook his head. "It's folly. She may wake; we don't know." He came over and crouched down, his strong hands on the boy's shoulders. "And I didn't bring you out of her prison for this. I don't want you to go."

"I have to." Kari's eyes were clear and cold; he looked like Gudrun, that secret, tense look.

Brochael stood up and stalked across the room to the door. He slammed his fist against the wood.

"We've never quarreled before," Kari said bleakly.

"And we're not now. If you go over the world's edge, I'm going with you, and you know that well enough. But we're walking into her trap. How could she steal the girl's soul?"

Kari was quiet for a moment. Then he said, "She's learned how. She's been powerful for too long."

Brochael's scowl deepened. He glared at the poet. "You're very quiet. You usually have some opinion."

The skald shrugged his thin shoulders. "I think Kari is right, we have no choice. And for a poet, such a journey is enticing. A dream road. They say there are lands of fire and ice up there. Someone would have to make the song of it, and it might as well be me."

"I won't be left behind either," Jessa said firmly. "Don't even think it. I'm coming."

Her scowl made them all smile, even now. When Jessa made up her mind, they all knew nothing would shift her.

Wulfgar stirred. "Then it's settled. A small group of us—we'll travel more quickly and secretly that way, and need less. . . . "

They glanced at one another, wondering who would say it. Finally Skapti did. "Not you," he said quietly.

Wulfgar stared at him.

"Skapti's right." Jessa leaned forward. "You can't come with us, Wulfgar. You know that. Your place is here."

"My place," he breathed, "is with Signi."

"It isn't. It can't be." She stood up and faced him. "Look. I'll tell you this straight out, as no one else will. You're the Jarl. You rule the land, keep the peace, settle the disputes. You order the trade, keep the frontiers, hunt down outlaws. The people chose you. You can't turn your back on them. If you came with us and we were away months, even years, what would be here when we came back?" She smiled at him sadly. "Famine, blood feuds, cattle raiding. Black, burned farms. A wasteland."

He looked away from her, such a hard, desolate look as she had never seen on him before. The room was silent. Only the flames crackled over the logs. Then Wulfgar looked back at her bitterly. "I think I'll never forgive you for this, Jessa."

"You will." She sat down and tried to smile at him. "And think of it this way. When she wakes, it's you she'll want to see."

FOUR

When Ymir lived, long ago.

All the next day Wulfgar avoided everybody. He spent hours sitting in Signi's room, watching her still face, or staring silently out of the window. At mealtimes he called for his horse and galloped away from the hold, riding hard for the hills.

Jessa watched him go, leaning against the corner of the hall. She could guess how he felt; Wulfgar was impulsive, always the one to act. It would be very hard for him to stay behind.

Over her shoulder, Skapti said, "The trouble with him is that he knows you were right."

"I wish I hadn't said anything. I should have let him think it out for himself."

The skald laughed. "Always spilling your wisdom, little valkyrie." He turned her gently. "Now let's go and see Kari, because I think he wants us. One of those spirit birds of his just came and croaked at me. The creature almost ordered me in."

She walked along beside him gravely. "Things are different in the daylight, aren't they?"

"Lighter, you mean?"

She thumped his arm. "You know what I mean. Last night, in all the confusion, everything seemed so unreal. Signi, those dreams, the cold. The idea of a journey seemed . . . exciting." She looked down at the longships moored at the wharf. A chill breeze moved them. "Now it's more frightening. It will be so cold up there. And no one has ever come back, and even if we get there . . ."

"There's Gudrun."

"Yes." She looked up at him. "Do you think it's the right thing to do?"

"I don't," he said abruptly. "But I think it's the only thing we can do."

"Skapti, you're mad."

"I'm a poet," he said, opening the door of the hall. "Pretty much the same thing." He grinned at her, lopsided. "You're not usually so wary."

"Dreams," she said absently. "Those dreams. They hang around."

Kari was out of bed and sitting at a table near the fire, carving a small piece of bone into a flat disc. He looked up at them.

"At last!"

"Feeling better?" Jessa tipped his head sideways and examined the cut critically. "Brochael was worried about you. He said you'd lost a pint of blood and you were a thin, bloodless wraith and couldn't afford it."

Kari shrugged. "He's given me orders not to stir out. That's why I sent the birds."

One of them flapped in at the window just then, hopping awkwardly down from the sill. It had a red, dripping object in its beak that might once have been a stoat. Delicately the bird picked it apart.

"Corpse carver," Skapti murmured ominously.

They were watching it when Brochael came back. Hakon was with him; they staggered in carrying a large wooden chest.

"Just here," Brochael grunted, putting his end down easily. Hakon dropped his with relief.

"No sword?" Jessa said sweetly, behind him.

He crumpled, breathless. "Not in the hall. Jarl's orders. I can live for an hour without it."

"Not much longer, though."

"Now." Brochael wrenched the key around in the rusted lock. "This should be what we want."

He put both hands to the lid and heaved it open; it crashed back on the leather hinges and a great cloud of brown dust billowed upward.

"What's all that?" Jessa murmured, looking down.

"Maps. So Guthlac says."

He began to rummage around with his great hands, tugging out rolls of withered brown parchment and skins, worn to dust at the edges, some of them tied and sealed with red, crumbling wax.

"Clear that table," he muttered. "Let's see what's in here."

Each of them dipped in and took a handful of skins, unfolding them carefully. Most were so old the dyes and inks had faded; there were deeds and agreements, land holdings, some old king lists that made Skapti mutter bitterly.

"These should be recopied." He held one up to the light. "This is a family list of the Wulfings; it goes back ten generations."

"But the poets know all those things, don't they?" Hakon said.

"Yes, passed from teacher to pupil. But there's always

the chance they'll be lost. I never even knew these existed."

"They were here before Gudrun's time," Brochael said, "but no one seems to have looked at them for years. There don't seem to be many maps."

They found land holdings for dead farmers, agreements swearing the end of blood feuds, promises of wergild, tributes and taxes from southland kings none of them had ever heard of. There were poems and fragments and even a piece of deerskin inscribed with tiny red runes that Jessa handed to Kari. "What do you think that is?"

"It's a spell," he said, staring at it in surprise.

"What for?"

"I don't know. I can't read it. But I can feel the power in it faintly."

Skapti took it off him and bent his long nose over it. "It's old. It's for making a goat give more milk."

"Useful," Jessa remarked drily.

"There are others." Brochael gathered a great sheaf out of the bottom of the chest. "As you say, not of much use to us."

"This might be." Hakon was sitting with something open on his knee. He lifted it onto the table and spread it out.

It was a map, drawn on ancient sealskin, dried out and

fragile. The corners were charred as if it had been once dragged from some fire. Jessa leaned forward, curious.

Marked at the bottom of the map was the jagged coastline of the Cold Sea, with the long narrow fjords they all knew so well reaching upward into the land. The Jarlshold was clearly shown, a tiny cross with the rune *J* underneath. All the ports on the coast—Ost, Trond, Wormshold, Hollfara—had their names under them, and rivers and larger lakes were marked with blue lines. Drawn in red dye was the old giant's road that led from the Jarlshold to Thrasirshall, and branching off from it, another red line north, straight up to the top of the map.

"What's that?" Jessa asked, putting her finger on it.

"It looks like another road," Hakon said.

Brochael nodded. "It is. I know where it begins, but like most of the giant road it's a ruin, lost under forests. Here and there are stone-built sections, poking through the snow. I've never traveled it. I don't know anyone who has."

"Now's your chance," Hakon said wistfully. "You could follow it north."

Jessa looked at him sidelong. He was scratching his cheek with his thumbnail and looking strangely at the map; almost a hungry look. She could guess why. Hakon had been a thrall for most of his life, a slave on a greasy little hold, and had never been able to leave it. Now he was free. But he was also Wulfgar's man, one of his war band. And if Wulfgar wasn't going . . .

Sadly she turned back to the map. The road ran north, clearly marked. Mountains and lakes and a large river were shown, but the farther north it went the more empty the map became, until there was nothing but the road, as if whoever had drawn it had no knowledge of what lay up there lost under the snows.

Or perhaps he had heard stories. For at the very top of the map, right across the sealskin, was a great black slash, as if some enormous chasm or crevasse opened there, and the road ran right to its edge, or into it. Some words were scrawled nearby, and Skapti read them out.

"The end of the road is unknown."

The black chasm also had a word in it, written loosely and untidily.

Gunningagap.

They stared at it in silence. Then Brochael looked up.

"What do the stories say?"

"You know what they say."

"Remind us. Earn your keep."

Skapti linked his long fingers together and flexed them. "Gunningagap is a howling emptiness," he said simply. "It's the place where the sky comes down to meet the earth. It's a great chasm that encircles the earth—here in the north its edges are heavy with ice; and eternal wind roars out of it, night and day. Long ago, they say, there was only the gap. Then a creature crawled out of it, a frost giant called Ymir. The gods killed him. From his body they made Middle-earth, the rocks from his bones, the stones from his teeth. His skull is the blue sky—four dwarves sit at the corners to hold it up. So the poets say. But one thing is sure, the gap is still there." He was silent a moment, then added some lines quietly.

"When Ymir lived, long ago,
Was no sand or sea, no surging waves.
Nowhere was there earth or heaven above,
But a grinning gap, and grass nowhere."

"So what's beyond it?" Jessa said.

He stared at her in surprise. "Nothing. That's what they say. Nothing. It's the end."

The thought of it silenced them—the frozen wastes of snow, the howling winter blackness of the world's brink. Jessa brought her mind back to the warm room with an effort.

"But everyone says the White People live beyond the world's end. And they come here, from time to time, so . . ."

"I don't know!" Skapti said, exasperated. "I'm a mere songster. A lackwit. A plucker of strings. How should I know? Perhaps there are worlds beyond this. No one has ever tried it and come back, that's the truth."

She tapped the map, its worn mountains and half-erased rivers. "Then we'll be the first."

"Well spoken, Jessa."

Wulfgar stood in the doorway, his face flushed from the wind, his eyes bright. He came in, brushing the dust from his hair, then tugged off his coat and threw it at Brochael. "You will. We'll make sure of that. This expedition will come back because none like it will ever have set out before. Sorcery, guile, strength, cleverness. You four have all those things. But I'd like to send one more thing with you. A sword."

They looked at him, uncertain, but he smiled at them, his old lazy smile. "No, not me. You were right about that." Sitting down, he leaned back in the chair, gripping the arms. "I am the Jarl," he said proudly, and a little sadly, "and I won't desert my people. No, I want you to take Hakon. You'll need another swordsman."

Amazed, Hakon gaped at him. "But I'm not . . . I mean, I've been training hard, but my hand is still not as . . ."

Wulfgar leaned forward. "Hakon Empty-hand, you'll

do as your lord tells you. Someone has to keep an eye on Jessa."

She glared at him, then laughed. "Five then."

"Five. And a better five I couldn't have. Because it all depends on you," he added softly. "Signi's life. All of it." He rubbed his hair again. "I don't know what I'll do when you're all gone."

In the silence Kari caught her glance. He was watching Wulfgar apprehensively, as if there was something else he had not told him, but when he saw her looking, he smiled and shook his head. She felt awkward. For a moment she had been wondering if Kari had changed Wulfgar's mind for him.

Five

Silence I ask of the sacred folk.

Jessa walked thoughtfully between the houses, through the noise and bustle of preparation. Outwardly the hold seemed to be back to normal after the bewildering spell storm; the smiths hammered, the fishing boats were out, women gossiped and spun wool in the sun.

And yet she had begun to realize that the dreams were still here.

Twice in the night she had woken from strange, tangled visions. Not only that, but the weather was cold. Too cold. Since midsummer a keen wind had whistled around the hold continuously; made drafts in all the rooms and corridors, moving tapestries, banging doors and shutters, touching the back of her neck like cold fingers.

She went in, past the sacks that were being packed with food, and up the stairs. Skapti was coming down, carrying the kantele, his precious instrument, well wrapped.

"You're taking that, then?" she asked, passing him.

"Some of us have to work, Jessa."

They were to leave in two days. Wulfgar and ten of his men were riding with them to the borders of the land, to the giant road. He'd insisted on that. As she ran up the stairs she clenched her fingers in her pockets, puzzled at how cold they were. Then she tapped on the door.

A woman opened it.

"Any change?" Jessa whispered.

Fulla shook her head. She was Signi's stepmother, an elderly woman. Her iron gray hair was bound in long braids; her dress hung with ivory charms. She let Jessa in, and they both stood by the silken hangings.

Signi lay unmoving, her beautiful corn gold hair brushed smooth. Her eyes were open, blue and clear and empty.

Jessa picked up the cold fingers. "Hear me, Signi," she said.

Nothing. No flicker, no turn of the head.

Slowly Jessa laid the limp hand down. "She seems cold."

"She is." The woman bent to touch the girl's forehead. "And I'm sure she's getting colder. I keep the fire well stoked, but the room has a growing chill. I've told the Jarl. It worries me."

Coming out, Jessa went back down the stairs. She was worried too, worried and restless. She went to the outside door and looked out. Wind caught her hair and whipped it up; the chill made her shiver. Something was wrong here. She looked around carefully, noticing other things. Most of the hens were inside, and very quiet. Up on the fellside the goats were huddled together in the shelter of boulders and tall trees. And now she came to realize it, there were no birds about the hold. None but Kari's ravens, hunched up on the hall roof like black carvings.

On impulse she ran between the houses and up the hillside and kneeled, looking closely. The grass looked shriveled. Small flowers of tormentil and thrift, bright yellow and pink two days ago, were brown wet stems. She picked one; it was rotten down to the heart, the leaves a blackening clot. Rolling it in her fingers she stood, looking over the fellside.

All the flowers were gone. Gudrun's unseasonal frost had seared the land here, though far off, well up the fjord-shore, it was still midsummer, the soft colors flaunting in the meadows. And there were no new green shoots. The raw wind flapped and gusted, but only in the hold; in bewilderment she stared up at the trees behind her; the forest was still, its dark fringe unmoving.

She ran back down, frowning.

Kari was sitting in his room with Hakon. As she came in she saw that he was carving another small bone circle with deft, skillful cuts.

"Why didn't you tell me?" she demanded.

Kari's knife paused in midair.

"Tell you what?" Hakon asked in surprise.

"He knows." She sat down between them. "It's still here, isn't it? Why didn't you tell us?"

Kari put the knife down on the bench and looked at it bleakly. "Keep your voice down, Jessa. If the holders know, they might panic."

Hakon had stopped burnishing his sword. "What's still here?"

"The spell. Whatever Gudrun sent."

"How did you find out?" Kari asked quietly.

"The flowers." She laid them on the bench. "The weather. The wind."

"It's not wind." Kari picked up the ring of bone and turned it over. "Those are dreams, moving around us."

"Can you see them?" Hakon asked, horrified.

Kari looked at him sideways. "I should have been ready for her!" he said, suddenly bitter. "Since she sent the rune creature last year, I've been gathering watchers around the hold. But she was too sudden, too fierce."

"Watchers?"

Kari looked at him. "Ghosts," he said.

Hakon paled.

Kari clenched his fingers on the bone disc. "You're right, Jessa, the rune spell is still here. It won't go. I can see it from the corners of my eyes, a coldness growing in the hold. It's wrapped around Signi, but she was just the first. It will spread, an icy sleep, and one by one, without warning, they'll all fall into it, their souls slipping away from them. Winter will close in. The fjord will freeze, the fires go out. Farmers, fishermen, thralls, they'll all lie down and the ice will cover them slowly, month by month. Even the beasts. She's wrapped the hold in its own dreams, and there's almost nothing I can do about it."

"Almost?"

He flipped the bone ring. "I have an idea. But most of all we have to find Signi."

"That's exactly what Gudrun wants."

"Of course it is."

They sat silent, feeling he had spoken prophecy, like a shaman reading the future. Perplexed, Hakon rubbed the dragons on his sword. "Have you told Wulfgar this?"

"Yesterday. As soon as I was sure. It's another reason he has to stay."

"But why should any of them stay?" Jessa said suddenly. "Why not clear everyone out of the hold—?"

His look silenced her. "No one can escape their dreams, Jessa. We five who go, I can protect. That's all."

"And those left?"

He spun the bone ring on the bench. "This."

She picked it up and turned it over. "What is it?"

The smooth white surface was carved with small running lines. They seemed to move before her eyes, as if they rippled. He took it from her quickly. "It's their defense. . . ."

A babble of noise outside interrupted him, raised, urgent voices. Jessa jumped up and went to the window. After a second she said, "Come and see this."

Hakon came behind her, Kari at her shoulder.

Below them a man was bent over in the mud; a small crowd gathering anxiously around him. He was shouting, his face white and desperate. As Wulfgar and Skapti came running up, the crowd moved back a little, and Jessa saw a small boy lying on the ground, curled up as if he was asleep. A handful of grain spilled from his closed fist; the hens still pecked at it hungrily.

"The children," Kari whispered. "They'll be the first."

"Come on!" She pushed past him, ran down the stairs and out, and they both followed her without a word. The crowd fell silent as Kari made his way in beside Wulfgar.

"Has it started already?" the Jarl murmured.

Kari touched the boy's forehead; the father glared, as if he would have pushed him away but dared not. For a moment Kari was still, his face remote, his colorless eyes watching the sleeping child. Then he looked at Wulfgar and nodded.

"What's the matter with him?" the father yelled.

The Jarl caught him by the arm. "Summon your courage, Gunnar. The boy is asleep, that's all. Take him home and put him to bed; I'll send you some help."

Watching him go he said, "It's beginning, then."

The door to the hall slammed wide, startling them all; inside they saw the tapestries billowing in the dream wind. A tiny flake of snow, no bigger than a shieldnail, sailed down and settled on Jessa's sleeve. It did not melt for a long time.

"Find Brochael," Wulfgar said grimly. "Tell him to get the men ready. We leave in the morning."

Then he turned back and looked at Kari. "You said this will spread. How far?"

"The hold first. It's already here—I can't stop that. Afterward, over the whole realm."

"Then we need some way to contain it, Kari. Anything."

Kari nodded slowly. "I'll do what I can."

Six

Wider and wider through all worlds I see.

Late in the night Brochael woke up and turned in the cramped sleeping booth. It was too small for him, as they usually were, but this time he was glad of the discomfort, because the strange dream of the cell had come to him again, and the memory of it disturbed him.

After a moment he sat up with a mutter of irritation. It

was cold in the stone room; the fire must have gone out.

He dragged the great bearskin from the bed, swung it around himself, and padded over the floor, scratching his tousled red hair. The brazier held a low glimmer of peats, and as he dropped new ones in, the light darkened even more, making the room a huddle of cold shadows. Still, it would blaze up eventually and last till morning.

He watched it sleepily for a moment, his mind avoiding the echoes of the dream. Gudrun's sorcery still lurked here. It was not often that he thought about her—he hated the woman for what she had done to her son. Apart from Kari only he, Brochael, knew the full evil of that. And he feared her. As for Kari . . . All at once he realized how quietly the boy was sleeping, and turned quickly.

The bed was empty.

For a moment, rigid, Brochael stared at it. Then he shook his head, dragged the bench up to the warmth, and sat down, leaning back against the wall. The alarm that had flared in him for a second died down—he knew Kari well enough. The boy had strange gifts, and they drove him strangely. Often at home, in Thrasirshall, he would walk the snowfields and forests all night, the ravens flapping above him. Brochael knew he spoke to ghosts and wraiths and invisible things out there, things he could tell no one else about. He tugged the bearskin tight on his broad back.

Wherever Kari was, it was his own realm. He was skillful there.

Under the oak tree at the edge of the wood Kari was digging, making a small pit with his knife in the moist soil under the leaf drift. Around him the night was silent, the wood a dank, rustling mass of darkness, rich with the smell of moss and wood rot.

When the hole was deep enough, he took a pouch from his belt, felt about inside for one of the small bone counters, and dropped it in.

"The last?" a voice croaked above him.

"Two more." He straightened, stamping the soil down quickly, rubbing it from his hands. "One more to close the ring. Near the shore, somewhere."

The moon glinted on his hair and face as he pushed through the tangle of bush and underbrush. Rowan saplings sprouted here at the wood's edge, thorn and hazel and great fronds of bracken between them, chest-high. In the dappled silver light fat stems cracked and snapped under his feet. He struggled through, noticing the frosted crisp ends of the leaves, already dying. About him the night whispered; the dream wind brought him voices and murmurs and crystals of snow; two dark shapes drifted above him from tree to tree.

Then he paused and looked back.

A small boy stood in the wood, watching him. Caught in the moonlight, the child seemed faint, pale as bone. Kari took a step toward him; the boy backed away. Dirty tearstains smeared his face.

"You're the Snow-walker," he muttered.

"I won't hurt you."

The boy looked up, bewildered, at the high, rustling trees.

Finally he came forward. His hand reached out to Kari's sleeve. "I can't get back in," he whispered. "I can't. And none of them can see me anymore. No one talks to me but you. Father tells me to wake up but I can't. I'm outside."

Kari crouched in the mud beside him. "I know that," he said gently. "Your name is Halmund Gunnarson, isn't it?"

The boy nodded, rubbing his face. "I was feeding the hens—"

"You will get back," Kari said urgently, "but I don't know when."

"My father keeps calling me! And I'm cold." He shuddered, and looked around. "And the others frighten me."

"Others?" Kari clenched his fingers. "People you know? People from the hold?"

"No. Shadow people. I don't know them. They're

worn thin, like ghosts. And there are wolves that flicker between me and the moon. Ships out on the water . . ."

"Have you seen a girl?" Kari asked quickly. "Signi. You remember her?"

"She fell asleep."

"That's right."

The boy shook his head. He took a step back, through a trunk of birch. "Has that happened to me? Am I dreaming this? I want to get out of the dream. I want to go home." Suddenly he turned and ran down among the trees to the hold, sobbing. Kari watched him go, fading to a glimmer of moonlight. Then he dropped his head and stared in despair at the leaf litter on the ground. His silver hair hung still.

"Not your fault," a dark voice said.

"In a way it is," he said without looking up. "She wants me. I should have gone with her when she asked. I knew she would never leave them alone."

He jerked up and pushed his way through and out of the wood, the two birds swooping above him, then ran down to the shore, where the black water lapped silently.

In the shingle he gouged another hole and dropped a bone disc in, then covered it with tiny stones and sand. A large boulder lay nearby; he tried to shift it but couldn't. "Help me," he muttered.

They came, one on each side of him, tall, dark men, their long taloned fingers tight on the rock. Together they dragged it over the buried talisman. Then Kari straightened wearily.

"That's it."

He looked back and saw the ring he had made around the hold, felt its power throb and tighten. The dream spell was held inside; none of it could escape. "The last should be left in the hall. A secret guardian over the sleepers."

He walked quickly through the sleeping hold, by shapes he knew, that lurked at the corners of the houses. Coming to the hall he went straight past the watchman, opening the door and letting himself in softly, blanking the man's mind and releasing it as soon as he was inside. The man scratched his hair, seeing nothing; the dog at his feet watched silently.

In the hall Kari moved between the sleeping war band to the roof tree. The ancient ash trunk rose high over him, the snake mark already half planed away by Wulfgar's thralls. Two raven shapes drifted after him through the high windows.

"Here," he said quietly. "This will be the place where the last of them gather. Whoever's still awake. This is the heart of the hold."

He took something small from the pouch and held it up for a moment, the moonlight glinting on its brightness. Then he bent and found a small slit in the seamed trunk, and pushed the shining fragment well inside with his long fingers. "Guard them," he whispered. "Till the time comes."

For a moment he stood there, winding it with spells and runes of protection, filaments of hope. Then he looked up at the birds. "I think you should stay too."

One of them seemed to laugh, a harsh grating sound. "We go with you, Kari. What could we do here, with these sightless men?"

"They see well enough. Differently from us, that's all." He pushed his hair away wearily. "Now I've done all I can for them. Her power is here already, though. Nothing can change that."

As he said it the tapestries rippled with a faint breeze. Some of the sleeping men turned uneasily in their fleeces and wraps. He watched them for a moment, tasting their dreams, then went quietly upstairs.

Brochael sat up as the door opened, his face a warm glow.

"All done?" he asked quietly.

Kari sat on the end of the bench and tugged his boots off.

"All done," he said.

They looked at each other, a flicker of understanding.

In the cold morning Jessa tied her bundle more firmly to the packhorse and swung herself up onto her own pony.

"Yes, but why not go by sea? At least to start with."

Skapti was picking at the upturned hoof of his horse with careful fingers. "Because of the ice." He put the beast's leg down and gave it an encouraging slap. Then he looked at her across the saddle. "If you sail around the coast, beyond Trond, beyond all the fjords, the coast starts to turn north, yes, but after a week or so, even in summer, you reach the ice. I've spoken to a few men who've tried it. Great floating bergs of ice. And if you manage to avoid them and sail on, the ice becomes thicker, smashed plates of it, jagged and sharp. The winter's teeth. Many ships have been eaten by them. Beyond that, they say, you reach a wall of ice, unbroken, higher than the Jarlshall. No one has ever crossed that."

Jessa laughed. "I'm convinced."

"Good." He swung himself up. "Are you all armed, Jessa Two-knives?"

"All armed."

She watched Kari come down the steps in his dark coat. He looked bone pale in the wan light, and tired, as if he had not slept. Brochael was behind him, the huge ax under one arm.

They climbed up onto their horses and waited, the courtyard an agitated clatter of hooves, whinnying, shouts for those who were missing. A drum beat quietly from the corner of the hall; an old man in a shaman's coat of feathers chanted luck songs and charms in a quavering voice.

Hakon came running around the corner with a bundle falling from his back and the precious sword under his arm; he fastened them both hastily onto the restless horse. His friends from the war band mocked him, and he got flustered and did the straps up wrongly. Watching him, Jessa saw how he had grown since he had been here. As a thrall he had been thin—now his arms were strong, his eyes quick from long sword practice with Wulfgar's men. As he scrambled up she said, "We thought you weren't coming."

He grinned at her. "Jessa, you won't get rid of me. This is my first real adventure, my first journey! I've dreamed of this for a long time."

She nodded, thinking that it was dreams they were escaping from. He was the only one who seemed really happy. Wulfgar, on his black horse, looked morosely around. Then he nodded to Brochael. "We're all here."

And he turned the horse and led the company out of the hold, riding proudly between the houses, past the ships on the fjord, scattering chickens and a bleating, long-eared goat. The holders watched them go, muted and somber; only the children waved and shouted, dancing alongside.

Jessa turned in the saddle and waved back to them sadly. She tried not to think about whether she would ever see them again.

Or they her.

She knew she was going too far to come back unchanged.

SEVEN

Men tread Hel's road.

They rode north, along the fjordshore. The path was broad, well used; it ran through the fringes of the woods and out over the wide grazing land of the Jarlsholders.

All through that first day the sun warmed the riders, and quiet warbles of birdsong filled the branches about them. Bees and maybugs and long, glinting dragonflies hummed over the shallows of the still water; occasionally a fish snapped upward, sending a plop of tiny ripples racing to the shore.

Twice they passed fishermen out on the blue water in their flimsy craft, who paused over their nets and watched the cavalcade pass, curious. On the fellsides goats and the long-haired sheep lifted their heads and stared unmoving. This was rich pastureland, owned by men who were respected, Wulfgar's firmest supporters. And it was still midsummer here, the air tinged with the scents of the innumerable flowers, so that the horses waded in clouds of blown seed and spindrift, and the crushed scents of water-mint and warm thyme.

If it could all be this easy, Jessa thought, struggling out of her coat and laying it across the horse in front of her. She laughed at Skapti; daydreaming, he had almost jerked from his horse as it stumbled.

Far ahead Wulfgar rode with Kari. They were talking, close together. Looking back, she saw Brochael joking with the men; they all roared with laughter. Hakon was just behind her.

"He's telling them horrible stories," he muttered. "I don't think you should listen."

Jessa grinned. "I expect I told him most of them."

She laughed at his shocked look, then watched a line of swans skitter down on the rippling water. "It's easy to forget, out here."

"Forget?"

"Signi. And the rest."

He nodded, brushing the swinging leaves away from his face. "I can't understand . . . how can her soul be gone?"

"Kari says so. He knows about these things."

"And what's to stop Gudrun doing that to us—to any of us?"

She looked at him. "Only Kari, I suppose."

Uneasy, he said, "It makes me feel useless. I'm only a swordsman, not even a very good one. Sorcery makes me shiver. Why did Wulfgar send me?"

For a moment she said nothing. Then she shook her head. "Kari needs us, just as we need him. Maybe more. Wulfgar knows that." Seeing his worried look, she laughed. "Anyway, maybe the Jarl wanted to get rid of you for a while."

He laughed with her quietly.

Late in the afternoon, with the long blue twilight barely beginning, the fjord had narrowed to a thin strip of water, the meadows on the other side drawn close. They stayed that night at a hold called Audsstead, the woman Aud riding out with her sons to meet them. Jessa went to bed early, yawning, leaving the talk and laughter in the great hall.

Next day the land began to change. They rode uphill now, and inland. The slopes were steeper, the grass short and sheep-nibbled, studded with boulders that broke the turf as if they were the land's bones, under its green skin. Here and there the slopes were boggy; the horses' hooves sank deep into soft peat, masses of lichen and bright moss matting the treacherous ground.

At last they stopped to eat, high above the fjord. Looking down, Jessa thought the sliver of water was a flooded crack in the land, as if the hills floated above reflections of sky and pale, passing clouds.

Brochael nudged her arm. "All well?"

"Just daydreaming." She snuggled up against him. "How long before we reach the road?"

He shrugged. "We're on it, Jessa, more or less. Only a path is left here, no masonry. We go over this hill ahead and down into a place called Thorirsdale. Beyond that, in the forest somewhere, the road divides. That's as far as Wulfgar will come. From then on, we're on our own."

She was silent for a moment. "Will we get there today?"

"Tomorrow. Tonight we'll stay at Thorirstead. I know Ulf. He used to beat me at wrestling, when we were boys."

Amazed, Jessa looked up at him. "You mean he's bigger than you?"

"He's a giant. He likes to boast he's the descendant of those who built the road. I, for one, believe him."

"I hope not!" Looking around she said, "Where's Kari?"

"Off with the ravens."

There was the hint of something odd in his voice but she had no time to pin it down; Wulfgar was telling everyone to mount up. He came and stood looking down at them.

"Comfortable?"

Jessa grinned. "Very."

He smiled, but briefly, and she knew the thought of Signi was weighing on him, and the dread of what he might find when he went back. She scrambled up, wishing she hadn't said anything.

"Where's Kari?" he asked Brochael.

"About."

"We'd better find him."

"There's no need." Brochael heaved his bag up onto the horse and fiddled with the saddle straps. "He'll come. He'll know we're waiting."

Wulfgar shook his head as Kari came over the brow of the hill just then and waved at them, the birds wheeling joyously around his head.

"Sometimes I wonder if there's anything he can't do."

"He can't steal souls," Brochael muttered. "At least, not yet."

★ ★ ★

When they rode over the hilltop they saw before them the green plenty of Thorirsdale, a wide valley, its tiny silver streams gushing down noisily. This end was pastureland, and they could see the smoke from the farmstead rising near the narrow river. Beyond that the land rose again to deep woods, dark against the sky.

As they rose into the valley the light lessened; the shoulders of the hills rose about them. Down here the air was warm and hushed, the last of the evening birdsong fading over the fields. By the time they neared the hold, the purple half-light had begun, and the weak sun was lost behind the hills.

There was a long low building which looked like the farmhouse, roofed in green turf to keep in the warmth. Smoke rose from a hearth hole near its center; Jessa smelled its sharpness. Other buildings clustered around it, barns and byres, all very quiet and dark under the rising moon.

The horses' hooves crunched down the narrow track.

"Perhaps they're all asleep," Jessa said.

"Not Ulf," Brochael muttered.

A dog barked ahead, then another. After a moment a slot opened in the dark house; light and smoke and cooking smells streamed out. The great bulk of a man clogged the doorway; then he strode out, others behind him.

"Who have I to welcome at this time of night?"

He glanced out at the riders through the eerie night mist, taking them in quickly, their numbers and strength; a tall, heavy man, his hair shaved close, a long sword held easily in his hand.

Wulfgar dismounted. "Me, Ulf Thorirsson."

"Jarl!" The holder turned, surprised. "What's happened?" he asked quickly, seeing Wulfgar's face. "What's wrong?"

"Plenty," Wulfgar said grimly. "But it'll keep until we're inside."

Ulf nodded, passing his sword back to a thrall. "My house is honored. In now, all of you. My men will see to the animals." He swept around and collided with Brochael, who had been standing close behind him. Halfway off her horse, Jessa giggled at the look on his face, half amazement, half delight.

"Brochael?" he breathed.

"Come for a rematch, Ulf." Brochael folded his arms and looked his old friend up and down. "You've been overeating. Running to fat."

Ulf grinned. "There's been no one here to challenge me."

"Until now."

They gripped hands, and Ulf slapped Brochael with a

palm that would have made most men crumple. "It's good to see you," he said warmly.

The hall was small, and heavy with smoke. Food was cooked here over the central hearth. The women of the farm were thrown into cold terror by the sight of the Jarl and all his war band descending on them out of the night, until Ulf's wife, a tall, gaunt woman called Helga, gave quiet, efficient orders.

The high table was cleared; Wulfgar sat in the center, his friends on each side of him, Kari next to Jessa. She knew he was uneasy. Once the excitement of their arrival had died down the people of the hold were only interested in him. They stared frankly, like animals, until he looked up, and then their eyes slid away.

"Center of attention," Jessa whispered.

He nodded, silent.

She trimmed the meat with her knife. "You must be getting used to it."

"You never do." He picked listlessly at his food. "It's not the way they look, but what they feel. Fear. Gudrun's shadow."

There was no denying that, she thought. In the silence that followed, she began to listen to Wulfgar. He was explaining what had happened at the Jarlshold, and Ulf was listening gravely. Brochael had been right; this man was enormous, a head higher than anyone else, even Skapti, his neck thick as a sapling. The coarse wool of his shirt strained over his broad back. Jessa saw that the chair he sat in was huge and old, its legs carved like wolves, their backs arched to bear his weight.

"Will it spread?" Ulf said urgently. "If the whole of the Jarlshold falls into the witch spell, what's to stop it spreading out here?"

Wulfgar looked at Kari.

Kari spoke quietly. "It won't leave the Jarlshold. I've made a binding ring of bone. The dream spell is trapped inside. It won't spread, as long as the people stay within."

"What sort of ring?" Ulf asked curiously. He stared down at Kari's thin face shrewdly, without fear. "Sorcery, is this?"

"You could call it that."

"And you trust it, Jarl?"

Wulfgar smiled slowly. "I trust it."

"Then that's good enough for me. But what about the people in the hold?"

Wulfgar's expression hardened. "We'll stay. That's the choice we've had to make." Then, as if to forget, he reached out a lazy hand for more wine and leaned back. "This is a fine hall, Ulf."

"My father built it. Now there was a big man, bigger even than me." He scratched his stubbly beard.

"Indeed he was." Brochael passed the wine. "They say he once carried a stray reindeer home, two days' journey. Is that true?"

Ulf nodded proudly. "Thorir Giantblood, they called him."

"Tell us about the road," Wulfgar said.

The huge man sat still, the firelight warming his face. Behind him his massive shadow darkened the hung shields.

"There's not much known about it. All the stories of the giants are almost forgotten; even who they were. Your friend here would know more about that than me."

Skapti nodded wryly.

"But the road," Ulf went on, "is real enough. It goes north. They say it runs even to the edge of the world, to a country where the snow falls all night and all day, and where in winter the sun never rises. No one has ever traveled a week's journey along it, to my knowledge, except Laiki."

"Laiki?" Wulfgar murmured.

"An old man now." Ulf stood up and roared, "Thror! Fetch Laiki!" and sat down again. "He went in his younger days. He tells strange tales about it, and they get stranger year by year. I don't promise, Jarl, that any of them are true."

The old man came up slowly. He was shriveled, his hair white as wool, long and straggly. A thick fleece coat covered his body, and as he grasped the chair and lowered himself into it they saw his hand had two fingers missing; two stumps were left, long healed.

"Well, Father, we hear you know something of the giant road." Wulfgar leaned forward and poured him a drink. "My friends will be traveling that way. Can you tell us about it?"

The old man's weak blue eyes looked at them all. He seemed delighted, Jessa thought, to have such an audience.

"Once, I went that way."

"Long ago?"

He wheezed out a laugh. "Forty years or more, masters. Forty years. Two other men and I, we set out to find the road's end. We had learned there was amber up there in the north, and jet. We wanted wealth. Like all young men, we were fools."

He smiled at Jessa and put a cool hand on hers. "Are you going on this journey?"

"Yes," she said quietly.

"Not just young men, then." He shook his head. "The road is paved at first, masters, whole and easy. After a while it becomes fragmented. It leads into a great forest, dark and deep. Ironwood, my friends called it, for a joke, but we were more than a week in that haunted, ghost-ridden place, and all the time we heard the stir and passing of invisible spirits, as if a great army of men whispered about us in the dark. None of us slept. We walked day and night to leave that nightmare behind. The air became colder. One night we came to a great ruined hall, deep in the wood. We were exhausted, and slept, and when we woke, one of my friends had gone. We never found him."

He gazed around at them soberly.

"After the wood, the ice. We struggled on, but our food was gone and our hearts were failing. Then wolves came. Alric was killed, and the horses that we hadn't yet eaten ran off. I wandered alone in the empty land, a place of glaciers, wide snow plains where the icy winds roared all night. I was lost there, starved and delirious. I do not remember, masters, how I got back through the wood. Sometimes it seems to me that I saw terrible sights, things I can't piece together, a great city in a lake, a bridge that rose up to the stars, but I cannot tell if these things were real or a delirium." He paused, sighing. "All I do know is that I came to myself in a shieling north of here, nursed back to health by a shepherd. For two weeks I had lain there, he said, babbling the nightmares of the wood."

He held up his hand. "And these fingers were gone. Bitten off, the good man thought. And to this day I do not know what happened to me."

He looked around at them all. "If your journey is not urgent, masters, take my advice. Turn back. That is no country for mortals."

They were silent a moment.

Then Brochael shook his head. "Lives depend on it, old man. We've no choice."

Eight

I tell of giants from times forgotten,
Those who fed me in former days.

The road was floored with great slabs, powdered with gray and green overlapping lichens. Here and there saplings had sprouted up through the gaps between stones, and bushes of thorn and rowan, but the way was still surprisingly easy to follow, leading downhill among the light-barred glades of trees.

Jessa sat herself down on the edge of it and looked

closely at the giants' handiwork. The slabs had been squared and laid close, each one flat and slotted in neatly to its neighbor. It would take many men and horses to lift even a few. No wonder people thought of giants.

"Are there such things?" she asked aloud.

"Indeed there are. Or there were." Skapti drew his long knees up. "Once, at Hollfara, I saw a merchant selling bones. Huge bones they were, immense, Jessa, bigger than any man or animal, except the great serpent that winds around the earth. What else could they be but giants' bones?"

She touched the amulet at her neck lightly. "Then I hope we don't meet any! Ulf's big enough."

She watched him saying good-bye to Brochael.

"Time to go."

Reluctantly the skald got up after her.

Wulfgar lifted her onto her horse and stood there while Hakon and Brochael mounted. Kari was already waiting, the ravens silent on a branch above him. Wulfgar looked at them all. "It hurts me bitterly to let you all go." He glanced at Skapti. "Especially you."

Skapti gave a lopsided smile. "You can get yourself a better poet. You've always wanted to."

"There is no better poet." He put a hand on Skapti's shoulder. "If you don't come back, and I haven't been caught in the witch spell, then I'll come looking for you. One day."

Skapti nodded. He climbed up onto the long-maned horse and the five of them looked at one another, silent among the crowd of men.

"Good luck," Wulfgar said simply. He glanced at Kari. "There are no others but you who could do this. Let the gods watch you."

"And you," Brochael rumbled.

"Good-bye, Wulfgar," Jessa said sadly. She turned her horse and rode out quickly over the gray stones, the others following, Hakon tugging the long rein of the packhorse.

They clattered down the slope, between the sprouting trees. When Jessa looked back she saw Wulfgar standing at the top, arms folded, watching them. He raised a hand. Then the bushes hid him, and all the men with him.

They were alone.

It was a silent journey, that descent of the ancient road.

None of them wanted to talk, and there was no sense of danger on them, so they rode in a long, straggling line, picking their way over the broken paving.

The road led down and up, winding over low hills, its gray line visible sometimes far ahead. Late in the day they rode over a high moor, with the gray scatter of broken paving stretching in front of them, mosses and peat spreading out over it, as if the land was drawing it back.

Hakon slowed his horse. "What's that?"

On the horizon a gaunt pillar stood stark against the cloudy sky.

"Dead tree," Brochael suggested.

"Too straight." Skapti narrowed his eyes. "A rock, maybe."

Cautiously they rode toward it. As they came close they saw that he was right, but that this rock too had been shaped, heaved upright. Sliced deep into its surface was a carving of three wolves, tangled together, their jaws agape. Behind them, his great hand reining them in, stood a huge man, his head roughly shaped, his eyes looking fiercely out. Unfamiliar words were carved at his feet.

"Can you read it?" Jessa asked Skapti.

The skald dismounted and went over to the stone, reaching up and fingering the carving thoughtfully. "No. These are no runes I know. And it's old, Jessa. Centuries."

"It could be a gravestone," Hakon said uneasily.

"It could. But I think it's a marker of territory. Or was."

"Giants?" Brochael wondered.

Skapti shrugged and climbed back onto his horse. "Maybe. But long ago."

Jessa looked at Kari. He was gazing up at the stone, his

eyes strangely distant. For a moment she thought he was listening to some sound, straining to catch it, but when he saw her looking, he said nothing.

They went on, but after that silent warning a sense of foreboding seemed to fall on them; they rode together now, and more warily.

Slowly the long day died, but still they traveled, not knowing where to stop. Finally, in a small copse of birch by the roadside, they saw the rise of a thatched roof.

Brochael drew rein. "I'll go and see," he said. "Skapti, come too. The rest of you, wait here."

But the ravens had come karking down about Kari in a flutter of noise; they perched on the gray stones, walking and pecking over them.

"They say it's empty," Kari said.

Brochael glared at him. "Are you sure?"

"So they say."

Everyone stared at the birds, but they knew better than to doubt him. Brochael urged his horse off the road. "This is going to be a very strange expedition," he muttered.

It was an old shepherd's hut, long deserted. Trees had sprouted in the doorway, and the walls had gaping holes, but the roof was more or less intact, and the floor seemed dry.

They hacked their way in and soon had a fire lit;

Hakon and Jessa rubbed the horses down and let them graze tied to a long rope.

"What about wolves?" Hakon said nervously.

Jessa gathered up her pack. "We'll hear them. And we can't take the beasts in with us, can we?"

"I suppose not," he said, grinning.

Later, as they ate around the fire, Brochael brought out the map. He opened it, the waxed sealskin crackling under his fingers, and spread it out on his coat. "We should add to this as we go. That stone, for instance."

"No ink." Jessa swallowed a mouthful of cheese too quickly.

"No." He scowled.

"Besides," Hakon said, looking at the parchment closely, "maybe the stone we saw is this." He put his finger on the faint ghost of a mark to the left of the red line; it was so worn it had almost gone, but now they looked closely it could once have been a rough suggestion of the stone, its carvings reduced to squiggles.

"So whoever made it got this far," Skapti said drily. "That cheers me."

"This hut"—Jessa waved her knife around—"could be the hut the old man talked about. It must have belonged to Ulf's people once. It's too small for giants."

The fire crackled and spat over the damp kindling.

Outside, the night was still, and through the doorway they could see the stars, faint and pale.

"It's colder up here," Hakon muttered.

"It'll get colder all the time." Brochael tapped the map. "This will be the forest."

Tiny scratched trees were massed about the red line of the road. In the midst of them Jessa thought she saw something else, a faint rune, but she couldn't be sure.

"How long before we reach it?"

"A day. Two." Brochael folded the skin quickly. "Now . . . from now on we have someone awake always. In turns. Kari first, then Jessa. We're out of the Jarlsrealm, and these are unknown lands. We should expect wolves, bears, outlaws maybe. Keep the fire going, Kari, but low. Not too much smoke."

They rolled themselves in cloaks and blankets on the uncomfortable floor, and as Kari sat outside, leaning back against the wall, the gradual sounds of their breathing drifted out to him. Deep inside each of them, he could feel the terror of his mother's spell, planted far down in their minds, ready to spread and trap them as it had trapped Signi and the boy. He knew each dream, and knew he couldn't destroy them, but only suppress them. So that each one would wake and forget.

Stretching out his legs he wrapped his dark cloak about

him and looked up at the stars. They glinted, in their strange, spread patterns. Did the same stars shine over the land of the Snow-walkers? And was Gudrun looking up at them now? Though he ranged the night with his mind's whole power, he could find no trace of her, or anything else either, in this strange empty land.

Except, far to the north, a sudden smudge of sound, which held him still for a moment, listening. A low murmur, like the beat of a drum. He stood up and looked out through the still trees, but he knew already it was a ghost sound, and not in this world.

"Did you hear that?"

The bird shape above came down and stood beside him. "We did. But far off."

Together they stared out over the unknown land.

NINE

Death is the portion of doomed men.

Two days later, early in the afternoon, they came to the edge of the wood.

For hours they had been riding through its outlying fringes, the scattered trees and sparse growths of hazel and birch, but now, coming down a steep hillside, they saw the sudden thickening of the trees, a massing of greenery. Below them lay a mighty forest, its millions of treetops stirring in the soft breeze. It stretched far to the north, beyond sight into mist and low gray rain cloud, as if somewhere it merged with the sky and dissolved there, at the edge of existence.

The road had dwindled to little more than a track, thin and muddy. It ran down among the trees and was swallowed.

Brochael ducked his head under a branch. "Someone must still use it."

Silent, they gathered beside him, letting the horses graze.

Jessa slid down and stretched stiffly. "So this is Ironwood. Easy to get lost in."

Hakon took a long drink and wiped his mouth. "I thought Ironwood was just a place in tales."

"So it is," Skapti said promptly, "but all tales are true. They're just the way we struggle with the world." He folded his thin arms, looking out over the forest. "The Ironwood of the stories is a very strange place. It lies far in the northeast. A giantess lives in its heart, and many troll wives. The giantess breeds sons able to shape-shift into wolf form. All the wolves of the world are descended from her. One day, they say, there will come an enormous wolf, called Hati, or Moongarm, who will strengthen himself by drinking the blood of all who die. Then he'll swallow the moon itself at the world's end, in the last conflict." He raised a thin eyebrow. "As the old man said, no place for mortals."

"But this isn't that wood, is it?" Hakon asked.

"Who knows. Perhaps every wood is that wood."

"If it's not, the old man gave it a bitter name," Brochael remarked. "And stop teasing the boy, Skapti, or he'll be no good to any of us."

The skald grinned. Hakon went red.

"But there are wolves." Jessa got back on her horse. "We've heard them."

"And other beasts, I hope. Some fresh meat wouldn't come amiss."

They picked their way down carefully. The remaining stones of the road were cracked and treacherous, poking up here and there through mud and leaf litter. As the riders passed silently into the wood they felt its rich scents wrap around them; tree sap and fungi, crumbling bark, centuries of decay and growth. High above, the spindly branches of silver birch rustled, the sky blue and remote through the windblown boughs. Birds whistled here, flitting among the leaves, but gradually the wood became thicker and darker. The birches gave way to oaks, then a mass of evergreens, pine and spruce and fir, clogging the light. Soon the riders moved in a green gloom, silent except for the soft footfalls of the horses.

Brochael rode ahead, with Kari and Jessa close behind. Skapti and Hakon came last, urging on the nervous pack-horse. The wood closed in. Branches hung over the path, swishing back into their faces; far off, the dimness was split by shafts of sunlight, slanting here and there between the crowded trees.

After only a few minutes Brochael stopped suddenly. Jessa's horse, always nervy, snorted and skittered sideways with fright, and she tugged its head around, trying not to back into Skapti.

Then she saw what had frightened it.

Skulls.

They were threaded, one above the other, hanging on long strings from the still branches, small skulls of birds and tiny animals—pine marten, stoat, rats, crows. Hundreds of them. In the faint breeze the bizarre hangings clicked and tapped against one another, the empty slits of their eyes turning. Half-rotten, green with mold and lichen, beaks and teeth and bones swung in the dimness. Feathers were knotted into bundles among them, and the stink of decay hung under the trees.

"What is it?" Hakon whispered, appalled.

None of them answered him. The sudden smell of decay brought terror, numbing and cold. Centuries of superstition rose in their hearts, fear of sorcery, sacrifice, unknown rites. Small flies buzzed and whined about Jessa's face; she beat them off in disgust.

Then Kari nudged his horse forward. He rode in under the long dangling lines of bone and caught one with his thin hands. Pulling it toward him he examined it carefully, the horse fidgeting beneath him.

His movement broke the stillness that held them. Jessa moved up beside him; the others came too, reluctantly.

"Look at this." Kari's fingers slid the skulls apart; he touched carved circles of bone, each marked with runes, the same angular letters they had seen on the standing stone.

"What do they mean?" Brochael growled. He had his ax in his hand; he glanced around at the clinking curtain of death as if it made his skin crawl.

"Looks like a place of ritual," Jessa muttered.

"Sacrifices?"

"Yes, but who left them," Skapti murmured, "and how long ago?"

Each of them kept their voices low; each of them noticed the human skulls, just a few, threaded here and there between the others.

Kari let the string of bones drop; it clicked and rattled

and swung ominously to and fro. He was the only one of them who seemed unaffected by the grimness of the place. "Some are old," he said thoughtfully. "They've been here years. But that—that's new enough."

It was the jawbone of a reindeer or some other grazing beast, snapped clean in half, impaled on the thorns of a bush. Strips of skin still hung from it. Around it, as if placed like offerings, were four small metal arrowheads, some black feathers, a broken bear's claw.

"This is sorcery," Brochael muttered, backing suddenly. He gripped the thorshammer at his neck and looked at Kari as if there was a question he didn't know how to ask.

Kari answered it. "I don't know for sure, but I think Jessa's right, in a way. The wood ahead of us is haunted by something. This is the barrier. Someone has made these offerings, built this curtain of power, hoping that whatever is in the wood can't pass it. I left something similar around the Jarlshold."

Jessa looked at him in surprise but Brochael nodded. He looked worried. "So what do we do?"

"We go on," Skapti said quietly.

"If the wood is haunted—"

"We have to go through, Brochael. Anything else would take too long."

Each of them nodded, silent.

"Then we keep together, and all armed."

"Let me go first," Kari said.

"No!"

"Brochael." Kari came up to him, his pale hair silvery in the dimness. "I'm the best armed of all of you when it comes to things like this."

For a moment Brochael said nothing. Then, with a grimace, he muttered, "I know that."

"So?"

"So watch my back."

He turned his horse and led them out of the grove, between the bones that turned and glittered in the draft. Jessa pulled a wry face at Kari, and he smiled and shook his head. She for one was glad to get away from the horror of the skulls, but fear had fingered them now and they could not shake it off. The wood was full of shadows, sly movements, unease. Branches rustled, as if invisible watchers touched them, and as the darkness grew to the dim blue of night, a mist began to gather, waist high, hanging between the dank boughs.

It became harder to keep to the path. Once, Brochael lost it, and they had to backtrack through an open stand of larches, bare of leaf below but black above. Skapti found a narrow track, but no one could tell if it was the remains of the road or not. Suddenly, in the great silence, they knew they were lost.

Lost. Skapti felt the word crisp like a dead leaf in his mind.

Brochael swung himself down. "Well, we had to stop somewhere; it may as well be here. We need daylight to see our way out of this."

But Jessa thought that this was not a place they would have chosen. The wood had chosen it for them. It was open, with no real shelter among the trees; they built the fire near a mass of holly that might be some protection, but the kindling was damp and the mist put the flames out twice before Kari intervened and made them roar up and crackle.

It was a miserable night. They were short of water, and the damp glistened on their clothes and hair however close to the fire they crowded. They tried to keep up a conversation, and Skapti told stories, but in the silences between the words, they were all listening.

The wood stirred and rustled around them. As night thickened, their uneasiness grew. Once, a low thud of hooves in the distance made Hakon and Brochael leap up, weapons in hand, but the sound had gone; only the trees creaked in the rising wind. There were other noises: cries, far off; long, strange howlings; the distant, unmistakable beat of a drum. And always the wind, gusting.

Late in the night they heard something else: a scream, suddenly cut off.

"That was a man," Hakon whispered.

Brochael nodded grimly.

"Shouldn't we go and see?"

"We're going nowhere, lad. Not until it's light."

They tried to sleep, but the damp and the eerie night sounds made it difficult. When Hakon finally woke Jessa to take her turn at the watch, she felt as if she had drifted from one nightmare to another. She sat up, stiff and dirty.

"For Odin's sake, keep your eyes open," Hakon muttered. "This place terrifies me. I see what the old man meant."

Irritably she nodded, tugging out the long sharp knives from her belt. "I know. Go to sleep, worrier."

The fire was low, the mist smothering it. She fed it carefully, squatting with her back to the others. The horses tugged restlessly at their ropes, their ears flickering as a murmur of sound came from the wood. Jessa crouched, listening. She wondered where Kari's birds were. There was no sign of them, but they might be roosting above, invisible in the black branches.

It took about half an hour for the kindling to run out.

Finally she stood up, brushing dead leaves from her knees. Gripping the knives tight, she ventured out cautiously into the trees and looked around.

The wood was a dim gloom, mist drifting round the dark trunks. She crouched quickly, snatching up anything that would burn—pinecones, snapped twigs, branches. Suddenly her fingers touched something hard, and she lifted it, curious.

It was an old war helmet, rusting away. One of the cheek plates was gone; the empty eyeholes were clotted with soil. As she raised it the soil shifted and fell, as if the eyes had opened.

And something touched her.

She looked down, heart thudding.

A hand had been laid on her sleeve softly. The fingers were scarred, pale as bone. And they had claws.

Ten

Nine worlds I can reckon, nine roots of the tree,
The wonderful ash, way under the ground.

Jessa screamed, twisting sideways. She jumped back, crashing into Hakon; he caught her arm and dragged her toward the fire, her eyes wide.

"Did you see it?" She gasped.

"There was a shadow . . . something."

The wood around them was silent. For a long moment they all stood listening, so tense that they barely breathed, Jessa shuddering from cold and shock.

Then Brochael hefted the ax in his hand. "Get some wood, Hakon. Plenty of it."

They kept watch as Hakon sheathed his sword and gathered quick armfuls of kindling, Jessa picking up what he dropped. Then all of them backed to the dying fire.

"Build it up," Brochael ordered. He stood warily, watching the dim trees. "So what was it, Jessa?"

She took a deep breath. "A hand. But the nails were long, really long. For a moment I thought . . ."

"What?"

She shook her head. "And there's this."

She held up the helmet. He spared it a glance, then looked again dubiously.

"That's familiar. Made at the Jarlshold, or Wormshold, surely."

Skapti took it from her. "Our people? Here?"

"Still here." Kari was watching something, his frost gray eyes moving, scanning the trees.

They looked at him and he said, "You remember.

Long ago an army from the Jarlshold marched north against the Snow-walkers. None of them ever came back, isn't that so? Except my father. And the witch was with him."

Jessa nodded, remembering all too clearly. "Mord told me that. He said the war band marched down into a strange white mist. No one ever knew what happened to them. Presumably they died." She looked into the fog gathering around the trees. "It happened here?"

"Near here."

"But the hand I saw . . ."

"Dead men's nails grow," Skapti said drily.

She looked at him in horror. But Kari said, "These are their ghosts. I can see them all around us. Gaunt, ragged men."

"How many?" Brochael asked quietly.

"Too many." Kari's voice was strained; he was glad they could not see as he could. The ghost army stood in the mist; wounded, filthy, their faces hard and unremembering, as if nothing of their lives or memory were left to them. They made no move, but their eyes were cold, and he knew they meant evil.

"Keep by the fire. I don't know what else we can do."

Behind him the horses whinnied; they too could see. One reared, and then another, struggling frantically with their ropes. Turning, he saw the wraith men had moved in behind, closer.

"Hold them!" Brochael snarled. "If they break out, we're in trouble."

Hakon threw himself at the straining rope; he dragged the horses' heads down and Jessa grabbed the leading rein of the packhorse, fighting to hang on to it. Slowly they calmed the beasts, talking to them, rubbing their long noses, but they were still terrified, Jessa knew.

"What do we do?" Brochael asked.

"Make a ring around the fire," Kari answered. "As close as you can. Lend me your sword, Hakon."

For a moment Hakon hesitated. Then he held it out. Kari took it and held it a moment; then he put the point to the soil and drew a great circle around them, horses and all. Where the circle joined he stabbed the blade upright into the muddy ground; it swayed but stood.

Even before he had finished, he saw the wraith army run forward, heard their hissing snarls of disappointment.

Outside the circle they stood close, bleeding from old wounds, their eyes cold. He saw rusted swords in their hands, smashed shields, helms black with old blood.

"Don't go outside the ring," Kari muttered. "Whatever you do, don't break it."

Jessa looked at his face, and the fear in it turned her

cold. She stared outward but saw nothing but trees, and mist, and faint movements in the corner of her eye, so that when she focused on them they were gone. But she knew they were out there. The concentration of malice and fear was like a rank smell about them; she gave Hakon one of her long knives and he gave her a quick, grateful glance.

Then Kari spoke. "I can hear you."

He looked outward, at one spot. "Leave us alone. These are your own people. Let them be."

"We have no people," the wraith voice snarled at him. "We have only the forest. We are its breath, its stirring. Our bodies feed its roots. We have waited years for you."

"For me?" he breathed.

"A sorcerer as powerful as she was. Release us."

There was silence. He knew the others were watching him; they had only heard his answers.

"What do they say?" Brochael growled.

Kari shook his head. Then he said, "I'll do what I can. How will I find you?"

The ghost warrior grinned, its broken face dark. "We will show you the way, rune lord."

"When the sun comes."

"Now."

"No. When the sun comes."

Silence answered him. He clenched his fists, alert for

what they might do. But slowly, they moved back and faded into mist, into nothing. He let his breath out painfully and turned.

"They've gone."

"Gone? Where? Will they come back?"

Kari pushed his hair from his eyes and sat down. "They'll be back."

All the rest of the night they sat alert around the fire, nervous at every sound. Kari seemed weary and preoccupied; he would say little about the ghost army or what they had said to him, and soon drifted into sleep, his head on Brochael's chest.

"He can sleep anywhere," Skapti muttered.

"He's lucky," Hakon said.

None of the others could. They talked in low voices, uneasy, Skapti making bitter, defiant jokes about dead men. Slowly the wood lightened about them, the dawn glint filtering through the massed leaves, but the mist still lingered, in pockets and hollows under the dark trees. Hakon's sword gleamed wet with dew.

Stiff, sore, and thirsty, Jessa untwisted her hair and tied it up again, tight. Somehow that made her feel better. Skapti handed out bannocks and some of the dry, crumbly cheese, and they shared the cold water.

"There must be a stream nearby," Jessa said.

"Probably." The skald ate quickly, his eyes on the mist. "But I'm not sure if I would care to drink from it."

"Why not?" Hakon looked at him in alarm. "What might it do?"

Skapti gave him a sharp sideways glance. "There are streams in Ironwood that turn men to ice, make them sleep forever, drive them mad—"

"Skapti!" Brochael growled.

Hakon looked away, his face hot. "I didn't believe any of it, anyway."

When Kari woke, Brochael made him eat. "Are they back yet, ravenmaster?" Skapti asked.

Kari nodded, swallowing. "We have to follow them."

"Follow them? Where?" Brochael demanded.

"I don't know. They've asked me to release them. Some sort of spell holds them here."

"And if you can't?"

"Then we'll never leave the wood, Brochael. None of us."

Jessa rubbed her chilled wrists. She caught Skapti's eye and he shrugged. "That's one tale you can believe, Hakon."

They mounted up, and Hakon heaved his sword out of the ground. At once Jessa felt unprotected, watched. They rode down the path that Skapti had found the night before. Around them the wood rustled, creaking with movement.

All through the morning the realization grew in them that a crowd of invisible presences surrounded them; behind the creak of saddle leather they began to hear the swish of feet through bracken and crisp drifts of leaves.

Soon Jessa grew wary of looking back; she had begun to see movements in the trees, to glimpse tall shapes that kept pace with them, and noticing Hakon's white, fixed look, she guessed he had seen them too. None of them spoke now; Kari rode ahead, the ravens flapping over him, Brochael saying nothing, but watching anxiously.

At midmorning they came to a hollow and rode down it in single file, the hooves crumbling the rich loam. At the bottom Kari paused, looking into the trees at the left of the path.

"In there."

The plantation was dark, thickly overgrown. A curious smell came from it, musty—a smell of old, rotting things. Gently he eased his horse off the path, ducking under low branches. As the others followed, Brochael muttered, "Weapons ready. All of you."

Behind them, all around them, the wood seethed with its silent army, crowding between the trees. Down Kari rode, almost lost ahead among the leaves, and then Jessa saw sunlight flicker on his hair, and she rode out after him into a great swath of open land choked with brambles and bracken.

They all stopped, looking ahead.

Before them was the mouth of a cave, huge, like the entrance to the underworld.

Jessa knew this was the place. It stank of death; flies buzzed in its windless silence. Among the bracken were heaps of rusted weapons, helms and shields, rotting into the soft soil. As the riders moved forward they felt as if the horses were treading among bones and snagged cloth and moss, sinking in deep. Disgusted, Jessa looked back. Among the trees she could see them now, the wraith army, long-haired and gaunt, their faces cold and remote.

At the cave mouth the travelers dismounted. Brochael peered into the dark. "In there?"

"Yes." Kari slipped past him, and the others followed, leaving the horses outside.

The cave was damp, dripping with water. Ferns sprouted from rock crevices, and other blanched, unhealthy growths dripped liquid from their cold fronds. The shuffle of footsteps rang in the roof.

"How far in?" Hakon wondered.

"I don't know!" Jessa grinned at him. "Worried?"

He pulled a face. "All this witchery terrifies me. You know that."

She nodded, thinking that not many people would have said it. But Hakon never pretended.

He slipped and she grabbed his elbow. "Don't collapse on me."

"It's getting darker."

It was. As they left the entrance behind, the dimness in front of them seemed thicker. Jessa stared into it, her nerves tight. Something was there, something dark, appalling.

Kari made some light. He lifted his hand and a glowing ring grew in the air, crackling with blue flames.

Hakon caught her arm. In the rune light they saw a tree. A huge, dead ash tree. It was enormous; it towered above them into the roof of the cave, and far up in its bleached bare branches hung helmets and shields and the skulls of horses, turning and creaking slowly in the stillness. At the base of the tree a ring of swords had been rammed into the ground, between the spread roots.

As Kari stepped toward it, Jessa began to feel afraid of it; its branches were twisted and strangely askew, as if it had had more than tree life, as if it had moved. Pulling out of Hakon's grip, she jumped from rock to rock and landed just behind Kari.

"Wait!" Jessa cried.

Kari turned.

"Don't go any nearer! I don't trust it."

Behind her Skapti said, "She's right. This is an evil

place. Only the gods know what went on here. And Gudrun."

"You recognize it, then."

They all did. The white snake was carved on the tree, into the heartwood, its lithe body winding around and around the dead, smooth bark, and the moss would not grow on it, as if the oozings of its skin poisoned them.

Kari took one step closer.

The crack rang in the roof; he and Jessa flung themselves aside, the branch crashing beside them, scattering sand and bark. Raising her head, she knew she was covered in dust; pain throbbed in her side where she'd bruised it against a rock.

Hakon hauled her up roughly.

"Be careful!" she whispered.

Kari stood up too, the echoes of the fall dying in the roof.

They looked at the huge branch, split with age, tinder-dry.

Brochael turned to Kari. "What do you want to do?"

"Burn it." His voice was bleak and cold and he looked at them unhappily. "This is the source of the spell. Burn it and they'll all be free."

Brochael unsheathed his knife. "At least there's plenty of kindling. . . ." He stopped as Kari laid a hand on his arm.

Glancing at the boy's face, he said, "I should have known it wouldn't be that easy."

"Nothing will burn it except rune fire." He glanced back. "Take the horses farther away."

Hakon went back and caught the bridles, dragging the horses to a safer distance.

Kari stood near the tree, tiny in its shadow. High in the branches his two ravens perched and hopped among the twisting shields. At his call they swooped down to him.

He stood still. A draft of air ruffled his hair and the collar of his dark coat. Then, suddenly, he stepped back.

The tree shivered, as if a wind had passed through it. Then Jessa saw a flicker of red spark along the dry bark. Smoke formed a haze; the almost invisible flame roared along the lowest branches, and suddenly the tree was ablaze, an inferno of hot, blackening wood, spitting sparks high into the cave roof. And the snake, writhing among it, came twisting and slithering down, unwinding itself as if it would escape, blackening and opening into a roaring hole of heat. She caught hold of Kari and drew him away; then they both turned and ran for the cave mouth, stumbling among drifts of smoke and the stench of burning. Coughing, her face smarting and her eyes sore, Jessa looked into the forest.

The wraith army waited.

"It's over," Kari said to them.

For a moment they stood there, watching the smoke stream from the cave. Then the ghost with the broken face nodded. "Our thanks, sorcerer. And a word of advice. The rainbow is not safe to walk on. Not for you."

Kari glanced at the others. He knew they had not heard.

"And this warning is only for me?"

"Only for you."

The wraith army turned. Silently they walked away.

Eleven

Boards shall be found of a beauty to wonder at,
Boards of gold in the grass long after,
The chess boards they owned in olden days.

All afternoon as they rode on, a mighty column of black smoke rose behind them, dissipating over the wood. Hours later, from higher ground, they looked back and could still see it, drifting east, the trees around them flexing and hissing in the rising gale.

"Why did she do it?" Jessa said thoughtfully.

"Spite." Brochael was watching the sky. "The same as with Signi. I don't like the look of this wind. We'll have rain. Maybe snow."

Down among the dim aisles of trees, they found a spring, bubbling cold and clear, and despite his wild tales Skapti was the first to drink from it. He sprawled against a fallen trunk and wiped his lips. "Heart ale. Sweeter than the mead of wisdom." He looked around, considering. "Why not stay here? It'll be dark soon."

"No shelter." Brochael filled his water skin absently. "We should find somewhere out of the rain."

Jessa and Hakon exchanged grimaces. They were both tired out—only Kari had slept much the night before, and since the tree had burned, he was silent and withdrawn, more so than usual.

Brochael must have noticed, because he said, "We need a place where these youngsters can have a good rest. And the horses."

"While we," Skapti muttered, stretching out his long legs, "we warriors, we Thor-like men of iron, travel tirelessly, I suppose?"

Brochael chuckled into his beard. "Spindly poets don't need sleep. They dream enough in the daytime."

For a while they sat there by the stream, eating the last

strips of smoked venison that Ulf had given them, listening to the roar of the wind in the high branches. Since the spell tree had burned, crashing in on itself into soft, powdery ash, the wood had changed. All that rustle and movement, the restless anger of the wraith army, had gone. Under the roaring of the storm, the wood was quiet. Its ghosts were sleeping.

They mounted up and rode on, now into squalls that gusted leaves and dust into their eyes. Jessa tied a scarf over her face and pulled her hood up, but soon the rain came, splattering between the trees. In minutes it was a heavy downpour, soaking them all, driving into their faces as they urged the wet horses on.

"This is useless!" Skapti shouted as the wind caught his cloak and flung it against him. "We need shelter!"

"Where?" Brochael roared back.

One of the ravens gusted down, landing with difficulty on a swaying branch. Kari watched it. Then he said, "Not far ahead, it seems. There's a building."

"A building? Here?"

"Some troll nest," Hakon muttered.

"I don't much care if it is; we'll look at it." Brochael wiped sleet from his eyes. He looked up at the raven. "Lead the way!"

At once it flew, low under the spread boughs and

splintered oak boles of this part of the forest, gliding like a shadow. They followed with difficulty through stunted hazels, and finally had to dismount and force their way through, dragging the reluctant horses.

Once off the path the undergrowth rose above them, a tangle of thorns and spiny bushes, menacing and almost impenetrable, as if they hid some secret place, lost for generations. Jessa was caught and snagged and tangled; she had to tear herself free more than once, and was ready to swear with frustration when she looked up and saw the wall.

It loomed high over the trees, a black, strangely gabled shadow against the stormy sky. Clouds streamed above it; ivy or some other creeping growth covered it. There was no light, no sound of life.

Behind her Hakon muttered, "I was right. No man built that."

The size of it silenced them, made them afraid. Sleet hissed into the trees around, tiny crystals of ice bouncing and scattering from leaf to leaf. The wind raged in their ears.

"What do you think?" Brochael said to Kari.

He shrugged. "It looks old. . . ."

Then he stopped. From far off in the forest had come a sound they all dreaded, that they had been awaiting for days, almost without knowing.

The rising howl of a wolf.

Others answered it, away to the east.

"That settles it." Brochael shoved his way forward. "Let's find the way in."

They forced their way through the tangled growth and came to the base of the great wall. It rose above them, huge black blocks of hewn stone, so high it almost seemed to topple outward. Saplings sprouted from it; ivy smothered it.

They groped their way along, searching for an entrance.

"It's ancient," Jessa said.

Skapti nodded in the dimness. "If this isn't a real giant hall, I don't know what is. What a size they must have been."

Brochael, in front, laughed grimly. "The bigger they are, the harder they fall."

Ahead the wall reached a corner; he put his head around cautiously. Then he beckoned them on.

This seemed to be the front of the building. They passed two huge embrasures, deep in shadow and choked with tree growth. Far above their heads they could dimly make out windows, immense and dark. Then they came to a small wall, knee high. It took Jessa a moment to realize it was really a step.

She raised her head and looked up at the doorway in dismay. A mighty wooden door confronted them, the handle higher than Skapti's head. Two sprawling metal hinges interlaced across it, the bronze rivets green with age.

On each side were three stone doorposts, the first carved into hundreds of faces—some dwarfish, others scowling, grinning, hostile, or ugly—a tangle of leering looks sneering down at the travelers, their huge noses and beards and lips crumbling into wet stone. All across the lintel too the faces crowded, and among them here were skulls, and on the second doorpost strange inhuman things—trolls and wolves and ettins and werebeasts, hideously open-mouthed. Dragons finished the design, writhing about the third row of posts, wormlike, biting one another's tails and slavering over tiny men carved into crevices.

Us, Jessa thought.

Over everything else, a great giant's face glared down at those foolish enough to knock; it wore a copper helm with nose and cheek guards; the face was stern, with a thick stone beard and deepset eyes that stared grimly from the shadows. Below it, in the same odd script as before, were five runes; perhaps his name. GALAR.

Rain splattered the carvings. The building was silent and black.

"Well?" Skapti murmured uncomfortably.

"We'll open it. Hakon, come up here with me."

Sword out, Hakon pushed through the horses to Brochael. He rubbed his nose nervously, then gripped the sword hilt tight with both hands.

They climbed the steep steps to the door.

Brochael reached up, straining, and grasped the ring handle. He turned it with all his strength, and then pushed at the door. It stuck, the wood warped and swollen. Skapti climbed up and helped them; together they shoved hard, forcing a crack wide enough for a horse to squeeze in. Then Brochael said, "Wait here."

Ax in hand he slithered through the dark gap.

They waited, alert, in the cold rain. In about five minutes he was back. "Seems empty. Come on."

They led the horses in one by one, the beasts clattering nervously up the steps, their ears flicking at unnameable sounds, balking at the damp black entrance. Jessa had to walk hers in backward, coaxing and cursing him under her breath. Once inside, she gripped the harness and stared around.

They stood in a huge darkness. Nothing could be seen of the hall but a glimmer of dusky sky here and there, far up in the roof, as if in places the turf or wood had worn and crumbled to holes.

"No windows." Hakon's voice came suddenly out in the dark.

"Must be. We saw them." They heard Brochael fumbling for his firebox.

"Smothered by ivy," Jessa suggested.

"Or shutters."

They heard Brochael mutter to Kari, and a small blue flame suddenly cracked into the darkness. It steadied into yellow, burning on the end of a thin beeswax taper. Brochael was grinning, as if at some joke.

"Now," he said, gripping the ax. "Let's see where we are."

"What about the door?" Skapti said.

"Ah yes. Close it."

But although they all pushed together, it was wedged now, immovable.

"Oh, leave it," Jessa said at last. "At least we can get out."

"And anything else can get in!"

"The birds will stay outside," Kari said. "They'll warn us."

"Right," Brochael said. "Follow me."

Carefully they moved out over the smooth dark floor. Judging from the muffled thump of the hooves, it wasn't stone but trampled earth, Jessa thought. The flame above Brochael's hand was tiny; it flung a huge distorted shadow of him back across their faces. The others were barely visible, glimpses of eyes and faces. As they crossed it she knew the hall was even more huge than it had seemed from outside. Here and there weeds and fat pale mushrooms sprouted, glistening wet in the candle flame. All around hung heavy silence, and far behind, the pale crack of the doorway glimmered.

"Over here," Brochael whispered. He shaded the flame with his hand and turned to the left, walking more quickly. He came to something dark and bent over it; then he picked it up.

"Look at this."

It was a carved horse, a chess piece. It was as long as his arm.

They gathered around it, fingering the rotting wooden mane. Other chess pieces lay on the floor, scattered around, broken and softening into the soil. Kari kneeled and touched one, lingering over it.

"Long dead," Brochael said stoutly, but there was a question behind it. Kari took his hand off the king piece and looked around in the darkness. "A wolf is listening," he said.

Far off, as if to answer him, one howled in the wood.

"They won't come in here," Jessa said.

He looked at her strangely, but said nothing.

Walking between the huge chess pieces, they crossed to the end of the hall. Here a doorway led off into another room, pitch black. Weapons in hand, they went in.

This room was smaller; a pale window at one end showed them a patch of stormy sky and two stars glinting. Wind roared through it. Debris was scattered here too, and in one corner a tree trunk had sprouted up and died and fallen years ago; now it lay in a sprawling tangle.

Brochael slapped it. "This will do. Plenty of kindling. We can watch the doorway to the hall."

"There's another door down there," Skapti muttered, straining his eyes into the gloom. "This place is a warren."

Brochael stuck the candle into a crack in the tree trunk and began to gather scraps of wood. They snapped easily, dry and loud.

It took no time to get a fire going; the flames lit the corner of the great room but little else. The travelers dried themselves out and ate wearily, then wriggled into blankets almost without a word. Jessa was glad to be warm. As she tossed to find a comfortable position, she thought of the old man, back at Ulf's. He had said something about a great hall. The thought eluded her; she was too tired to chase it. Sleep swallowed her instantly, like a great wolf.

Hakon had first watch.

He propped his chin on his sword to keep awake, but that was no use; soon he was nodding and had to get up and prowl about in the dark.

He crossed to the doorway and gazed out, into the

black spaces. For a moment he had thought that something had shuffled out there, but everything seemed still. Far across he could see the crack of the outer doorway, paler than the surrounding blackness.

The others were asleep; it would be better not to wake them unless he was sure. If it was nothing, Skapti would have something bitterly sarcastic to say. Jessa too, if he knew her.

He stared out, puzzled, into the hall. The silence of the great ruin was complete. He thought of the warped doors, the dust over everything. No one could be still here.

Then, this time nearer, he heard it again. A chink of sound.

Gripping his sword hilt with both hands, Hakon stepped cautiously out, sliding his foot against rubble and stones. Out in the invisible heart of the hall, a patch of moonlight fell briefly through a roof hole and vanished; he glimpsed sleet spiraling down and for a moment something long and gray that moved through it and slid into the dark. His heart thumped. It had looked like a wolf.

He waited, breathless a moment, then took a silent step back. At once a cold hand slid around his mouth and clamped down; a sword point jabbed in his back.

"Don't move. Make a sound and I cut your throat."

The swordpoint was a cold pain between his shoulder blades; even breathing out made him wince with the sharp stab. The hand lifted from his mouth and took his sword quickly. Rigid, Hakon squirmed with fury. He wanted desperately to call out, but dared not. And yet the others were depending on him. He opened his mouth but it was too late; the hand clamped back.

"How many of you are there?" the hoarse voice whispered.

Hakon shook his head.

"How many?" The hand lifted slightly.

He managed a yell, half-stifled, but loud; then he was turned and shoved face-first into the wall, a bruising blow that burst in his forehead, and to his astonishment and fear the room growled about him; it rumbled and shook, and the floor tilted and he fell into a slither of stones.

Twelve

A wind-age, a wolf-age, till the world ruins;
No man to another shall mercy show.

Jessa woke to a roaring and rumble that made the floor shake. Pain sprang in her fingers; for a moment she thought they had been bitten off; memory and sleep confused her. Far off in the building something slid and smashed. One of the horses was whinnying with terror; as she watched, Brochael's pack slipped from the tree trunk and crashed down, spilling water and food and coins that rolled and rattled.

Skapti hauled her up.

"What is it?" She gasped.

"Keep quiet!"

Silent, they waited, letting the long echoes fade. The walls quivered once, and were still.

"An earthquake?" Skapti breathed.

Something crashed out in the hall, settling to stillness.

"Could be." Brochael stood tense. "If so, we should get outside. There'll be others."

"It could have been something else," Jessa muttered.

"A giant, walking?" Skapti suggested.

They were silent, despite the scorn in his tone, imagining the great figure of Galar pacing through his hall. Then behind them, in the firelight, Kari said, "Brochael. Hakon's missing."

They all turned instinctively. "The fool!" Brochael said. "What was he thinking of? Has he gone outside?"

"No. The birds would say." Kari looked preoccupied. Abruptly he said, "I think there's someone else here—out there in the hall."

They gazed apprehensively at the black archway. Then Brochael walked up to it, and even his great bulk was tiny in its shadows.

"Hakon?" he breathed.

A small, strangled murmur came out of the darkness. Then Hakon's voice, sounding strained. "I'm all right, Brochael, but there's someone with me."

"Who?"

Only silence answered.

"Get me some light," Brochael snapped.

Carefully Skapti went and pulled a smoldering branch from the fire; he lit the candle with it. Light glimmered on the wild eyes of the horses as they backed and snorted.

"Leave the boy alone," said Brochael hotly. "If he's hurt . . ."

"Listen!" Hakon sounded breathless. "He's got a sword at my throat. He says he's alone and wants no trouble, but if you attack, he'll kill me."

"We should all get outside," Skapti muttered. "That earthquake . . ."

"I know! But Hakon first. Come on."

They stepped out behind him, through the arch.

The candlelight was weak; eventually it showed them Hakon, crouched among a pile of stones with his knees up under him and his head dragged back; a blade glimmered under his chin. In the faint light, someone else stood behind him, gray and shapeless. Dust was spiraling everywhere, and what looked like snow drifted through the roof gaps.

"Let him go!" Brochael snarled.

Hakon was dragged, clumsily, upright. The shadowy figure was tall and lean. But no giant.

"If I do," a low voice said, "then we meet as friends?"

"For our part." Skapti was dangerously quiet.

They waited. Then Hakon stumbled forward and stepped away quickly, as if he had been released, and they heard the long shiver of steel returning to its sheath.

The man gave Hakon his sword back and lifted his hands. "No weapons."

Reluctantly Skapti put his sword away and Jessa her knife. Brochael let the ax swing from its strap around his wrist. Kari did not move.

"Come to the fire," Brochael said gruffly. Turning, he muttered, "And let's have a look at you."

The man came behind them gradually, into the light. He was tall and hooded, and as he pushed the hood back they saw that his hair was gray and long, swept back to the nape of his neck. He had bright, amber-colored eyes and a fine gray stubble of beard. He would be about forty, Jessa thought, quite old; a strong, lean man, in colorless clothes.

He wore no amulets, no brooches, no metal of any kind except his sword in its battered leather scabbard.

"Are you really alone?" Skapti asked.

"I am now." The man spoke huskily; his front teeth were sharply pointed, as if they had been filed.

Brochael glanced at Kari, who nodded, almost imperceptibly. The stranger gazed warily around at them. His glance caught on Kari just for an instant, and a flicker passed over his face but he said nothing. Jessa had noticed it, though; she knew Kari would have too.

"I'm a traveler through this wood, as you are," the stranger said, taking the food that Skapti held out to him. "I came from the west; I've been searching many weeks for the giants' road. When I found it, I followed it. It led me here." He looked round wryly. "I watched you come. I needed to be sure you were indeed men."

"What were you afraid we might be?" Kari asked unexpectedly.

The gray man gave him a shrewd glance. "Anything, lord. Trolls, werebeasts. Even Snow-walkers."

There was a tense silence. Jessa fingered her knife hilt.

Kari nodded. "You know I am one of that people."

"I see that."

"You've known others?"

"I've had dealings with them." The man's voice was

almost a growl. He said no more; no one pressed him.

Instead Skapti said, "We're traveling to the country of the Snow-walkers. Do you know where that is?"

"Over the edge of the world. No one can get there." But even as he said it, Jessa saw the considering look in his eyes.

"You haven't told us your name," she said.

He looked away. "I have no name. Not now. I'm an outlaw, without kin."

"But we have to call you something."

He looked at her strangely. "Do you? Then I choose a name. A name out of this wood. I choose Moongarm."

They stared at him in silence. Jessa remembered Skapti's story of the wolf that would devour the moon. Moongarm. And to be an outlaw meant the man was a murderer at least, or under some curse.

"You choose a grim name," Brochael said heavily.

"I have a grim humor."

He held out his hands to the fire; the backs of them were covered with fine gray hairs, the nails blackened and broken. "Will you allow me to travel with you? The forest is no place for a man alone."

Instantly they all felt uneasy. "We need to speak about that," Brochael said stonily.

"Then do." Moongarm stood up. "I'll fetch my goods,

out there in the hall." He walked out with long strides.

Brochael turned. "I say no. An outcast—probably a murderer. He has that look. We'd never be able to trust him."

"Not only that," Skapti said, "he's cheerless as the grave."

"Be serious!"

"Oh I am! But if you don't trust him, Brochael, we should have him with us. Or do you want him out there in the forest following us, as he will; not knowing at every night's camp which tree he's looking down from?"

Jessa nodded. "Skapti's right. We need to keep an eye on him. And there are five of us."

"Hakon?"

Hakon scowled. "I don't want him. If I'd been on my own, he'd have killed me."

Somehow they all felt that was true.

Brochael shrugged and looked at Kari. "It's up to you."

For a moment Kari said nothing. Then, quietly, "I think we should let him stay."

"But why?"

Unhappily he looked beyond them, his eyes bright and frost pale. "I don't know yet. He has something to do with us. And like Skapti, I would rather know where he is." A change in his expression warned them and they saw the man come back through the arch, a heavy pack in his arms. He threw it down in a corner.

"Is it to be?"

Brochael rubbed his beard with the back of his hand and breathed out, exasperated. "It seems so. But I'm warning you, Moongarm—"

"I hear you, tawny man." He smiled then, showing his teeth. "To show faith I'll even take the first watch."

"You will not," Brochael snarled. "Besides, we're moving out. That earthquake—"

"Was no earthquake." Moongarm spread a moth-eaten blanket out in the corner calmly. "I know a little about this hall. Traveler's tales. They say the giant who lived in it still lives; that he was buried alive near here by the gods themselves, centuries ago. He struggles and squirms to be free, and his struggles shake the ground."

They were silent a moment. Then Skapti said, "A good tale."

"It's true. Tomorrow, I'll show you the place."

"Where?" Jessa asked.

"A little north of here."

She nodded. "And if you came from the west, how do you know about it? How long have you been living in this hall?" Sharply he turned and looked at her. Then he smiled and shook his head, rolled himself in the blanket, and turned his back on them.

As they settled down, Jessa moved nearer to Kari. "Is he safe?"

"For the moment." He lay on his back, staring up at the black spaces of the roof. "There's a lot he hasn't told us. Did you notice his ears?"

She shook her head.

"Look at them tomorrow."

"But he's got no horse. He'll slow us down. And we need to hurry, Kari. Anything could be happening back at the hold." She wriggled into the woven blanket, trying to get warm. "I wonder how Wulfgar is managing."

"So do I," Kari said softly.

Later, when he was sure they were all sound asleep, he unfolded from his body and left them, stepping soundlessly past Brochael at the door. It cost him too much strength to do this often, but tonight he was restless. Moongarm worried him. There were scents and tastes and tingles about the man that were alien; he smelled of sorcery and rank, animal things.

Kari could have reached into the man's mind, but he held back, as he always did. That was how Gudrun had started, controlling the men around her. He feared that for himself. And so far the stranger had done nothing except lie. And yes, the flicker of recognition. Kari had felt that, like a feather across his face. And more, a flash of old hatred, instantly snapped off.

Now he walked, silent as a ghost across the empty hall, through an enormous doorway to the base of a stair, each step high as his waist. Quickly he hauled himself up, his spirit body light and frail as a cobweb, and as he climbed, the air grew colder; the steps froze under his fingers.

At the top was a great platform, covered with a thin crust of snow, the parapet cracked and broken. He crossed to the edge and looked out over the forest, high above the trees.

Closing his eyes, he moved into the distance with a great effort. He saw the Jarlshold, the dark houses, the watchman coughing outside the hall door.

Things were worse.

He knew that at once. Signi still slept, and of her soul there was no sign. But others were here now, wandering the purple twilight, trapped in the power of his spell ring. Two old men, a woman, a warrior—he knew all their faces, one or two of their names. They had been well enough when he left. The little boy was with them. He watched them walk restlessly between the houses, and the wind of dreams that blew there was stronger; it rattled doors and gusted against the walls of the hall.

He dragged his mind back to the giant hall and opened his eyes.

Jessa was right, as usual.

They would need to hurry.

Thirteen

The brood of Fenris are bred there,
Wolf-monsters.

"Near here," Moongarm said abruptly, "is the burial place I told you about."

They looked at him curiously. It was the first time he had spoken since they'd left the giant hall after another, milder ground shake had woken them all. Since then the gray man had walked tirelessly beside the horses. Brochael had grudgingly offered him the pack pony but he had refused, saying the beast disliked him. Jessa had noticed that all the horses did, whickering and rolling their eyes whenever he came too close.

Now, remembering what Kari had said, she looked at his ears. They seemed oddly placed, hidden by his hair. She glanced at Kari but he was gazing into the wood, lost in his thoughts.

The morning was bitterly cold; a thin layer of snow lay where the trees were sparse. It struck her how the weather was changing quickly—too quickly—as they traveled north. At the Jarlshold it had been midsummer. Now they already seemed to be riding into winter, as if they traveled in time as well as distance.

They came to a wide place which had been cleared of trees long ago. Saplings had sprouted up, but the frequent earthquakes had toppled and uprooted them; the whole area was a mass of tumbled rock and earth piled high, without shape, as if it had been shattered and heaved up over and over.

"This is it," Moongarm said.

Brochael gazed around. "It seems like an ordinary landslip," he said coldly.

"And that." The gray man pointed. "What does that seem like?"

To their left, in a patch of sandy soil, something stuck out from the earth. It was big, a hard, shiny thing, curved like a shield, split and broken, blackened with dirt and age. As she stared at it Jessa saw it move, just a fraction.

At once soil slid; stones rattled. The ground began to rumble, a far-off deep tremble. The forest floor quivered, a tree crashing behind them.

"Out!" Brochael yelled, wheeling around; then they were all galloping for the trees, Moongarm racing after them.

The ground bubbled; it heaved and bucked as if something huge was indeed raging and struggling underneath, and only when they were well into the trees did it stop, and they felt safe.

"Did you see that?" Jessa gasped, fighting to control her horse.

"I did indeed." Skapti looked at her slyly. "What did it look like, Jessa?"

She flicked her hair from her eyes reluctantly. "You know what."

"Tell me."

She glared at him, annoyed. "All right, if you're all too scared to put words on it. It looked like a thumbnail. A huge thumbnail sticking up out of the ground. As if the rest of the hand was buried down there. Not even poets could make that up."

Skapti grinned. "What a poem this will be."

"The poem can keep." Brochael turned his horse and glared darkly down at Moongarm. "This is no place for us."

All that day, and all the next, they rode north through the endless wood, keeping to what remained of the road, and the air became crisp with frost. Already they wore thicker clothes; the packhorse traveled light, all the food almost gone. On the second evening Hakon caught a hare in a snare; they stewed it with mushrooms and puffball, and the juices were hot and sweet, a welcome change from dry meat and salt fish. But there was barely enough.

Even the length of the days had begun to shorten; winter was closing about them, the eternal cold of the north. Snow drifted often between the trees; the nights were bitter, uncomfortable times, spent as close to the fires as was safe.

Moongarm traveled tirelessly, easily keeping up in the tangled undergrowth that slowed them. On more open stretches, where the horses could briefly run, he loped behind, the ravens above him. Jessa was sure they were watching him. Brochael's glance too often followed him suspiciously; Moongarm was well aware of this and seemed not to care. In fact she thought Brochael stayed awake through Moongarm's watches, despite the ravens on the branch overhead. But the stranger did nothing. He walked silently and ate his food to one side.

On the third afternoon after the giant hall, the wood became such a tangled murk that they had to dismount and hack their way through, dragging the reluctant horses. The road, all that was left of it, was completely lost under leaf litter; the black gloom of the crowding, silent wood made them all uneasy. They felt they were deep in the forest, lost in it, that they would never come out. Far behind, a wolf howled, then another, nearer.

"That's all we need." Hakon stumbled over a tree root and rubbed dirt wearily from his face. "Gods, I'm filthy. What I wouldn't give for a bed. And hot food. And wine!"

"Wine!" Jessa said scornfully. "A few months ago you'd never even tasted it!"

"It doesn't take long to get that hankering," Skapti muttered. "Wine. Odin's holy drink." He slashed a branch aside with his sword. "What do you say, gray man?"

Moongarm looked at him briefly. "Water is my drink."

"Water's good enough," Skapti observed. "For washing."

Moongarm smiled narrowly. "As you say." He looked into the trees on his right. "But I hear a stream nearby, and I'm thirsty."

He shoved his body into the mass of leaves and almost disappeared; after a moment Kari led his horse in after him.

"We'll catch you up," he said.

The others struggled on, deeper into the wood. "Aren't you going to stay and watch him?" Jessa teased.

Brochael frowned at her. "Kari can look after himself. And besides—"

A twig cracked, sharp, to his left.

He spun around.

A flurry of men in green, a sudden, bewildering ambush, were leaping and falling from trees and rocks, swift as thought. Hakon crashed down; Skapti yelled a warning. Already Brochael was struggling with two of them; another grabbed Jessa from behind. She screamed; the horse reared and as the man glanced up at it she saw his face, hungry, mud-smeared, leering. She drew her knife and struck without a thought, slashing his arm, the blood welling instantly.

Brochael was up, swinging his ax; there was a wary space around him. As she turned she saw something flicker at his back; her eyes widened with fear.

"Behind you!"

But the arrow, swifter than words, was in him. He slammed back against a tree, crumpled up, and lay still.

Fourteen

At the host Odin hurled his spear.

"Brochael!"

Kari's voice was a scream of anguish.

He ran from the trees; already the archer was fitting another arrow. Jessa yelled at him, wild, desperate. She saw Kari kneel, his face white and cold, and then he turned and struck—she almost saw it, that savage, flung bolt of power.

The archer crumpled with a scream. Facedown in the mud he smacked, and the searing crackle of that death rang in the wood.

For one shocked instant the attackers were still; then they were gone, as if the trees had absorbed them.

It had been so quick. Jessa was dizzy with the speed of it.

Skapti picked himself up and hobbled to Brochael, turning him gently.

"Is he dead?"

"No, Jessa. Your shout warned him enough. It's the shoulder. But it'll have to come out." Working quickly, Skapti staunched the blood.

She glanced at Kari. He was white, his hands knotted together.

Moongarm bent over the outlaw. He glanced up at Kari with a strange fear on his face. "Well, this one is."

The Snow-walker looked over at Moongarm, at first as if he barely understood. Then he went and stared down at the man and rubbed his hand over his forehead.

"I didn't mean this."

"It looked final enough to me."

Kari gave Moongarm a fierce look and went back to Brochael.

"Can't you keep quiet?" Hakon muttered.

Moongarm shrugged.

"Get the horses," Skapti said over his shoulder. "We can't stay here. They may come back."

"I doubt it," Moongarm said.

"So do I!" the skald yelled at him, suddenly furious. "But I'm taking no chances! Get Brochael on my horse. Quickly!"

They rode warily, hurriedly, deeper into the tangled wood. Hakon was in front and Moongarm watched their backs, sword drawn. Jessa kept near Kari, who was silent. So was she. She hardly knew what to say.

When they found a defensible cleft in some rocks, they eased Brochael down, Skapti and Hakon taking his weight. They lit a fire, and the skald worked on the wound, probing it with his fingers and a thin knife, muttering to himself.

Kari watched bleakly, and when it was over and Brochael slept, he went and sat against a tree trunk. The ravens hunched unnoticed at his feet.

Jessa went and sat with him. "He's strong. He'll be all right," she said.

He nodded.

"You had to do it," she went on awkwardly.

"I killed him, I wanted him dead."

"Easy to understand."

He gave her a glance that chilled her. "Yes. Many people feel that. But I can do it, just by a thought. I let myself do it."

He was shaking with shock and misery. She put her arm around him and they sat there for a while, watching Skapti build up the fire.

"Hakon will be jealous," Kari said at last.

Jessa stared in surprise. "Will he?"

He almost smiled. Then he said, "When Brochael went down like that, Jessa, I felt as if it was me, as if it had struck me, right through the heart."

She nodded. She knew that already.

Later, when Kari was asleep, she said to Skapti, "Who were they, do you think?"

He shrugged. "Outlaws. Kinless men."

She looked at Brochael, restless and flushed in the fire's heat. "He will be all right?"

The skald ran a thumb down his stubbly chin. "I'm no expert, Jessa. I'd say so, if we can keep the wound clean. He's a strong man. But we need a place to rest up, and I don't know if it's safe enough here."

"I can make sure of that." Moongarm squatted beside them in the dimness. "I'll go and prowl around. Make sure we've not been followed."

Skapti shook his lank hair. "It's too dangerous. We can't afford to lose you too."

"So you need me now?"

"We need everyone"—Skapti stared at him levelly—"if we're all going to get out of here alive."

"I'll be safe enough. No one will see me."

He turned away into the shadows; Skapti muttered, "Fool."

He started to get up, but Jessa put her hand on his. "Let him go."

He looked at her.

"Let him go. I think he knows what he's doing. I think he knows this wood better than we do."

They stayed in the clearing by the rocks for a day and a night. Moongarm came back soon after daylight, saying he had searched the forest around the camp as far as he could; there were no signs of the outlaws. The body they had left behind still lay there.

"Let the wolves have it," Hakon muttered.

Moongarm gave him a searching look. "They already have."

Brochael slept for a few hours, then ate the food Kari

brought him. He was cheerful and joked about the pain. Skapti had told him what had happened, but he said nothing until Kari did.

"Death comes to us all. That's fate."

"Not his death. It wasn't a fair fight."

Brochael snorted. "You think it would have been, if you'd fought him with a sword?"

"It wouldn't have been fair to you then," Jessa said.

Kari glanced at her irritably. "Thank you for reminding me."

"We use one another's strengths," Brochael said. "A sword for some of us. Jessa has her brains, Skapti his lore."

"And I have sorcery."

"Many would envy you," Brochael said quietly.

"Not if they knew."

On the second day, they left, traveling slowly. Brochael did not complain, though Jessa guessed the wound must be hurting him. But he laughed at her sympathy.

"Don't worry about me, little valkyrie. I've had a hard life."

By midday the trees had begun to thin; finally Skapti pushed through a thicket and stopped. His voice came back to them strangely unmuffled.

"Look at this!"

Jessa broke through the cover quickly, and grinned as

the cold clear air struck her face and lifted her hair; behind her Hakon gave a whoop of delight.

At last the forest had ended. They were on a high fell-side, and below them spread a new country of lakes and open slopes, white with untrodden snow. Mountains rose to the north and east, huge and astonishingly near, their tips scarlet with the smoldering sunset.

Brochael and Kari emerged behind them, leaves in their hair. Kari looked tired and Brochael gruff-tempered, but their faces cleared at the sight of the wide, bare country.

"Thank the gods for that," Brochael roared. "Another day of trees and I would have run mad!"

A flock of birds scattered at his shout.

"You're mad already," Skapti said mildly. Then he whistled. "Have you seen what you're standing under?"

He reached into a hollybush and pushed branches aside carefully, and they saw that a great archway rose over them, almost completely masked by growth. The same strange runes ran around it, and on the top, glaring down at them between the red berries, was the stern, helmed face that had guarded the hall.

"Galar," said Jessa. "I wonder if he's the one who's buried."

"If it is, I'm glad he can't get up." Hakon looked at Skapti. "This must mark the end of his land."

"The end of the wood. The wood is his."

"So where now?"

Brochael grimaced. "Down. Before night."

But it was dark well before they reached the bottom of the steep, unstable slope, winding down on the broken path, between rocks and stunted trees to the silent land below. In the end Hakon's horse slipped suddenly and crashed heavily onto its knees. He fell clear, but the horse did not get up. It struggled bitterly, but the foreleg was broken, everyone could see.

"It's finished," Brochael said grimly. "Get your pack off it, Hakon."

When his gear was off, Hakon loaded it onto the pack beast; they led the other horses carefully down the rest of the ravine.

Brochael stayed behind.

When he came down into the camp they had made, some time later, the long knife he wore had been scrupulously cleaned. He carried a sack under his arm.

Stiff and sore, he sat down. "No spare horses now." Jessa gave him some smoked fish; he chewed it thoughtfully. "At least we've got some fresh meat. Tomorrow, we'll cook it. You, Moongarm . . ."

He looked around quickly. "Where is he?"

The man's pack was there, but there was no sign of him.

"Now where's he lurking?" Brochael growled. "I don't trust him. Not even when I can see him."

"The birds are with him," Kari said quietly. "He won't be far."

Later, deep in the night, Jessa rolled over and saw Moongarm come into camp and talk to Skapti quietly. The gray man looked sleek somehow. He refused any food and lay down, on his own as usual.

Jessa caught Skapti's eye and lifted her eyebrows. The skald shrugged.

Not far off she could hear wolves snarling and fighting over the carcass of the horse, where it lay under the stars.

FIFTEEN

Fairer than sunlight, I see a hall,
A hall thatched with gold.

The village was floating on the water.

That was Jessa's first thought as she gazed down at it from the deep snow of the hillside. Then she realized it was built on an island, or on some ingenious structure of high poles out there in the misty lake. A narrow wooden causeway linked it to the bank, built high over the marshlands, leading to a gate, firmly shut. A tall palisade guarded the village from attack. From one or two of the houses smoke drifted into the purple sky, up into the veils of aurora that flickered like ghost light over the brilliant stars.

It looked safe, snug behind its defenses.

And very quiet.

Brochael shifted, pulling the stiff, frosted scarf from his mouth. "Well?" he said gruffly.

They had been four days now living off horsemeat and herbage and melted snow. The horses limped with the cold; their riders ached with weariness and hunger. Each of them knew the settlement was a godsend.

Only Moongarm seemed uneasy.

"Are you coming with us?" Brochael glared at him sourly. "You don't have to."

The gray man turned his strange amber eyes on him. "You know how much you'd miss me, Brochael. Don't worry, I'll come."

"You would!" Brochael scowled.

As they picked their way down, Jessa wriggled her toes with relief. She was starving, and stiff with cold. Hakon grinned at her. There was no doubt what he thought.

Snow fell silently about them, small hard flakes that rolled from hair and shoulders and melted slowly, soaking through cloth. It fell on the dark lake water and glittered, the northern lights catching the brief scatter of crystal. On the hillside it lay thick, banked in great drifts, and the horses' hooves drove deep holes into it, compacting it to ice with careful, crunching steps.

Long before they reached the marsh they were challenged. A question rang out; Brochael stopped them at once, very still.

"Travelers!" he roared, his voice ringing in the hard frost. "Looking for a welcome."

There was silence. An aurora whispered overhead.

Then two figures stepped out of the darkness, well muffled, with flat snowshoes strapped under their feet. One carried a long glinting spear; the other, whose eyes alone were visible in the wrappings about his face, had a peculiar weapon—a wand of wood, studded with quartz and crystals and tiny silver bells that tinkled in the cold.

They looked up warily at the travelers.

The man with the wand had bright, sharp eyes. He raised his hand.

"We give our hospitality to anyone, strangers, but especially at this time. Tomorrow is a great feast day for us, so you've come at a good time."

He came forward and offered his hand to Brochael. Brochael leaned down and gripped it. "Our thanks."

The man nodded. "You'll need to lead those beasts of yours. The causeway is slippery with ice. Follow me."

They dismounted into the soft snow.

"Can't see much of them," Hakon muttered.

"Well, they can't see much of us." Jessa winked at him. "They might not like your face when they do. Keep your sword handy."

The causeway began in the snow and stretched out over the bog, a narrow, railed walkway, built of split logs caulked and spread with what smelled like resin or pitch, a sharp smell. The horses thudded over noisily. Below them the marsh spread, its stiff stalks and frozen rushes purple in the aurora light, with strange wisps of blue that rose and drifted in the mist. Somewhere waterfowl quacked. The marsh smelled dank, of decay, of a million rotting stems.

As they walked farther out, black water glinted beneath them. Jessa saw how the snow lay in a thin film across it, already freezing in patches. Tomorrow the lake would be sealed under a frozen lid.

At the end of the causeway was the gate. The wand man knocked and called; the heavy wooden door swung open. Inside, figures came running out from nearby houses, some to stare, others to help, pulling the horses into a low building lit with lanterns, its empty stalls spread with fresh rushes and shavings.

"Unload your goods," the man said, "and bring them with you, whatever you need. These men will see to your horses."

He waited for them, after whispering something to a small figure who slipped out at once. A girl, Jessa thought. She slung the bag on her sore shoulders and moved up next to Kari.

"Are we safe here?" she asked quietly.

He pushed his hood off and looked at her gravely. "I don't know, Jessa! I don't know everything."

"Sorry." She grimaced. "We'll find out soon enough, I suppose."

"No one attacks their guests." Hakon sounded shocked.

Skapti shrugged, behind him. "It's been known."

"Only in sagas!"

"Sagas are real, I've told you that. As real as your sword, dream wielder."

The stranger led them out of the byre, across the trampled snow. A low, rectangular building was nearby, the door so sunken that the snow was already banked against it. The man stopped and opened it, trudging down a pathway. He beckoned them in.

The smoke caught Jessa's throat as she straightened, making her eyes smart; as she coughed, the light of many candles flared and danced around her. Then they steadied. She saw a small, airless room, acrid with smoke. After the clear cold air outside it felt stiflingly warm. The hearth was in the center; a great bronze cauldron hung over it on a triple chain. Above, the thatch was yellow, pale as gold.

Sitting around the cauldron, staring at her, was a small group of men and women, obviously one family. They were all heavily tattooed. Each of them had some thin blue creature crawling down his or her cheek, a boar or a fox or a fish. A small, elderly man, the man who stood up, had a strange coiling beast of curling dots. Their hair was dark and glossy, their clothes brilliantly colored—woven wool and dyed sealskin in reds and greens and blues, all hung with knots and luckstones and feathers.

"Welcome," the chieftain said warmly, his accent strange. "Come to the fire, all of you."

For a moment no one moved. Then Brochael dumped his pack against the wall and came forward. The others followed, pulling off coats and wrappings and gloves, scattering snow on the floor and benches.

"Come close, come," the old man insisted, waving them in. He said something quietly; a woman and a girl got up and poured out a drink for each of them, handing out small horns of yellow-colored liquid.

Skapti tasted it and smiled in surprise. "Mead?"

"We call it honey brew. Sit down now, be comfortable."

There were low benches near the hearth; the travelers perched themselves in a thankful row. The man who had brought them in pulled off his own faceguard and coat; now he came and sat near them, laying the quartz-headed wand carefully at his feet. The bells gave a strange, silvery chink. Not a weapon, Jessa thought suddenly. Something magical.

She looked at him curiously. He had a lean, sharp face, with a ragged fringe of brown hair. A tattoo uncoiled on his cheek, ran down his neck and under his clothes. Two others crawled on the backs of his hands. The silver bells showed that he was someone special, a shaman, she thought firmly, noticing the strange pierced bones that hung from his belt.

Food was set before them and they ate hungrily. Hot roast spicy meats, possibly duck; fish, fresh from the lake; crumbly oatcakes and honey; cheese and beer. It was a feast, and Jessa enjoyed it to the full, despite the stifling smoke. It had been weeks since they'd eaten properly; she noticed how thin and gaunt they all looked, how travel worn. Filthy, long-haired, wild.

The chieftain watched them. His eyes were light blue,

his face beginning to wrinkle. He smiled. "My name is Torvi, father of the people. This is my wife, Yrsa, and my daughter Lenna. The Speaker is our wiseman, our shaman to the dark. His own name may not be known."

As he said that, the family made a brief sign, a touching of their lips. Jessa nodded to herself. Knowing his name would give them power over him. Or so these people would believe.

Skapti gave their own names courteously and the tattooed people gazed at them all. If they recognized what Kari was, they said nothing. Jessa had the feeling they didn't, which was surprising. Although, a lake people like this had no reason to travel far. They had all they needed here.

"It's fitting you came tonight," the woman was saying. "Tomorrow is the feast of giving; the opening of the darkness. We'd be honored if you would join us."

"If the food is as good as this," Skapti said drily, "I'm sure we will."

They all laughed, and there was an awkward silence.

Then the Speaker leaned forward. "So you're traveling. From beyond the wood, by the look of you. And where do you travel to, may we know?"

Skapti shot a look at Brochael, who shrugged.

"A long way," the poet said carefully.

"To my country." Kari's voice was unexpected; the shaman turned to him. A strange look passed between them.

Then the Speaker nodded. "A long way indeed, to the land of the soul thieves."

Jessa caught her breath. So he knew, at least.

Kari nodded but said nothing. He drank from his cup.

A woman came in and spoke to the chieftain; he turned to Skapti. "A guest hall is ready for you all; Sif will show you the way. Sleep well, sleep late. Rest and eat well. Tomorrow we will talk."

"Tomorrow we should leave," Brochael said uneasily. "We have an urgent errand."

The old man shook his head. "I fear the weather will keep you here. But the choice is yours. Do exactly as you wish. We will sell you food and ale and grain, as much as you want."

Awkwardly Brochael stood and nodded. "We appreciate that."

The guest hall was a copy of the eating hall, but smaller. Equally smoky, Jessa thought irritably. "It's a wonder these people can breathe," she said aloud.

Hakon fingered the brightly woven hangings and lifted one aside. "Furs!" He flung himself down with a groan of comfort.

Jessa crawled scornfully into the next booth and dumped her bag. She lay down, just for a moment, to try out the bed.

In seconds she was asleep.

Kari lay in the darkness. Slowly the absence of feeling came to him. He saw nothing, heard nothing.

But there was a tightness about his neck; he put his hands up and felt for it, and touched rope, a great noose of frayed, damp rope. Desperately he pulled at it, but it was coiled and cabled with heavy knots, and something crisp, like feathers, were stuck and threaded into its skeins.

He spread his hands out into the darkness, fighting down fear. This was no dream, he knew that. It was a vision. But of what? Terror touched him; he tried to sit up, and couldn't, and then he knew the darkness on top of him was heavy, wet with peat and matted lichens and the seeds and spores of generations. It weighed on him, suffocating him like a dark hand over his mouth and nose, and though he writhed and struggled and flung his head from side to side, she would not let go of him; she was drowning him in soil, her hand forcing him down and down.

He choked and retched and the darkness broke; it shattered into glints of candle flame and a fire red roof, and Jessa and Moongarm bending over him.

"Are you all right?" Jessa whispered anxiously. She pulled him up, knowing he wasn't; he was white, his lips a strange blue; he struggled to breathe, bent over, dragging in long, painful, choking breaths.

"Shall I call Brochael?"

He shook his head. After a moment he managed, "No . . . I'm . . . all right."

"You don't look it."

"I . . . will be." He looked at Moongarm.

"You seemed to be stifling in your sleep," the gray man said somberly.

"He woke me," Jessa whispered. "He was worried. Was it a nightmare?"

"I hope so."

"A warning?"

Kari shrugged, rubbing his throat with thin fingers. "I don't know. They seem friendly."

"Very friendly," Moongarm muttered.

Jessa glanced at him. "You don't trust that?"

"I'm wary. The comfort here will be hard to leave. And if your errand is so urgent, you should beware of that."

Kari looked up at them suddenly. "There's one thing I do know about them, and that's strange enough."

"What?"

He coughed and swallowed painfully. Then he said, "They were expecting us. They knew we were coming."

Sixteen

Chess in the court and cheerful.

The old man had been right.

They woke late, to a blizzard that howled around the village all morning, blotting out even the wall of the nearest house in a storm of white driven flakes. Travel was impossible. Hakon took one look outside and went back to sleep. He had a lot to catch up on, he said.

Jessa and Kari played Hunt the King on a board made by scratching out the squares with a knife. Kari did it; he was clever at carving. For counters they used some of Brochael's coins. The chieftain's daughter Lenna, who brought breakfast, stayed in the house to watch, fascinated. Jessa explained the rules.

Brochael had nothing to do. His shoulder no longer bothered him; he prowled restlessly for a while, and then pulled on his bearskin coat and went out into the flying snow.

"Where's he gone?" Skapti muttered absently.

"To look at the horses. What else is there?" Moongarm was sharpening his sword with a long whetstone borrowed from the villagers. He gazed curiously across at the poet, who lay on a bench, wrapped in his blue cloak. Skapti had the kantele out and had tuned it carefully, adjusting the harpstrings and checking the birchwood frame for damage. Now he plucked notes with his supple fingers.

Jessa looked up from the board. "Out of practice?"

He grinned at her. "A feast needs a song. Even from visitors." He looked at Lenna. "You must have poets of your own. Storytellers? Rememberers?"

She looked confused, her long black hair swinging. "The Speaker. He knows the past."

"Is he a shaman?"

The girl nodded, reluctant. She pushed back her hair nervously and gathered the dishes. Skapti let the notes fade. Then he said, "I have a good song of thanks for hospitality. Would they let me sing it tonight?"

Lenna paused, her head bent. "I don't know. . . . It's not that sort of feast." Kari raised his head and looked at her quickly, and she scrambled up. "I'd better go. My mother will want me."

They watched her hurry across the hazy room, the brilliant reds and blues of her dress delighting their eyes.

She pulled on her coat and went out.

"She was scared," Jessa said. "Now why was that?"

Kari moved a piece. "Skapti's song. The prospect of hearing it."

Jessa giggled, but wondered what he really thought.

The skald ignored them. He wrapped his cloak tight around him and leaned back against the wall. "Don't disturb me. I'll be working."

Then he closed his eyes and was still.

Jessa had seen him do this before. Making the song; fitting the words and notes and kennings together, knotting them into intricate lines and rhythms, charging them with power, memorizing them—it was an intense, concentrated process. He would lie there now as if in a sleep for hours, with just the soft touch of a finger on a string now and then to remind them he was alive; later he would begin the music, working out patterns of sound to weave with the words.

For a long time the room was quiet. Just the click of the moving coins, the whirr of the whetstone.

Then Brochael stormed in, scattering snow. He stamped it from his boots, looking more cheerful. "It's clearing up. I've been buying supplies from the old man— they're surprisingly generous." He dumped three sacks in a corner. "We should be able to leave tomorrow."

From his bed, Hakon groaned.

Jessa laughed; she knew what he meant. The warmth, the food, the chance to rest were enticing. And just being indoors without having the eternal wind and sleet in her face, chapping her skin, stinging her eyes, without the constant stumble of the horses, the stiff, freezing nights. But they had to keep on. Signi was depending on them. She thought suddenly of the slim girl asleep in the dim room, her hair spread. Wulfgar too; by now he must be aching with worry.

"I could show you how things are there," a voice said. "If you want."

She looked up at Kari, startled and furious. "Don't do that to me!"

He looked down. "I'm sorry, Jessa."

"It's too dangerous. . . ."

He shook his head bitterly. "You don't need to tell me. But sometimes, I can't help it. That picture of Signi was so strong."

Something in his look calmed her down. Grudgingly she said, "Show me then."

He cleared the pieces from the table and carefully poured water from the jug the girl had left. It spread, making a thin pool.

After only a moment Jessa saw images drift on its surface. She saw the Jarlshold; it looked quiet, eerily empty. Smoke came from only two—no, three—houses, and from the hall where glimmers of light showed in the high windows. Snow lay everywhere, blanketing the roof, piled high against the doors, almost untrodden, as if no one was there to venture out. On the fjord shore the ships bobbed in a line. Deserted.

Then the water seeped through the cracks of the table and drained away.

"Where are they all?" asked Jessa.

"Inside. Those that are left." He looked up at her strangely. "Did you see anyone?"

"No. That's what's worrying."

For a moment he didn't reply. Then he said, "I did. I saw their souls, Jessa. Almost half the people now. Wandering between the houses, wrapped in their dreams like mist. They're lost. Her spell has them—even here I can feel it, feel her."

She nodded grimly. "She knows we're coming."

"Of course she knows. She wants us . . . me. The closer we come to her the more I can feel her delight. And the more scared I am."

"Why?" she asked quietly.

"Because I don't know what to do." His voice was low, strained. "You're all depending on me to release Signi, but

I don't know how. And I don't want to see her . . . Gudrun. I don't want to see her."

He looked so distraught that Brochael had come over and was listening.

"We'll worry about that when we get there," he said gruffly. "If I find the witch I'll know what to do."

Kari shook his head. "Swords are useless. You know that."

In the afternoon the snow stopped. Jessa and Hakon went outside and explored the settlement; no one seemed to mind.

The sky was iron gray, the lake frozen hard. They skittered flat stones across it, watching them ring and rattle and slither to a stop far out on the ice. Already the sun was low, a sullen red circle. Geese flew across it, honking.

"A good bow would get one," Hakon muttered, staring up.

The village was busy with its secret preparations. It was also very well defended, Jessa thought. The timber wall around it was higher than a man, and only two wharves jutted out, where several frail wicker and skin boats were drawn up out of the ice grip. The only other way in was the causeway, and that was guarded at both ends.

They wandered out onto it, slipping on the frozen logs. In the marsh, men were bending. They saw the shaman rise from among the bulrushes and see them. He came over, smiling.

"What are you doing?" Jessa asked, curious.

"Preparing." He waved the carved wand at the sky and its bells chinked. "The weather is better. Tomorrow you'll be able to leave, if you want."

"We will," Jessa said firmly. "Though you've been very kind to us. It was a godsend, finding you."

He looked at her, his eyes amused. "For us too, lady, it was a godsend. The dark mother brought you."

He touched his lip in that strange way they did, and walked along the causeway. Then he turned abruptly.

"One question. Your friend, with the pale hair. He's a sorcerer?"

They gazed at each other. Jessa said, "Not exactly. He . . . can do certain things."

The Speaker nodded, smiling. "I knew it. He and I have that in common. He has the look of one who speaks to the dark."

The feast began when the last edge of the sun closed up and died; darkness came instantly. The villagers and their guests, all unarmed, watched it from the wharf, then they all walked in silence to the hall. There was no music, no singing.

Inside, the room was cold. They sat around the walls on benches; the hearth in the center dark and unlit, stacked with fresh logs.

No one spoke.

Jessa glanced at Brochael, who raised his eyebrows at her; this was like no feast she had ever seen. Uneasy, she became aware of a sound, a low humming, and realized the people were making it; it grew, slow and ominous, and then they began to beat their hands, pounding out one rhythm.

The Speaker came forward. He wore a green shirt open at the neck; she saw the coiling tattoos that covered his chest and forearms, and now he cupped his hands together and crouched low, whispering and rocking to himself.

The beating rose to a climax, then stopped instantly.

A flame had appeared within the man's hands; the people murmured in awe. He carried it carefully through the silence to the kindling; a fire grew, steadying to red. Around her the people began to sing, a high, excited chant, with words she didn't know.

Kari can do this, she thought. But she was beginning to feel uneasy; the ritual was unfamiliar, and unnerving.

The fire grew. Red light and smoke gathered in the hall. It lit eyes and faces and hands. Blood light, she thought.

Servers came quickly and brought everyone bowls, small wooden bowls. All empty.

"Hardly a feast," Skapti muttered.

"I don't like this," she said. "Something's wrong."

"It's too late to get out now."

They were passing around a great board, and on the board was a cake, a huge round thing, cut into thin wedges, one for everyone. The people took a slice each, gravely, almost reluctantly, placing it in their bowl. No one ate it. The travelers, puzzled, did the same.

The room was full of strange, unspoken tension.

When everyone had been served, the Speaker stood by the new fire, wand in hand. He raised it slightly, and the crystals and bells glinted with fiery hearts.

"Dark one," he said, his voice low, "you give and you take. Now, in the time of the sun's death, choose the one you will have."

He nodded.

The people, reluctantly, began to eat.

Uneasy, Jessa looked at the others. Suddenly she felt afraid. She did not want to touch the cake—a rich crumbling mass of oat flour and berries and fruits—but everyone else was, so she picked it up and nibbled a corner. It tasted good. Rich and honey sweet; delicious. She ate more.

People were looking around, watching their neighbors. Beside her, Skapti coughed; then he coughed again, almost choking. Hastily she slapped his back; he retched and spit something into his hand.

It was a large hazelnut, baked hard as stone.

They stared at it, astonished.

And in that moment everyone moved. Jessa was grabbed, forced still. The Speaker had a sharp knife at Skapti's chest—two other men held him from the back.

"So it's you," the Speaker breathed, his eyes bright. "She's chosen you, poet."

Hakon was struggling; Moongarm and Brochael held tight. No one touched Kari, but they surrounded him where he sat, white with shock.

"Do something!" Jessa screamed, struggling. "Kari!"

"I'd be grateful," Skapti breathed, trying to smile.

"I can't." Kari was amazed. "I can't reach him."

The Speaker grinned at her. "I have a spell about me, lady. I told you he and I had things in common."

Seventeen

Oaths were broken, binding vows,
Solemn agreements sworn between them.

The guest hall was their prison now. Each of them was bound firmly, hand and foot, with ropes of hemp. Where Skapti had been taken none of them knew; the villagers had dragged him from the hall. He had been silent and dignified, with only a quick, hopeless glance at the others. Now the Speaker came in and looked down at them all. His eyes were bright, his face flushed. But his words came clear enough.

"I regret it had to be your friend; there's never any way of knowing. You won't be harmed, any of you. Tomorrow, when the giving is over, you can go."

"Where's Skapti?" Brochael roared. "What are you doing with him?"

The shaman looked at him gravely. "The darkness will eat him."

He glanced at Kari. "As for you, enchanter, I've made sure you can't harm me, and I'll be with him from now until the end. If there's any disturbance, any hint of trouble, I'll kill him at once. Do you understand?"

Kari nodded unhappily.

The Speaker turned and went out. They heard the door being bolted behind him.

Silence hung heavy around them. Finally Moongarm broke it.

"They'll kill him anyway, and it won't be a clean death."

Brochael shook his head. "I've heard of this," he said heavily. "The victim is chosen by chance—whoever gets the sacred seed, or whatever. Skapti would know more. They'd say the earth mother chose him. Then they give him to her—I don't know how."

"I do." Kari leaned his head back against the wall. "They'll take him to the bog, tie a garrote about his throat, and choke him—but not to death. Then they throw him in."

Aghast, Jessa said. "Is that what you dreamed?"

He nodded. "I didn't know what it meant till now."

"But when? How much time have we got?"

"I don't know."

"They might be doing it now," Hakon whispered.

The door bolt slammed; they were silent instantly. The girl Lenna came in, carrying a heavy tray of hot, steaming food. The feast must have really begun now, Jessa thought, now they all knew they were safe. Two men with spears were behind her.

She put the tray down.

"How are we supposed to eat?" Hakon asked.

She looked at him. "I'll untie one hand for each of you—the left. But not him." She glanced at Kari, a frightened look.

He shrugged. "I'm not hungry."

She undid the ropes very carefully, keeping well back. They looked at the food but no one had any appetite.

Then Brochael reached out. "Eat it," he ordered. "We need to be ready for anything. Starving won't help."

The girl crouched by the fire, putting on wood. The flame light shone on her glossy hair, the thin fox outlined on her face.

Jessa said, "Don't you care about him?"

The girl paused, her hands sticky from the fresh logs. Then she went on piling them up. "It will be for the best," she said in a low voice. "His blood will enrich the land. He'll nurture our crops, feed our cattle. Because of him the dark one will be pleased."

Jessa felt rage swelling in her; she wanted to shake the girl and scream at her. "But he's not one of your people!" she yelled. "He belongs with us, and we came here as guests; we trusted you! You lied to us. . . ."

"No."

"Yes! Lied! And now you'll murder him!"

"Not murder . . . no." The girl shook her head hastily.

"And he had no say," Hakon said, watching her closely. "He didn't know. None of us did."

"He has to do it!" Lenna jumped up, her eyes wide with terror. "If he doesn't, it will be one of us; don't you see? One of us! And everyone is so happy now, so relieved. Every year this terror comes around . . . if the dark one isn't given her choice, there is famine, death, disease. It's for the best. I'm sorry. But it's for the best."

She hurried to the door, saying to the guards, "Tie them up. Quickly."

"Wait." Jessa looked up. "One question."

The girl did not turn.

"When will it be?"

Lenna paused, her hand on the door. The long ends of her hair swung down and hid her face; her dress swished around the soft boots she wore.

"Dawn," she said. Then she opened the door and went out.

They waited till the men had tied up their hands and left before anyone spoke again.

"Neatly done." Moongarm looked at Jessa and Hakon. "Quite a team."

"I can't do anything with the ropes," Kari said simply. "There's some sorcery about them—they won't burn or untie for me. Someone else will have to untie us."

"Where are the birds?" Jessa asked.

"Outside. They can't get in."

"Even if we could get free"—Moongarm pointed out from his corner—"how could we leave the village? There's a man outside, and the only way off is across the causeway. That will be guarded. So will the skald."

"You seem keen to point out difficulties," Brochael muttered. "Can't you do anything else?"

"These are truths, tawny man."

"There's another way out." Jessa had an idea; her face lit with thought. "Listen, Kari, we have to get free, but not yet. After all, they may look in on us. It needs to be just before dawn. Is there anything you can do then?"

He smiled at her sideways. "Oh, I can do something, Jessa. No matter what the Speaker says."

It was difficult in the dim room to keep track of time. The night seemed endless. Outside the wind had dropped; the faint sounds of voices and music drifted from the hall. Later a drum began, just one, a low muffled beat like a pulse from somewhere nearby. Kari recognized it; he had heard it before, like a warning. They all lay awake listening to it, a shaman's drum, like the beat of a heart. They came to wait for each beat, dreading it, yet fearing it would stop. Lying in the dark, Hakon thought it was the beat of Skapti's heart, and he wondered in what hut the thin poet was lying, and if he had guessed what was happening to him. Knowing Skapti, he had. And he must know they wouldn't desert him. Hakon smiled sadly. The skald's acid remarks had cheered him up many a time; his sly teasing, his songs, his endless, useless knowledge. Already they were missing Skapti.

Finally Moongarm, who had some strange instinct about time, told them it was near dawn. Jessa sat up, restless. "Right. We go now."

Each of them looked at Kari, not knowing what to expect. But he sat against the wall, unmoving.

"What can you do?" Hakon asked at last.

"Quiet!" Brochael growled. "Look!"

The door was being unbarred, quietly and smoothly from the outside. A figure slid around it, well muffled against the cold. It was the guard. He leaned his spear against the wall and came forward; they saw his eyes were wide with terror.

"Don't make me do this," he pleaded hoarsely. "How can you be here in my mind?"

"I'm sorry." Kari shifted from the wall. "I have no choice."

The man bent; despite his own will his hands went to the ropes about Kari's wrists.

"Hurry up," Jessa said, "or they'll notice he's missing!"

When they were all untied, the man stood still, as if Kari had forbidden him to move. His eyes watched them as they gathered their belongings, buckled on belts and weapons, picked up the sacks of supplies.

"Now," Kari said to him gently. "Outside."

At the door, he picked up his spear again; Hakon looked out cautiously. "No one about."

In the snow the man bolted the door and stood against it. Even in the cold he was sweating. Kari reached out and touched him lightly, once, on the forehead.

"I'm sorry," he said again.

Then he turned and walked away between the houses. The others followed; they paused in the shadow of a wall.

"Will he remember?" Jessa whispered

"No. When they find us gone, he'll be as surprised as the rest." He sounded disgusted with himself. Moongarm looked at him with a strange respect. "I fear you more than them, Kari."

Kari glared at him, his eyes cold as frost. "So you should," he said bitterly.

The village was silent, held in frozen night. Only the drum still beat, an ominous reminder of time passing. Jessa led them to the wharves; there she crouched down and nodded out onto the lake.

"That's our way off."

"The ice!" Moongarm raised his eyebrows. "Ingenious. But will it bear our weight?"

"I don't know, but it's our only way off this island."

"And Skapti?"

"We wait until they bring him, at the bog. We'll see them coming. Then we attack."

"Yes, but the horses!" Hakon was aghast. "We can't leave them!"

There was silence. Each of them knew they could never get the horses out without rousing the entire village.

"It's a heavy choice," Brochael said grimly, "but Jessa's right, this is the only way. I think we're on foot from now on."

They climbed down over the edge of the wharf to the timbers beneath. Jessa stepped off first, carefully. The dawn cold was bitter; her breath clouded and froze on her knotted scarves. The lake lay before her, a rigid, shimmering mirror, white under the crescent moon, with the long blue shadows of the buildings stretching across it.

The night was silent. Stars glittered, clear and hard.

As she put her toe on the ice she felt the coldness underfoot, expected the slab to tip, to crack, but although her growing weight made strange wheezing sounds deep under the surface, it stayed solid. She stepped out and stood still, her footsteps ringing.

"It's thick."

Carefully, testing every step, she walked out into the lake, the others slipping behind her. In the hard frost every step and creak sounded loud, every slither enormous. She found herself holding her breath, and let it out in a cloud of mist. Every moment she expected the crack—the darkness underneath to open and swallow her. And why not, because it was the darkness they were defying, the darkness that wanted Skapti.

You won't get him, she thought. Looking back, she saw the others; Kari was light, and Hakon too. But Brochael was taking careful steps, as if he feared his own weight would bring him down. Silent and surefooted, Moongarm was a gray shape under the moon.

Halfway over, she heard voices. Lights flared on the causeway.

She crouched, hearing Hakon slither up beside her. "Brochael says hurry. They're coming out."

She nodded and crawled on, keeping on hands and knees now, until the plate of ice under her wet glove suddenly shifted, and she stopped. "It's the edge."

"Be careful, Jessa!"

They were already among the rushes on the edge of the bog. Here the ice thinned to a lace-fine fringe that crackled and splintered under her. Then her feet were in brown brackish water, knee-deep, the reeds high above her.

"Why doesn't it freeze?" she breathed.

"I don't know and I don't want to know," Brochael growled out of the dark. "Keep to the edge. It'll be treacherous farther in."

They waded through the ice-cold muck, working their way around to the causeway. Once Hakon's foot went deep and he staggered; Moongarm hauled him out silently. Shadows among the reeds, they crouched and watched the torches approach from the village. The stink of stagnant rotting growth hung about them.

A small group were crossing the causeway.

"How many?" Brochael said.

"Four."

Behind, well back, the villagers stood, as if they dared come no nearer.

"Where is he?"

"In front," Moongarm murmured. "With the Speaker."

She saw him then, his thin, upright figure, that lanky walk. They had taken his coat off; his shirt was open and about his neck was a great noose of hemp, knotted strangely. He was silent, maybe gagged. He was alert though, she thought. He was probably wondering where they were.

But Skapti knew exactly where they were. He also

knew what was happening; as Brochael had guessed, he had heard of such things before. And as he stumbled on, pushed from behind and shivering with cold and fear, he tugged and twisted his bound wrists uselessly to red sores until the voice spoke quietly inside his mind.

"Get ready, Skapti. You weren't afraid we would leave you?"

He grinned, unable to help it.

The voice had been Kari's.

The Speaker and his prisoner and two torchbearers came right on into the swampy ground, the morass of clotted peat and moss squelching under them.

"Ready," Brochael whispered.

Each of them had their weapons to hand; Hakon gripped his sword tight.

"Here's your chance to name that," Jessa breathed.

He wondered how she could joke; his own chest was tight with tension.

"I'll take the Speaker," Brochael said. "You two, the others. Jessa, get Skapti." He looked at Kari. "You'll have to deal with the rest—the people on the causeway. If they cross . . ."

"Leave them to me." The ravens had come down; one was perched on his shoulder, gripping the dark cloth with its great talons.

"What will you do?"

"Keep them back."

"Yes, but how?"

"Like this."

As he said it the night seemed to crack open. The Speaker spun around as a white gate of searing flame leaped up to bar the causeway; it spat and sparked like lightning. People screamed.

"Now!" Brochael urged.

They leaped out, yelling, flinging the torchbearers aside, the flames falling and hissing out in the black water.

The Speaker cried out something in rage. Jessa saw him turn at her, but Hakon was there; he sliced the air with his sword between them and the shaman jerked back, stumbled, twisted away from Brochael's ax. He fell, full length, floundering in the black ooze.

Jessa grabbed Skapti, sliced his bonds. "It's us!"

He grinned. "Thought you'd abandoned me."

"Not us."

As she turned she thought the Speaker would be up, but he wasn't; instead she saw the marsh was bubbling and churning around him, and a blackness seemed to rise and gather from it, covering him as he screamed and struggled, bending over him, a dark form. His voice choked, broke, bubbled. Half a cry hung endlessly on the silent air.

Skapti grabbed her arm. "Come on!"

As they fled, the sudden silence behind chilled them. Only Kari's fire gate crackled under the moon, the people behind it watching, without a sound.

Along the road they raced, into the darkness, laden with packs and weapons, always looking back. Snow, deeper than before, slowed them, and then, just ahead, they heard the howl of wolves, a pack, hungry

Jessa stopped dead, the others slamming into her.

"Get up the hill!" Moongarm yelled. "Leave these to me." He flung his pack at Hakon and drew his sword.

"Not alone," Brochael growled.

But the man was gone, transformed suddenly to shadow.

Kari turned away. "Let him go. Come on!"

Uphill they raced, to a stand of pines that rose in a dark line against the stars. Once there, they leaned against the trees, gasping for breath.

The rune gate still burned below, the searing light from it crackling above the lake. But Kari was looking elsewhere, at the wolves hurtling after them up the slope, at least ten low, misty shapes.

"Give me my sword!" Skapti yelled.

"You won't need it." Kari pointed. "Look down there."

A gray shape sat waiting on the hillside. It too was a

wolf, but larger than any Jessa had ever seen, and it sat as still as a stone under the stars. Its amber eyes glinted in the rune light.

The wolf pack saw it. They slowed, stopped, yelping.

Then one by one they slunk away from it, in terror.

Eighteen

The wolf is loose.

Miles away and hours later, huddled under an overhang of rock, the travelers watched the sun strengthen.

They were silent, breathless from the long scramble into the hills. No one wanted to ask the question; it was Hakon who finally couldn't bear it anymore.

He turned to Moongarm abruptly. "That wolf," he said, clenching his hand nervously. "What was it?"

The gray man stared at him, expressionless. "Just a wolf. It came from nowhere. A pack leader, I would say. The others seemed to slink off when they saw it."

His amber eyes challenged them all, levelly. Then he went back to eating the villagers' bread.

Hakon turned a bewildered look on Jessa. She glanced at Brochael.

The big man was glaring at Moongarm, his face set with a grim, hostile fear. "So where did it go," he asked harshly, "this convenient wolf? Does it still follow us? Has it been with us all along?"

The man did not turn. "It went into the dark," he said quietly.

Brochael was livid; Jessa knew Moongarm's coolness made him want to explode with rage. It was only Kari's urgent shake of the head that kept him silent. Intrigued, she kicked snow from her boots. So the man was a shape-shifter. A werebeast. All of them seemed to have guessed that now, and all of them, she thought drily, were terrified of it. Except perhaps Kari. You never knew what Kari was thinking. And she liked Moongarm, had come to like him. He was quiet, watchful, yes, but shy, a man with a great secret. Now they knew what it was. And he obviously wasn't going to explain anything.

"At least," Skapti said quietly, "we're all alive."

"Without the horses," Hakon said.

"There was no help for that. And I have to say I'm grateful to you all for getting my neck out of that noose. Especially Jessa." He put a long arm around her shoulders and squeezed her. She grinned.

"Kari made the fire gate."

He nodded.

"I know you wouldn't have worried," Brochael said gruffly. "Not with your courage."

Jessa giggled.

"Thank you," Skapti said lazily. "I was, of course, terrified. And did you also know, or haven't you worked it out in your snail-shell of a brain yet, that I wasn't chosen by any earth goddess, but by the shaman?"

They all stared at him. Only Kari nodded.

"The ravenmaster has, I see." Skapti sat up, rubbing his cold hands together. "They knew we were coming, didn't they—the Speaker knew. So we were a godsend. He made sure one of us would be the gift to their earth hunger. I had plenty of time tied up in the hut to work it out. He chose me, probably because he thought I was the cleverest." He grinned. "They didn't know about Jessa."

"So they knew where the seed was?" Hakon said. "In which piece?"

"Not all of them. He knew."

"And what about afterward? That thing in the marsh that dragged him in . . ."

For a moment they all saw it again, the dark bubbling of the peaty water.

"Ah, now. That's beyond me." Skapti sat back. "Kari's

the one for spirits and earth wraiths. Something came out of there for him, that's sure enough. Something out of the dark."

They sat silent, thinking about it. Then Brochael sighed and reached for his pack. "Let's get on." He glanced at Moongarm, as if to say something. Then he turned away.

Already they were high in the foothills, the snow here deep under a frozen crust. As they traveled north all vestige of the giant road was lost; they waded up bare white slopes, leaving a blue tear of shadow, through gloomy stunted firs whitened with thick snowfalls frosted into place.

The cold became intense; the daylight always shorter. For two days they struggled over the high passes, stumbling and falling and pulling one another up, soaked and shivering, trying to keep the food sacks dry. Their lungs ached with the tingling air. Without Kari's rune fires they would have frozen; as it was, each night was an ordeal of cold, a quest for kindling and a place out of the raw winds that seared the exposed skin about their eyes. The world had turned white, had become an endless tilted plateau, and they seemed always to be climbing, their toes and ears and fingers raw with pain.

On the second night a blizzard swept down; a howling fury of stinging ice that drove them into the only shelter they could find, a narrow cleft where all of them huddled together shivering, the ravens perched mournfully above. There was no fire; Kari had sunk into sleep at once and none of them had the heart to wake him, but at least they were out of the eternal wind.

One by one, the others drifted off to sleep.

Jessa couldn't; she was shivering, and the rough knobbly floor stuck into her back. She shifted, restless.

"Awake?" Brochael murmured.

"Too cold."

"Come closer."

She moved against him, and he put his great arm around her, just as his left held Kari. "Better?"

She tugged the blanket close. "You're warmer than the floor."

"That's not saying much."

For a moment they were silent; then she whispered, "Brochael, do you think we'll get through?"

"Of course we will." His voice was gruff. "They're depending on us."

There was no doubt about that.

"Still . . . ," she murmured.

"I'll tell you what worries me more than the snow, Jessa. It's that werecreature we're dragging with us like a shadow. What does he want? What sort of a thing is he?"

They both watched Moongarm's lean huddle in the corner; he slept silently, breathing deep.

"He's one of us now," she said.

"Oh no! He'd like to be. But I'll never have that—I'll never trust him, not until I know where he's going and why, and how this curse came on him. A man who can slither into wolf-shape is no fellow traveler for me. He could turn on any of us. Is he man or animal?"

"Kari is more than a match for him," Jessa murmured sleepily.

When he didn't answer, she opened her eyes, surprised. "Don't you think so?"

"Kari sometimes worries me more."

She sat up then and looked at him. In the pale shimmer of the reflected snow all the russet of his hair and beard seemed drained from him; he looked thinner, with a gather of lines between his eyebrows.

"Why?" she whispered.

He looked at her. "Jessa, where are we going? To Gudrun, if we get there. To some land of sorcery and soul theft that's not even in this world. And all the time I can feel him gathering himself, summoning all the skill and mind craft that's in him. His mind is often away somehow—back in the Jarlshold, talking to ghosts and spirits and the birds . . . I don't know where. I'm afraid of what it's doing to him."

She shook her head. "He's done this before, the fire gate. . . ."

"Oh, lights and fires, that's nothing. It's the rest. The outlaw. That guard."

She pulled a face. "Moving minds?"

He nodded, wondering. "Imagine the power of that, Jessa, the secret, tingling power! Making everyone around you do just what you want. And they—we—would never know."

"He won't. He wouldn't." Jessa settled back firmly.

"He may have to. To defeat Gudrun he may have to become like her. Almost certainly, he will have to kill her."

Appalled, she stared at him. On his other side Kari twisted in his sleep, the long hair falling from his eyes.

"Or she him," Brochael murmured.

In the morning they went on, weak from cold. It froze on their eyebrows and lashes; all the brief afternoon the snow fell, relentless. Only after nightfall did the sky clear and reveal the breath-catching steely glitter of millions of stars, the aurora shimmering over them.

By the third day the travelers were worn to numbness. They were high in the mountains, a place of bare rock, frozen, icy chasms and passes, clattering rockfalls and the eternal howling wind. They rarely spoke now, plowing on in a straggling group, their thoughts wandering, lost in their own pain and hunger. There was only snow to drink; they gathered handfuls and sucked it. The food from the village was almost gone, and Brochael handed it out rarely.

Jessa's eyes ached from the snow glare; her lips were chapped, wind sores chafed her face. Hakon was limping badly, perhaps with frostbite, but he kept up and said nothing.

They hardly knew that the land had begun to descend beneath their feet; they reached the treeline with a vague recognition, and trudged wearily in under the frost-stiff branches.

Kari stumbled and fell. For a moment he did not get up, and Brochael went back and bent over him. When they caught up with the others, the big man said, "Time to rest." His voice was hoarse with cold.

Under the silent trees they sat and ate the last scraps of food. Skapti flung an empty sack away; the ravens came down and picked it over. Even they looked skeletal, Jessa thought.

With an effort she said, "We're over the mountains."

Brochael nodded. None of them answered; their relief was deep and unspoken. Below them broken forestry descended into the snow-filled glacier. On the horizon faint fog drifted. Hakon stared at it through red-rimmed eyes and roused himself. "Is that smoke?"

"Could be. Could be just mist."

Brochael glanced at Kari, who shrugged. "I can't tell," he murmured.

Jessa looked at him. He looked bone weary, and frail as ice, but his pale skin and hair fitted here; he belonged, more than any of them. And the farther north they went, the deeper into frosts and whiteness and sorcery, the more he seemed to have a strength that the rest of them lacked, a power not in his body but deeper. He was a Snow-walker, she thought suddenly.

By the next day, weak with hunger, they had come to the region of smoke. It had not faded, or blown away, and now Brochael thought there was too much of it to be a settlement.

As they journeyed toward it over the bleak tundra, the air changed, became warmer; a strange dry breeze sprang up. Jessa pulled the frozen scarf from her hair and scratched wearily, looking ahead. Surely the land was gray; bare of snow.

"What are we coming to?"

Behind her Skapti shifted the kantele on his bony shoulders. "Muspelheim."

"What?"

"The land of fire. Or to be exact, Jessa, a volcano."

Nineteen

Fumes reek, into flames burst,
The sky itself is scorched with fire.

The volcano probably saved their lives.

Jessa realized that, standing knee-deep in the gray, bubbling mud, the incredible warmth thawing her toes and legs. It was wonderful.

All around her the ground bubbled and heaved, puffing up globules that burst with strange, popping sounds; insects whined around them. The air stank of sulphur and unknown, steamy gases, but it was warm, even hot in places. Bizarre plants grew here, things she'd never seen before, and birds too flew in flocks over the warm land.

Standing next to her like a long-legged stork, his boots around his neck, Skapti was studying the map.

"Not much marked. We could be here, I suppose." His finger touched a faded rune in the sealskin, on the far side of the mountains. Neither of them could read it.

Jessa looked at the emptiness above it. The great gash of Gunningagap was all that was left.

"We're getting close," she said.

"We need to." Skapti rolled the map. "Time's going on." He sighed blissfully, as if he was wriggling his invisible toes in the volcanic heat. "Flame tongue, Loki-land, dwarves' furnace. Matter for poetry."

"It would be if we had something to eat."

"Animals will come here. We'll set snares."

They had made camp on the edge of the lava field; the rock there was contorted and twisted, forced from the earth hot. Cinders littered the soil; tiny plants sprouted between them. On the opposite side of the valley the snow still lay.

Kari sat by the fire, his coat off, watching the steams and mists churn from the mud. Hakon lay beside him, eyes closed.

Skapti took one look at Brochael and said, "What's wrong?" The big man sat wrathfully cleaning his ax with a lump of pumice, each stroke a slice of anger. It was Kari who answered.

"Moongarm has gone hunting."

"Good! So?"

Kari nudged the gray man's pack with his foot. They saw the hilt of the sword jutting out—Moongarm's only weapon.

"Without that?" Then Jessa understood. She sat down thoughtfully.

"He said we needed food and that he would get it. Then he was gone, into the smoke."

"If he thinks I'll eat any of that . . . filth," Brochael burst out.

"You must." Skapti sat down, his knees pulled up. "Signi and Wulfgar—all of them—are depending on us. We eat, Brochael. Even wolf carrion."

Brochael spit, but said nothing.

"While he's gone," Jessa said, "we should talk. Has he said anything to any of you? About what he wants?"

They all shook their heads. Hakon opened his eyes and propped himself on one elbow. "Is he safe?"

Kari shook his head. "Not altogether. He becomes an animal, in body, perhaps in mind. There are sudden surges of wildness about him."

"And that means sorcery," Skapti put in.

"No." Kari shook his head. "Not of his own."

"Well, I don't care whose!" Brochael said fiercely. "We watch him! All the time!"

It was late, just before dawn, when Moongarm reappeared. Hakon was awake, and he saw the lean figure stride suddenly out of the sulphurous fogs and rumbling red glows of the lava field.

Moongarm squatted by the fire. His eyes were bright, with a wild, satisfied look in them that Hakon avoided. When he spoke, his voice was rasping and hoarse.

"Cook this. Wake the others when it's ready."

He flung down a dripping carcass, already skinned and gutted. What it was Hakon wasn't sure—it looked like goat. Feeling briefly like a thrall again, he prepared it. For a while the werebeast stayed there and watched him lazily, by the fire. Finally it made Hakon uneasy.

"Stop staring at me," he muttered.

Moongarm grinned. "Bothers you, doesn't it."

Spitting the meat, Hakon glanced up. The man's lips were drawn back; his sharp teeth gleamed. Blood was on his hands and clothing.

Hakon put his hand on his sword.

Moongarm laughed then, and stood up. "Don't wake me," he murmured. "I've already eaten."

The smell of the cooking meat woke Jessa; once she realized what it was, she sat up quickly and stared across. Hakon was turning it on a rough spit; the fat dripped into the flames, crackling and hissing. She hurried over.

"Wake the others," he muttered. "It's ready."

"Moongarm's?"

"Yes." He frowned at her. "The gods know how he got it, Jessa."

"I don't care," she said firmly.

They all ate hungrily, even Brochael, though he was unhappy and silent. It was goat, or some wild relative, although they'd seen no sign of any animals.

Behind them Moongarm slept easily under his blanket.

Kari threw scraps to the ravens; they swooped out of the dusk and tore them up and gobbled them.

"Those birds don't look as scrawny as they did," Skapti remarked.

"They went after Moongarm," Kari said. "Ate his leftovers."

"And he was in wolf shape?" Jessa asked quietly.

"Yes. A great gray wolf, the ravens say. His body slept and it rose from him like a wraith."

Everyone touched their amulets; Brochael grasped the thorshammer at his neck. But no one said anything. They didn't know what to say.

Before the weak sun rose, they were moving on, trudging over the lava field, picking out a way. To their left the ground bubbled and steamed; yellow, flung splashes of sulphur seared the rocks. The air was dry, full of fumes; it made Jessa cough.

Coming over a small rise they felt the ground tremble;

they stopped, alarmed. It vibrated under their feet, as if huge pressures were building up.

"It's erupting!" Jessa hissed.

Brochael grabbed her. "Run!"

But the floor shook, toppling them all; the noise rose to a hiss and a whistle and a scream, and suddenly it was released, and a scalding fountain of water shot straight up out of the mud into the sky. Astonished, they picked themselves up and gazed at it; their faces wet with the steam and hot droplets. Then it was gone, instantly. Far off another burst out.

"What are those?" Brochael marveled.

"Waterspouts," Skapti said, unpoetic for once. "That much is clear. It must build up underneath. It's a steaming cauldron down there; the earth forge, Hel's anvil. The crust we walk on is weak; in places it breaks."

Crossing the lava field took almost all day; the ground was ashen, choked with cinders, and fumes and plumes of smoke drifted from it. In places it had cracked and fallen away, and they saw in deep ravines below them the slow red magma, flowing and curling and hardening in dark, crusted clots.

Gradually, late in the afternoon, the air became cooler; they came to soil of black cinders. The rocks here were bigger; their surfaces pulverized and pitted with holes, riddled with tiny lava tunnels. Leaning against one for breath, Skapti said, "Look there."

It was a small circular pool of water, clear as glass. The weak sun gleamed on it, making its surface glitter.

They were all thirsty, so they scrambled toward it over the rocks. Jessa's foot slid into a crack and wedged. Kari waited for her while she tugged it out.

"I feel filthy," she said irritably. "Covered with dust."

"It hangs in the air," he said, looking up.

They hurried after the others, who had reached the pool and were bending over it.

A raven squawked above them; it flapped past, brushing their faces with the draft of its wings.

Kari stopped dead.

She bumped against him.

"Look," he murmured.

Astonished, she gazed over his shoulder. Skapti and Hakon were lying still, sprawled; as she watched, Brochael crumpled and fell, the water spilling from the leather sack in his hand onto the dry rocks. Moongarm lay beyond him.

Jessa clenched her fists. "It's poisoned!"

"I don't think so." He nodded. "Over there."

Jessa stared into the smoke. Slowly she made out a shape standing among its drifts and swirls; a woman, a young woman, her black hair tied back. She came forward, picking her way over and staring down at the sprawled men. Then she bent; when she stood up, she had Hakon's sword in her hand. She stood over him, considering.

"No!" Jessa stepped forward. The woman turned, like an animal turns. She said something, moved her hand in some gesture, but Kari ignored it and came on, jumping down among the lava. Jessa followed.

Up close, the woman was strange. Her skin was shining with grease rubbed into it; her eyes were narrow and slanting. She wore thick furs, right up to her neck, and boots of the same, enviably warm. She stared at them both curiously.

"It won't work on me," Kari said.

"So I see." The woman looked down at Skapti and laughed. "Pity. Three of my goats have been stolen. These are the thieves, I thought." She looked back at him. "Do you pursue them?"

"They're our friends."

"Are they? And why has one of the Snow-walkers crossed the rainbow?"

Kari looked at her, unmoving. The words of the wraith soldier in the wood flickered into his mind, a glimmer of colors, a warning, a long fall into the dark.

Jessa glanced at him, then at the woman. "Have you killed them?"

"No. I can wake them. Or your friend can."

"We didn't mean to steal," Kari said quietly. "We've come a long way. We're looking for the land of the Snow-walkers."

For a moment she looked at him, puzzled. Then she snapped her fingers; the sprawled sleepers stirred and she looked down at them scornfully.

"Get them up," she said. "Bring them."

twenty

The old songs of men I remember best.

"She's a skraeling," Skapti whispered. "I've heard of them."

From the back of the room the woman emerged, carrying cheese and fish. "So the barbarians of the south call us," she said coolly.

She put the food into the sack and pushed it toward them. "This is for you to take tomorrow. It's all I can spare."

"Thank you," Jessa said in surprise.

"Oh, I have a price."

They looked at one another uneasily. The woman's dark eyes noticed; she smiled through the smoke of the fire. "But first, tell me how you came to the ends of the earth."

It was to Jessa she spoke, and Jessa told the story, as quickly and clearly as she could. The woman listened, sitting close to the flames, once or twice nodding her glossy hair. The smoky tallow dips that lit the small house reeked of goat fat; they showed only shadowy corners, a loom, a scatter of skins.

"And now," Jessa said, "we need what you know."

"Indeed you do." The woman put her fingertips together. She looked at them all. "You are a strange company, to have come so far. Beyond the wood is a land of legends."

"As is this land for us," Skapti said, smiling.

"So all legends are true, then. But as for what lies before you . . ." She shook her head. "All I know is this. Two days' walk to the north of here is the great chasm. Even before you see it, hours before, you will hear it, a raging of blizzards, a roaring of the elements. The wind will be a wall before you. Crossing the chasm is a bridge, a mighty structure of ice and crystals, lifted by sorcery. It comes and goes in the sky. It leads, they say, to the land of the Snow-walkers. Of that place I know nothing."

She looked at Kari. "But I have seen them, once or twice, glimpsed them in the blizzard. They are white as ice, and have strange powers. Like gods."

Kari shook his head. "Not that."

"You should know, traveler."

"What about you?" Jessa asked. "Why do you live here alone?"

The woman smiled again. "There are many of us. The others travel between sea and pasture, in the blizzards and the ice floes, with the flocks. This is the place of memory, the place between heat and cold, light and darkness. One of us is always here. I am the memory keeper, the story weaver. Here I weave the happenings and hangings of my people."

"Their history?"

"Their memory. What is a people without memory? Nothing but a whisper on the ice. Later, Jessa, I will show you, all of you."

"But your price for the food," Brochael growled.

She looked at them silently. Then she said, "I have an enemy."

"And you want us to . . . ?"

"Ask him to leave."

"And if he won't?"

"Kill him."

Skapti threw a worried look at Brochael.

The woman smiled, mocking. "The idea appalls you."

"We're not murderers, nor outlaws," Brochael said heavily. "At least not all of us. Who is he? What has he done to you?"

She laughed, amused, and her laughter shocked them until Kari said, "Don't tease them. Tell them what you mean."

Touching his shoulder lightly, she said, "I mean to." Then she lifted her eyes to Brochael. "He knows why I laugh. This enemy of mine is not a man."

"A woman?" Hakon was appalled.

Her dark eyes lit; she shook her head. "Not a woman either."

"An animal," Moongarm said quietly.

"I thought you would know." Spreading her hands to the blaze, she said, "Every night, in the starlight, a great bear prowls about this house. It hungers for the goats. It kills anyone that travels here. If it will not go, I would have that bear's skin."

She looked at Kari. "You must speak to it for me."

Worried, Brochael said, "Look, a bear is a dangerous creature—"

"So are wraiths and ghosts and spirits. The Snow-walkers move among them, speak to them as I speak to you. Isn't this true?"

Kari nodded. "I'll try," he said simply.

"And if it won't go, we'll do what we can," Brochael muttered.

"You should. Or tomorrow it will be hunting you."

Brochael stood up. "We'll go and get things ready. Jessa, you stay here." He flashed her a look; she knew what it meant and sat down again, warming her hands and hiding her annoyance. The others went out; Hakon closed the door.

The woman bent closer. "You have strange companions."

"Some of them."

"One is a shape-shifter, I see that. And the two bird wraiths that sit on my roof, did you know that they are also sometimes like men, tall, cloaked in black?"

Jessa stared in surprise.

"The Snow-walker is the strangest of all. He has an emptiness deep inside, a blank space where his childhood should be." She put both hands around herself, hugging. "And all of you are hung about with dreams; they're snagged and caught on you, as if you had burst through a web of them."

Jessa nodded, silent.

After a moment the woman went on. "There is something else. Your story put me in mind of it. Many weeks ago

I heard a sound in the night and opened the door of my house, just a crack. I saw a tall white woman coming north over the snow. Behind her a girl walked—a girl with fine yellow hair and a blue silken dress. They were joined, hand to hand, by a silver thread, and the thread was made of dreams. Then the moon clouded. When it passed, they had gone."

"Signi!" Jessa breathed.

"I would say so. The other one was your friend's image."

Jessa nodded gloomily, and the woman watched her. "Be warned, Jessa. These Snow-walkers are not people like us. How can he defeat her without using the same powers as she does?"

Astonished, Jessa looked at her, remembering Brochael's fears; then the door opened and Hakon and Moongarm came in. Behind them Skapti ducked under the low doorway.

"We've tied a goat outside," Brochael said shortly.

The woman smiled. "I would prefer not to lose it."

"Lady," Skapti said graciously, "we'll do our best."

The bear did not come. As night fell they lay listening, wrapped warm in furs. Brochael and Skapti discussed tactics; Hakon sharpened his sword. His hands shook a little, but Jessa knew he would forget his nerves if it came to a fight.

Moongarm said, "What do you want me to do in this?"

"Go to sleep!"

The gray man did not smile. "This is a bear, Brochael. You'll need all the help you can get."

"Not yours!"

"Brochael . . . ," Skapti muttered.

"No!" The big man thumped a fist stubbornly. He glared at the werebeast. "I won't fight alongside a man I don't trust. My friends, yes, but not you. You stay here."

For a moment Moongarm gazed at him calmly, his strange eyes unblinking. "You're a shortsighted man, Brochael."

"I see far enough. I see through you."

Moongarm's eyes narrowed, but he said nothing. He turned and lay down, a huddle in the dark. Jessa glanced at Hakon, who shrugged. They both hated this.

The night gathered slowly. After the bitter journey Jessa found it hard to stay awake; without knowing, she drifted into sleep. The others must have done so too, because a great snarling and roaring woke them all in sudden terror.

She grabbed her knives and heaved the furs off. Moongarm's blanket was empty.

"The fool!" Brochael raged.

He flung the door wide; Jessa stared under his arm.

The sky was black; ablaze with stars. The wolf and the bear, each glinting with frost, circled each other warily, the tethered goat bleating and squealing with terror.

The bear was huge, its pelt creamy white, splashed with mud. It bared long teeth, snarling with hunger.

"Moongarm!" Kari's voice was sharp. "Not yet!"

The wolf slavered at him, its eyes cunning. It crouched in the snow, its tongue hanging over wide jaws. Ignoring it, Kari came out of the house, Brochael close behind him.

Kari came forward over the snow. A little way from the bear he too crouched, still.

The bear did not move. Neither did the Snow-walker. None of the others heard their conversation.

For Kari the bear's mind was a white cave, a swirl of sharp scents, cold, the tang of blood. He reached in deeper, fascinated by the stream of instinct that drifted around him. In a place beyond words and speech, the bear's thoughts moved.

The bear was winter, it was white, it was huge. Wherever winter is, it said, there is terror, there is cold. The cold comes from inside me. I am the ice; I am the vast frozen plains; they are all here, deep inside me, and yet I walk on them, cracking my thoughts with the weight of my wet fur.

I am winter, said the bear. How can you kill the cold, the frost, the wide, empty wind? I am all these. I am the stars, the aurora, the pain in your fingers and ears. I am the world's edge.

The bridge, Kari asked, struggling to keep his thoughts clear. What is the bridge? Is the bridge a rainbow?

But the bear answered no questions; its mind did not move that way. Its long chant began again, endless, as if its mind revolved on the same matter hour by hour. It snarled at him. Kari felt Brochael's anxiety; he dragged his mind out of the cold, reasonless hollows.

Standing up, he said, "It won't leave; it can't. Animals have no reason but their hungers. And this is a beast of myth. You'll have to do what you must."

As he spoke, as if it had waited for this, the wolf leaped. It seized the bear's loose throat and dragged at it, snarling.

With a yell Brochael ran out, Hakon behind him. Claws slashed; blood splattered the snow. The big man heaved his ax up and sliced at the bear's thick pelt; it roared in rage and tried to turn on him, but the wolf jaws held it.

Then the bear shook the wolf off like a piece of rag; it turned and lumbered toward the men.

The wolf that was Moongarm staggered up, snarling, head low. Brochael, Hakon, and Skapti stood, shoulder to shoulder. The bear paced toward them, growling.

"Ready," Brochael muttered.

The wolf yelped; the bear swung clumsily. The men yelled; they attacked together, defending one another, an ax and two swords, avoiding the fearsome claws and teeth, the great muscular limbs. In an uproar of fury the bear swung back; again the wolf leaped at its throat.

Hakon's sword slashed down.

The bear crumpled, dragging the wolf with it, striking at it, rolling on it, crushing it.

"It'll kill him!" Skapti gasped.

Breathless, Brochael gave a hiss of frustration and swung the ax high over his head. It caught the bear full in the neck; the beast shuddered; bones snapped under the blow.

It twitched and made a small, low rattle.

Then it lay still.

Silent, they all looked at it. Its fur lifted in the faint breeze. The wolf struggled out, gasping and wheezing; it stood, eyes blazing, blood dripping from its jaws.

It stepped toward them.

Brochael raised his ax.

For a long moment the tension hung. The wolf was battle worn, savage; there was nothing human about it. Jessa felt her fingers clench; she wanted to shout, to warn Brochael to step back.

Then the wolf turned, as if with a great, silent effort. It loped into the smoke and mist.

"Moongarm!" Brochael snarled.

"I think," the skraeling woman said quietly, "it would be better to let him be. These shape-shifters carry the wildness in them for hours after a kill. They are not safe."

"I'd be happy if we never saw him again," Brochael muttered.

The skraeling looked down at the bear. "This one and I have long been enemies." Kneeling, she touched its muzzle. Perhaps she saw, as Kari did, the way its soul gathered on the snow, the white ghost-bear that wandered away into the frost. "I honor you, bear," she whispered. "Your memory will not be lost."

Later she showed them the loom. It was dim, until the woman held the tallow dip over it. Then they saw the cloth was colored with brilliant dyes. There were battles woven in it, and voyages over blue seas, and great death struggles against the trolls of the dark. An old hero made the earth from an eggshell, made a kantele of pike bones and sang the trees and clouds and mountains into being. And as Jessa looked closely the hanging moved before her, and she smelled the salt of the sea and heard the leaves rustle. She saw herself and the others, and all their journey was there, all its fears and doubts, and now they were walking into the white, unwoven spaces. But the candle guttered, and she knew she had imagined that, and that none of them were there yet.

The woman turned to the poet. "You will recognize this."

He nodded, his sharp, lean face alight with pleasure. "All poets weave this web, lady."

They smiled at each other.

Moongarm did not come back. When they were ready to leave, the travelers gathered, looking across the snow to the horizon.

"We can't wait for him," Brochael said grimly. He turned to the woman. "I hope we haven't left you with a greater enemy."

"We can't just go," Jessa murmured.

"We can and we are."

Skapti shouldered Moongarm's pack. "I'll take this."

"Leave it here."

The skald shook his head. "It's not heavy. He may catch us up."

"I hope so," Jessa said.

"I don't. We're well rid of him."

"He may be hurt, Brochael!"

Brochael snorted. "That one!"

The woman looked at him then. "There are all sorts of pain, Brochael. Maybe there are some you do not recognize."

He turned away.

They said good-bye, and the skraeling woman watched them go, the wind lifting the ends of her black hair. She folded her arms and called, "If you come back, I'll be pleased."

"We'll come back," Jessa said.

The woman shook her head. "You walk into the whiteness now. Into dreams. Only wraiths and sorcerers can live there."

She turned and went back into the low house.

Jessa turned away. "We never even asked her name," she said.

Twenty-One

On Hel's road all men tremble.

All day there was no sign of Moongarm.

The travelers walked through a perpetual twilight; for the first time the sun never rose above the horizon. Over them the icy stars swung in a great wheel, the polar star bright overhead. They walked on ice, immense tilted slabs of it, smashed here and there into jagged spars and shards that jutted up and had to be climbed and scrambled over.

A light snow fell on them, dusted them white with its touch. They saw nothing. No animals, no trace of anything alive in the long, pale blue shadows of the ice cap.

"He's staying behind," Hakon joked. "He's wise."

After long hours they were frozen with cold; they ate the skraeling woman's food, and it put some heart back into them. Kari made a white rune fire spark and crackle on the bare ice, but it had no warmth; there was nothing here to burn. They seemed to have lost all idea of time; the perpetual twilight confused them, as if time was something they were walking away from, leaving behind.

They tried to sleep there but the cold was too bitter.

"We'll carry on," Brochael mumbled, scraping ice from his beard. "If we stay here we'll freeze. Come on."

They staggered up and walked, almost uncaring. The wind rose, roaring from somewhere ahead over the empty miles and crashing against them. They were no longer a group; each one dwindled deep within himself, daydreamed and imagined and sang silent songs. Speech died; their lips were too numb to shape words. At last, bone weary, they dug a snow hole and risked a short sleep there, out of the wind, but even that was dangerous. Blue and shivering, Jessa could hardly lift the food to her mouth.

Later, as they trudged on, she imagined that they were walking into the great white spaces at the top of the map, walking into blank parchment that no skald had ever written on, that held no words to make itself known.

Stumbling, ears throbbing, the skin under her scarves seared with the wind, she thought of Signi in that room, lying still on the bed with its silken hangings. She felt those furs and blankets now; she was walking over them, up to Signi's mind, and they were warm, and all she had to do was lie down among them, like Signi, and sleep and sleep. But some nagging part of herself wouldn't let her; it ordered her, angrily, to shut up and keep walking.

Then Brochael murmured something in awe.

Jessa stumbled, opened her eyes. Sleet stung her face like grit. And through her blurred eyes she saw, rising in a great arch against the dark sky, a bridge, glinting white. It was breathtaking; already it towered high above them, and she saw it glittered as if made of millions of crystals fused to a solid mass. Rainbows glinted deep within it; it shone against the snow squalls.

The sight of it brought them back to themselves; they stood still, their breath ragged in the wind.

Then Skapti said, "This will be my best song yet."

"If you ever get to sing it," Hakon muttered.

The skald wiped snow from his eyes. "You're getting cynical, Hakon. Like me."

They approached slowly, bent against the wind that tore at them. The ravens flew above, dim shapes against the stars, knocked sideways, squawking.

The ice here at the edge of the world was pitted with great cracks; they had to help one another over, scrambling and climbing, and all the time the scream of the wind increased; it raged in the terrible gap ahead of them, sending storms of snow and cloud churning high against the stars.

With an effort they gathered together, steadying one another. They had reached the foot of the bridge.

It was a fantastic, trembling structure, solid ice hanging in pinnacles and icicles of every thickness and length, frozen droplets bright as stars. The roadway itself was smooth as glass and looked slippery. On each side a delicate rail rose up, made of thin spines of ice spun in a fine paling, knotted with glassy balls.

Somewhere under the bridge, hidden in the falling snow, was the gap. The edge must be within feet of them, Jessa thought. Out of it there rose a howling and raging of wind; a stir of snow that twisted and burst.

The bridge rose into the storm and vanished. Of the other side they could see nothing.

"Right." Brochael gathered them round him and spoke loudly. "I'll go first. Keep your heads down or the wind will blow you clean off. Hands and knees might be best."

Skapti slapped him on the back, nodding.

Brochael put his hands to the slope and began to pull himself up. At each step he slid back a little, his boots scrabbling for toeholds on the smooth glassy floor.

"It's possible." He gasped. "Barely."

"Go on," Skapti called. "We're behind you." He pulled Hakon over. "You next, swordsman. Take your time."

Hakon settled his sword hilt and smiled at Jessa.

"Be careful with your hand," she said.

"I will. Good luck."

He stepped up behind Brochael, bent low against the screaming wind. They both climbed slowly, gripping onto anything they could. Under their feet the bridge was a glass hill, treacherous, beautiful. The others watched, the wind flapping their hoods and hair, until Brochael was a fair way up, the snow squalls hiding him now and then.

Dragging his knees up under him he squirmed round and looked down at Hakon. "Keep in the middle!" he roared. "In the middle!"

But Hakon's foot had slipped; he slid sideways with a yell, sending a shower of crystals into the air, and began to slither, slowly, unstoppably, toward the frail ice uprights.

"Hakon!" Jessa screamed.

He scrabbled with his hands, with feet, with fingers, but nothing held. Brochael, scrambling down to him, cursed in the raging wind.

Hakon's foot met the ice pinnacles; for a moment they held him, but as all his weight slid down on them they splintered; one snapped with a great crack, and with nightmare slowness he felt his legs sliding through the gap. Squirming, he grabbed at an icicle and heaved his sword out of the sheath, slamming it down flat on the wet surface. Then he drew himself up, and with all the strength of his terror he stabbed the blade down hard, ramming it into the ice.

It held, and he clung on, the sword grip so close to his face that the tiny red dragons blurred and moved in his wet eyes.

The wind tore at him. Below him was nothing; he hung over the edge of the world, swinging, clinging desperately to the sword that held him.

"Brochael!" he whispered.

"I'm coming. Hold on!"

Birds flew above him; the ravens. The glossy ends of feathers brushed his face, but they were wraiths, they couldn't help. No one could. Numb, he knew he had been here before, long ago, in his dreams. He knew how it ended. And his hand, his weak right hand, was aching to the bone, unclenching on the leather hilt, the fingers opening, loosening.

"Brochael!" he screamed.

Closing his eyes, he felt the gale drag at him. Suddenly the sword slewed sideways; he yelled, grabbed at nothing, at a hand, a sleeve, warm fingers.

"Got you!"

Brochael's whisper was close, his face, huge, taut, the sweat freezing to crystals on his beard. He began to squirm back, and Hakon felt himself move. He was hauled up over the wet ice, swinging, until his knee came up and found the solid edge, and he heaved himself over and collapsed against Brochael, all breath knocked out of him.

For long seconds they lay there, dizzy, the sky glittering above them.

Only Jessa's desperate shouts stirred them.

Brochael waved. At this distance his words were lost, but the others saw he was safe.

"Thorsteeth!" Jessa breathed. She unclenched her gloves, felt the ache loosen between her shoulders. "I thought they were gone."

"So did I." Skapti looked white. "You next."

She scrambled up quickly.

"Keep your head down."

She struggled up the glassy slope. It was very difficult. The wind forced against her; she crouched low, feeling for every treacherous, sliding step.

"Kari?" Skapti said.

But the boy had turned; he was looking back into the snow. Something moved in the squall, a great gray shape that leaped by him; with a snarl it had Skapti down and was standing over him, paws splayed, slavering at his throat with white teeth.

"Moongarm!" Jessa yelled. She stopped, looking back. Above her on the bridge Brochael roared with rage.

The wolf turned its head and looked at Kari, and there was something deep in those eyes that Kari knew, but it was lost, almost lost.

"All right," Kari said. "Let him up."

The creature backed, snarling. Skapti scrambled to his feet, shaking.

"He wants me to go with him!" Kari yelled. He moved away, a small dark figure on the snow.

"You can't!"

"Go with the others. I'll be close behind."

"Kari!" Brochael thundered.

Kari looked up at him; too far to hear, Brochael heard the words clearly, sharp with pain. "Cross the bridge, Brochael. You must get them across the bridge."

The squall blinded them for a moment; when they could see again, the ice was empty.

"Kari!" Jessa yelled furiously. "Don't do this to us!"

But in all the miles of snow, there was no one to answer her.

Twenty-Two

A third I see, that no sunlight reaches,
the doors faced northward,
Through its smoke vent venom drips
serpent skins enskein that hall.

They crouched in a snow hole, the blizzard lashing them. Shards of snow stung Kari's face; he tugged the scarves tighter.

The wolf had brought him here, leading him through the snow. Now it dissolved; became gray rags of mist that the wind whirled away. The man's body lay half-buried; Kari scraped snow from the eyes and mouth, and lifted the head.

"Moongarm!"

He was cold, almost lost. Putting his thin fingers on the man's wrist, Kari searched desperately within him for the frail soul, dragging it to the surface. Ravens descended around him.

"He's gone," one of them said harshly, crouching beside him.

"Not yet."

The man gasped, his eyes flickered. Slowly the taints and wildness of the wolf were gathered into him; Kari felt them enter and flood the man. For a moment he had the impression of someone gentler, older; now it was gone, submerged. Moongarm's amber eyes watched him, intent. Snow roared between them.

"I have to get back," Kari said. "The others—"

"No!" He struggled up, his cracked fingernails gripping the boy's shoulder. Kari waited, uncertain. The man was still savage with the beast nature that tormented him, but under that was fear, almost terror.

"Help me." The words were quiet, nearly lost. "Only you can."

Kari shook his head. "This power is your own."

"I don't want it!" Moongarm snarled. "It's taking me over—you can see that, you with your ghost sight." His face was gray, his hair streaked with ice. He crouched, head bent.

"When it began, I could control it; I could change my shape and my nature as I wished. I was free, Kari! I could become something else, something wild, strong, fierce, without the troubles men have!"

"Without reason either."

"Yes. But free."

"You still can."

"It's destroying me!" He paused, as if struggling for calm, his eyes wild and bright in his tangled hair. "Every time, it takes me longer to come back. Gets harder. And even when I fight my way to man shape, the rage is still there. I'm changing. I think more and more like an animal thinks. Moods sway me, hungers, fears. I can't control them. After the boar died, I was savage; those three men were just enemies, scents; I slavered for them. I didn't know their names, that they were Hakon, or Skapti, or even Brochael the Stubborn. I have to get the wolf out of me, Kari. I have to!"

Kari wiped snow from his face. He was chilled to the bone, desperate to get back to the bridge. "Why now?"

"The bridge. Once we cross it, anything might happen."

"To me," Kari said bitterly. The rainbow shimmers of the ice bridge came back to his mind.

"I need your sorcery. Reach in now and take the wolf

out of me." The man's eyes were close; his fingers closed tight as claws on the boy's arm. "Now, Kari! Before it devours me altogether. Before I run mad."

Kari shivered, trying to think. Then he moved out of himself into Moongarm, walked down the trackways of wolf sight, saw the long loneliness of the man, the flung spears, the barking dogs, the blood on the snow. He tasted endless arctic nights, the itch of fur, irrational terror. Then the wind splashed him with ice. He shook his head.

"I can't. Or if I did, it would kill you. It's too deep in you, Moongarm. You welcomed it in, and it's tangled about you. Why?"

"A woman once offered me a chance of strength and courage. I was a weak man, of no family, no importance. Like a fool I took it." Numb with cold and hopelessness he stared up at the ravens. "Take it out, Kari."

"No. One man is dead already because of me."

Moongarm leaped up, sudden and supple. "Then if you can't help, the gap will have me. The world's throat can take one more morsel."

"No!" Kari jumped up quickly.

"You won't stop me, ravenmaster."

"Won't I?" Kari gave him a cold, amused look. "I may seem frail, Moongarm, but I can hold you to life. And I will!"

The wind blew his hair into his eyes; he shook it away. The shape-shifter stared at him through the scatter of snow.

"Then you will. And I must fight and struggle with myself. But if I can, Kari, I'll escape it, wherever I have to go. To have a power you dare not use is worse than having none."

"I know that," Kari said bitterly. "Better than anyone."

"Not much farther!" Brochael yelled.

He was lost in the snow squall ahead; Jessa couldn't see Hakon either. Behind her somewhere, Skapti slithered. She rested for a moment, crouched, her head low. Inside her frozen gloves her hands were blue and numb; her legs and back ached unbearably. She felt exhausted.

The bridge had been endless; first the climb high into nothing but sky and storm, and now the long scramble downward, slipping and stumbling on the glassy slope. Briefly she thought of Kari and her anger and worry flared. Where was he? She was uneasy without him. Brochael must be too.

She looked up again; the bridge led away into blown snow, but through that she thought she could glimpse something else now, a shimmer of colors.

"Come on." Skapti gasped behind her. He settled the

bag with the kantele in it more firmly on his back. "Not the time for dreaming, Jessa."

"We're all hung about with dreams," she said, scrambling up.

"Are we? Well, this wind will blow them off. They'll go sailing over the world's edge like spindrift." A gust rocked him; he grabbed at her. "Us with them, if you don't get on!"

She felt her way on, one hand on the frail ice rail, the abyss roaring below. Her foot slid, testing the ice. Snow blinded her; she wiped it away, twice, and opened her eyes. The world was blurred. For a moment she stood still, in a sudden place of rainbows. Her hair and skin tingled; colored lights moved all about her, they crackled, spit blue and green and purple sparks, glimmered, rippled over her face. She shivered with the eerie charge.

"What is it?"

"Surt's blaze. The aurora!" Skapti yelled. "It's all around us."

Blue and scarlet waves flowed over him; his clothes rippled gold and green. The crackle of colors enfolded them both, and under their feet the ice bridge broke the uncanny light and refracted it in a million tiny rainbows, deep within.

Not far ahead, someone called.

"That's Hakon." Jessa scrambled forward, slid, fell on hands and knees.

Skapti hauled her up. "Be careful!" he warned.

The bridge descended; they walked blindly into the colored air, and wonderfully, after a few steps, they came out the other side, straight into a sudden cold stillness, the wind ending abruptly, as if an invisible wall of power held it back. The shock of that stillness, the relief of it, was enormous, and they both stopped, high in the sky.

Below them, they saw the land of the Snow-walkers.

Astonished, Jessa stared out at it. The sky here was black, the stars brighter than she had ever seen them, a shining dust flung to the horizon. Stretching from the foot of the bridge for miles and miles was an unbroken ice sheet, smooth as marble, empty and featureless. Mountains rose in the distance, strange jagged peaks shining in the starlight, and among them, huge even from here, a building, a hall or fortress, tall and white and smooth behind a great encircling wall.

In silence they looked at it, across the miles of ice, at Gudrun's hall, in its silent, empty land, long sought, long feared.

At the foot of the bridge Hakon and Brochael were sitting wearily.

Skapti said, "So this is the land of dreams." His voice

was oddly choked; she looked at him sideways and he smiled uneasily. "Poet's visions, Jessa. Rarely do they come true."

"Visions? Isn't this real?"

"I don't know anymore. I think we left the world behind a long time ago. This is somewhere else, beyond the edge. The spirit realm."

"I wish Kari was here," she muttered.

When they got down to him, she knew Brochael was thinking the same. He gazed anxiously up at the rainbow bridge, arching into light. "Where is he?"

"He'll come."

"If he doesn't, I'm going back. We can't do anything here without him." He looked around uneasily. "Even the air smells of sorcery."

It did. It was bitterly cold, and still, and had a strange tang of fear that Jessa found unnerving. Once or twice she thought she saw something move, out there on the ice, but the surface seemed empty, glimmering white.

Nothing would start a fire here, not even Brochael's tinderbox, and they were so tired that they lay down and slept as they were, in a dirty, wind-tangled huddle at the bridge's foot.

And it was then, in their sleep, that they knew the terror of the White People. Voices whispered around them faintly. Cold fingers touched their hair and faces. The Snow-walkers came walking through their dreams, touching, laughing, mocking. They made Jessa dream of home, her farm by the sea, and in an instant she saw it dwindle to a black, charred ruin, open to the rain. She saw Signi, in thin chains of ice, calling her name. She saw Wulfgar sitting alone in his hall, with a silvery woman at his shoulder, holding her hand out to him.

With a shiver of fear she opened her eyes.

They had been foolish to sleep; she knew that at once. Something had changed. Something was wrong. She stared around, dumbfounded.

A cage had been spun about them; fine spindly bars. They seemed easy to snap, but when Brochael struggled up and saw them, he tried to wrench them apart with his huge strength. Nothing happened. He couldn't even grasp them. He swore, and looked at Skapti in alarm.

"It's no use," the poet said quietly. "Look out there."

They turned and saw.

Sitting watching them was an old, old man, his face wizened, his hooded eyes evil and bright. Coats and cloaks muffled him; the blue starlight played over his face.

He smiled at them.

Jessa recognized him at once.

Twenty-Three

Breath they had not, nor blood or senses,
Nor language possessed, nor life-hue.

"Grettir!" she breathed.

The old man smiled at them, a toothless grin.

"What have you done to us?" Brochael roared.

"What my people do, loud man. What my people do. I've caught you." He scratched his head with a long hand. "You haven't changed, girl. Still the fiery one. And here's Brochael Gunnarsson too, and the Wulfings' poet. All so far from home."

Jessa sank down in despair.

"Who is he?" Hakon muttered.

"Grettir. Gudrun's counselor. He was with her when she ruled in the Jarlshold—a sly creature, nearly as evil as she is. Did you never see him?"

He shook his head, staring at the pile of their weapons out there on the ice, the dragons on his sword hilt gleaming.

"I suppose," Skapti said drily, "you don't intend a feast of welcome?"

"Clever." Grettir coughed, a harsh, racking cough, and spat. "No indeed. I've caught you in a cage of your own dreams. You can stay in there until you die—in this cold, very quickly. Then I might release you, and you can wander this land like all the other stolen souls. Unless of course . . ." He edged a little nearer, wheezing. "Unless you tell me where the boy is."

They were silent, glancing at one another. Jessa knew no one would speak.

"I see." The dwarfish man nodded. "Misplaced loyalty, I'm afraid. Do you think I would harm him? His mother wants him alive."

"We gathered that," Skapti said.

Grettir nodded, grinning. "Ah, I'd forgotten. Yes, we took the girl, if only to bring you here. If you knew that, I find it strange that you should have come."

"You would," Jessa said scornfully.

"So then. Where is he? Why is he not with you?"

"He came before us," Brochael said. "He may be with Gudrun already.

Grettir laughed slyly. "Now, that does not become you, my friend. I've been waiting here for you for many of what you call days, though here the stars are eternal. And no one has come this way. I watched you come over the bridge, remember. I tasted your anxiety. He's not with you."

"Maybe he's dead," Skapti said gravely.

Grettir looked at him. "Maybe. In which case you can tell Gudrun, for I dare not. But I think we'll wait and see. I know this, that he has her powers, and he'll feel the cold gripping you, the agony of your deaths. He'll know your danger. So we'll wait. In this land there is no hurry."

They turned away from his smug grin and squatted miserably on the frosty surface. Jessa felt so cold, a bitter cold that seemed to pass right through her. The frost cage held them firmly trapped.

"This is a nightmare," she whispered.

Hakon nodded. "And we're helpless."

"If Kari comes," Brochael muttered, looking up at the bridge, "he'll walk straight into a trap. The old man must have something ready."

"Kari might know."

"And he might not. If only we could warn him! And Moongarm! What treachery has he brewed up?" He clutched his hands in frustration. "If only I could get out!"

"Kari's grown, Brochael," Skapti said. "Grown in power. The old man might not have realized that."

"It's too late anyway." Hakon dropped his gaze from the bridge. Then he said, "Take a look, but don't turn your heads. Don't let him know."

Above the bridge two tiny black flecks had soared

out of the aurora light, becoming shadows among the starlight.

"The birds." Jessa flicked a look at Grettir and saw with despair that the old man had noticed them too.

He chuckled and stood up unsteadily. "Ah. About time."

"What are you going to do?"

He grinned at them. "Let me give you a lesson. Do you know the time to steal a soul? The best, easiest time? As a man dies. It comes loose then, comes free. Almost anyone might reach out and take it—valkyrie, demon, sorcerer, Snow-walker. To take a soul from a living man takes great skill, enormous sorcery. Of all of us, only Gudrun can do that. I can't. I must be content with a dead one."

"You're going to kill him?" Jessa gripped the frost rails. "But you said—"

"I lied. His body will die. His wraith I will take to Gudrun. That's all of him she wants."

His eyes lit; his long finger jabbed at the rainbow bridge.

"There!"

Two small figures had emerged from the nimbus of light; for a second they stood still up there, poised on the glassy arch. Jessa knew they were staring down at the empty land as she had done, feeling the relief of being out of the wind. Even from here she could recognize them—Kari's shining hair, pale in the moonlight, Moongarm just behind him, gripping the rail.

"Kari!" she screamed, leaping up. The others were shouting too, wild, useless warnings. For Grettir lifted his hand and spoke one word, a strange, ugly syllable.

And the bridge faded.

Like a rainbow fades, she thought, gripping her hands into hopeless fists. Through wet eyes she watched it go, lose substance, solidity, melt to a thing of light, through which the figures of her friends slipped, grabbed, fell, plunging down and down like small broken things into the mist. The storm of Gunningagap swallowed them abruptly.

Their fall had been silent.

"Kari?" Brochael whispered.

Jessa turned away, sick and furious. Grettir was still, eyes closed, as if listening for something, reaching for it. She gripped the bars and wanted to scream at him, to kill him, and then she stopped, drawing a tight, painful breath.

From the pile of weapons, Hakon's sword was being lifted, lifted by an invisible hand. It came floating through the air to the back of Grettir's neck and jabbed.

The old man stiffened, eyes wide. Astonishment and

dismay passed over his face. Then he nodded appreciatively. "Clever," he murmured.

Jessa grabbed Brochael's arm and forced him around. "Look!" She gasped, warm with joy. "It's all right! They're alive!"

Slowly Moongarm became visible to them all. He held the sword point against the old man's neck. "Sit down," he snarled, "and do nothing, sorcerer. I wouldn't like to soil my friend's sword."

The old man crumpled. He seemed ruefully amused. "She said you were unpredictable, Kari. I had not guessed how much."

"Hadn't you?" Kari stood on the ice, the ravens flapping out of nothing about him. "Are you sure about that?"

Grettir looked up at him, and his face changed. After a moment he said gravely, "You have grown so much like her."

Kari said nothing to that. He came over to the cage and gripped the bars.

"Can you do it?" Skapti asked.

"I think so."

Hakon shook his head. "We saw you fall!"

"I'm sorry." Kari looked at Brochael. "I had to make it look like that. We'd crossed earlier. I had a warning. Long ago."

Brochael nodded, numb with cold. He reached out and touched Kari's sleeve. "I should have known," he said, his voice gruff. "Get us out of here."

The bars dissolved; they melted to nothing. And all the world went with them, into darkness and cold.

Someone was chafing her fingers and hands; numbly she felt the pain throb back into them, the hot pulse of blood.

She opened her eyes slowly. Brochael's bulk loomed against mist and starlight. He said, "You're all right. You're back."

She was wrapped in blankets, chilled to the bone. A fire was burning on the ice, crackling and sparkling; for a moment she wondered how, and then realized Kari must have made it, a rune fire, but giving out wonderful heat. Then she saw the sack burning in it, and the thin, familiar spars of wood. It took her a long moment to realize what they were.

Appalled, she sat up.

Skapti brought her a cup of warm water and some salt fish. She took it, staring at him. "How could you?" she asked gently.

"No choice. We had to get warm." He smiled wanly toward the burning wood of the kantele. "There'll be plenty more songs, Jessa, if we get out of this, don't worry.

They're in me. She won't undo them. Not the trees in my forest."

She nodded sadly, wondering what he meant. Her body felt strange, cold at the edges, like a house no one has lived in for a while. She flexed her toes and fingers, her shoulders.

Grettir was sitting quietly by the fire, Moongarm close beside him. They were taking no chances, but the old man seemed content just to sit, as if he accepted his plan had failed. But his bright eyes gleamed at Jessa under his hood, and she knew he was laughing at them all.

She must have been asleep a long time; the stars had moved around in their great silent wheel. Otherwise everything looked the same. The land glimmered, pale and empty.

Kari was talking. "Halfway over I knew something was wrong, but not what. We had to come unseen."

Skapti shook his head. "It's cost me a year off my life."

Brochael said nothing; he put his big arm around Kari and squeezed him.

"And now what?" Hakon asked.

"Now we go to Gudrun," Kari said firmly. "Alive."

Grettir shook his head and smiled slyly. "For now, little prince. For now."

Twenty-Four

The planets knew not what their places were.

They walked through an empty land, without time. It was a country where nothing grew, where even the wind dared not come. Soft snow fell silently through the long, arctic night; it was a realm of starlight and sorcery, beyond the world. Since they had entered it, each of them had felt a constant fear, a strange diminishing of themselves. They were no longer sure who they were or how real this was—in this place anything could happen. Even the air was alive, tingling with power.

They walked together in a group; only Kari walked a little way in front, the birds above him. He said nothing, but all his old apprehension seemed to have fallen from him. He had put on that coat of power, that air of remoteness they knew. He was ready now, Jessa thought. And for whose death? Because only he or Gudrun would survive. Once they had walked away from each other. But not now. This would be the end.

The fortress loomed nearer, a hall built from icy

blocks, fitted together with sorcerous skill. The gates were open. They were entanglements of ice, sharp shards of bright crystal. Grettir walked in between them, limping; the travelers followed him with drawn swords.

A great courtyard stretched before them. They crossed it quickly, watching the high windows. Hakon glanced back. Only their footprints marred the smooth snow. And yet they all knew they were being watched.

Only Kari saw them, as he passed by; the great host of the Snow-walkers, talking, laughing, amused, curious. They were a pale people, their faces as thin and delicate as his own. Children among the crowd stared at him; men and women with white snake marks in their skin. Gudrun's people. His people. It moved him; apart from Gudrun he had never seen anyone who looked as he did. Turning away bitterly, he faced the doors.

They were open.

Grettir stopped on the bottom step. When he got his breath, he wheezed, "From here you go in by yourselves."

"While you lock the doors?" Brochael grabbed the old man's arm roughly. "Oh no. Show us where Signi is."

Grettir shrugged. "It makes no difference in the end."

"It might to you, if you want to live. Where is she?"

"Through the hall. Up the stairs."

The hall was bitterly cold, a palace of ice. It was bare of

furniture; snow lay in tiny waves on the floor, crunching as they walked over it, but its splendor was in the light that came through the ice; a pale shimmer of blue and green, a refraction of stars and snow, eerie and cold. On some of the walls were hangings, all white and silver, and shields of strange metals. Ice girders held up the roof; thin spindles of ice hung from each windowsill, and great curtains of it, formed over years, massed here and there, sprawling out into the floor to make pillars and columns of intricate crystal. It was a frozen house, without sound, or welcome.

On the far side of the hall were some stairs leading up.

"These?" Brochael snapped.

Grettir nodded.

Kari leaped up the first steps lightly; the others clattered after him.

"Where are they all?" Hakon breathed to Jessa. "We're walking into a trap, I'm certain."

"I know that. We all do. Stick behind me if you're scared."

He smiled, but it was a wan effort.

The ice steps led up between glinting walls. Then they came out into a room at the top. Crowding into the doorway behind Hakon, Jessa caught her breath.

The room was a blaze of candles; white candles of every size and thickness. The flames burned straight, with no breeze to flutter them. In the center of the room was a white chair, and Signi was sitting in it, staring at them. She held out her hands.

"I almost hoped you wouldn't come," she said sadly.

"We had to." Skapti crossed to her.

"Is Wulfgar . . . ?"

"He's not with us. He had to stay at the hold."

Her dress and hair seemed paler here, drained of color; her skin had a strange, glistening tinge. The back of the chair was a network of ice strands, hung and looped, great chains of it. They dropped from her sleeves and wrists, unwound and slithered after her as she stood up and crossed the room.

She tried to touch them, but her fingers passed through Brochael's and he shook his head.

"How do you like your sword, Hakon?" she asked.

Puzzled, he glanced down at it. "Very much, but the gift was a long time ago."

"Was it?" She looked at them carefully, at their worn clothing, and windburned, unshaven faces. Fear crept into her eyes. "How long?"

"Weeks."

She pressed her fingers together, pale and trembling. "I didn't know. There's no time in this place. Nothing but silence and cold, no one to speak to or touch . . ." Her eyes darted to the doorway, where Grettir stood. He smirked at her.

Kari fingered the chains thoughtfully.

"Can you?" Jessa asked him.

"No. This is Gudrun's spell. Only she can."

"You should leave here!" Signi put her wraith hand on his; only he could feel her, frail as a leaf. "You shouldn't have come, Kari. It's you she wants! She only brought me here to bring you."

"I know that." He turned to Grettir reluctantly. "Where is she?"

"Waiting for you."

"Then show me where. But I want to know that nothing will happen to my friends. Either way. I want to be sure of that."

"Oh no!" Jessa said firmly. She caught his arm tight. "You're not vanishing on me again! We're all in this."

He tried to tug away, but she had been expecting this; she held tight.

"Jessa—"

"No, Kari."

Grettir watched them, amused. "Touching," he murmured.

"Keep out of this," Brochael growled. He put his hand on Kari's shoulder. "She's right."

Kari glanced at them both. "I don't want to hurt you—"

"Nor will you."

"But you have to let me go! Please, Brochael!" He squirmed away from them.

"Not without us." Brochael caught him again firmly. "Listen, Kari. Jessa is right. We're all in this; it isn't just you. You can't take it all on yourself."

"And what good do you think you will be to him?" a cold voice mocked. "The boy is no kin of yours, Brochael Gunnarsson. He's nothing of yours. He's mine. And always will be."

Brochael stood still. His face hardened, and as he turned he put his arm around Kari and they stood together, looking at the woman in the doorway.

Twenty-Five

His hands he washed not nor his hair combed.

She looked older.

She was still tall, though, and pale, her long hair

braided and caught in a shining net. Her coat was the color of snow shadows, blue and dim in the strange ice light, her eyes colorless and impossible to read.

She stepped quickly into the candlelight, her silks and furs swishing, and she smiled at them, that cold, indifferent smile that had terrified Jessa so long ago.

Glancing at Kari, she said, "You only have to look at us."

They all watched her, uneasy. Gudrun had worked her spell on each of them, Jessa thought. She had once made Hakon a thrall, crippled in one hand, useless but for slow, endless labor. She'd sent Jessa herself into the terror of Thrasirshall, stolen Wulfgar's kingdom, made Skapti an outlaw scavenging for years on favors and carrion. Brochael she had banished to die with her son, and from him, Kari, she had taken everything, left him unable to speak, walk, even to think, not knowing what people were. His very father had never seen him. And then she'd murdered his father.

Each of them had deep cause to hate her. Only Moongarm stood aside.

Gudrun crossed the room and put her hands out to Kari. "I knew you would come home."

"This isn't my home." He stepped back.

"Yes it is," she said seriously. "You've seen that, seen

the people here. My people and yours. I heard you think it, Kari. You can't deny that."

He turned away, then back to face her abruptly. "You've offered me this before. I don't want it."

She nodded and smoothed her dress in the old gesture that Jessa remembered. "Then let me show you something that you do want. All of you. What happened in the Jarlshold was my spell, yes, but the dreams that destroyed you were your own. Dreams of mortals. Destructive, dangerous. Look here, and see what you do to yourselves."

In the middle of the room she opened her hands, almost carelessly, and spread a coldness about her, a darkness in the air that surrounded them all swiftly. The room faded, they seemed to be standing in snow, knee-deep in it, somewhere outside.

Jessa looked around fearfully. It was the Jarlshold, she knew. But how it had changed!

The silence was deathly. Thick snow coated everything; icicles hung over shutters and sills. Between the riven clouds a few stars glimmered, and showed her that the snow was unmarked. The settlement seemed totally deserted.

Gudrun opened the door latch, the familiar door to the hall. It opened slowly.

"It was cunning of you to leave a guardian," she said,

glancing at Kari. "Otherwise I should have had them all by now."

They stepped warily into the hall.

It was frozen, stiff with ice. Gloom hung in its spaces, a silence of sleep. Walking in the vision over the stone floor, Jessa saw sleeping forms all around her, huddled up, barely breathing in the searing cold. They were all here now—the fishermen, farmers, children, thralls, the women and the war band, some crumpled where they had fallen, others covered with blankets or furs.

Ahead of her, deep in the gloom, a glint of red light showed, smoldering, barely alive. Someone was still awake.

As they came closer Jessa saw it was the embers of a fire, the dull peats giving out a faint heat. Over it one man was huddled, wrapped in a dark blanket, and as he raised his head and looked at them, she saw it was Wulfgar.

His appearance shocked her. He was thin, almost gaunt. A dark stubble covered his chin and his red-rimmed eyes looked weary and unfocused. He smiled bitterly when he saw them. "Now I know I'm delirious. Are you dead then, all of you? Are you ghosts, come to haunt me?"

"A vision," Kari said, crouching by him. "Nothing more."

Wulfgar did not seem to hear him. He shook his head

and gave a low, bitter laugh. "Of course you are. Dead at the world's end, where I sent you. And all of us here caught in her spell, except me. Gods, I wish I was too."

He clasped his hands around his sword hilt and turned away from them, staring into the flames.

Skapti stood rigid, watching him. Then he turned on Gudrun. "I could kill you myself for this."

She smiled coldly at him.

"He can barely see us," Kari murmured. "He thinks he's imagining us."

"But why is he still awake?" Jessa asked.

Kari crossed to the roof tree; the great ash trunk rose above him, glinting with frost. "Because of this."

They gathered around him and saw, wedged into a deep cleft at the base of the tree, something that shone in the firelight. Jessa moved back to let the light through and suddenly they saw what it was: a small piece of crystal, covered with spirals. For a moment she wondered where she had seen it before, and then the memory came to her of Kari's strange tower room in Thrasirshall. The crystals had hung there in long strings from the roof. She remembered them turning in the sun.

"This protects him?" Brochael asked.

"Yes." Kari turned defiantly to the witch, who stood a little back. "You'll never get it out. I made sure of that."

The vision of the hall vanished instantly; they were in the candlelit room, and Signi was crying quietly into her hands.

"That doesn't matter," Gudrun said easily. "None of that matters now. I wanted you to come and you have."

She touched his sleeve, teasing. "This is where you belong. Stay here, and I'll release them, all of them. These can go; the Jarlshold will be free. I have no interest in them."

"Kari, no," Brochael warned.

The boy was silent.

"And think about this," Gudrun went on quietly. "Here, you are one of us. No one will point you out because you're different, or stiffen in terror if you look at them. I always enjoyed that, but I think it pains you. Among them you'll always be an outsider, and that will never change, Kari, never, no matter how much they think they know you. Can you live with that all your life?"

For a moment they stood together, two identical faces, Gudrun's watchful, Kari's downcast. Then he pulled his arm away from her.

"Leave me alone!" he said bitterly. "You've done this to me before! I won't let it happen again. We've come too far, been through too much. These are my friends; I trust them. They trust me." He gripped his hands together and went on rapidly. "And I need them. I need them to keep me from becoming like you. I care about them, and about Wulfgar, and all the people you've stolen from themselves. I can't turn my back on them. Not now."

"Well said," Brochael growled.

"Can you understand that?" Kari went close to her, almost pleading. He was as tall as she was now, Jessa noticed with surprise. Face-to-face he confronted her, snatching her thin hands. "Can you?" he breathed.

Gudrun smiled at him, almost sadly. "No," she said. "And you know that means death for one of us."

Her words were like a blow.

Brochael stepped closer but she looked through him, unconcerned. "I've never known you, Kari," she said. "You and I have always been on opposite sides of the mirror."

"We don't have to be," he whispered.

"I see now that we do. It's too late, my son. Too late for everything."

And they were gone instantly, both of them.

Jessa gasped with shock and rage; Brochael swore in fury. "Where are they?" he roared, swinging around. But the old man had gone too.

Twenty-Six

What do you ask of me? Why tempt me?

Kari was standing in darkness.

Around him were many invisible people; he could feel their thoughts crowding him and he pushed them away. He knew this was the spirit world, the dream realm. Anything could happen here, so he made some light; it flooded the room.

He was in a small place, little more than a cell. A dirty bed lay on the floor in one corner, and on the hearth the ashes were cold. A tiny window let in starlight over his head.

He knew where he was. The memory came over him, sharp and bitter, and then it was a weariness, a familiar relentless numbness that crept over his mind.

He went across and kneeled on the gray blankets, fingering the scrawls on the wall, the marks made with a charred stick, all blurs and spirals.

"Why here?" he murmured.

"Because of all the places in the world this is the one you fear most." She leaned against the damp wall looking down at him, as she always had. "They don't know, your friends, about this terror, do they? About the nightmares of this room? Not even Brochael?"

Kari sat on the worn blankets, knees up, hugging himself. He rocked back and forth a little, saying nothing.

"How empty they were," she said softly, coming to stand over him. "All those years in here."

"You locked me in here. Abandoned me . . ."

"Years of silence. Fear. You remember them?"

"I can't forget." He looked up fiercely. "Why did you do that? It could all have been so different. For both of us."

She shook her sleek head, kneeling before him, her silk dress rustling in the straw. "Among us, there can be only one soul thief. I knew that from the beginning."

Kari barely heard her. He was fighting to stay calm, to beat off the terrors of his childhood. All around him he felt them coming out, from the walls, from the blown ashes, from the marks he had drawn years ago, a child without thoughts, frightened and cold, unable to speak.

He knew every inch of this place, had fingered every crack of it, crawled in every corner, watched the slow forming of frosts every winter, the moving wand of sunlight that stroked out the dreary days. Now it seemed as if he had never left. All that had happened since grew faint and unreal; he knew this place was the emptiness in him, the yearning, the source of all her power over him. As he crouched there he began to forget them all, Jessa, Skapti, even Brochael; speech began to die in him, so that he groped for words and had forgotten them, even their sounds. There was only the woman, the tall woman, and he could never escape from her, never. He had been here too long.

Far outside him, something flapped and squawked; he looked up with a great effort and saw a raven's beak prising at the window bars.

Gudrun smiled. "Even those I can keep out."

Miserably he put his hands out to her, and she took them. And with a strength and suddenness that astonished him, he felt her reach into him, deep among his thoughts and terrors and memories, until she touched, with a cold finger, his soul. And she began to tug at it, and he felt his personality quiver and fail, and as he slumped away from her against the stone wall, he knew numbly that she was drawing out his very being, dragging it from him, and he crumpled to his knees, clutching the gray blanket with a child's thin fists.

"Stay with Signi," Brochael ordered.

Moongarm stared at him. "I'm surprised you trust me."

"So am I," Brochael snarled. "Keep the door shut."

He slammed it from the outside himself, the others behind him.

"They could be anywhere," Skapti muttered.

"Not even visible."

"I don't care, Jessa!" Brochael was aflame with wrath. "We'll tear this place to pieces till we find someone, somewhere! She won't take him away from me. Never!"

He raced down the stairs; the others followed, reckless.

The ice hall was bare and silent; the rooms on each side of it deserted. Skapti flung their doors wide, one after another.

"Nothing!"

"She's here!" Rubbing frost from his face, Brochael stopped. He slammed a fist into the wall. "She's got to be."

"She'd have a room," Jessa said thoughtfully.

"What?"

"A room. A place of her own . . ."

"For her sorceries, yes, I know! But where?"

"High up, like Kari's." Jessa turned decisively. "There must be other stairs. Split up, quickly. Try every room."

She ran into the nearest narrow entrance; it led her to a small storeroom piled with chests of strange white metal. Putting the point of her knife under the lid of one, she forced it open. A sudden yellow glow lit her face; she gazed down at huge lumps of amber, gloriously colored. A treasure beyond price. And the other chests would hold jet and ivory and silver, all Gudrun's hoard.

But there was no time for it now. She slammed the lid down and ran back out. Skapti thumped into her. "Anything?"

"No. What about—?"

Hakon's yell silenced her; it was distant, far across the hall. When they got to him, he was leaning against a wall of frost, breathless.

"There," he managed.

The doorway was small, hung with icicles. Beyond it, steps descended into darkness. A cold, sweet smell hung in the air.

"Down?" Jessa muttered.

"She's his opposite, remember?" Hefting the ax in his great hands, Brochael led the way grimly.

The stairs ran deep into the ice. As they clattered down them, the air grew colder, bitterly cold, their breath a glinting fog. Light faded to blue-green gloom. They knew they were far down in the ice layers, deep inside the glacier. On each side of them the walls became opaque, then mistily transparent; far inside them bubbles of air were trapped, like soft crystal shimmers.

Brochael stopped abruptly. "We were right."

The doorway at the bottom was a small one, but carved deep in the ice above it was a great white serpent. It curled around the lintel, its sightless eyes glaring down at them. From within came sounds, a murmur of voices.

"They're in there," Hakon muttered.

Brochael gripped the ax. His face was set. "Ready?"

"Ready."

"Brochael!" Jessa's scream of warning was just in time. He turned and in the corner of his eye saw the movement flash; then the snake struck at where his head had been, its venom sizzling the ice.

"Gods!" He jerked back, shoving Hakon aside.

The snake hissed; a thin tongue flickered from its ice lips. Then quickly it unwound itself from the doorway, slithering down the pillars toward them.

Hakon was closest; he struck at it in disgust, and the sword sliced deep into the cold, impossible flesh. But it came on, slipping around his blade, his wrist and arm, and he yelled and squirmed in terror.

"Keep still!" Brochael roared.

He and Skapti tore at the wet, slippery body; it hissed and spat at them, darting at their eyes, tightening its muscles around Hakon with a fierce gripping pain that made him cry out. Jessa slid behind Brochael, knives in hand. The pale scaly back rippled before her. Choosing her time, she pulled her arm back and thrust, deep and hard.

★ ★ ★

Like a distant shock, Kari felt the stab.

For a moment his mind cleared; he reached out and pushed her away, knotting darkness and runes to a wild web of protection that she tore to fragments in seconds. Fierce and hungry, she dragged at him, and he struggled to fight her off, to stand. Outside, something thumped and thudded. From an immense distance a voice yelled, "Kari!"—a voice he knew, a voice that stirred him. And he remembered. He remembered the day when the door had opened and the stranger had come. A man such as he had never seen, huge and red and bearded, a lantern gleaming in his hand. And he knew that the man's name was Brochael, and grasping that, he felt his life flood back to him, his thoughts and speech, the faces of his friends. Power surged in him; he stood up shakily.

Gudrun grabbed his hands again, her nails cutting deep.

"Stay with me," she hissed.

Numb, he shook his head. Then, summoning all his sorcery, he tore her spell apart.

The walls soared upward, the window rippled, became a wide casement of glass, open to the sunlight. With a cry he let the cell split open; it became a tower room hung with long strings of threaded crystals that twirled and glittered in the cold, brilliant light. With a shrill kark of triumph the ravens broke through. They flapped through the window and perched, one on a table, the other on the rim of a bowl.

Kari sat down in his usual chair. He was weak with the effort it had cost him.

And Gudrun gazed around at it all, furious.

Twenty-Seven

The children of darkness, the doombringers.

"Perhaps this is the place you fear most," he said quietly. He felt drained already, weary from the desperate struggle to hold on to himself. Now he reached out and touched the hangings of quartz, setting them swinging. The bird wraiths stood behind him; he knew she saw them as he did: two tall men. One laid a narrow hand on his shoulder.

"Where is this?" she demanded, her voice clotted with wrath.

"You know where, though you've never been here. This is Thrasirshall. The place you sent me to die." Shaking his head, he smiled wanly. "The strange thing is, it was here I learned how to live."

Gudrun looked coldly around her, at the sparse room, at the bird wraiths. "I see. And now you think you're a match for me?" She laughed at him, her eyes bright, and he felt his heart sink, as it always did before her.

"My powers are too much for you, Kari. I've had years of practice. Try if you like, but remember this: Of all our people, only I can steal souls."

He looked up at her, and knew his danger.

"Until now," he said.

Moongarm looked sidelong at Signi. "What does it feel like?" he murmured.

She shook her head, the pale hair swinging. "As if I'm adrift. Nowhere."

He crossed the room and picked up the ice chain. "That's a feeling I know about." He ran it through his hands, over the sharp, broken nails.

"So why did you come with them?" she asked quietly. "Why here?"

"You've guessed why." He flung the chain down and turned away from her, a lean uneasy figure in the white room. "Because the spell that's on me came from here. I didn't know that at first, didn't know who the woman was.

I never saw her again. But as I wandered north, an outcast, hated, chased away from every settlement, I heard the tales of them, the sorcerers at the world's end, a pale, dangerous people. I thought then she must have been one of them. When I saw the boy, I knew. But he can't help me. And then, just now, there she was, standing in that doorway. The same woman."

"Gudrun?"

"It was years ago, but I knew her. She looked at me, but I saw that she's forgotten me. Forgotten."

"She's hurt us all. . . ."

"But I asked her for this. I asked her! And I was glad of it. At first I thought she had made me more than a man. Not less."

He brooded bitterly, watching the floor with his strange amber eyes. She felt sorry for him, and suddenly afraid.

"Moongarm . . ."

He crossed to the door. "I have to go. You'll be safe enough."

"Moongarm, wait!" She stood up, the ice chain tinkling. "Leave it to Kari!"

Sword in hand, he looked back at her and shook his head. Then he opened the door and slid out.

★ ★ ★

Painfully Jessa picked herself up off the floor, where the thrashing of the snake had flung her. Hakon lay on his stomach, coughing for breath; he rolled over and stared at her.

A long wet stain scored the ice between them; it froze as they watched, into a stinking shimmer of crystal. The knife too was coated with ice; she wiped it in disgust against the side of her boot.

"All right?" Brochael asked.

Hakon nodded, getting up. "Was it alive?"

"As alive as I wanted," Skapti said. "I could even have done with a little less."

"Don't waste time!" Jessa snapped.

"She's right." Brochael turned to the door. "Open it."

She lifted the latch and pushed suddenly. The door swung wide without a sound, but despite their hurry none of them made any move to enter. Because what lay beyond the door was not a room, or a place in any world they knew. It was a nothingness, a mist of light, and figures loomed and moved in it, receding into distances that were too far. They knew this was the spirit realm, the place where Kari sometimes went in the darkness, under the stars. But if they were to go in, how could they ever get back? Jessa thought.

She glanced at Skapti. "Do we?"

"No!"

Brochael turned. "We have to! Kari is in there."

"And Kari knows far more about it than we do." The skald crossed to him, took his arm with long, firm fingers. "I know it's hard, Brochael, but we can't just blunder in. We might not be helping him. We'd be putting ourselves in danger."

"He's right," a sly voice muttered.

Grettir stood behind them on the stairs, a tiny, hunched figure in his coats and wraps. He rasped out a chuckle. "Go in there and you'll wander forever."

"You would say that!" Brochael came back and caught the old man by the throat, all his frustration infuriating him. "Tell me the truth now, before I squeeze the life out of you. What's happening to them?"

Grettir still smiled. "A contest of souls, axman. And only one of them will come out of it alive."

He reached out at her, through sunlight and mist. Through unbearable coldness into empty places, into nothing. With all his power he reached for her soul—and touched ice. He took out his knife and began to dig at it, chipping and stabbing, kneeling on a glacier, out in the cold. Somewhere, she was laughing at him; he ignored that. A little way off, dark against the stars, all the Snow-walkers watched.

It was hard, tiring work; fiercely he chipped at the ice

and shards of it flew up in his face. He jerked back, afraid for his eyes. Hands pulled at him, voices murmured, but he shrugged them off.

"Keep them away!"

The bird wraiths moved behind him, menacing.

And now, deep in the glacier, something gleamed; he pushed his fingers in among the crushed slush and tugged it out: a stone, a diamond, hard and glittering.

It burned him and he almost dropped it. It became a snake winding over his fingers, a bird fluttering in his hands, a flame, a drift of vapor, a stinging wasp, but still he held it, through all the pain and the woman's growing anger all around him.

"Even though you've found me," she whispered. "You won't keep me."

"I will. This time."

She was there, feeling for his hands, opening his fingers, but he flung her off and held on.

She came again, her hands soft on his. "I'm your mother," she said. "Remember?"

"I know that." Despite himself, tears blinded him; he held the stone fiercely, huddled over it. "But that's over. All of it. Everything is over."

Then she knew. With a scream of rage and fear she struck at him, became a coldness that closed about him tight, tearing at his life, but he held the diamond tight. And it was her soul that he held, and her power and anger and amazement, and he let it flow into himself, feeling that he knew her for the first time, knew all of her, and it terrified him.

"Let me go!" her voice screamed. "Let me go!"

Dragging all his energies about him, Kari began the webs; he conjured with runes and blackness and cold, pulled out every shred of power he had to wind about her, to hold her, to keep her still. Murderous with rage she tore at him, became a flame that burned him, lava that seared his hands, but he knew he was holding on, that he was winning, and the power in him grew and he wound the spells tighter, fiercer, binding them about her.

Somewhere, someone was shouting, but he couldn't think about that now, he had to imprison her; his hand slid to his pocket and he pulled out the crystal he had brought for this.

Deep within it he embedded Gudrun's soul, deep in the sharp glass facets, weaving spells about her with words that came from nowhere into his mind, as if all the sorcery of the Snow-walkers rose up and flooded him now. And when the spell was finished, when he was sure it was safe, he closed his eyes and let his mind empty, and there was silence, and exhaustion swept over him like a wave.

"Is it done?" a harsh voice croaked in his ear.

Numb, he nodded.

"Then you must get back. This is nowhere. We're lost here. Now, runemaster!"

"Later," he murmured.

"Now! It must be now, Kari!"

They crowded him close, anxiously. All he wanted to do was sleep, to lie down and rest, but he knew they were right, and he staggered up, his hand gripping the crystal.

"Which way?"

"Any way! It's all one."

Nodding, struggling to think, he stumbled forward into the dark, into a mist that swirled purple and green and then white, ice white.

And as the others stood at the door, they saw him drift toward them, loom suddenly out of nowhere, and Jessa swore that for a moment two men were with him, until the mist swirled and she saw they were only the ravens swooping out, eyes bright.

But Kari was indistinct; he stumbled as he came, and just as he reached the threshold, he almost fell. Brochael caught him, but at the same time Moongarm pushed from behind and snatched something out of Kari's hand, snatched it fiercely, hungrily, a small, glittering stone.

"No!" Kari gasped.

Brochael grabbed the man's sleeve.

"Let me finish this," Moongarm said quietly.

"No!" Kari struggled to stop him. "Brochael!"

"You know it's best," the werebeast said. "I'll take this where no one will ever find it. Where she'll never get back. Call it my revenge. And it's what you want, Brochael."

Slowly Brochael let go of his sleeve. Then he said gruffly, "It's taken me too much time to come to know you."

"And now you do?"

"I think so."

Moongarm nodded at him. "I'm glad, my friend."

And then he turned and walked through the doorway, deep into the mist, and as he walked his body twisted and blurred into a lithe, gray creature, shimmering, gone in an instant.

Kari turned away, silent.

And over his shoulder the others saw nothing but a small frozen room, every surface of it seamed with ice, and in a white chair Gudrun was sleeping, just as Signi had slept.

Twenty-Eight

Unsown acres shall harvests bear,
Evil be abolished.

Kari slept for a day and a night, almost without moving.
The others stayed alert. They gathered in Signi's room, not
knowing what to expect, and Brochael prowled about
uneasily, ax in hand. But no one came near them. The ice
fortress stayed as it had always been, cold and silent.

Finally Jessa and Hakon ventured out. Food was running short, and they needed to find out what the Snow-
walkers were doing.

Creeping silently into the hall, they saw a strange sight.
Grettir was huddled in a small chair, his palms flat on the
carved armrests. On a white bier before him Gudrun lay
asleep; she lay still, barely breathing, her long hair loose,
her dress smooth and white. Icicles already hung from her
sleeves; crystals of frost had begun to form on her hair and
skin.

They walked up to her, and looked down in awe.

"She looks as though she'll wake up at any moment,"
Hakon whispered.

"She won't." Jessa looked down at the old man. "What
happens to you?"

Grettir stirred and looked up. His face was lined and gray. "That depends. Does the boy live?"

"Yes."

"Then we're all in his hands. He has the power now."

He stood up and shuffled toward the sleeping woman, and looked down at her thoughtfully. "She was cruel too often, but she was strong. She knew all the secrets; she took what she wanted. Until the end, she was never afraid."

He glanced at Jessa, who said, "She was evil. We all knew that."

"And now Kari comes into his inheritance. How different will that be?"

"Very different," she snapped.

He laughed wheezily. "I'm glad you think so. But I know better. I know how their power gnaws them till they must use it; how it changes them. Even she was different once."

"But Kari's got something she never had."

"What?"

She smiled at him. "He has us."

For a moment he looked at her gravely, and at Hakon, and then he smiled too. "So he does," he said sadly. "I hope that it will be enough."

He turned and hobbled away. "I'll bring you some food."

"Thank you."

"We didn't even ask him," Hakon murmured.

"That's how this place is."

"And it's Kari's now. Will he stay here?"

"I don't know." Thoughtfully she walked to the door.

Grettir brought the food; strange stuff, most of it, but they ate it and saved some for Kari. When he finally woke up, he sat by Brochael for a while, listless and silent, no one wanting to bother him with questions. Finally, with an effort, he got up and went over to Signi.

"You must go home now," he said.

The girl smiled at him, her silken dress pale. He touched her wrists briefly and the ice chains began to melt, dripping away rapidly.

"Don't be sad, Kari," she said. "It's all over."

Surprised, he managed to smile back. "Yes. It's over. Tell Wulfgar what you've seen. Tell him we're coming home."

Fading before their eyes, she reached out to touch him. "All of you? Are you all coming?"

"All of us."

And then the chair was empty, and Jessa imagined with sudden clarity the girl lying in that bed in the hold—how she would be waking now, sitting up, stiff and hungry; how she would stumble downstairs, into the silence and cold of the hall, to Wulfgar. . . .

"What about the others?" she asked aloud.

"Gudrun's spell faded with her," Kari said. He sat down against the wall, knees up. "They'll all be waking now—the noise and warmth will come flooding back. All their souls will return to them; the hold will be as we always knew it—busy, warm, alive."

"In fact, by the time we get back," Skapti said slyly, "they'll have forgotten about it."

"And us," Jessa muttered. "It's a long way."

"Indeed it is. And there are places we'll go a long way around," Brochael rumbled.

They all laughed and fell silent.

After a moment Kari got up and went out into the hall. Brochael gazed after him uneasily.

"Let him go," Skapti muttered.

"He's too quiet. I thought he'd be . . . happy."

Skapti rubbed his unshaven chin. "Give him time, Brochael. All his life she's been there, a threat, a torment. When a weight comes off your back, you're often too stiff to stand up at once."

It was Jessa who went after him, much later. She found him standing at the side of the bier, looking down, quite still. Beside him, Jessa was silent a moment. Then she said, "Where is she, Kari?"

He twisted the frayed end of his sleeve around his fingers. "I don't know, Jessa," he said finally. "I stole her soul and locked it into a crystal, locked it deep, with tight spells. But he's taken it back into that world, it's lost there, and I don't know how to find it again." He looked up intently. "Perhaps Moongarm was wise. Now she's neither dead nor alive. Because I couldn't have killed her, Jessa."

They turned and walked back into the little room. Brochael looked up at them.

"We leave tomorrow, after we've all slept. Unless you want your kingdom."

Kari laughed suddenly. "Grettir can have it. Thrasirshall is my kingdom. And you're its only subject."

They all laughed then, Brochael hearty with relief, and the sound echoed in the empty rooms and halls of the palace. Jessa thought that it was a strange, new sound here, and wherever they were the White People heard it with surprise. She caught Hakon's eye.

"You never got around to naming your sword."

"Ah, but I have."

"Tell us then."

Awkwardly he touched the hilt. "You'll laugh."

"No, we won't."

"Well, at first I thought of Bear-bane. . . ."

Despite herself, Jessa giggled.

"Not bad," Skapti conceded.

"And then Snake-stabber. But I didn't think that was any good. . . ."

"It's not."

"So I thought of Dream-breaker."

"Why that?" she asked.

"Because in my dream I fell from the bridge, but the sword saved me." He smiled at them shyly. "What do you think?"

"It's a fine name," Skapti said.

Kari nodded, and Brochael laughed. "I never thought we'd make it then."

"Oh, I did," Jessa said, putting her arms around them both. "I always did."

Acknowledgments

Chapter-opener quotations in Book 1 are from "The Words of the High One"; those in Book 3 are from "Voluspa" (translated as "The Song of the Sybil"); both from *Norse Poems*, edited and translated by W. H. Auden and Paul B. Taylor (Faber and Faber Ltd, 1983); reprinted by permission of Faber and Faber. The Book 2 chapter-opener quotations are from *Beowulf*, translated by Michael Alexander (Penguin Classics, 1973), reprinted by permission of Penguin Putnam.

Read on for a preview of

Catherine Fisher's

electrifying book

The Oracle Prophecies:
The Sphere of Secrets

So the rumors were true. And *these* were elephants.

Their enormous bodies amazed Mirany. In the evening heat they stood in a great semicircle, twelve beasts, tails swishing, vast ears rippling irritably against flies. On their backs were towers, real towers of wood with gaudy painted doors and windows, within which the dark-skinned merchants sat on jeweled palanquins tasseled with gold.

From her seat before the bridge, on the left side of the Speaker, she watched the animals through the twilight. A huge full moon hung over them, the Rain Queen's perfect mirror, its eerie light shimmering on the emptiness of the desert, the fires on the road, the black ramparts of the City of the Dead. A breeze drifted her mantle against her arm;

someone's thin silver bracelets clinked. There was no other sound, except, far below, the endless splash of the sea against rocks.

The central elephant was lumbering forward. Its great feet, heavy with bangles, thudded into the soft sand, the swaying mass of silver chains on its neck and ears and back brilliant in the moonlight. It wore a scarlet harness of tiny bells and immense pearls, the largest dangling between its eyes, a fist-sized, priceless lump.

Behind the mask, Mirany licked sweat from her lips. The eyeholes restricted her view, but she could see the Speaker, Hermia, and the rest of the Nine, the girls sitting rigid as if in terror, their bronze masks smiling calmly as the enormous beast neared. Next to her in the line, Rhetia fidgeted. The tall girl was alert, watching the crowd. Her fingers, light as dust, touched Mirany's wrist. "He's looking at you," she whispered.

On his pale horse, Argelin should have been easy to find. But he sat in shadow, armor gleaming, the bodyguard of sixteen huge men that never left him now, armed and facing outward. Mirany smiled sourly. There were probably others in the crowd. The general was taking no chances. And yes, his helmeted eyes were turned her way. Quite suddenly she felt exposed, unprotected. But she was as safe here as anywhere, these days.

Hermia stood. Hurriedly, Mirany and the rest of the Nine rose with her, and as the elephant came closer over the cooling sand, the smiling masks glinted under their feathers and jeweled headdresses, all color draining in the pearly light.

The great beast reached the bridge, and bowed its head. The smell of it was hot and rank, of dung and perfumes, and Mirany saw the myriad folds and wrinkles of its dusty skin, the sag of its belly as it lowered itself. She drew her breath in. For the elephant was kneeling before the Speaker. It knelt clumsily, and the thud of its great limbs in the sand sent vibrations across the wooden bridge. The rider, hidden behind the vast headdress, flicked a hand and spoke; the elephant lay right down and lifted its trunk; then it made a sound that chilled the night, a terrible brazen roar.

Hermia did not flinch, though one of the Nine— probably Chryse—made a moan of terror. Argelin's horse started nervously. The elephant looked along the crescent of the Nine. Its eye stopped at Mirany.

It recognizes you, the god remarked in her ear.

Recognizes?

As a friend. They are considered very wise, Mirany. Their memories are older than any other beast.

It has such small eyes, she thought, deep-set and

shrewd. As she answered she seemed almost to be speaking to the animal. "Where have you been for so long? I thought I'd never hear you again."

Gods have a world to run. I have been busy.

"We need you! Things are going wrong."

From the wooden howdah on the elephant, a ladder unraveled and a man climbed down. He was tall and bearded, wearing a robe of white and gold, so stiff with pearls it looked almost rigid. He put his hands together and bowed over them.

"What is it you seek here?" Hermia's voice rang across the desert.

"I seek the wisdom of the Oracle. I seek to hear the words of the god."

"From what land have you traveled?"

The answer was solemn, and measured. "From the east where the sun rises. From the Islands of Pearl and Honey, over the deep sea we bring the gifts and request of the Emperor, the Exalted, the Wise One, to the Bright god of the Oracle."

The masked face nodded. "How have you prepared?"

"By fasting, by lustration, by purification. By three days of meditation. By washing three times in the silver pool."

"What is your name?"

"Jamil, Prince of Askelon, companion of the Peacock Throne."

Hermia raised her manicured hands. Crystals glinted from her fingernails. "The wisdom of the god is infinite," she said. "The day is auspicious, the hour a sacred hour. Enter the precinct of the Mouse Lord."

Formalities over, the Prince turned and beckoned, and two more men, identically dressed, climbed down from the elephants and joined him. Behind them, Argelin's line of soldiers closed up.

The pearl merchants took out jewel-handled swords and thrust them dramatically into the sand; then they walked forward to the bridge. Without a word Hermia swept around and led the Nine and the three strangers on to the Island. They had sailed in a week ago, a fleet of vast caravels that were anchored now in the harbor, all but blocking it. Their wives wore brilliant colors, their children bracelets of pearl. The whole population of the Port had been thronging the wharfs for days, fingering the bales of merchandise, the cloth, foodstuffs, gems, ivories, exotic fruits—bartering, stealing, arguing, tasting. Even on the Island Mirany's sleep had been broken by the bizarre trumpeting of the elephants, terrible and fascinating.

Walking now under the moon, she said in her mind, "Do you already know what they want to ask?"

I know.

"And will she give them the right answer?"

He laughed, a quiet sound. But all he said was, *The palace is full of such wonders, Mirany, and all for me. Music and silver gaming boards and food—such sweet tastes! And there are tiny fish in the garden pools with snouts and trailing whiskers!*

For an instant the voice was a boy's, full of delight. Mirany shook her head, dismayed. "Listen to me! Don't you know Oblek is missing!"

Also by Catherine Fisher

Hc 0-06-057157-8
Pb 0-06-057159-4

Hc 0-06-057161-6

Read Books One and Two in
the Oracle Prophecies trilogy

The Oracle Betrayed

When timid Mirany is chosen to serve the High Priestess, she is unprepared for the dangers of her exalted position. She joins forces with Seth, a young tomb-robbing scribe who knows the secrets and hidden passages of their land. Every twist and turn in this heart-stopping epic is filled with unforgettable surprises.

The Sphere of Secrets

Mirany. Seth. Oblek. The Jackal. The Fox. Hermia. Rhetia. Their futures are in the hands of a small child with a soul that is older than time. Will the secrets of the silver sphere be revealed in time to save the Two Lands?

www.harperteen.com

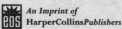
EOS *An Imprint of* **HarperCollins**Publishers

GREENWILLOW BOOKS
An Imprint of HarperCollinsPublishers